A COUP OF TEA

TEA PRINCESS CHRONICLES BOOK 1

CASEY BLAIR

A COUP OF TEA
Tea Princess Chronicles: Book 1

Cover design by Hampton Lamoureux of TS95 Studios, 2021.
Author photograph by Mariah Bush, 2013.

Ebook ISBN: 9798985110104.
Paperback ISBN: 9798985110111.

www.caseyblair.com

To everyone who believed in this story.

Special thanks to Django Wexler, Raf Morgan, and A. T. Greenblatt for persuading me my reach would not exceed my grasp.

CHAPTER I

I WALK ALONE THROUGH a hallway of strangers.

Ceremonially approaching the Grand Shrine is surreal in a way I didn't expect. No one is permitted to guide me, but hundreds of people line the halls to watch my progress.

I must not walk too quickly. That would indicate I don't value their presence and dismiss them. But if I walk too slowly, I show disrespect for their time and take advantage of the honor they do me in attending.

As the fourth of five daughters, I'm not used to being the focus of so much attention, but my steps don't falter. I know what outward appearance is expected of me.

But somehow it never occurred to me to practice this barefoot walk across the hard, cold stone. I wonder if anyone's feet have ever frozen in the dedication process.

On one hand, this makes me want to rush my approach. Once I've completed the rituals I'll have to meditate alone, so I can tuck my feet under me to warm them up.

On the other, the walk is unpleasant but not impossible. Not so the decision I'll need to make at the end of the ritual meditation.

My older sisters' paths were clear. There were obvious services people needed from them, and each is shockingly well-matched to her chosen task. I'm expected to follow in their tradition—a low enough expectation, to only need to continue behind them, to make no waves and fade quietly into the background.

Yet the weight of the prospect makes me feel smaller, heavier every time I contemplate it. I seem to be the only one who realizes how thoroughly I don't fit, the only one who worries trapping myself in ill-suited service will twist my spirit, who thinks that will matter not just for me, but for the people I'm ostensibly to serve.

I wonder if I'm the only royal of Istalam who's ever gone into the Grand Shrine to dedicate their life to service with so many doubts. It ought to be unlikely, but no royal since our house's founder has walked out of the dedication ceremony without a clear path of service ahead of them.

After what feels like a lifetime, I reach the end of the hall. Here, at last, are people I know.

I do not feel any less alone.

I bow first to my only younger sister, Karisa. She's just a few years younger than me, but it's clear she'll remain shorter than the rest of us. Each of us but my oldest sister bears some physical mark of my father's foreign heritage, and that is hers.

Karisa bows in return, and murmurs snidely, "Your fingers are blue."

Of course that makes me notice the heavy silver cuffs I wear every day are freezing against my skin.

It's a blatant goad, her attempt at political posturing against me of all people, who holds no sway over her life—and at a time like this, when I'm embarking on arguably the most spiritually significant moment of my life. This is the first time since I began the walk that I wish I were not forbidden to speak except as part of the ritual. In theory she isn't either, but I'm not surprised she doesn't care.

I ignore her baiting and turn to my oldest sister, Iryasa. I'm spared Karisa's famous temper on a day-to-day basis, but it's no great mystery why she's lashing out: even with Karisa in a gown finer than she should be wearing, Iryasa's regal bearing in clothing only slightly more adorned than my ritual garb—a plain white, tight-fitting floor-length tunic worn over loose pants—outshines her. Iryasa is the pinnacle of Istal beauty: the lanky limbs, the perfect shade of brown in her skin, the sleek, dark hair. She would be the model for every artist in the city if she weren't so busy doing the work of crown princess.

As crown princess, Iryasa is far too important to be a safe target for my youngest sister's ire. Unlike me.

Iryasa is enough older than me that we haven't spent much time together. She was already thoroughly occupied by learning the intricacies of statecraft when I could barely talk. But although I don't know her very well I recognize Iryasa's barely-embroidered choice of tunic as a form of wordless solidarity, so I bow to her a little lower than strictly called for.

Then I turn to the figure standing in front of the Grand Shine's enormous wooden doors: my mother, Queen Ilmari of Istalam.

She may be more a stranger to me than anyone in these halls.

My mother's expression doesn't change as she faces me, and mine doesn't either. No gestures of common feeling here.

I bow to her, and my royal silver cuffs feel somehow heavier.

I open my mouth, and my chest tightens as if my whole body conspires to keep the air from my lungs, to keep me from uttering the next words that I must.

Somehow I manage anyway. "Your Majesty, I come to dedicate myself in service to Istalam or be cast out to make my way alone."

The words are ritual and familiar, but now my heart pounds.

I don't know my mother well personally, but I know her incredible political sensibility has held Istalam together through rocky times. Every word she utters is chosen precisely and with care.

And to me she says, "Go with honor, Princess Miyara."

The doors open. I go.

The Grand Shrine has been cleared for my dedication ritual. I've never seen it in its simplest form, and it takes me a dizzying moment to orient myself. The dome is empty but for the priestess and the three guides I've chosen to advise me.

Unlike most shrines, the Grand Shrine at the Royal Palace of Miteran isn't dedicated to one element or manifestation, but to all three elements that govern life: earth, water, and air.

I walk to the bed of earth first, sinking my feet into the soil. Even that helps me feel warmer, until I look into the face of my father, Cordán the Consort.

I know as little of him as I do of my mother, which is by design. The contract between Istalam and Velasar for their marriage stipulated he could be as involved in his children's upbringing as the queen. Velasar thought to gain a generation sympathetic to its goals.

Instead, until Karisa, my mother refused to spend any time with us as children. And so nor could my father.

My father is stocky, with bright blue eyes and tightly-curled hair. Those curls are my inheritance, tempered down into a less energetic, thick wave. I don't know what other parts of my father I inherited.

He doesn't either. At last he says, "I don't know why you chose me for this."

Then he goes silent.

I've given him a chance to talk to me privately before I reach my majority, and he has nothing to say to me.

I don't know what I would say to him either, but I'm still not allowed to talk.

The silence stretches on, and my father finally rumbles, "Do your duty. That's all any of us can do. That's the lesson of earth I'll leave with you."

He has spent years doing his thankless duty, so he should know. But his is not a fate I would wish on anyone, let alone myself.

I know my royal duty is to serve. My spiritual duty, too—serving people serves the spirits.

I just don't know *how.* Is my duty first to uphold the nation of Istalam? Is it to support my family? Is it to the Istal people? If I've learned nothing else from my father's life, it's that those three do not overlap as much as my tutors have taught me.

But I bow and move to the pool of water, where my sister Saiyana waits.

Saiyana is the closest to me in age, only three years older, and she's spent more time with me than any of my other sisters.

"Your softness will be the death of you," Saiyana says without preamble. "The first time you have the chance to make a statement about who you are and what kind of public servant you'll be, and you waste it on pity. Transparent pity, at that. You clearly feel bad because our father played no part in any of his previous daughters' dedications, so you gave him a chance in a way that wouldn't elevate him over the queen's authority by your other two choices for guides. Don't think I don't realize what you're up to."

Probably no one knows me better than Saiyana does, but our personalities are so far apart it's difficult to tell we're related at all.

Her blue eyes are hard like rocks. "What you need is to stop wasting time on nonsense like that and bother to apply yourself to what matters, Miyara. There's a lot of work to do, and you could do a lot of good if you would just set your mind to it. So that's my advice to you, sister. Surge like the water."

From Saiyana, this is almost shockingly sweet. She's not one for compliments, so it's a remarkable admission of her confidence in my abilities. She's the most effortlessly brilliant person I've ever known, and that she thinks I could do what she does twists the knife in my gut, making me feel worse about my doubts.

But I don't miss what that confidence is predicated on: first stop caring about other people. Just do the work.

Not, ultimately, so different than my father's advice.

Yet I can't help feeling that if I have to ignore the parts of myself that make me *me* in order to dedicate myself, then who am I really dedicating into service?

I take my leave of Saiyana for the final station: air.

Saiyana was right about my choice of guides. To balance the choice of my father: first my sister, who knows me best.

And last my grandmother, the retired queen Esmeri, now in her seventies and seated behind a waist-high candle. The queen so fierce she'd bowled over anyone who opposed her in her reign.

She'd also been so polarizing that she'd retired to leave her careful daughter to manage the fallout in her wake.

I spread my hands over the air above the candle and watch her face behind its flickers as my fingers begin to thaw.

"You have an interesting choice to make," my grandmother says.

My fingers still. This is the first I've heard anyone hint I might do anything other than follow Saiyana's footsteps into stewardship, the thankless work of going around the kingdom solving administrative problems.

"Iryasa will rule. Reyata has dedicated herself to the warrior's life and commanding Istalam's armies. Saiyana devoted herself to magecraft to prepare for her role as steward. How else can *you* serve that they don't already have covered?"

I only realize my expression has betrayed my surprise at her words when my grandmother chuckles. "Let me leave you with this, then, as the lesson of air," she says, and stares at me intently over the rim of her spectacles.

"There will always be work for those who know how to listen."

What is that supposed to mean?

She winks at me. "Careful with the fire, dear."

I snatch my hands back from the candle—too long hovering and my silver cuffs will burn my skin.

But removing my hands is also the signal that my time for guidance has come to an end.

I want to shout at her, but I'm not allowed to talk until I speak my dedication. So my father, sister, and grandmother file out of the shrine, and the priestess seals us in.

"Take as long as you need to reconcile yourself, your Highness," she says, retreating to the side of the dome opposite the great doors I'd entered through. "The rest of your life is ahead of you, but we have until sunrise."

As if that will be enough time to decide the course of the rest of my life. As if I will have an answer today when I haven't in all my years before.

I lower myself to the cold stone, tucking my feet beneath me at last.

After a minute I decide the priestess won't tell anyone if I don't observe correct posture, un-tuck my feet, and use my silver cuffs to warm them.

If I'd really wanted advice, maybe I should have chosen different guides. Although I had more than one reason, ultimately all my choices were political. Being a princess means everything I do is political, though; I don't know people for nonpolitical reasons.

No matter what I choose, that will still be true.

I will still have to do my duty, to move at the exact pace prescribed for me.

There will still be no space for compassion. Any attempt will be viewed as a sign of weakness, a waste of resources.

I will still be the fourth princess, redundant after my illustrious sisters.

There will always be work for those who know how to listen, my grandmother said.

Listen to what? To whom? *How*?

How can I possibly serve people if I can't even answer those questions?

I blink. Stare at my royal cuffs in a moment of sudden clarity.

I *can't.*

I can't possibly serve people if I don't know what they need from me. If I don't know what I have to offer them.

And... maybe that *is* the answer.

My heart pounds.

I'm not like my sisters, always pushing. I always do my duty. I always stay within the prescribed lines, fading quietly into the background. I never make a fuss.

That may be exactly my problem.

I sit there for another minute wondering if I've gone mad, if the pressure to choose has finally snapped my wits.

But this feels right. Righter than anything has.

And if I have any hope of pulling this off, I need all the time I can get.

Shakily I stand.

"Priestess," I call softly.

"Are you ready to dedicate yourself, your Highness?" the woman asks.

I swallow. "More than anything, I wish to serve my people, priestess," I say. "But I do not know how."

Her eyebrows rise. I'm not supposed to have said anything other than the path I'll spend the rest of my life devoted to. "I'm afraid I don't under—"

She breaks off as her breath catches, her eyes widening.

I slide the cuffs off my wrists and hand them to her. It's strange to hold them, like I've never realized how heavy they are.

"No one has done this in hundreds of years," the priestess blurts as if she can't quite believe this is happening on her watch.

"Not since the founder of Istalam herself," I agree. "But it is within the scope of the ritual."

"Your Highness, this can never be undone!"

"I know." I meet her stunned eyes before pronouncing my fate. "I will make my way alone."

Outcast from the royal family.

A moment passes after my pronouncement, and then another.

"Priestess?" I finally prompt her.

She presses a hand to her forehead. "Oh, my dear. I suppose we'd better get you out of here then, haven't we? Quickly, now. Follow me, your High—"

The priestess breaks off, and we stare at each other.

No one will ever call me 'your Highness' again.

I've chosen not to dedicate myself in service. I've forsaken my life, and once I leave the shrine I start again with nothing. No support. No family.

No expectations.

I'm not a princess anymore.

I feel around the edges of the thought, testing my reaction to it. Renewed relief at my escape, thrill at what lies ahead, and not a little fear of the unknown, of how quickly I've made the biggest decision of my life—they're all there, but muffled, like my mind is still scrambling to make sense of the course my spirit has set me on.

The priestess ushers me to the back of the Grand Shrine. The dome gives the illusion of being stone all the way around, but we walk through what appears to be solid stone to an actual corridor. The priestess hesitates at a coat rack, grabs a serviceable gray shawl off it, and hands it to me.

"Put that on," she instructs. "You're too conspicuous in all white."

While I'm ducking into it she must notice I'm barefoot, because when I look up she's thrusting her own slippers at me.

I bow in gratitude. The slippers aren't sturdy, but they're more than she owes me.

No one owes me anything.

That thought is only just beginning to terrify me. I quash it as we keep walking.

Once I see the sun breaking through the early afternoon clouds I expect the priestess to leave me, but instead she motions for me to wait and pulls three candles out of her robes.

As she lights them, she says, "You realize your family will not be pleased."

I nod. "This will bring them a great deal of embarrassment. They will probably try to bully me into making a different choice."

"And attempt to push the shrine into thwarting tradition and letting you have a second chance to dedicate yourself," the priestess says.

"But they can't do anything if they can't find me," I say softly.

The priestess nods. "Exactly. Get as far away as you can. Lie low. If you truly mean to make your way alone in the world, that's where you start."

The priestess begins chanting. I didn't pursue magecraft like Saiyana, but all the princesses are required to learn the basics so we can tell if someone uses magic against us. The cuffs are primarily intended as emergency devices to summon aid—and also to find us if we're lost or kidnapped.

My mind keeps stumbling on each realization, and here's another one: no one will be able to find me if something bad happens to me.

And here is a mage clearly intending to spell me somehow with this construct of candles.

I pay attention and work out that it's an illusion spell of some kind right before I feel a wave of warmth wash over me.

The priestess says, "No one will pay you any mind while that illusion is up, and it's good until the candles burn down."

The exhaustion in her voice tells me this is the end of what she can do for me, even if she were willing to help more.

I look at the candles. They're not very tall.

The priestess points down the street. "See across the square—"

"The train station?"

She nods. "Exactly. Get yourself on a train as fast as you can. May the spirits guide your way."

I stare across the Royal Square of Miteran, the only place I've ever lived. I wonder what I'm supposed to be feeling about it—sad to be leaving? Excited?

I don't quite believe yet there's no 'supposed to' for me anymore.

I step out of the Grand Shrine onto the dusty mosaic-tile road of the Royal Square.

I have all the time in the world to work out what I feel.

Then I hear a loud horn and see a train pulling in at the station.

There are others in the station, but this train is a big one.

Big trains are more likely to travel farther away. And I need to get as far as possible.

They also don't arrive that often, and this illusion spell will only last so long.

I sprint.

I barely take in the gardens, the beautiful shops, the stages for players and music.

I ought to need a ticket, but I have no money to buy one with.

But I do have an illusion, so I sail past the crowds, the ticket masters and conductors and guards, and fling myself onto the train just before the doors close and it pulls away.

Only then does it occur to me that I never looked at where it's headed.

I have no idea where I'm going. But as I watch through the window as the train picks up speed, I know I'm on my way.

As I walk through the train car I spy one of the other passengers' tickets indicating this train is eastbound. This is more than I knew before, but it doesn't tell me much: the capital Miteran is on the western side of Istalam, so heading east leaves a lot of ground to cover.

More importantly, I don't have much time until the candles run out. I make my way to the car with non-reserved seats and scoot to the end of a bench.

I now have plenty of time to figure out my next move, but the train car is warm and all at once my energy drains out. I have enough time to realize the illusion spell has probably just worn off and sapped the remainder of my energy with it, and then I'm asleep.

CHAPTER 2

I STARTLE AWAKE TO hands shoving me roughly.

"Hey, grace, where's your ticket?" someone is asking.

I blink rapidly into the face of a conductor. "I'm sorry?" I respond automatically, while part of my brain wonders if I have ever been addressed as "grace," a common address of respect, rather than "highness."

"Where's your ticket?" he asks impatiently as the events of the morning come flooding back into my awareness. "We're pulling into the transfer station now. This train turns north, so if you're heading south you need to get off here. Where's your final destination?"

If he finds out I have no ticket, he'll arrest me, and my family will find me before I've been gone a day.

He's blocking the aisle.

I shoot to my feet as if in panic, and he automatically takes a step back.

I squeeze past him before he has a chance to keep me there, demanding to see my ticket.

"Oh, thank you for waking me," I say, and then I dash for the exit.

He calls after me, but in the press of bodies I have the advantage. I slip away into the darkness, darting out of the station before he has a chance to follow, listening to the sound of the horn as the train departs behind me.

Wherever I am now, I'm stuck here until I come by money for a ticket or another illusion spell.

I glance back at the train station and do a double-take at the name: Sayorsen South Station.

Sayorsen is *all the way* east. I'm on the other end of the country, right at the edge of the Cataclysm.

Which explains why it's dark: I must have slept off the effects of the illusion spell the entire day long.

No sooner do I notice the dark than the sky seems to open up and dump down a sea of water.

I trip over the cobblestones as I run across the street looking for a place to take shelter.

Iron streetlamps dot my path, but they're barely visible in the onslaught of rain. After a few minutes, I finally stumble upon a building with a light coming through the window.

A good thing, too, since my gifted slippers are now so soaked they're sliding off my feet. I pick them up and scamper up the steps to the door—

Only for the lights to blink off.

A man walks out and is turning to lock the door when he sees me. "Can I help you?"

"Please," I say. "Could I come in for a few minutes? Just until I dry off?"

I can't make out his face in the darkness, but I get the feeling he frowns. "I can't stay any longer, and I can't leave you alone in the shop. Sorry. Where's home?"

I freeze.

"Hello? Where are you headed?"

I have no idea, and this time no clever answer comes to mind.

"If you have nowhere to go," the man said slowly, "the police—"

Definitely not. That's the fastest way back to everything I just left.

It occurs to me that there may be forms of help that are worse than none at all, even when sincere.

"Sorry to bother you," I mutter, and when he reaches out as if to hold me back I slosh away into the night.

A block later and walking on the cobblestones is hurting my bare feet. I pause to shove the slippers back on—at least they offer some protection. I make out another illuminated building, but from the haze come three figures, all scantily clad, swaying and smelling of smoke and wine.

I am just worldly enough to understand what this suggests about the lit venue they're staggering from.

"Hey there," one of the figures says in a voice made husky by smoke. "Want to join us?"

I am also sheltered enough to understand I will have even less idea how to handle such a situation than the one I just fled from.

"No, thank you," I say, "but I hope you continue to enjoy your evening."

They laugh, and I stumble onward.

At this point I'm not looking for a place that's open—it's clearly late enough that most everywhere is closed for the night—but maybe I can find an overhang to keep me out of the rain. A large tree to sit under. I'm increasingly less picky.

Then I see one more light.

I can't see anyone inside.

Should I bang on the door? Probably someone left a light on by accident. Even if someone is inside they're likely to put me in a difficult position.

I stand there debating, staring at the possibility implicit in the light through the window until the door is flung open.

A woman stands there—around my age if I were to guess, early twenties. She's wearing a blood red sweater that's far too big for her, but it's hanging dramatically off one shoulder like she planned it that way. Combined with her tight leggings and the black boots that lace up almost to her knee, the effect makes her frame look gamine. But her face is utterly feminine, with full lips and black-lined eyes that stand out in the frame of her short-cropped, artfully disheveled hair, light gray-gold like frosted sand.

With hair that color, she is likely a refugee of the Cataclysm from Gaellan. Gaellani aren't common in the west, but here, on the border of the Cataclysm, they would be.

A woman born a refugee who looks totally together, while a woman born a princess stands sodden and aimless before her. There's irony in this.

"How long are you planning on standing there?" the woman asks casually while I drip.

"I hadn't decided," I say. "Am I in the way?"

"There aren't many good reasons to be lurking outside a business where only one person is inside," she says. "And lest you find the odds of robbing me reassuring, I promise I can maim you in any number of ways if you try."

That statement should probably worry me, given how calmly she says it, how unconcerned she is with a bedraggled visitor on her doorstep.

I'm too preoccupied with freezing to concern myself.

And she did open the door.

"I was looking for a place to warm up and dry off."

The rain continues to pour on top of me, and not on her.

"You are rather sopping," she agrees.

"Your powers of observation are remarkable," I say.

Her eyebrows lift.

Chagrined, I open my mouth to apologize for my rudeness—

But she huffs out a breath that sounds almost like a laugh.

"Come in," she says, stepping back from the door.

I stare at her, disbelieving, but only for a moment, and then I duck inside.

I strip off the slippers once again and, standing just inside the doorway, try to wring them out over the street. This fails; they just get wetter as the rain dumps on top of me.

"That was a really poor choice of footwear for around here," she says.

"I agree," I say. "This has been educational."

She makes that small huffing sound again. "Leave them there. Better take off your shawl too; spread it out over the coat rack—no, the other side. Yeah, there. Spirits, you wore *white* this time of year too? What's your name, anyway?"

The question startles me so much I answer honestly, "Miyara."

It's a mistake—I'll be easier to find using my own name—but I can't remember the last time I met someone who didn't know my name already.

"I'm Lorwyn," she says. "Sit over there and don't touch anything."

I follow her instructions, sitting on a wooden stool at a round table without question until she's vanished through a back door.

Only then do I look around. The room is still pretty dark—the light I saw is apparently coming from the back—but there are small tables and stools throughout, with colorful cushions and patterned tablecloths. With that much fabric everywhere, it's no wonder she wanted me planted at this one table near the door—I'll soak the whole place if I move.

I squint into the darkness in the direction Lorwyn went—there are shelves on the walls with things on them, but I can't make them out. I think I see a teapot?

Lorwyn comes back in with bundles of cloth in her arms.

"Towels to clean up spills," she says, tossing me one. "May be tea-stained; I think one of the boys put used towels in the clean pile by mistake."

I don't care. All I care about is being warm.

My hands shaking, I wipe myself down. Lorwyn then produces a large tablecloth and wraps it around me.

"There," she says. "Back on the stool. Tuck your feet under you—yes, like that. Better?"

I stare at myself, huddled in a tablecloth, and back at her. I'm reasonably sure she's mocking me, though I am, in fact, better. I'm no longer getting sloshed with water, I'm indoors and absurdly grateful for it, but somehow I can't wrap my mind around my current situation.

This morning I was a princess. Now I'm a vagabond in a tablecloth.

Maybe tea will help.

"Good," Lorwyn says. "Sit there and thaw for a while. Don't touch anything, and don't bother me. I'm going back to work."

"Wait," I say.

She turns back, and now she looks suspicious. I'd disarmed her mistrust, somehow, at the door, but now she's considering me as a potential danger again. Or maybe just wondering how much of a nuisance I intend to make of myself.

"Please," I say. "I smell ginger. I don't suppose—is there tea?"

She stares at me. Sniffs obviously at the air. "You can smell that out here? Really?"

I start to nod; stop. "Well. It smells *like* ginger, but there's a subtle difference I can't place."

Mentally I kick myself. Lorwyn is not one of my tutors. I'm allowed to give her incomplete answers. I'm tired and falling back on old habits.

A smile spreads on Lorwyn's face.

It is not the sort of smile I consider comforting.

"You," she says, "are going to earn your keep. Yes, there's tea, and you're going to taste it for me. Wait right there; I'll be back when it's ready."

It doesn't take her long, but still long enough that my hands are beginning not to shake. She clatters down a tea service in front of me.

"Is this a tea shop?" I ask. "I couldn't see signs in the rain."

"Talmeri's Teas and Tisanes, yes," Lorwyn answers as she arranges the kettle, the small pots, a cup in front of each. It's clear she knows her way around a tea set—her movements aren't the deliberate ones I learned for tea ceremonies, but this is a woman who has poured an awful lot of tea and is confident she won't break anything.

She pours water from the kettle over the tea pet—an exquisitely crafted clay dragon that moments later spouts out water as if it were breathing fire.

Lorwyn smirks in satisfaction. A tea pet only spouts water once it's at the correct temperature—she has a good sense of timing to guess that accurately.

"What kind of tea are we having?" I ask.

She pours. "You tell me."

A tea pet only works for specific water temperatures, and the correct temperature for brewing green tea is not the same as for white, or for a tisane. Even if she chose tea randomly from a shelf, to make use of a tea pet she obviously has to know what tea this is.

So this is a test for me.

"My main job here," Lorwyn says, "in theory, anyway, is to prepare tea blends. Talmeri, the owner, just got a new ingredient in stock that's posing a particular challenge. But for reasons that can't possibly be good enough, she bought crates of the stuff. So we have to find a way to sell it or else cut a huge loss. So." She hands me the first cup. "Tell me what you think."

Right up front I get the full-bodied floral taste in an overpowering blast—that still somehow manages not to cover the slick, almost oily note underneath.

"Well?" Lorwyn asked.

"White tea and fairy dew extract are commonly paired together," I say evasively.

"And I'm clearly not trying to do something common here," Lorwyn says impatiently. "What do *you* think?"

My thoughts. Who has ever been interested before?

And of course I'm asked by someone who's not going to like the answer.

But I'm not a princess anymore, and I can share whatever thoughts I want. Perhaps not without repercussions, but all of a sudden I desperately want to know what it is to experience fallout for speaking thoughts of my *own*.

"I think you're failing to cover whatever else is in there and abusing the fairy dew in so doing," I say. "I'm not sure what sort of tea blends you usually sell, but I would never choose to drink this."

Silence.

And then Lorwyn smiles again, that uncomfortable, predator-like smile.

"So you can taste after all," she says, and although she doesn't seem upset I feel a spike of unease. "Try the next one."

This one is a tisane, no tea at all. It contains the ginger I smelled before, along with ground peppers that only long training in not visibly reacting to Nakrabi cuisine in public prevents me from coughing as my throat tries to close, that other mystery flavor slithering through in a slick trail.

When I'm sure that my mouth is under control, I say evenly, "Please understand, I say this with the utmost gratitude for the tablecloth and the dry space. But I can only consider someone who would ask another, unsuspecting, to drink this as being an unkind person."

Lorwyn throws her head back and laughs, or perhaps cackles.

"Sorry," she says, not sounding sorry in the least—more delighted. "I thought the Nakrabi death peppers might burn through the—the new ingredient—"

"They do not," I say firmly. "They burn, but your mystery ingredient slides underneath until everything is terrible."

"Noted," she says, clearly not offended in the slightest. After that cup she has no grounds to be offended, anyway.

She hands me a third cup, though, and I eye her mistrustfully, that unease back again and sharp.

"Earning your tablecloth," she reminds me.

I smell the grassiness of the green tea before I taste it. But the flavor is so strange I can't immediately identify the elements—she's used aloia nectar not just as a sweetener, but to bind this mystery ingredient, and the result has a strangely smooth, nutty element. I frown at the cup and take another sip, swirling the tea in my mouth.

"So?" Lorwyn asks.

It's much better than the other two, but this tea gives the impression of oozing—no, *crawling* through the grass—

I set the cup down abruptly. "Please tell me your mystery ingredient is not insectoid."

Her eyebrows rise in surprise. "Wow. Okay, I'm impressed. Apparently the trekkers named them sleekbeetles. New species discovered in the Cataclysm. Talmeri bought crates of their scales."

I am drinking beetle scale tea.

This morning I was a princess, and now I sit sopping in a tablecloth drinking *beetle scale tea.*

"Why?"

Lorwyn shrugs. "I'm sure they were cheap—even in a place as used to weirdness as Sayorsen, beetles aren't exactly a much sought-after commodity. Talmeri's always on the lookout for novelty items to boast the most unique tea flavors in the city, and she also likes torturing me. Who can say which was the primary factor this time?"

I grimace. "Wonderful. A hitherto untasted bug. I hope it's at least magically inert and you haven't poisoned me?"

"Of course I didn't poison you," Lorwyn says. "I tasted it before you did. You didn't tell me what you think of this one, though. How could you tell it was beetle?"

"The grassiness of the green tea," I say. "It's too sharp. You need something mellower that's still robust enough to hold up to the aloia nectar."

Lorwyn slumps back—I'm not entirely sure how she manages to, since she's sitting on a stool.

"Aloia is tricky," she grumbles.

"Maybe it needs another note," I say. "The aloia manages the beetle flavor into something nearly salvageable. Now you need a bridge between the aloia and the tea."

Lorwyn bolts out of her stool before I'm done talking. "Wait there!"

I blink, then smile just a little. Her commanding presence gives her a sophisticated air, but it falls apart when she gets distracted.

She returns with another small pot and a cup, adds them to the tea service. She lifts the pot to pour, and all at once I realize, beetle scales aside, what's been bothering me.

It's not her smile that's triggering the bolts of unease—that's my mind reacting to unexpected magic use, perceiving a threat.

The water from that kettle should not have correctly brewed different kinds of teas and tisanes. The temperature of the water has to have changed, and there are no cooling or heating devices anywhere near the table.

I glance around for a structure, anything she could have used to anchor magecraft. The stools aren't in any particular order around the table, there are no candles, and the tea cups are arranged for the taster's benefit alone.

Which means this isn't magecraft at all.

It's witchcraft.

Which is supposed to be closely regulated.

I promise I can maim you in any number of ways, she said.

Brewing me concoctions with unknown ingredients from the Cataclysm she is sure are magically inert.

A mysterious air of confidence and sophistication.

Lorwyn holds a cup of tea out to me with an excited look on her face.

I've lost my wits. After realizing what she's doing, it's the only explanation for what I do next.

I take the cup, and I sip.

It's the same tea leaf, but it's been brewed with roasted rice—mellow but rich. And not only that, she's added a sunny note light enough not to overpower the tea but robust enough to moderate the aloia—and most importantly it does not at all make me think of beetles.

"Marigold," I say. "Perfect. Maybe even a touch more. This tea can handle it."

Lorwyn studies me. "Which flush of leaves?" she asked.

I cock my head to one side, not sure why she's asking. "Second," I say. "It has to be, to balance these flavors correctly."

"So you're a professional taster," Lorwyn says bluntly.

This startles me. "No, I'm not."

"A tea master, then. Or at least an aspirant."

"What? No, I mean—I can perform tea ceremonies, but I'm not certified or part of the tea masters' guild. I've never taken any of the exams."

It's strange to think about my education that way. Of course I'm not a tea master—a princess can't be compared to a person who works in service.

That thought takes my breath away.

Lorwyn pushes on. "You've done some of the same training though! That's practically the same thing."

"Is it?" I ask. And then: "Is that how it is for witches?"

Silence.

Lorwyn has gone utterly still. "Are you implying I'm a witch? Just because I'm a woman, and—"

"Not all witches are women," I say automatically. Our current understanding is that all witches are born with female reproductive organs, but that isn't the same.

Lorwyn's shoulders tense, as if she's clenching her fists, hard, under the table where I can't see them. "I'm aware of that," she growls.

"The water temperature," I explain.

She closes her eyes. "Of course. If you know tea this well, of course you'd notice that. Curse you."

She sounds bitter, but also resigned.

"I take it that means you're not registered," I say.

The registry is the rare piece of legislation my grandmother had been forced to approve or face a popular uprising, even though she was against it. Ever since the Cataclysm, witches have been required to register with the state to be regulated. Because unlike magecraft, which anyone can learn but has natural limits imposed by the need for physical structures to anchor it, witchcraft is innate. The registry enables mages to watch over witches—and if their power is considered too great, they can be executed.

What this means, naturally, is that witches notoriously don't register. Which means the mages have a greater mandate for laws that crack down against those who disobey, and people come to mistrust witches, and then witches are even less likely to come forward even if their power is minor.

But since Lorwyn heated water in this kettle without even appearing to think about it, I do not think her power is minor.

"No, I'm not registered," she says evenly, confirming my assumption. "I prefer living. Do you?"

My heart races, and I know I need to think very quickly. "I do," I say. "You have no more reason to maim me now than you did in the doorway."

"Don't I?" she asks. "I can never trust you won't get in trouble and decide to give me up to ease your way, can I?"

It occurs to me that I wouldn't. That should bother me—I barely know this woman, and she has threatened to hurt me.

But she also brought me in out of the rain and wrapped me in a tablecloth.

Saiyana always grudgingly admitted my snap judgments of people are usually correct. I can't help wondering what she'd think of this one.

"Do you think," I say, "I would have been standing out drenched in the rain, in the dark, if I could appeal to local authorities for any kind of assistance?"

Her gaze sharpens. "Are you in trouble of some kind?"

"Of some kind," I agree. "And it's the kind that is in no danger of vanishing for the rest of my life."

"A lot can change," Lorwyn points out.

"Not this," I say firmly. "And I'd be more distressed than you if it did—this situation is of my own making, and I don't want it reversed."

"Even if it means freezing in the rain."

I hadn't even considered going to the police and having them send me back to Miteran. That reassures me—deep down I'm more confident in my choice than I fully understand yet.

"Yes," I say. "Even then."

"Yet we're still unequal," Lorwyn points out. "I have to take you at your word that you won't betray me, with no insurance. I don't think that will work."

She says this matter-of-factly, not like she's looking for excuses to maim me but as if we're haggling over a business contract. But her complete surety in turn leaves me sure this is a sticking point. She has to have more of a hold on me to let alone the hold I have on her.

Spirits guide me.

"If the police ever have reason to investigate me," I say, "it will be the end of my life."

Not in the literal sense, probably. But I will never be allowed any agency in my own life again, not after what I've done. And thinking of returning to the palace, to be carefully managed forever, turns my stomach. Already I'm not sure how I lived so long with it.

I hope it is easy to live a life where the police will never have a reason to investigate me.

"That's not good enough," Lorwyn says. "I need to know why."

"No," I say. "You do not. And it is good enough."

I say this with authority, as calmly as I pronounce judgments on tea. And I see this makes a difference: she believes me. But she's not quite prepared to let the point go.

"For whatever it's worth," I add, "I also think the law is egregiously immoral on top of being counterproductive and should have been repealed years ago. I have no trouble behaving as though that wrong has already been righted."

Lorwyn throws her hands up in exasperation. "Who talks like that?" she demands as I blink in confusion. "And anyway, you can't behave that way—can you imagine how quickly I'd get noticed? Keep your head down and pretend everything is as it should be. That's how hiding works."

Hiding. For someone who's spent her entire life in the background, it ought to be more natural for me. I need to learn that better, fast.

"And," she says, "I'm going to keep you where I can keep an eye on you, I think. You don't have a place to stay or work, correct?"

Cautiously hopeful, I say, "That's correct."

"Tomorrow I will bring you back here, and you will convince Talmeri to give you a job."

"How will I do this?" I ask. "And why do you want me to?"

"Self-interest," Lorwyn answers easily. "My main job, as I said, is making tea blends. The entire lab is mine. I work here because I can experiment with whatever I want, whenever I want, without interference. Since Talmeri knows I'll never give that up, I also end up with any other jobs she can't be bothered to deal with. Bookkeeping is bad—how are you with spreadsheets?"

"Fine?" Were spreadsheets dangerous somehow?

"Fabulous. Anyway, bookkeeping is bad, but it's not as bad as supervising the boys who serve tea. Or having to serve customers myself because one of the boys is too incompetent. You know tea, you need a job, and I have all these jobs I don't want. So you're going to persuade Talmeri that you should run the tea room."

"And why," I ask slowly, "do I want to do this? Aside from the need for income?"

"Because in exchange, I'm going to arrange free lodging for you for half a year," she says brightly, and I am now completely sure I should never trust this particular smile from her.

"How?" I ask.

"Do we have an agreement?" she presses.

"Tentatively," I say, and knowing she won't mind clarify, "as this sounds rather too convenient for me all around."

I'm right. My honesty makes her laugh, and the tension that's been in the air eases a bit.

"Oh, it won't be convenient at all," Lorwyn promises. "Just you wait. No, you know what, we're getting this over with—are you dry? Let's go see if you approve of your housing arrangements."

"Now?" I ask, glancing habitually up, where the room remains dark.

"No better time," Lorwyn says with her predator's smile.

CHAPTER 3

LORWYN BORROWS AN UMBRELLA from the shop and loans me her coat. It's far too big for me, but, in her words, "It's not as if you could look *more* bedraggled." I'm too grateful for the additional warmth to care what image I present, and Lorwyn isn't concerned that my appearance will adversely affect her ability to arrange housing for me.

The place Lorwyn takes me is farther away than I'd like, given the rain and the state of my slippers, but not, ultimately, too far of a walk from the more urban part of Sayorsen and the tea shop.

I can hardly afford to be choosy, but I'm surprised when we stop at the side gate of a park.

"A... park?" I ask, certain I've misunderstood something.

"No," Lorwyn says, peering intently into the darkness, scanning for something. "Grounds."

She bends down and scoops up a handful of rocks as I squint until I make out a looming mansion.

A mansion with a crest, no less. That means it's not a wealthy merchant's, but a noble's.

There can't be more than a dozen nobles with homes in Sayorsen proper, and Lorwyn has brought me directly to one of their estate houses. This is possibly the last place I should be—a noble is more likely to recognize me than anyone.

And Lorwyn proceeds to throw a rock at one of the mansion's nearby windows.

"What are you doing?" I hiss.

Lorwyn throws another rock, and then another. "Getting someone's attention," she says.

With an effort, I hold my ground and do not hide behind her. "I hope," I say, "you didn't bring me here to get me arrested taunting the nobility?"

She grins, a cut through the darkness. "I can't deny taunting the nobility has its charms, but no. Getting arrested isn't on the agenda for tonight."

I fight the urge to throttle her—she enjoys making me work for answers entirely too much—and finally notice her foot is tapping in a steady rhythm.

No sooner have I realized that the sound of the rocks thumping against the mansion are falling in a looping rhythm than a side door opens from the mansion.

Whomever Lorwyn has been summoning has answered.

"A friend?" I ask.

Lorwyn's face is inscrutable. "Something like that."

Not a friend, and someone who lives at a noble mansion besides. Perhaps all the nobles of this family are at court this season, but my heart is racing again. "Then I hope you're certain this person can be trusted not to turn me into the police?"

Lorwyn frowns at me. "Why should she?"

I want to scream, but she may not have understood what I meant when I said 'local authorities'. Frantically I whisper, "I should not have dealings with nobility. In the interest of hiding."

Her gaze holds mine searchingly for a moment. "I'll keep that in mind," Lorwyn says, and I know I've inadvertently rekindled her interest in my story. "But you'll be fine with this one, I promise."

Then it's a noble she's called after all.

I don't have time to ask how she can be so sure because the noblewoman in question arrives at the gate.

There's so little light I can't make out much of her features, just the shape of her body moving silently in the night. Lithe and rangy. But she wears a rich cloak and her hair falls in a long, thick braid, so I don't doubt she's Istal nobility.

"The guards will be back this way any minute," the noblewoman says without preamble. "You shouldn't be here, Lorwyn."

"I could enter House Taresim's grounds without telling you or anyone noticing any time I want, as you know perfectly well," Lorwyn says, her voice cutting.

The noblewoman's braid flips in irritation. "So you want something. What is it? And who's this?"

"I'm calling in the favor you owe me," Lorwyn says softly, and somehow it feels as if the world has gone still with her words.

The noblewoman certainly has.

"Guards incoming," Lorwyn says, and the noblewoman whirls. "We shouldn't be seen lurking at the gate. Come around to your grandma's summer cottage."

Without waiting for a response, Lorwyn grabs me by the elbow and pulls me away with her.

"We're going around to a secret gate on one of the other sides," Lorwyn tells me. "Risteri will let us in and show you where you'll be staying."

Under duress. "You're blackmailing her."

"She blackmailed me," Lorwyn says, her voice hard.

I can imagine with what.

Still. I'm not sure how I'd thought this was going to work; but profiting off old bitterness leaves me more than a little uncomfortable.

I slow. Lorwyn tugs at my arm, and unthinking I yank it back.

We both stop.

"Look, it's not what you're thinking," Lorwyn says, sounding irritable again. "We're not friends anymore, but whatever else you can say of Risteri, she'll keep her word. She promised me a favor of comparable magnitude in exchange for what she needed from me, and I'm holding her to it. That's all. Okay?"

I read anger and anxiety in her face, which I do not equate with "okay." "And I'm worth it?" I ask. "A sizable favor from a local noble house, the leverage you have over someone who's tried to take advantage of you before?"

"You *have* spent time with nobles, haven't you?" Lorwyn asks. Apparently rhetorically as she continues, "It's not exactly easy for someone like me to cash in favors like this one. The only things I might need are too small or big to qualify. This favor's been sitting around unused for half my life now. I can't think what else I'm going to do with it, so someone might as well benefit. Are you coming or not?"

An answer to my second question, but not my first.

But I start walking again.

Half Lorwyn's life means she's known this noblewoman—Risteri—since they were both young. Childhood friends.

I wonder how it came to pass that a noble daughter met a refugee witch, but then again, *I* had just wandered into her tea shop tonight.

And I think of my sister Saiyana, who arguably knows me better than anyone. I think of how over time our impressions of each other, our goals and priorities, can become unbearably tangled, twisted from a place of understanding.

And I decide not to ask.

As the minutes pass, Lorwyn's shoulders relax a touch, realizing I'm not going to press any further into this wound.

We trudge up a path through some trees, and I see why Lorwyn called it a secret gate. Even in the daylight, if I didn't already know there was a gate here, I wouldn't see it.

"Let me do the talking," Lorwyn says. "Trust me."

"Says the woman who fed me beetle scale tea," I say mildly.

"And ultimately you got a drinkable cup of tea, didn't you?" Lorwyn responds unapologetically.

But not with irritation, and I'm relieved as we approach Risteri at the gate.

She doesn't open it, standing there with crossed arms.

"I know you, Lorwyn, but how do I know I can trust this person?"

"Seriously?" Lorwyn's voice drips scorn. "Because if I had any interest in causing you or your family trouble I've had years to do so in a way you'd never be able to connect back to me. Come on, Risteri, surely you haven't gotten hit on the head that many times in the last decade."

"You'd be surprised," Risteri mutters, but she does open the gate.

I follow, nonplussed at what kind of situations a noble daughter can get into that would get her hit on the head more than once.

A stone path winds through a copse of trees to a small cottage. I see why Lorwyn wanted to talk here: there are so many trees no regular guard patrol will see us coming or going.

The inside of the cottage isn't much warmer than outside, but it's not wet. Risteri claps a magelight system on, and a fire blooms in the corner.

Risteri blocks the doorway, making a face as she gets her first good look at my slippers. "What were you thinking, wearing shoes like that in fall in Sayorsen?"

It's so like what Lorwyn said to me earlier I want to laugh, but I don't think Lorwyn will appreciate it. "If nothing else comes of tonight, I can at least count on this shoe experience to be memorable enough to not bear repeating," I say.

"Take them off," Lorwyn instructs. "The coat too. You're shaking with cold again."

I didn't notice until she mentions it, and now that I have I shake so hard Lorwyn and Risteri have to help me into a chair by the fire. Suppressing discomfort has been necessary as a princess, but it occurs to me that it might not be entirely healthy.

Lorwyn forced me to notice what I was feeling. It occurs to me now too, belatedly, to reconsider what kind of reaction my youngest sister Karisa had wanted when she forced me to feel the cold of my hands and feet this morning before entering the Grand Shrine.

This morning. Spirits, that had only been this morning.

"Is she in shock?" Risteri asks.

"She's been half frozen most of the night, as far as I can tell," Lorwyn answers. "But she's thinking clearly enough."

I focus. I'm huddled in a large chair in front of the fireplace, but Lorwyn and Risteri are hovering around me.

I finally notice it's not so much out of concern for my wellbeing, or at least not entirely, as the fact that there aren't other chairs. There's a small kitchen, with a single stool at a bar. It's quaint, clearly designed for only one person, and not at all where I'd expect to find the grandmother of a noble house residing. Maybe referring to it as her 'grandma's cottage' is a joke of some kind?

"Bathroom's behind you," Lorwyn says, jerking her head in the direction around the other side. I crane my neck to see the wall blocking it and the beginning of a staircase. "The attic is basically a closet with a bed."

I blink. "Is the closet or bed particularly large?"

"Not particularly," Risteri says.

"The closet," Lorwyn says at the same time.

They glance at each other and then away again.

It finally occurs to me to take a look at Risteri now that she's taken her cloak off. My assessment outside was accurate but incomplete: she's dressed in silken pajama pants tucked into very sturdy, well-worn boots. More than that, her arms are well muscled: not huge, but defined, far more so than I'd expect of a noblewoman outside the armed forces. She's about our age, maybe twenty; no wrinkles in her face, but her skin tone is dark brown, like someone who spends considerable time in the sun. Not typical for a noblewoman at all—but then again, most noblewomen our age live at court. Clearly, she's not typical.

"Are you going to tell me what this is all about?" Risteri asks.

"I told you, I'm calling in my favor," Lorwyn says. "On your honor."

Risteri's braid swishes again. "Yes, I heard that part, but you haven't said what you want."

"This is Miyara," Lorwyn says, gesturing at me, where I watch quietly. "She needs a place to stay, and I happen to know this cottage is unoccupied."

She means for me to stay *on a noble estate*? Is she mad?

"Why can't she stay with you?" Risteri asks, and I see that the second the words are out of her mouth she regrets them.

"And stay where?" Lorwyn asks. "You know how many siblings I have. We already don't fit. If I knew of another place for someone to stay, don't you think *I'd* be living there?"

"I could find you both a place, instead," Risteri says.

Lorwyn shakes her head. "No. First, she needs a place now. And that wouldn't be an equal exchange."

"What about this is equal?" Risteri asks. "I'm not exactly on great terms with my father, and you think I'm just going to explain away someone taking over my grandmother's cottage?"

Lorwyn doesn't even move, but her voice cracks like a whip. "I'm asking you to help someone hide, and to do so in the shadow of your noble family home."

Risteri reels back like Lorwyn has struck her in truth. There's a meaning there I don't understand, presumably related to their past exchange.

"Since you will have to deal with your family," Lorwyn says, biting every word, "the deal is that Miyara will only stay until spring, when your grandmother arrives. After that, she'll be out of your hair, and your debt to me will be clear. You can't tell me that isn't a comparable exchange."

Risteri crosses her arms, scowling at me. I'm still trying to wrap my mind around the notion that Lorwyn is forcing a noble daughter to go against the head of her house at all, let alone that Risteri isn't dismissing the very idea out of hand. Whatever Lorwyn did for her, it must have been serious.

And Risteri is going to have to make it stick for six months—apparently even Lorwyn doesn't think Risteri can stand against the house matriarch after that.

"It's not like you to be so compassionate," Risteri says—to Lorwyn, apparently, though she's looking at me when she says it. "What are you getting out of this deal? You don't do anything without getting something in return."

Lorwyn's expression has twisted, and I know Risteri has pushed too hard against an old wound. Before Lorwyn can answer, I blurt, "I think there's a lot of beetle tea in my future."

Both of them look at me.

Then Risteri's eyes narrow and she looks incredulously at Lorwyn. "She doesn't mean sleekbeetles, does she?"

Lorwyn rolls her eyes. "It wasn't my idea."

"You're spending your time making sleekbeetle tea," Risteri echoes. "I don't believe this. Lorwyn, what are you *doing* at that place? You could leave—"

"No," Lorwyn says, "I can't."

They stare at each other some more, the weight of old arguments hanging between them, thickening the air.

I'm abruptly too tired to be patient with the drama not quite unfolding in front of me. It's clearly so important to them, and just as clearly not going to be resolved tonight, and at this rate Lorwyn is going to push Risteri to throw us both out and then my feet really will freeze.

"I don't suppose," I say, "I might be able to find a kettle in the kitchen for some tea? Perhaps a, ah, more conventional cup."

Lorwyn doesn't laugh as I'd hoped, but she does break their staring match to look at me. "Risteri can show you where everything is. I'll be back to pick you up tomorrow morning."

She's walking away, grabbing her coat off the hook by the door, as Risteri says, "I still haven't agreed to this."

Lorwyn replies, "You agreed to this a decade ago," and the door shuts behind her.

Leaving me alone with a noblewoman who certainly does not want me here.

On the other hand, Lorwyn's continued presence was likely to make our interaction even more awkward.

We regard each other in silence for a long moment.

"I didn't realize the sleekbeetles were common knowledge," I say.

Risteri's eyebrows shoot up. "Lorwyn didn't tell you?"

"I suspect the list of things Lorwyn hasn't told me is quite long."

A smile ghosts across her face. "There is that. But she will always tell you what she thinks of you." She shakes her head. "I lead tours of the Cataclysm for work."

I blink rapidly, trying to process the wealth of information in that single statement.

First and foremost, there is the fact that she *works.* For *money.* For a noble, performing labor at all, let alone being seen to, is practically obscene.

And she does it of her own volition.

No matter her reasons, that would all be shocking enough, but her choice of vocation is another matter entirely.

What we now call The Cataclysm once comprised the bulk of Istalam's empire, as well as a number of countries that used to lie on the other side of our borders.

We're not certain how many continue to exist. We don't know how far the Cataclysm stretches.

Fifty years ago, magic exploded somewhere to the east. No one agrees on what caused it, though many people fear it was witchcraft gone rogue.

In the end, the magical detonation left a huge swath of land uninhabitable. The Cataclysm destabilized reality; within its borders, magic is wild. Not only do the rules that govern our physical world not function there, there *are* no rules except that everything is changeable. Up becomes down, solid land morphs into fiery miasma, fruit evaporates or becomes angry creatures with claws once eaten, tsunamis form in places with no water, and there is no way to navigate to north. Anyone caught within the Cataclysm before the border had stopped expanding died.

The scale of loss is incalculable.

Lorwyn's people, the Gaellani, were the biggest group that managed to flee the devastating effects, rushing west ahead of the spreading magical effects as fast as they could. Most others weren't so lucky.

It's possible to cross the border into the Cataclysm. On the edges, the effects aren't so pronounced. Daring tourists go to see wild magical novelties—shifting glimpses into other landscapes, beasts that have never existed, vines that are conscious and hungry, weather that travels in pockets that burst without warning—in a relatively controlled setting. But the deeper in you go, the harder it is to find your way back. Teams of trekkers regularly fail to return, but those that do bring back with them magical treasures that can make them fortunes.

If Risteri leads tours, she's ventured into the Cataclysm so often she knows the layout of its rim well enough to be a guide. She also has enough experience in the Cataclysm that she's trusted to deal with magical anomalies and random attacks that may crop up, trusted to defend the hapless tourists and bring them back across the border safely. Only on the rim, of course, but that she can at all implies she's spent considerable time deeper inside the Cataclysm, too. But even as a tour guide, she risks her life every time, and by the sound of it, every day.

It is common wisdom that only the very brave or the very stupid venture into the Cataclysm.

Of course this is the kind of noble daughter a witch made friends with as a child.

"I think I see why your relationship with your father might be strained," I say.

"You don't know the half of it," Risteri says. "Come on, let me show you around."

She leads me around the cottage, pointing out spell anchors and how to activate them.

"The magetech isn't slick by modern standards," she says, "but you won't have trouble with the oven or anything."

As if I would know what to do with it. It's a marvel that she does.

"The cottage was built for a favored steward generations ago," Risteri explains as we head up the stairs, "but more recently it was used for the occasional visitor as a guest studio. More privacy and functionality than an inn, and it's convenient on the grounds. But Grandmother inexplicably decided she liked it and would rather have privacy than stay in the main house all the time, so now it's reserved for her use when she stays with us for spring and summer."

Lorwyn wasn't kidding about the second floor. Most of the space is devoted to clothing storage—chests of drawers and empty racks. It's not large as noble closets go, but it's adequate for a season's wardrobe. If Lorwyn shared a small space with her family, I can imagine how her standard for size would be different than Risteri's.

But my attention is drawn to the bed. It's not large at all, but it is piled high with blankets and plush pillows and never has anything looked more inviting in my life.

"Here, sit down," Risteri says.

I ignore her, afraid that if I sit down I'll never stand up again, and watch as she goes to one of the chests of drawers.

"Grandmother always leaves some clothes here, in case her luggage gets delayed on the way from the capital," Risteri explains, pulling out some cloth. "It won't fit you super well, but it has to be dryer than what you're wearing."

I take it hesitantly. It's soft, almost fluffy, and I can feel a lump inside that I dearly hope is socks.

Socks. I have never appreciated them as well as I do today.

"Are you sure this is okay?" I ask.

She shrugs. "Sure. It's not like my grandmother ever needs to know."

Risteri must be the strangest noble girl in the world.

Then again, although she's clearly rebellious, of the two of us she hasn't actually abandoned her family.

"That's not what I meant," I say. "You know nothing about me."

She nods slowly. "That's true. But I do know Lorwyn, and it's not like her to go out of her way for people. So either she knows enough about you to make you trustworthy, or she's learning compassion. Unlike her, I *do* care about the wellbeing of people I've never met, so that's enough for me."

Lorwyn as uncaring—the characterization doesn't sound wrong, exactly, but certainly incomplete. Whatever happened between these two as children ran deep.

"Lorwyn told me," I say, "that no matter what, I could trust you to keep your word."

Risteri goes rigid, and then she takes a deep breath and changes the subject. "We can sort out more of the details of your stay tomorrow. Do you need anything else tonight?"

I start to say no automatically, but pause, remembering how I keep forgetting that I'm cold, and think.

"I don't suppose," I ask, "there might be any food the main kitchen could spare? It's been some time since I've eaten."

Risteri frowns. "How long?"

I'd started fasting the night before the ceremony, so— "A day, about."

Risteri winces. "Wait here."

I succumb to the temptation of socks before realizing she's only going downstairs.

"This is all I have on me," she says when she returns, handing me a sack containing nuts and a hunk of cheese.

"You keep snacks in your cloak?" I ask.

Risteri shrugs. "Sometimes you don't notice a magic pocket on the horizon until you're caught in it. Best to be prepared."

That sounds like wisdom. I suspect in the future I will never find myself without snacks, trustworthy tea leaves, and a sturdy pair of boots.

With *socks.*

"I'll see what I can find at the house," Risteri says. "Munch on this in the meantime and start getting ready for bed. You look like you're about to keel over."

I'm having trouble keeping my eyes open, the exhaustion creeping up on me almost as suddenly as it did on the train. I manage to finish the snacks and pulling on the nightclothes, but I'm asleep before she returns.

CHAPTER 4

I WAKE WITH THE birds and stare, disoriented, at a ceiling that is not covered by mosaic depiction of the three great spirits of the world. Instead it's plain and white.

I look around, see the line of trees outside the window. This is not my view, and yet, now it seems to be.

I have a room with a window. That's always been considered too ill-advised for a princess' rooms, even in secure Miteran.

The events of the previous day filter back in. I don't remember getting into bed, but either I must have, or Risteri moved me and I didn't notice.

I rub my bare wrists. I need to be more attentive. Perhaps I can be forgiven for letting my guard down my first day on my own, but for exactly that reason I can't make it a habit—it's no longer anyone's job to protect me. Only mine.

I've been exceedingly fortunate, but I can't keep depending on the goodwill of others.

Sitting up, I feel crusted layers of mud crinkle on my skin.

I am downstairs in the bathroom instants later.

I take a breath, thinking back to the night before and all the instructions Risteri gave me. I wasn't processing very well, but I did, at least, listen. Twisting nobs tentatively, I manage to get the tub filled with hot water and find bottles of liquid soaps stashed in a cupboard.

As I sink down into the tub, I revel in the feeling of being surrounded in warmth. It's a facet of water I've never truly appreciated before.

Then I go about figuring out what to do with the soaps, relieved they're labeled.

I step out regretfully when the water begins to cool, pulling on a robe hanging from the door. It's lavender silk, delicately embroidered with violet birds flitting across, and I love it immediately.

Then I remember it isn't mine. Nothing is mine. I rub my wrists absentmindedly again.

I find a comb and attempt to use it on my hair, but after a few fruitless minutes my stomach rumbles. I've barely eaten in two days now, and I'll need food before I can be good for anything—beginning with being able to stay awake in the presence of strangers, and ending with no longer being dependent on their charity.

In the kitchen, there's a note from Risteri left on the bar, right in front of the stool: she's left soup in the cooler.

Splendid, as I have no idea how I'd have found food otherwise. I have no way to contact Lorwyn or Risteri, no money to buy food, no idea where I could even obtain it.

The magnitude of my impulsive decision the day before threatens to drown me. It's not that I didn't understand I'd have to find food for myself, but there are so many *details.* I will have to relearn completely how to live.

I take a few deep breaths. Air, for calm.

I'm rubbing my wrists again. I stop.

I figured out the bath. I will figure out food, too.

The soup is cold, congealed; it will need, I assume, to be reheated. If I can heat water in a kettle, I can probably manage this.

I rummage through cupboards, surprised anew by the wealth of wares needed to outfit a kitchen for one person—glasses, plates, serving bowls and measuring spoons, many other utensils I can't identify that must be for cooking. I eventually land on pots, use a large utensil I don't recognize to pry the soup into one, and have clapped the magical stove fire on before I've realized I've done it.

Strange that it's cooking, an expression of earth and nourishment, that comes easily to me today, when I've never felt so untethered from my roots. It's like I'm a whole new Miyara.

No: I'm myself for the first time.

As I search for an appropriate bowl and spoon, I wonder if Risteri's grandmother uses this kitchen. Has the kitchenware sat here unused for years? Does she have a servant come by every day? Has a noblewoman of my grandmother's generation taught herself to cook?

Maybe I can too.

Soon enough, I'm seated on the stool with a bowl of hot soup. It's milky yellow, rich with mushrooms, cabbage, and noodles speckled with peppers. It's all I can do to keep from inhaling it, but I can't afford a burnt tongue—I may need my tasting skills again today.

So I take a moment to study the cottage a little more closely. I've been moving through it like a ghost, but this is the place that, if I'm successful today in securing a job at the tea shop, I'll be spending the next half a year.

It feels cozy to me, which is not at all what I associate with grandmothers—though it must be said mine, as the most dominant queen of Istalam, is perhaps not a customary standard for grandmothers.

Then again, what do I know of grandmothers? Perhaps they are all inscrutably wise and terrifying.

It's not at all what I associate with a place that I live, either. After all of one day of cold, I think I will make it a point to embrace coziness in my new life.

The kitchen, with its bright white cabinets and brass nobs, stands out at striking odds with the sitting room: there the floor is covered in rugs, deep burgundy with burnished yellow floral patterns; the oversized chair in front of the fireplace is a cream with the same pattern embroidered around it. A bronze table with a ruby and gold mosaic surface sits next to it in front of the fireplace, where a thick, saffron yellow blanket rests invitingly.

There's no altar to the spirits, though. I'm sure I didn't see one upstairs, either. That's highly unusual—at least, to the best of my knowledge; it's not as though I've been in many private citizens' homes over the years.

So maybe having an altar in every home isn't as normal as I think, but it's still important. You invite the spirits into your home, and you invite their blessings and balance into your life. That matters.

Perhaps, once I have money, I can make a small one myself. There aren't many open surfaces in this cottage, but it occurs to me there should be flowers here.

I've finished the soup and am attempting to find a vase when Lorwyn barges in without so much as a knock.

She kicks the door closed and glares at me.

I frown back at her.

"How are you awake this early?" Lorwyn demands.

"How are you this rude at any time?" I return without hesitation.

Lorwyn pauses in the act of shedding her coat, looking at me sidelong. "I'm always equally charming, even before I've had sufficient cups of tea."

Aha.

"And you are even sassier when fed and bathed, I see," Lorwyn continues. "But I hesitate to ask what you've done to your hair."

Did I make it worse? "I tried to comb it."

Lorwyn sighs, the sigh of a thousand sighs. "You have older sisters, don't you."

I'm not sure how that's relevant, but nod regardless. This seems safe enough.

Lorwyn throws up her hands. "Of course you do. I am cursed with younger sisters. Let's go upstairs and get this sorted out, though I'm warning you, I'm not helping you with your hair every day. You'd do better to cut it off."

My face betrays my horror before I think better of it.

Lorwyn sighs again, and I follow her numbly up the stairs.

It would make it easier to hide, but... surely it won't come to that. Surely I'll be able to figure out how to care for it without servants?

Upstairs, Lorwyn goes straight to the closet and starts rummaging. "We need to convince Talmeri you're as good as a tea master, even if you don't have the credentials, which means you need to look the part," she says, then freezes. "Curses. Anyone will recognize this as one of her grandma's formal tunics, won't they? I didn't think of that."

"No," I disagree. "They're at least a season old, which means, as a noble, she'll have been seen, the pattern disseminated. I'll merely look behind-the-times. But are you sure it's fine to borrow?" Nightclothes were one thing, but formal dress—

"It's not like I have formalwear lying around," Lorwyn says. "Come on. Try this on."

She waves a bolt of pale, sunny yellow cloth with hints of purple embellishments at me.

“Is that the only one?” I ask.

She glares at me. “Are you picky? We don’t have all day.”

“That is not a color I should ever wear, and in particular it’s not one I can wear in autumn if you want your boss to take my knowledge of etiquette seriously.”

Lorwyn throws her hands up. “Fine. Come look. I’ll go get the combs and clips.” She tears downstairs in a whirl, and I feel a moment of sympathy for her younger sisters.

It is perhaps the strangest moment of the morning yet to go through the formal tunics and pants in the closet. Not so much because they belong to another person, but because this feels familiar. With dress, at least, I know how to present myself—except, again, I don’t. I’m not a princess anymore.

This is the first time the thought hasn’t sent me reeling. Good.

I choose a cream-colored dress shot through with a design of coppery feathers and the orange pants from a different set to wear underneath. The orange, being intended for spring, is the wrong shade, but paired with the cream the discrepancy is offset. I’m pleased I can manage to struggle into the dress alone—but already I realize the problem.

Risteri’s grandmother is apparently taller than me, and also a bit stockier. The high neck of the dress falls loose at the top; the long sleeves are longer than my hands; the flaps of the dress hang too low and the slits on each side don’t hit at my waist.

I stare at the travesty in the mirror, feeling a sharp sense of dread.

And then while I watch, the fabric tightens around me, magically fitting.

I turn to see Lorwyn watching me from the top of the stairs with narrowed eyes.

“There,” she says. “That’ll do for now. I’m not experimenting with witchcraft to unsnarl your hair, though. Sit on the edge of the bed and let’s get this over with.”

“Experimenting?” I echo.

She waves her hand vaguely. “Not like I need it for my own. You want me to practice on you?”

"No, thank you," I say quickly, resisting the urge to cover my hair with my hands.

"That's what I thought. Now hold still."

In the light of day, Talmeri's Teas and Tisanes doesn't look nearly as inviting as it did when I was freezing wet. Its pale green façade and the gold lettering of the shop's sign give it a veneer that separate it from the plain stone apartments nearby, but it looks cold, faded.

I'm disappointed. I want to remember it as a beacon of light and hope, drawing me in from the darkness.

Inside, at least, it's warm, and a little bell tinkles above our heads as Lorwyn unlocks the door and ushers me in.

This time, the magelamps are lit, and I can make out the interior of the shop.

At the back of the room I see the door to where Lorwyn's lab and supplies are. There are two other doors—one around the corner from the front door and one tucked away on the side—and I can't tell where they lead.

The front, at least, is mostly reserved for round tables of varying sizes, covered in pastel-patterned tablecloths, each with a small arrangement of woven flowers and candles in the center. There is a booth against the side wall, behind where I sat the night before, outfitted with a stove and multiple kettles, a special drawer unit with miniature compartments that I hope hold tea, and cabinets arrayed behind with tea utensils stuffed inside, cups and pots separated from their sets to fit wherever they can.

And the rest of the room is covered in shelves: the highest display expensive pots and china, as well as frames of pressed high-grade tea leaves.

A simple, classic tea set is on sale, but the lower shelves hold a stranger assortment: paper pads emblazoned with the title "tea recorder"—to keep track of teas customers try?—candles and incense, jewelry with charms that look like cups or pots and some with little jars that hold dustings of tea leaves. And—

"Does that say tea *soap*?" I whisper to Lorwyn.

"It does, and no I can't explain," Lorwyn says. "Are you ready?"

I don't ask why she didn't wonder this before and simply nod.

At that moment, the door around the front corner bursts open.

The woman who emerges is well into her middle age; possibly older. She's Istal like me and Risteri, but stockier, and her facial features flatter. She holds herself proudly, and her knee-length, loose dress over cropped pants is finely made. At a guess, she's a successful merchant, not a noble.

"Lorwyn, what a pleasant surprise, seeing you at the store so early! I almost couldn't believe it when I heard that door unlock. Now, before you get to whatever you came in for, if you could just help me—"

"Actually, I have someone for you to meet, Talmeri," Lorwyn says, stepping aside to gesture more obviously at me.

Talmeri pauses, as if noticing me for the first time. Her polite waiting smile is too affected, too forced. "Oh? A... friend?"

I hear the implication in her words, the unlikelihood that Lorwyn could have friends. I barely know Lorwyn, and still this galls me.

Perhaps because no one would ever believe I could have friends, either.

"No," Lorwyn says, a tightness in her voice and a strained smile. "Not a friend."

Talmeri nods, clearly having expected no less. "So, do tell. I do have quite a lot of work to get to this morning—"

"This morning?" Lorwyn cuts her off. "Does that mean you're planning to leave the shop—and the untrained boy on shift today—unsupervised *again*?"

Talmeri looks at her reproachfully. "A dear friend is ill, Lorwyn. Of course I'll go tend her. You'll manage—"

"Not and produce palatable sleekbeetle tea at the same time, I won't," Lorwyn says. "Which if you had given me any *notice* of, I could have—"

"Well, it's a good thing you're here early then, isn't it!" Talmeri says with obviously false brightness.

Lorwyn grows tenser beside me.

I, on the other hand, relax.

I grew up at the court of Istalam with this sort of biting smile. I don't have the full measure of Talmeri yet, but this I can handle.

"My pardon for interrupting you at such a busy time," I say. "I had not realized the situation here was so precarious. I can return again at a later—"

Talmeri's head snaps back to me. "Precarious? No, not at all. Please, how can I be of service?"

I bow low, careful not to smile. That was the easy part. "Grace Talmeri, I have some experience in the preparation and serving of tea. I hoped you might do me the honor of allowing me to serve you."

As I stand, Talmeri looks slowly from me to Lorwyn. "What's this?"

Lorwyn says, "I think she should work here."

Drat it, I'd just hooked Talmeri—Lorwyn is moving too fast!

Talmeri shakes her head. "No. I'm sorry, I don't know what Lorwyn has told you, but she knows I don't hire female servers."

To me, Lorwyn says, "Part of what Talmeri does here is train well-off boys in service and etiquette so they can make better matches. Having a nice young gentleman as your server is part of what Talmeri's is known for.

"But," she turns back to Talmeri, "you're comfortable with women for other positions. I'm in charge of the back, and you take care of the customers in the front."

"And what other position do you think needs filled, precisely?" Talmeri asks, her smile fixed.

"Yours," Lorwyn snaps.

The beat of silence that follows is deadly.

"I beg your pardon?" Talmeri says, her façade of good humor vanishing.

I can practically see my promise of lodging for the next half year, and any possibility of income, let alone self-sufficiency, going up in flames in front of me.

Not to mention my barely begun notion of making an altar, a space of my own.

"You haven't been present for a full shift in over a month," Lorwyn says. "Who do you think is promoting the image you want for your customers? The boys who're barely trained? Surely you don't think it's a good idea to leave *me* responsible for service? At a time when we need more revenue than ever, why do you think our business is dwindling?"

"I might ask you the same," Talmeri said. "You have no idea how much I do."

"I do, since I end up doing most of that too!"

Enough of this. "Grace Talmeri, please forgive me."

They look up surprised and chagrined to be caught arguing in front of a stranger, which makes me wonder how often that happens.

"I was not fully aware of Lorwyn's plans," I say, "but I believe I can be of use to you regardless. I respect that this is your establishment, and you more than anyone know its needs. I'm sorry to have caught you at such a busy time. Before any further discussion or decisions, I would be honored to serve you tea."

Talmeri watched me through narrow eyes, clearly distrustful.

Lorwyn adds, "Please let her, and I promise I'll find a way to have sleekbeetles on the menu by tomorrow no matter what."

"That quickly?" Talmeri pounces on her words. "Aren't you the one who told me you'd need at least two weeks, and that it possibly couldn't be done at all?"

"I didn't just pluck any old person off the street," Lorwyn says, though of course this is patently false. "Miyara's trained to taste, and she pointed me toward a major breakthrough yesterday."

"Oh, is that so?" Talmeri asks, turning back to me, and I can practically feel her thoughts spinning as her false smile returns. "Lorwyn is notoriously picky. If you two worked well together, perhaps you'd be willing to stop by and help her from time to time?"

I open my mouth to answer affirmatively, but Lorwyn says, "While I'm sure she would dearly love to offer her services for free, alas, she also needs money to eat."

Talmeri glares at her.

Aha. Talmeri hadn't been offering me a job, but trying to cheat me out of one.

I incline my head in a way that indicates both acknowledgement and regret.

"Well, now, look at those manners," Talmeri murmurs. Folds her arms. "All right. You have one chance to impress me, Grace Miyara. What tea will you serve me?"

And now it begins.

I don't know what tea she carries or what accoutrements are available, so I'll assume the best and work from there.

"If you'll permit me, I'll perform the tea ceremony," I say.

Talmeri's eyebrows creep up, and even Lorwyn looks surprised. Practitioners of tea ceremony train for years. It's possible to do poorly, but for my confidence that I can impress her with it, they intuit I must possess some actual skill.

"You didn't say you were a tea master," Talmeri says.

"I regret that I'm not." I incline my head again. "However, you may judge my skill for yourself. Sadly, I can't prove my pedigree with credentials. There are no records of the masters I've trained under, nor have I taken the requisite certification exams. But I don't think you will be disappointed with my performance."

"Why do you think I'll hire you for a tea master position when a noble household wouldn't?" Talmeri asks.

"I'm not applying to be your tea master," I say. "I am not so presumptuous. But I can see you run a special kind of business and you're not afraid to take measured risks—either with sleekbeetles or with a brewer as unconventional as Lorwyn. So I don't expect you to hire me, but I hope you might consider the notion."

"Hmm. An answer that's to the point, indicates a firm understanding of your place, and is still polite." Talmeri flashes that false bright smile at Lorwyn, and I realize Lorwyn's own unnerving smile is a perversion of this one. "A skill we don't see much of day to day, don't you think?"

"You don't say," Lorwyn says dryly.

"Very well," Talmeri says. "We shall take tea in the ceremony chamber. Let's see what you can do."

Lorwyn looks hesitant for the first time. "Talmeri, we haven't used that room in a while."

"Then it should be clean, shouldn't it?" she says, holding out her hand.

Lorwyn winces, handing over a key. "That's not, exactly, how—"

She breaks off as Talmeri opens the door, and dust wafts out of the room.

"You see?" Talmeri asks from inside. "It will do nicely."

"She has never had to clean a day in her life," Lorwyn mutters in explanation.

"Lorwyn," I say quietly. "Do you have any aloia incense in the back?"

She glances back at me quickly, catching on. The combination of aloia nectar and fire will suck the dust away. "I can whip some up quickly," she says.

"Three, if you can," I say. "Let's draw the dust away from her, before she starts coughing."

"On it," she says. "I'll be back in a minute."

So now I'm on my own.

I step across the threshold, and my test begins.

I place both hands palm down on my thighs and bow at the waist.

There's an altar on each of the other walls, and I bow to them in turn, then to my guest, kneeling on a cushion at the low square table in the center.

Her expression is pinched, but she won't cough, not yet. Nor will she admit she erred—at least not without blaming Lorwyn.

"All the materials you need are in the closet on your right," Talmeri says.

I bow once more and slide open the door. There's a sink, a small stove with a kettle, and a case underneath that holds all the tea ceremony utensils—much more organized than the front room's, thankfully, and the case has protected them from the dust. There is a shelf with several canisters of tea.

This is the next part of the test: not only setting up the ceremony on my own in an unfamiliar setting, but selecting the appropriate tea.

I look over the shape of the leaves in each before pulling down two canisters. After sniffing, I make my choice. Talmeri has work to do now but will have a calm afternoon sitting with her friend: I'll make her the classic green water blend, for adaptability.

I hear the door open again, which must be Lorwyn coming in with the incense.

I start the water heating in the kettle and arrange the wooden tea tray: the clay pot with the stylized wave swirling around it, indicating it pairs with the water blend; two cups lined with porcelain; scoop and tea pet and kettle stand. It's not just a matter of what's on the tray, but how each piece is positioned, distinct for each tea ceremony.

When I have them all set appropriately, the door shuts again.

With a breath, I lift the tray carefully and carry it out.

Lorwyn is nowhere to be seen. Talmeri must have asked her to leave us. I don't mind: Lorwyn would probably only antagonize her accidentally.

And the tea ceremony is a sacred ritual. It's right for it to be just Talmeri and me.

I bow at the waist again, still holding the tray out, parallel with the table, demonstrating to my guest that I possess the skill to take care of her.

The tray's angle is perfect, and it never wavers.

I set it down on the table, bow, and on cue the kettle begins to whistle. I fetch it, deposit it in its place, and kneel.

The tea ceremony is a series of stylized movements that serve multiple purposes. Part is practical: the method of brewing that draws the best flavor from the leaves, priming the pot and cups, discarding the first steep. But even this is to feed into the main purpose of the tea ceremony, which is an experience.

The guest must always feel that they are taken care of, that they will be well served.

They must feel comfortable, and they must feel special.

They must feel the ceremony is a sacred oasis.

The particular movements are a ritual to bring them into this experience. Every turn of a cup, every splash of water, every bow creates that space.

Bows are second nature for anyone at court. But that's not my only strength.

Although I have a tea pet, I know exactly how long it takes for this amount of water to cool from the boiling point to be at the correct temperature for this tea without having to time it.

I know how long each of my movements must take in that time so there is never a lull during which my guest might worry or their attention wander, and I know how to make the best effect of the formal dress I wear as I move.

I know how much tea to scoop without a measure, and I know how long it must steep for.

I know how to kneel in this position for hours if I have to, if that's what it takes to serve all my guests.

When I serve Talmeri the tea, I know that while she might not hire me despite my and Lorwyn's hopes, it won't be due to my lack of skill.

Talmeri takes a deep sip of the tea. Her eyes close, and she takes a deep breath.

"Well," Talmeri says, and sighs softly, setting the cup back down. "Well. I can't deny I'd like to hire you, Miyara, after a performance like that."

Despite my calm moments before, I feel a spike of panic.

I *don't* know how else to persuade her, nor how to get a job elsewhere.

"But?" I ask quietly.

"This area is under a lot of pressure," Talmeri says. "We need every coin we can bring in. Lorwyn makes a salary, but our serving boys don't—their education is a service I provide to their families. You need to make a living wage, and I'm not willing to pay you one."

I steady my breathing, watching her, trying to think.

No. I need to *listen.*

I've heard how easily she manipulates her tone—she should have pronounced that with finality, and she didn't.

This is the opening sally to bargain.

Saiyana once told me diplomacy and bargaining are the same thing.

"I don't need a living wage right away," I say. "I need enough for food, general household items, and to style myself in a manner befitting your shop. Lodging rent is not an immediate concern, so I'd be comfortable starting with a low salary initially until I've proven to you how useful I can be."

It's a risky statement, with undefined parameters. But I need to turn the 'no' into a 'yes' before I impose conditions.

"A possibility," Talmeri allows. "And what if I never decide you're worth a full salary?"

"I'm confident you will," I say.

Talmeri laughs. "I appreciate that kind of confidence, but I'm looking for a plan of action here, Miyara."

Certainty in her voice. "You already have one in mind."

Her eyes narrow, though she doesn't look upset. "So I do. In three months my lease on this building expires. What do you think that means for a struggling business, when prices are rising?"

I think for a moment. "If your profits have been dwindling, then it isn't enough to make as much as you used to. You need to be more profitable to compete."

Talmeri nods. "Just so. Good, you understand the basics of commerce."

"Lorwyn intimated she hoped I might assist with the business spreadsheets."

"Ha! Clever girl, dropping that in. And just like her, to try and pass those off. But one thing at a time, Miyara."

"Yes, Grace Talmeri," I say demurely.

"Good," she approves. "Now. You understand that even if you took on more of the work around here, that wouldn't be enough to turn our fortunes. I have some plans in the works, but if I can't count on customer revenue exploding beyond my wildest dreams, what does that leave me to bargain with?"

"Providing a valued service to the community," I say.

"I already have that. No, stop, I realize I can add value or services. That's not the answer I'm looking for."

I cast around, thinking of what else I'd heard from her this morning. She's leaving her business to see a friend, she values her image, she's proud—

"Reputation," I say.

Talmeri nods slowly, eyeing me with more appreciation.

It occurs to me that until that moment she wasn't sure I was actually intelligent.

She waves her hand at me, indicating my body, my clothes, my poise. "Yes. Reputation. With a reputation, I have bargaining power. It affects the network I have access to—where do you think these serving boys come from, after all?—and the degree of investments. And you know what would bring me one?"

"A tea master," I say. And: "Which you can't afford."

"But you, with no credentials, references, or paperwork to your name, I can," she says. "Because I can pay you whatever I like."

I keep my expression even. She wants a reaction from me at that, the implicit threat. She knows I'm desperate or I wouldn't accept less than a full wage.

"But I'm still not a tea master," I say. "And if you try to use my position as leverage for investments, every noble will know you for a liar. Which won't be good for your reputation at all."

"Ah, you know how the game is played. We'll get along fine." Talmeri smiles. "And that won't be a problem if you become a tea master in the next three months."

I blink.

She's serious.

"Three *months*?"

"Three months. You clearly have a thorough background in the ceremony already, so that should be sufficient. I will sponsor your study materials, of course."

I'm intrigued despite myself. This is mad, but if I can pull it off, I won't need this job anymore—as a tea master, I'll be sought after wherever I go. Since it's likely I'll need to move eventually to hide from my family, that holds a lot of appeal.

"The exam has multiple components, if I recall correctly," I say. "I'll also need to practice, and it's clear that this room is not in regular use. Shall I add a service of value to your shop in the course of my studies?"

Her eyebrows shoot up, but she remains smiling. "An interesting idea. You're amenable, then?"

"With some qualifications," I say.

This is the next part of the test.

"Oh?" Talmeri asks politely, her smile fixed.

"If I'm to work here, I'll have to be studying on my own time," I say. "That's a great investment of my time up-front. Accordingly, I would like an advance of my salary up-front."

"You think I should pay you before you've done any work?" Talmeri inquires, as if to point out how ludicrous the very notion is.

"Yes," I say, pressing the point. "Every week, we will both put in either money or time and effort at the start. If you're not satisfied with my progress, or I experience difficulties with my degree of compensation, then we will adjust before more work begins."

"And I will agree to this because...?"

"Once I'm a tea master, I won't demand compensation equal to the value I bring."

Her face tightens, and I know I'm right to address this now. Did she think that wouldn't occur to me in the next three months, or did she think she'd be able to lock me into a bad arrangement while I was desperate?

"Lots of vagueness in those terms," Talmeri points out, as if regretfully broaching an uncomfortable issue of etiquette.

It's my turn to nod. "Yes. I'm taking a risk trusting you now, and your risk will come later. But so will the fruits of this arrangement, for both of us."

"Unless you leave me in the lurch," she says doubtfully.

I amend my assessment. It's not that she didn't think I would realize this—it's that, overcome with the possibilities, she hadn't thought her plan through.

I remember that she mass-purchased sleekbeetle scales for tea. Talmeri understands her business and is a woman of many fine ideas, but she does not consider consequences thoroughly in advance of their eventuality.

I'll have to keep this in mind.

But she's also a woman who takes risks.

"Grace Talmeri, I would like to be of service," I say. "I think I may be able to do that better here than anywhere. You have my word that I'll stay as long as I'm able, and you will not regret our arrangement. And if you're not willing to take this opportunity, my word is all I will ever be able to offer you."

Talmeri considers the tea service between us, the image I strike in formal dress, and she stares at me, hard.

Then she stands. "Let's go to my office, then, and look at the numbers."

And with that, I have three months to pass the most restrictive exam in the post-Cataclysm nations and become a tea master.

Only once Talmeri leaves the room do I have a moment to reflect in horror at what my impulsive bargain means, how impossible that task truly is.

What have I done?

CHAPTER 5

"THAT'S THE CENTRAL MARKET," Lorwyn says, pointing at a shining, tidy, open street lined with shops and vendors, bustling with activity.

I take a step toward it, but Lorwyn yanks me back.

When I look at her in confusion, she jerks her chin over her shoulder. "We're going to this way."

Then she turns on her heel and rounds a corner.

I scramble to track all the turns she takes down narrow alleyways and don't have confidence I've managed it. But soon enough we emerge in a courtyard, surrounded on all sides by crumbling stone buildings covered in ivy, like ruins of old, abandoned castles.

It's clear, however, that this place, while in disrepair, has not been abandoned.

I can scarcely hear anything above the clamor in this courtyard, and I lose track of Lorwyn in the sudden press of bodies jostling all around.

Then a hand closes around my bare wrist, and I tense before I realize Lorwyn has located me and is now pulling me through the crowd.

Suddenly there's space again; it's only around the edges of the courtyard where it's a fight to move. But on the inside, like we've passed into a bubble, I can hear again.

And I notice the majority of people in this courtyard are Gaellani.

"Two noodle plates," Lorwyn calls to a man in a booth at the center, then looks at me. "You're paying."

My eyebrows shoot up as I pull out the pouch of coins Talmeri gave me. "Do I have enough?"

Lorwyn swears and covers the pouch, pressing it back against my tunic. "Don't wave money, or anything valuable, around like that," she says. "At least make the thieves work for it."

I nod. "That doesn't answer my question." I'm sure I can afford a meal of some kind, but this money needs to cover all my expenses for the week.

Lorwyn rolls her eyes. "So you grew up rich and not in a city, I take it. Yes, you have enough. You can count money, can't you?"

"Yes." I know precisely what each coin should weigh, its metal content, the symbols of my house's history and images of my ancestors and all the political maneuvering that led to the decision for each. But I've never actually used one before.

"It'll be two marks for each," Lorwyn says.

"That little?" I ask, but quietly, in case this is the sort of place where merchants raise their prices for certain people.

"That's why we're here," Lorwyn says. "If Talmeri's going to be cheap, at the very least her money can go to Gaellani."

I pass a five-mark coin to Lorwyn and watch carefully how she handles the transaction with the vendor. Now that I'm not startled by the new place and the sheer quantity of people, I see that in front of the booth there's a drawing of three dishes next to a number, presumably the cost in marks for each of the day's specials. I'm glad I won't have to magically intuit prices every time I purchase a meal.

In short order we're seated at stools around the side. The noodles are a different texture than I've eaten, fried noodles that are twisty, round and of medium thickness. The sauce is sweet rather than spicy, and the vegetables are all ones that I know from the yearly crop yields are among the most common and least expensive.

"This is delicious," I say. "Thank you for bringing me here."

Lorwyn snorts. "For cheap Gaellani street food? No problem."

It *is* wonderful, though, and new, but possibly it's too normal for her to see it that way. Sensing she'll scoff at any further compliment of the food, I instead say, "It's a far tastier meal than I could have made."

She waves her chopsticks expansively in between bites. "Anyone can make this. I don't care if you haven't done anything more than boil water for tea, this dish is the easiest thing in the world to cook."

I'm not sure she realizes I have literally done no more with a stove than boil water and decide not to mention it. I'll have to learn how to cook for myself, but it's not her responsibility to teach me. She's already done more than enough.

"Why not take me somewhere more expensive, then, if you were planning on paying with Talmeri's money?" I ask.

Lorwyn eyes me sidelong as she chews, as if weighing how much to tell me. Then she swallows her food in a big gulp and says, "Okay, two reasons. The first, which you'll start hearing about soon enough, is that Gaellani businesses, and even businesses that serve Gaellani customers, are being charged higher rates."

That would make it harder to bring enough money in to run businesses or to buy the products that are suddenly more costly too. Maybe the fact that the courtyard is mainly full of Gaellani isn't entirely by choice. "If I'm going to start hearing about it, does that mean it hasn't always been that way?"

Lorwyn salutes me with her sticks. "You're quick. It has always been that way, and the costs have risen over time as costs do, but there's been a steep increase in the last year. So we support each other as much as we can."

"Then I'll have to make sure I can find my way back so I can contribute, too," I say. "Thank you for letting me know."

"How can you miss it?" she asks, and I can't tell if she's joking or just that entrenched in living here before she looks a challenge at me. "And I may have been angling for that."

I cock my head to one side. "Why wouldn't I help if I can?"

Lorwyn shrugs. "You're a sheltered rich girl with no ties to anyone here. You might be more comfortable at nicer places, and you have no reason to care about anyone here."

I have no reason to be notably comfortable at a "nicer" place, either, as I have no standard for what a commercial dining place should look like. The idea that I should need a reason to care about people's wellbeing is so reminiscent of the life I've abandoned that I refuse to address it.

"You remember I'm the girl who sat sopping in front of you in a tablecloth just last night."

"So it's gratitude, then?"

I frown at her. She's asking the question, but I don't get the sense she's actually interested in the answer. More that she feels she ought to challenge me. So I respond in kind.

"For gratitude, I tasted your beetle scale pepper tea," I remind her, and she laughs.

"The second reason," Lorwyn says, "is that if you shop Gaellani you can save some money. That apparently didn't occur to Talmeri, since she only gets her food at 'respectable establishments'. It'll help you get around this horseshit about justifying every purchase to her."

I blink, and then it's my turn to laugh. "You hate manipulating people, don't you?"

She glares at me. "What makes you say that?"

"Not only did you tell me what you were angling for, you did so before you gave me an extra reason to be grateful to you."

"Maybe I was judging what kind of person you were before making sure you had a reason to do it anyway."

I shake my head, still smiling. "You already knew I would."

Lorwyn regards me for a moment, and then stands abruptly. "Are you done? We should get moving."

Sudden longing strikes me. She's brought me to a place unlike any I've experienced, and I'm to catch just a glimpse and then be spirited away again?

In a way, it's not so different than the life I've abandoned. I recognize that's dramatic, but my hesitation remains.

I know I'm prevailing on her time, but I take a breath and ask, "Is there a reason I can't walk through here first?"

Lorwyn looks at me strangely, like she can't believe I want to. Is it her bias about the place, or about what I must think of it?

"We have to get you a full set of formalwear and get back in time for me to start teaching you what to do at the shop before customers arrive," Lorwyn says. "You really think we have time to spare now?"

I have no idea how much time any of this will take. I've chosen formalwear before, of course, but I don't know if my experience will be comparable to visiting a tailor in the city. I don't know how long it will take me to be ready for customers, but I'm inclined to think an afternoon won't suffice in any case.

"I suppose not," I say, casting a wistful look around. I can hardly make out everything being sold here; just people. People who know each other, who trade jokes and shouts and are *here*, and that is more compelling to me than all the things I can't see.

"It's not like the courtyard is going anywhere," Lorwyn points out, already striding back toward the edge. "You can always come back. Hey, that's Glynis. Glyn, hold up!"

Lorwyn takes off, and as I hurry after her I decide I think I will enjoy coming back here—if I can find the courtyard again—without Lorwyn. This isn't a place she thinks is worth showing me for its own sake, so I will discover its character on my own, without needing to justify my attention with every step.

Lorwyn hauls me through the press of bodies, and we're back in an alley, still running—and then Lorwyn stops abruptly.

"I'm in a hurry," a new voice says, higher-pitched and bored. "What do you need?"

From behind Lorwyn, I lean as far to the side as I can and see an adolescent girl. Her ashen hair is shoved up in a hat, and her boots are sturdy but have clearly seen lots of use. Her clothes are worn but neat and well cared-for: trousers and a buttoned vest over a crisp shirt with the sleeves rolled up right above the elbow, revealing that one of her arms stops there.

Lorwyn turns, leaning against the wall of the alley casually so the girl can see me. "Glynis, this is Miyara. She's staying at Risteri's grandma's cottage."

Glynis nods as though this is a completely normal thing to tell a stranger while I stare at Lorwyn askance.

"You remember I'm trying *not* to announce my presence?" I say to her, letting a hint of anger bleed into my tone.

Lorwyn holds up a hand—to Glynis, I realize, who's frowning at me. "Glynis is a messenger," Lorwyn explains. "See the guild patch on her sleeve? If you need to reach me, or Risteri, or anyone else, you either flag down a messenger or you drop by the messengers' guild headquarters and leave your message with them, and they'll see it delivered."

I hadn't noticed the patch; sloppy. With everything so new and thus noteworthy to me, I'm not sure how easy it will be for me to notice, so I'd better learn where the guild is based, too.

In the silence I realize Glynis is staring at me, and I'm not sure if it's because she thinks I'm rudely staring at her arm or if she's suspicious why Lorwyn thinks she needs to explain how the messengers' guild works to me, but I step back and nod briskly as though nothing's amiss.

"What kind of privacy do you want?" Glynis asks, and my façade fails.

Much? Some? I turn to Lorwyn at a loss for how to begin to answer that question.

Lorwyn says, "Personal for now—she'll accept messages from anyone who knows her by name."

I shake my head quickly. Giving Lorwyn my name last night was a big mistake, but it's too late to undo. "No, there are people who know my name that I don't want to know where I live, or where I am."

"With all due respect, *grace*," Glynis says, drawing herself up to her full height, "I assure you, no one can track a messenger."

Saiyana could, but Saiyana is also one of the best mages in Istalam, so this is perhaps not an argument worth making aloud.

Glynis glares at Lorwyn. "Anything else?"

"No, that's it," Lorwyn says with a wave. Glynis nods perfunctorily and vanishes down the alley.

"I didn't mean to offend her," I say, "but is this really a good idea?"

"Yes," Lorwyn says, resuming walking at a more normal pace. "Maybe it's different wherever you're from, but the messengers' guild out here is serious about being incorruptible, since people rely on them to communicate. And no one will find out your whereabouts from them—you don't get to be a messenger by being stupid. If people start sending you messages or packages you don't want, you can set up a system for the messengers to filter your mail. This is totally normal, Miyara, and it would be more suspicious if you tried to go around without getting set up with the guild."

I don't want to be isolated, but I can't help but feel uneasy about an organization that everyone believes can't be corrupted. I hope my suspicions are never substantiated. "And am I now? Set up with the guild?"

"Yeah, Glyn will take care of it."

Glyn. Lorwyn knows this girl well enough to feel comfortable addressing her by a diminutive. I hesitate for a moment, and then ask, "Do you know what happened to her arm?"

Lorwyn cocks her head to the side for a moment, thinking while we walk. "I can't remember if it was an accident when she was little or if she was born that way," she finally says. "Her arm's been like that as long as

I remember. It annoys her that she can't sew as fast as her mom—I mean Glyn's still faster than almost anyone I know, but her whole family's seamstresses—so she decided to join the messengers' guild early. Why, does it bother you?"

"No, of course not," I hasten to say, because it shouldn't, and if it bothers me in the way she means that is a problem with me, to work out on my own. But then I pause, because that's not why I asked, and add, "Well. No, it does bother me to think she might have lost her arm due to the lack of available quality medical care, and I hope that wasn't the case."

Istalam has been blessed with talented mage healers, but the Cataclysm and the influx of refugees strained our resources. Although I never made policy, I know even Saiyana feels measures to ensure the communities with the greatest influx of people are being adequately served are insufficient.

"Oh," Lorwyn says. "No, definitely not. If it had come down to that, for a serious injury to a child—we'd have worked something out."

She means witchcraft.

I'm not sure if I should feel better, knowing the Gaellani have witches to call upon when needed, or worse, that they should be forced to because the state is failing them. But it seems at least Glynis is not a victim of Istalam's failures, and that's all I really meant to ascertain.

To my surprise, Lorwyn returns us to the Central Market. For the most part, the Central Market is lined with indoor shops, though there are a few carts and booths set up alongside. After the shock of the courtyard, it feels calmer, almost sedate in comparison. It is, I admit, more what I expected a shopping district to look like—neater, more orderly, and above all quieter—but although in a way it's more soothing, I find I already miss the raucous atmosphere of the courtyard.

Lorwyn drags me along. There is an entire shop for crafts made from mulberry paper—boxes, stationery, art—and another selling fine inks of every shade. That shopkeeper catches my eye and bows, and I return her regard automatically before Lorwyn tugs me onward.

I smile as we pass the display of whimsical glass statuettes, bowing in return to another shopkeeper's greeting, until I catch Lorwyn's scowl, and I finally notice something else:

They are only bowing to me.

I stop all at once, going cold as panic seizes me. I look all around, and my dread grows. They aren't bowing to anyone else either. I should be glad that they're not disrespecting Lorwyn specifically in their greetings; this isn't anti-refugee sentiment at work. But.

Lorwyn appears directly in front of me, hands planted on her hips. "What now?" she demands.

I swallow and whisper, "Why are they all bowing to me?"

Lorwyn rolls her eyes. "You know how rare tea masters are. Talmeri's spread the word among her contacts that she'll be sponsoring your tea assessment, clearly, and they're treating you with the respect due an aspirant."

Talmeri had said she would arrange for an assessment with a tea master, hadn't she? And only someone who seriously expects to pass the tests for tea mastery schedules one, so of course this news would be worthwhile for her to spread. My breath escapes me in a rush of relief, and a little irritation with myself.

Of course, why should shopkeepers in Sayorsen recognize the fourth princess of Istalam, anyway? My secret is still safe.

Except that Lorwyn narrows her eyes and asks, "If you weren't expecting this reaction, why weren't you bothered by all the bowing before?"

She's right; I should've expected this, given how rare tea masters are, but I've been trying not to dwell on that for fear I'll daunt myself out of the task before of me.

Tea masters fill a unique role in our culture. In a way, they're more respected than royalty or priestesses. Not only are they highly sought after as guests, a certified tea master can travel through any country, regardless of national treaties, and sometimes are called upon to help establish those treaties in the first place. Although it's sacrilege to refuse the request of a tea master, they're supposed to be too wise, too deft with people to create such a situation. Tea masters are experts of etiquette and poise, of history and diplomacy, of art and craft. They transcend borders, and they specialize in bringing people to a greater awareness of themselves and their place.

Becoming a tea master is, in a way, symbolic of everything I want for myself, and everything I have no idea how to achieve.

It's not enough to be able to brew tea. That, at least, I have a head-start on, or the task ahead of me would be impossible rather than merely improbable. But how to accomplish the rest? Aspirants to tea mastery spend decades in study and practice.

I have three months.

But if nothing else, I am well-practiced at presenting a façade of calm and partial truths to the world, so I shove down my rising panic and address Lorwyn's question.

"Formal manners were a matter of great concern where I grew up," I say. "Reciprocal bowing is such a habit I sometimes forget that my upbringing was nonstandard in that regard."

Lorwyn snorts. "You sometimes forget how to talk in a standard regard, too. Come on."

But I don't follow her, instead drifting a few paces away, because I've noticed a store filled with all sorts of equipment I don't recognize in between pots and spoons and tea kettles.

I could have a tea kettle of my own.

The force of that sudden want is staggering, and I swallow to hold it in.

"What are you looking at now?" Lorwyn asks, and my eyes dart around the display for a likely distractor and find confusion.

"I have no idea," I admit, entranced by the breadth of gadgetry on display. "These things are all—for cooking? What do you do with them?"

Lorwyn laughs. "You don't. Most of these things are totally unnecessary if you have a good knife and a steady hand. And the ones from this store you could reasonably use are either overpriced or overly concerned with being pretty at the expense of stability."

"So they can then sell you another one later," I murmur. "I see."

"Also so they can keep their profit margins high," Lorwyn notes dryly.

A rough chuckle sounds from the booth next door. "Such cynicism from one so young," he says in a rich voice weathered with age.

He doesn't appear so very old, but he's striking nonetheless: his skin is light, but not like the Gaellani's—there is more gold in it, and his straight hair is a thick, true black. His eyes are sharp as he drums long, heavily ringed fingers on a display table while lounging back in his seat in a way that somehow conveys his weariness with everything around him and yet utter confidence.

It's a demeanor every person I've met from the Isle of Nakrab has possessed.

"Don't even try with her, Thiano," Lorwyn says. "She has to justify every purchase she makes to Talmeri."

It clearly bothers Lorwyn, but despite my newfound commitment to never let my life be controlled I decide that, for now, I'm actually relieved by an externally supervised budget to keep me from buying items I don't need. I don't expect to spend frivolously, but my ability to judge what is useful or what may be a scam is limited.

"Talmeri is bearing the brunt of the risk in this venture," I point out. She's the one who will be putting up money for a task I might not be able to accomplish, and she has only my word that if I do I won't leave her in a lurch. But I don't say this out loud, because Lorwyn already knows; my words are for the benefit of Talmeri's reputation and thus the tea shop's, and not undoing the groundwork she's laid spreading the word of my tea assessment.

"But Talmeri's not going to be doing the work," Lorwyn says.

"It's not unreasonable for her to be strict with her investment up-front," I say, mindful of our interested audience.

"And if she never loosens up?"

Lorwyn is not, evidently, quite so mindful. "By then I intend to have a greater ability to negotiate, and regardless, this is perhaps not the best place for this conversation?"

"Oh, don't mind me," Thiano says with a smirk. "I'm well aware Talmeri has the soul of a mercenary, and no amount of careful words will convince me otherwise. But if you're to be studying the ways of tea, perhaps I can interest you in a tea set?"

He gestures to a white porcelain pot, delicately painted with exquisite flowers. As I watch, the flowers dance, shifting around the exterior, and I smile, delighted.

"Don't even think about it, Miyara," Lorwyn says. "Thiano's no less mercenary than Talmeri, and he'd grin at you merrily while counting every last coin of your life's savings. Which would also be at least twice as much as the value of his merchandise."

"Lorwyn, you wound me," Thiano says, and with a wink at me adds, "As though I'd settle for payment less than three times the value."

"Not if you're selling pottery to anyone who knows their business," Lorwyn says easily. "Anyone in Sayorsen knows perfectly well not to pay more for pottery from you when it's not on the level of what Deniel makes."

"Deniel?" I ask.

Thiano sniffs. "An ungenerous Gaellani artisan of some renown."

Lorwyn smirks. "You're just sore he won't sell to you so you can re-sell for more."

My curiosity is piqued. "Does this Deniel have a shop nearby?"

Lorwyn snorts. "In the Central Market? Not hardly."

"As I said, he's ungenerous, and also miserly," Thiano says, shaking his head. "Deniel hoards every coin of his success for himself and won't spend a mark that doesn't benefit him in some way."

Lorwyn is set to erupt in outrage, but I beat her to it. "So keeping a storefront in the Central Market is expensive, and his skill is known enough that he can afford not to pay for the placement here?"

Thiano smiles toothily at Lorwyn, who scowls. Ah, so he was deliberately trying to get a rise from her.

She crosses her arms and tells me, "He set up shop in the same district as Talmeri's. Don't bother visiting unless you want to torture yourself, though. You won't be able to afford his pieces anytime soon."

I now want to visit simply because she's told me I shouldn't, and I wonder if I've always been this quietly contrary, or if it's a result of exposure to freedom and the urge will lull with time.

I sense more than see Thiano watching me—and in fact his eyes aren't on me at all, but although he banters with Lorwyn I can tell he's aware of every movement I make. This is a man of deliberation, who has allowed me to become aware of a competitor for my interest. Why?

The shop behind him contains all manner of items, from vases to exquisite time-pieces. Not, in truth, a surprise: it's rare for Nakrabi to spend any length of time on the continent, and I assume this shop is a sort of trading outpost to funnel goods considered exotic in either their culture or ours.

But when I look at the table between us, the selection is more limited. There is the tea set, there are heavy bracelets not unlike the cuffs I wore in the palace, there are scarves of rich, royal purple. And there is a small painting, a tree with shades of leaves falling as though in autumn, but all of them are green.

I finger the edges of it gently, and look up to find him watching me. "Why green?" I ask.

Thiano shrugs. "A color of harmony and new beginnings, I suppose. Who can say? I'm not the artist. Maybe she was just feeling overwhelmed by all the oranges this year."

Shades of green aren't out of season, but they're not the common trend for this year's autumn in Sayorsen. If I'm to distinguish my wardrobe in a way that will serve my role at the tea house, this is information I can use.

"Miyara, we've lingered here too long. We should get going," Lorwyn says.

Holding my gaze, Thiano says, "You may not be able to afford any of my wares now, but perhaps you should stop by sometime to check."

I smile. "I'd like that very much," I say, and we exchange a bow of understanding before Lorwyn leads me away.

My grandmother was right. I know how to listen, and so, clearly, does Thiano.

He knows who I am, and I now know he's a spy. I only wonder what he thinks helping me will gain him.

CHAPTER 6

THE TAILOR'S SHOP IS like nothing I've seen before. That revelation probably shouldn't still seem so surprising to me, and perhaps over time it won't. But it is still hard for me to reconcile how leaving the palace has caused me to enter an entirely new yet parallel world. There are commonalities, but so many of the details are utterly foreign. In some ways it's the similarities that are the most jarring when I encounter them in the sea of all the difference.

This tailor's shop is pristine, wide open, and huge, with much of that space devoted to the meticulous storage of fabric.

And I can tell right away that Lorwyn hates it by the fixed scowl that appears on her face as soon as we enter.

"Why are we here?" I ask her softly.

"You need formalwear fast," she says in a clipped tone.

I narrow my eyes, quelling my initial urge to respond that yes, I'm fully aware of that, and that's not what I meant and she knows it.

Because perhaps it is what I meant. Seamstresses Lorwyn knows and respects probably can't afford to keep the kind of fabric on hand in substantial quantities for formalwear, not least because the demand for it among their clientele is likely low. So despite her preferences, she's brought me to a place that will.

A woman glides in from around a corner. She smiles when she sees me and bows. "The tea aspirant! Talmeri mentioned you might stop by today. Please, be welcome."

"I'm honored to make your acquaintance." I bow once toward her, and then again at Lorwyn, who frowns at me. "I'm Miyara, and this is my companion, Lorwyn."

It's a subtle trick of etiquette, but one that indicates I expect the shopkeeper to treat Lorwyn with the same degree of respect she bestows on me. Lorwyn clearly doesn't recognize it, but the shopkeeper does, tendering Lorwyn a bow without missing a beat.

"The honor is mine," she says, her smile just as warm, and I'm satisfied I can do business here after all. If she disrespects Lorwyn as a Gaellani, it will be by accident, not design. Today I will bear that, and judge whether it is worth bearing again when expediency is less of a priority.

"I understand you're looking for formalwear," the tailor says, bowing as she backs toward one table in the center of this front room. "I took the liberty of gathering a few samples as a starting point."

I follow her, motioning Lorwyn to do the same. She rolls her eyes but complies, and the tailor has pulled several fabric samples from a shelf beneath the table by the time we've arrived.

My eyes narrow. Thiano was spot-on. Oranges indeed.

"The deeper shades contrast well with cream, though you may also want to consider some lighter, more sophisticated shades," the tailor says.

I shake my head. "No, not this season, I think."

She looks up at me quickly, masking her expression to one of polite, pleasant curiosity. I hear the quiet huff from next to me and know Lorwyn is already amused.

"I assure you, these colors—"

"—are perfectly in line with the palette fashionable this season, yes," I agree. "I can already see your eye is very keen. But since you know Talmeri, I feel more comfortable explaining part of what we hope to accomplish with my service at her shop, and that is to distinguish it. My style must convey both a sense of sensitivity and awareness of what my guests care about so they feel comfortable, but must also be set apart. A statement, but one of exquisite elegance."

"I see," she says, eyes crinkling at the corners which I take to mean she is considering my words. "Do you have an idea in mind?"

"Green," I say, and Lorwyn looks at me sharply.

"Hmm," the tailor says. Skeptical, but the challenge has piqued her interest. "Perhaps a design of delicate falling leaves across the front?"

"For at least one," I agree. "Perhaps the leaves can be in a shade of orange that complements this season's palette?"

"Maybe a burnished yellow," she muses. "Or perhaps the under-pants can set that off. Please wait a moment while I see what we have in the back."

"One more thing," I say. "The fabric—"

The tailor nods quickly. "Silk if I can find it, yes. But you understand that will cost more?"

I smile. "I'm making extraordinary demands. It seems right that I should pay for them."

Her façade cracks, and I see a slight smile break through before she bows again and backs away.

"Why silk?" Lorwyn demands promptly. "Do you realize how much that costs? Your budget—"

"It's a good thing you've just shown me how to conserve money at lunch," I say. "And as time is of the essence and I intend to be very particular, it's unlikely she will have a sufficient variety of fabric on hand for me to purchase only silk from her."

"It's still a waste of money."

"No, silk will be ideal to strike the right note of sophistication while still being comfortable enough for daily work."

I'm pleased that I thought to consider the latter until Lorwyn says, "I hope your image is worth it, because silk's still a pain to wash."

I blink. Stare at her.

Lorwyn sighs. "You have no idea how to wash silk, or anything else, do you?"

I blush and shake my head, too embarrassed to reply.

"I can show you the basics later this week, but don't expect me to do it for you."

Another thing I'll owe her, and a rush of despair strikes me sharply. *How will I ever be in a position to give more to the people whom I should serve than I've taken?*

But Lorwyn seems more relaxed, perhaps at having found a way to contribute in this setting that otherwise makes her feel like an outsider.

I take a breath and hold it in, letting the spirit of air suffuse me, and when I release it I'm calmer. I've been away from the palace only a day, and already I have a monumental task in front of me. If it's not the right path for me, I will change, because that is what I've dedicated myself to: not a particular well-trodden path, but to making my own.

The real work will begin later this afternoon, I know. But this is part of what will make that work possible, which means it's important to do well. Lorwyn may not know Istal formalwear thoroughly, but she does know fashion.

"Shall we look at some of the fabric until she gets back?" I ask Lorwyn, gesturing around us.

She snorts. "Why bother? It's not like I can afford anything here."

"According to you, neither can I," I say, wandering over to a shelf where a soothing deep green catches my eye from well above my head.

So many choices! At the palace, tailors would never bring so much at a time. I chose fabric from sample images in booklets, and even those, I realize, must have been carefully edited.

I glance around until I find a step-stool, then tug it over. I hesitate before climbing it, but Lorwyn looks considering, not like I'm doing something untoward. Though I'm not sure she'd stop me if I were.

The green cloth that had caught my eye is for under-pants only, and regrettably the top designed to match it has a pattern that won't suit—a shade too childlike in its playfulness. I discard it and carefully begin sifting through other piles.

"You've worn formalwear a lot, haven't you?" Lorwyn asks from across the room.

I nod distractedly. "I take it you haven't?"

"Not much call for it," she says wryly. "But I don't exactly feel the loss."

I glance down at her and nod. "You would look very striking, I think, but in general I can see it wouldn't suit your attitude as well as your own style does."

Istal formalwear consists primarily of two components: flowing pants designed to be seen through a waist-high slit in a form-fitting, floor-length tunic with a high collar. With Lorwyn's gamine frame, formalwear would accentuate all her angles, but it also covers so much and is tight enough that the clothing shows to best effect with smooth movements; I can imagine her finding that too constraining.

"You really like formalwear, though, don't you? I'd have been annoyed when Talmeri said she was only going to pay for formalwear, but you seem totally comfortable with it, and with the idea of wearing nothing but formalwear all the time."

I pause, considering. My likes and dislikes have never been relevant before, but even as a princess I'd had the ability to make style choices in my wardrobe. Within a very specific set of limitations, but Lorwyn is right. I do like formalwear, and I am most comfortable in it—and in my ability to perceive and convey subtleties of style in this arena.

Saiyana always thought my style too traditional, but she'd take advantage of that effect when dealing with older nobles. Karisa would conform to the letter of the instructions for our wardrobes and flout all other aspects as blatantly as she could.

I had always been subtler, and that skill will serve me well now. But it's also going to hold me back, and I will have to keep in mind that not only *can* I be bolder now, for my role at the tea shop to work I *must*.

I can't be guided just by others' ideas anymore. There is pressure that comes with this, but somehow I can't stop smiling.

Here, now, is the first step I can take to define who I am and who I will be now that I am no longer a princess.

"Help me find some warm, dark purples with gold embellishments," I say to Lorwyn.

She huffs, but to my surprise doesn't argue and obligingly goes over to another shelf and begins sorting through fabric samples.

"We're not going to be done here anytime soon, are we?" she asks.

"I'm sorry. This matters to me, and since it will be expensive, and this is all I'll have to wear for some time—"

"You're picky," she summarizes. "I did wonder, after that getup you arrived at the tea shop in, but far be it from me to judge elaborate attention to fashion detail."

Aha! So her outfits aren't effortless after all. I feel better already.

"When we run out of time, have her send the clothes to your house and I can help you with any adjustments," Lorwyn advises.

My house.

I want to dwell on the warm rush I feel at those words, but I can't help but ask, "Why are you telling me this now?"

"Because she's going to try to pressure you to make a decision faster, and I don't think art should be rushed."

This time, the warmth spreads more slowly, but I feel as if it suffuses my whole body, like the thaw of drinking a warm cup of tea after coming in from the cold. "Thank you," I say, and it feels inadequate to convey the depth of my gratitude. For her understanding, her help, her patience. For her faith in me.

"Remember how nice I was now," she adds, "because when we get to the tea shop, believe me, there will be plenty of rushing."

I fear she means that to sound exactly as ominous as it does.

"Welcome to Talmeri's Teas and Tisanes." I smile and bow serenely for the thousandth time in the last several hours. My posture is perfect and the smile is as precise as it has been from the beginning, but each time takes a greater effort than the last. "How can I serve you?"

One of the two women in front of me frowns. "What's this, Talmeri's having women to work the front now? That's not the service I've come to expect from this establishment."

She's middle-aged, clothes simple and elegant over a plump frame, and probably knows more about the shop than I do. "No, grace," I begin for the hundredth time today. "I—"

"Well, I think it's delightful!" her companion announces. This woman looks similar enough in feature and stature that she must be a close relation of some sort—sister, perhaps, or else cousin. But she's chosen shockingly bright, angular fabrics, her hair is in disarray, and where her relative's jewelry is tasteful hers appears as though she simply decided to wear every single bracelet that makes her happy.

Sisters. The stark difference in their togetherness decides it.

"I've always thought Talmeri's should have some girls on staff to appeal to all their clientele." The colorful sister winks at me.

"Timasa, you wound me!" a young man calls over his shoulder as he passes. "I'm equally charming to everyone who comes through."

"Oh ho, so I'm not special?"

At eighteen, Meristo is the oldest "tea boy" currently working as a server at Talmeri's, the most experienced, and the only one on the schedule for this afternoon. Lorwyn convinced Talmeri to add him to the shift schedule today while she showed me the ropes, and instead Talmeri exchanged the shop's newest tea boy for him because, in Lorwyn's words, "she's insufferably cheap." But Meristo is built like an athlete, cocky as can be, and, thank all the spirits, as distressingly charming to our customers as he thinks he is.

He grins. "Of course you're special, grace. But I can't go admitting that aloud in front of all other customers, now can I?"

While Timasa laughs, I finish explaining to her sister that no, I won't be a regular server, but today I'm learning how the shop is run.

And I have so much learning to do. I'm no longer convinced that becoming a tea master will be my greatest challenge.

"Well, that's all right then," she allows. "I'll have my usual."

I bow slightly. "Your usual, grace?"

She stares at me like I'm stupid. "It's the tea I have every time I come here."

I restrain the urge to bite my tongue. The poor organ has already been much abused today.

"Oh, come now, you know the one," she says in a reproving tone. "It's the best black tea you carry. What have you been doing all day, if you don't know that?"

I smile again, careful it is not so bright as to reveal my actual thoughts. "I've learned that our customers rarely agree on which tea is the best, and I myself still haven't sampled anywhere near all our stock. But I think I know the one you mean."

I do not. But she clearly doesn't either, so I'm off the hook for the next minute.

What I have truly learned today is to seize these breaks as they present themselves. It seems somewhat dishonest, but I've already ceased caring.

She nods approvingly and nudges her sister. "Timasa, stop giggling and order."

"Oh, choosing is always the hardest part! What would you recommend?"

At first, I found the sheer number of people who, after learning I'm new to this shop and haven't tried most of the stock, promptly ask me for recommendations rather shocking, and then irritating. I've moved onto weariness.

I hear Meristo snicker as he passes behind me, and this time restrain the impulse to roll my eyes. It is becoming almost comical.

"What have you liked in the past?" I ask her patiently.

"I'm easy," Timasa laughs. "I like just about everything. I know, why don't you bring me a blend you've just gotten in recently?"

This is, of course, the least easy request she could have made. As if I, who have been here less than one afternoon, have any idea which blends are new.

Fortunately, I've been eavesdropping on Meristo all afternoon and heard him suggest two that Lorwyn has created in the last month.

"We have a new rose blend with lyala sap—"

"Oh, but that one's so sour! And no, I mean newer than that."

"Have you tried the sage and sorrowseed green as well?"

"Yes, I had that one two weeks ago. Not lively enough for my tastes. You don't have anything newer than those?"

Of course she has specific tastes that she can't define and yet considers herself an easy customer. This, I have also learned, is a common misconception.

"Why don't I see what Lorwyn has brewing in the back?" I ask. With their assent and attention already turning to comfortable bickering, I bow and retreat.

But the elegant sister is watching me narrowly when I arrive at the brewing station. Fortunately, the skill to pass information while under public scrutiny is one I developed as a princess, and so I'm able to covertly murmur to Meristo as I start a new kettle, "Do you know what her usual order is?"

He glances up, directly at the sister, and I close my eyes in a moment of irritation at his lack of subtlety. But when he flashes a grin at her she turns back to Timasa, so perhaps it's not so bad.

"Sanava? Yeah, she always gets Bloodbean Black."

I blink, then feel my lips quirk. "You've all deliberately never told her what it's called, haven't you?" I can't imagine Sanava, who takes herself so seriously, ordering a tea with that name.

Meristo winks at me as he finishes loading his tea tray. "Definitely not. Not that I don't enjoy having a joke on her, but I hope that's one of the things you'll be taking over."

"Naming?" I ask, startled. "I don't know anything about how to choose names." I barely know myself, let alone other people. How can I be expected to know what sorts of names will appeal to them?

"You can't possibly be worse than Talmeri," he informs me, before setting out again for another table.

I turn, looking at the compartments behind me in vain for one labeled "bloodbean." I can no longer tell if I'm so tired it's affecting my ability to read, or if the compartment simply isn't labeled—most, I've learned, the tea boys simply learn to find by habit.

Feeling the weight of Sanava's scrutiny on my back, I don't waste more than a few seconds looking before heading back to Lorwyn.

Every time I enter her lab something new is happening. Currently there's a blazing fire, a metallic contraption creaking as it extracts vials from a bubbling pot, and Lorwyn is attacking some sort of thick, tentacular root wider than my leg with an axe. She strikes it with shocking force, and the resulting sonorous gong and lack of dent gives the impression she's attempting to chop metal.

I've also learned that, long ago, Lorwyn witched the door between the lab and the storefront to block sound.

"What do you need?" she yells, I assume over the ringing of her ears.

"Bloodbean Black and something new."

"How new?" Lorwyn shouts louder, already stalking across the warehouse and hauling a box off a shelf for me.

"Newer than the lyala rose or the sorrowseed sage green." I pause, thinking of Timasa. "Something with more warmth if there is one, maybe sweeter?"

Without looking, she points backwards. "Take that white tin on the side of my desk."

I make it two steps before the large root twitches, snaps up, and is suddenly looming over me.

Another shout, and I feel the abrupt clench in my gut that I now know indicates Lorwyn is performing witchcraft.

The tentacle falls back, limp. I remain utterly still.

"I take it back," Lorwyn says calmly, now in a normal volume. "There's one on the shelf right by the door. Take that for now."

I nod as if what I'd thought was an inanimate root did not just rise up from a slab and try to attack me, backing slowly toward the door.

"What is it?" I ask.

"Tortoiseshell marrow white tea. You can brew it at a standard white tea temperature, but it should steep for an extra minute."

I meant the root, but she's clearly talking about what's inside the tin. I locate it, open the top and sniff. It's creamy but robust—perfect.

Then I frown. "Wait. Do tortoiseshells even have marrow? Shells—"

Lorwyn appears beside me, thrusting a small bag of tea at me. "Trust me, you don't want to know," she says grimly.

I think of the tentacle behind me, decide she may be correct, and head back into the store without more than a thank you.

By the time my two pots of tea are ready, I've washed three trays worth of tea serveware, restocked four teas stored in compartments I can actually locate without magical knowledge, smilingly answered a question from a customer who wandered up to the brewing counter to ask me for the shop hours that are posted prominently on the wall, another about the reason to brew a tisane at a particular length, deferred one about the shop's history to Meristo, and emptied a trash bin not full or smelly but that appeared to be flowering.

I purse my lips, consider Timasa, then add small pots of cream and honey to her platter, with a cinnamon stick in the cup. No embellishments for Sanava; she won't want them. Her tea, I've made sure to brew with exacting precision.

I note my additions on the shop log, review the cheat sheet for customer costs, and carefully balance the tea trays with all the grace I can muster as I weave through the maze of tables, dancing around the chairs that shift into my path.

I've barely finished delivering their tea services—to a grudging nod of approval from Sanava and Timasa's hands clapped in delight—when the bell above the door chimes. Four customers—apparently not together, it is immediately evident, and I hope Meristo knows how to handle that because we don't have that many available tables to seat them all at once and separately—enter the tea shop.

Above the door, I see the clock that reveals I'm only halfway through my shift.

I straighten; stretch a smile across my face; hope it looks human and not like whatever creature of customer service I've become. "Welcome to Talmeri's Teas and Tisanes! How can I serve you?"

CHAPTER 7

THE SHOP IS, AT LAST, closed for the day.

I have abandoned dignity and sit slumped over a table in the center of the shop.

"I have never been this exhausted," I mumble.

"Pretty sure you were in worse shape last night," Lorwyn says, clearly amused and infuriatingly not even a little tired. "Then you were too worn-out to even know how tired you were."

I manage to lift my head long enough to glare at her, but decide it's too much trouble to respond and settle back down.

"If every day at the shop is like today, I'm surely doomed," I mutter. "I can't possibly have the energy to prepare for the tea mastery examination and work like this every day."

Lorwyn snorts. "You'll be fine. You just need practice."

A chair scrapes, and I hear Meristo—for surely it must be, with the forceful sound of the flop—drop into a chair across from me at the table.

"Don't look for sympathy from Lorwyn," he advises me. "She has no tenderer feelings, and definitely not sympathy."

"You don't deserve sympathy," Lorwyn drawls. "Only a sharp kick in the rear to wipe that smirk off your face."

"You see? No respect. And try it—I'll smirk harder, just for you." I can practically feel his grin and Lorwyn's ensuing eye roll as he continues, "But it's always like this at the beginning. You did way better today than Iskielo."

"That is an extremely low bar to clear," Lorwyn says.

"Iskielo is the newest tea boy working here, right?" I ask.

"Yeah, Talmeri just brought him on a couple weeks ago," Meristo says. "He's mostly been working shifts doubled with me or Taseino, which you'd think would make things run smoother, with more people, but doesn't, because Iskielo has no idea what's going on. It's faster to do something myself than to give it to him, but if I don't give him anything to do he finds things that someone ends up having to clean up."

Lorwyn elaborates, "Iskielo's all of, what, fifteen? Full of enthusiasm, not a drop of common sense. But he practically worships the air Meristo passes through, which is useful for reining him in."

Aha. "And Taseino?"

"Not good with customers, even after all this time," Meristo says with a hint of frustration. "It's like smiling is some kind of torture for him."

"On the other hand," Lorwyn says pointedly, "Taseino is quiet, focused, and not susceptible to distraction like certain others I could name Meristo. There's more parts to this job than dazzling smiles, and you can actually trust Taseino to, you know, do them."

"You're just jealous because everybody likes me better than you," Meristo says smugly.

Weary of his cockiness now that I'm not relying on it to distract customers, I say, "If you are using the customers most impressed by youthful muscles and grins as a standard for whose regard is worth acquiring, I too might question the merits of your charisma."

"Hey now," Meristo protests, laughing, "what's with the formal rebuke?"

Drat it all, I'd been doing so well at keeping my more formal speech patterns at bay most of the afternoon, too.

Lorwyn apparently takes this as an indicator that I'm tired in truth, because she says, "It really will get easier, though. I promise."

Meristo mock-gasps. "Be still my beating heart—common human sentiment in Lorwyn! She really must like you, Miyara."

I open my eyes, see Lorwyn's jaw set, and sigh. "I wish people would stop commenting on how remarkable it is that you like me," I say as I lay my head down and close my eyes again. "It makes me feel as though I'm some rare magical creature you're secretly fattening to end up as a trophy on your proverbial wall, and before I know it I'll be laid out on your laboratory slab and you'll be going at me with an axe like that tentacular root."

A beat of silence, and then Meristo is laughing uncontrollably, and I watch him nearly fall out of his chair.

"I guess that's why," he finally gasps, then jumps out of the way as Lorwyn makes as though to throw something at him. "Anyway, I'm off now. See you next time, Miyara!"

Meristo bursts out the front door, and silence reigns in his wake.

"He amuses you," I finally note.

"I'm endlessly astounded by the imperviousness of his ego, but never tell him," Lorwyn replies.

I half-smile, sitting up at last. "Will it really get easier, or are you trying to make me feel better?"

"I wouldn't bother," she says dismissively, taking Meristo's vacated chair. "I've worked here a lot of years, and I've seen too many boys on their first shift. There's a lot to learn at the beginning, and a lot to keep track of, but trust me, you're a natural. To be honest I wondered whether the whole management part of the deal would work out with you, but after today it's clear you'll be fine."

"I can't even *find* all the tea," I protest.

She huffs. "Well, get used to that. We're not exactly highly organized around here. But you're totally unflappable, you have an answer for everything, and you never let any of the customers tell how totally out of your depth you are or how totally ridiculous they are. And you're not above, you know, doing actual work. Everything else you need you'll get with experience."

It's unexpected, that years of training as a princess to always pay attention, know the correct response, and project the image of serenity and poise for hours at a time have served me so well today.

Saiyana would probably be disgusted by the "waste" of those skills; Karisa, too. But I find myself wondering what Iryasa would think and can only imagine her nodding gravely.

Somehow I think my grandmother would be amused.

"You're just saying that because as long as I work here you never have to deal with customers again, aren't you?" I ask.

"Oh yeah, no question," Lorwyn answers easily, and I'm laughing quietly when I hear a knock.

"Oh spirits, not another customer," I mutter, expecting Lorwyn to laugh. When she doesn't, I look up and see her glaring at the doorway.

Through the window Risteri waves at me and gestures pointedly at the lock.

I glance a question at Lorwyn, but she just shrugs and looks away.

"Miyara, you look half-dead again," Risteri laughs by way of greeting when I open the door for her. "Ready to go home?"

"What," Lorwyn says behind me, her voice a thousand times more caustic than it was when she was teasing Meristo, "don't you trust me not to abandon her? Or is it that you think no one can find their way without your personal guidance?"

Risteri crosses her arms, but unlike last night it's clear that this time she's the one prepared for a confrontation.

"You're the one who brought her to me," she reminds Lorwyn, breezily ignoring the weighted malice in her words that makes me wonder, again, what went so badly wrong between these two people who are both going out of their way to help me. "And since I do actually live in the same neighborhood as Miyara, I thought I'd show her where to get groceries. Unless you think someone like me can't handle that?"

The last is clearly a challenge, one that Lorwyn ignores with a scoff.

"Don't be ridiculous," she snaps. "Miyara has no idea how to handle herself in a night market, she's exhausted, and everyone will try to take advantage—"

"She'll be with me," Risteri says, "and no one will bother her."

There's a beat of silence, and then Lorwyn makes a sound of utter disgust. "You clearly haven't changed."

"Neither have you. Miyara, shall we?"

I look between her and Lorwyn.

And, after a long moment, shake my head.

"I very much appreciate the offer, Risteri, I truly do. But I don't appreciate being used as a weapon in the battle the two of you are waging against each other."

"It's none of your business, Miyara," Lorwyn tells me.

"If that's what you wanted, you perhaps shouldn't have involved me in settling your score while flinging scathing innuendo over my head as if I'm not supposed to notice," I say, keeping my voice even.

Lorwyn stands abruptly, pushing her chair back. "You know what, just go with her. I have things to do here without you anyway."

And with that she stalks away and slams her lab door shut behind her.

I want to go after her and apologize, but I'm not sure exactly for what. In any case, I'll see her again tomorrow—perhaps it will be easier with some time between us.

Then again, perhaps it will be worse.

I look back at Risteri, half-waiting for her to storm out the opposite door, but she looks apologetic.

"You're right," she says. "Sorry, I didn't think how you would feel about this."

"It's fine," I say. "I really do appreciate the offer and would be happy to take you up on it. It's just hard to mind my business when yours seems to encroach on it."

Risteri nods. "That's fair. Lorwyn and I barely see each other anymore, but when we do it's almost always like that—just without witnesses. We'll both just have to try not to snipe at each other when you're around."

As one, we both glance toward the lab door, then back at each other. My expression must look doubtful, because Risteri snorts and says, "Yeah. Or maybe we'll just have to try not to be around you at the same time."

That doesn't seem like a solution, so I refrain from condoning it. "I don't suppose you're still willing to take me to this night market?" I ask tentatively.

And then she beams at me, openly and easily and honestly, and it's almost shocking how different her utter forthrightness is from Lorwyn's underhanded caution.

Perhaps I do, in fact, have an inkling of what went wrong between them.

"Absolutely," she assures me. "Just wait, once we get there you'll forget how tired you are."

I remember Lorwyn's earlier observation of that as a symptom of being truly exhausted and manage to contain my amusement as I follow her out the tea shop.

❧

Risteri was right, the night market is glorious, and I do forget how tired I am because I never want to leave.

The street is lined with booths crammed up against each other, lanterns lighting the way, full of people bartering—not angrily, but as though it's a game, albeit a serious one, between friends. It is full of bright colors and laughter that light up the night, and after a day of careful words and smiles I can practically feel the atmosphere suffusing me with warmth, putting me more at ease.

If I were truly ready to be a tea master, that is the feeling I should have been generating for others all day.

I do gawk. Quite a lot, but Risteri was right about this too. She doesn't snap at me to contain my reaction, and no one tries to take advantage of me—in fact, they seem greatly amused by my wide eyes. Perhaps in a mocking way, but I can't take offense—I'm sure I do, in fact, look ridiculous.

But I am getting a lot of stares. At first I think it's the tea aspirant news again, but few people bow—so it's not my history as a princess, either. Although this market is mainly Gaellani, too, no one is staring at Risteri, so it's not that I'm so plainly ethnically Istal, either.

"Is it because I'm new to this market?" I ask her. "Everyone seems to know everyone here."

She shakes her head. "They don't really," she says. "Or at least, not all of them. But no, I think it's your hair."

I make to touch my hair, but my arms are laden with bags of food I have no idea how to cook and it seems like too much effort to lift them that high. "My hair?"

"Because it goes all the way to your waist," Risteri explains. "For most people, hair that long would be too troublesome to take care of, and it would get in the way of work. They probably think you're a noble and are wondering why you're here."

Of course. Some of that mockery I sense must be because they think a noble has come to gawk at the way they live, and now I feel acutely embarrassed because they are not entirely wrong.

But Risteri, although she must be known to be noble, isn't garnering the stares. Her hair is tightly contained, and she wears clothes no one would mistake for noble garb, and that, no doubt, helps people treat her as though she's not so different from them. Because she has taken real steps to elide the differences she can control, at least in this one, outward fashion.

The only clothes I'll be wearing for some time will be formalwear, as it's all Talmeri will pay for, so that's not a step I can take.

But. My hair.

When Lorwyn first mentioned cutting it, I couldn't control my horror at its loss. But that meant Lorwyn had to help me take care of it. And it means now that Risteri, who has been made responsible for hiding me in plain sight, can't disguise that I'm a noble.

My hair is not so important that it should cause me to be dependent and a burden on those who are already doing so much for me.

"You've gotten quiet," Risteri says, jolting me out of my thoughts. "Everything okay?"

I think for one more moment, steel myself, and let out a breath. "How hard is it to dye hair?"

Her eyebrows lift in surprise. "I have no idea, but I bet we could find dye here. What are you thinking?"

"That I want to be the one to shape how others perceive me, and not have it decided for me," I say, and it feels right. "This won't be enough, but it's a start, and every time I look in the mirror I'll remember to forge my own path. Will you help me?"

Risteri clasps my wrists and looks me in the eye. "Absolutely," she says fervently. "Now, are you ready to answer the most important question?"

My eyes widen. "What question?"

Reflected lantern light dances in her eyes, and they're bright in the darkness. "What color?"

I laugh, already glad of my decision. "Emerald green, if I can. So I will match the wardrobe I ordered today." I swallow, and add, "We should also find scissors."

"Cutting your hair, too? Are you sure?" Risteri asks, and I'm bolstered by the concern in her voice.

"Not too short," I say. "Maybe just to my shoulders. That shouldn't be too bad, right?"

"That's a lot all at once," she says seriously. "I mean, don't let me stop you if you're sure, but maybe start with, like, mid-back-length. You can always take more off."

I let out a breath, and some tension goes with it. Yes. I don't have to take all the steps at once. But I do have to start.

"True," I agree. "But, for now. How do I begin?"

Risteri claps me on the shoulder. "We," she says. "Let's go."

Risteri shows herself inside the cottage the next morning while I'm practicing the tea ceremony on the floor of the living room. "I brought breakfast," she announces, and then, "Spirits, we really do need to touch that up, don't we?"

"Oh yes," I say fervently, and we both dissolve into giggles for a minute.

Our attempt to cut and dye my hair last night involved a lot of giggling, but as attempts go, it was not unequivocally successful.

In the light of day, and with my hair now dry and its waves returned, the length of my hair is a bit jagged; perhaps even ragged. This is less than ideal, given the image I'm to present at the tea shop, but more of a problem is my hair color. It is extremely uneven, and shows poorly. We realized too late that perhaps the thing to do would have been lightening my hair first, and now it simply looks like I dipped my head in a vat of oil and have not yet managed to get the stain out.

Still. "Let me finish this," I ask, adjusting the angle of my head just slightly. I've been making minute changes in movements and drilling them into muscle memory for hours already, making sure my hair sweeps correctly now that its length and weight are so different.

I wish, fervently, that I had a proper tea set to practice with. I've commandeered several items of approximately the right weight or shape to stand in for the objects I'm more familiar with, so I sit on the floor with a sturdy mug, a delicate sugar jar, what I believe is a soup bowl, and various utensils that have nothing to do with tea ceremony.

But although it's turned out rather badly, and I should have thought how this change would affect my ability to execute the tea ceremony beforehand, I don't wish we hadn't made the attempt at all. As I've repurposed kitchenware, I'll adapt.

Risteri is still unloading breakfast pastries from a bag when Lorwyn bursts in the door and then freezes there.

"You," she breathes in disbelief and horror, pointing a shaking finger at my hair.

Which Lorwyn then promptly transfers, more firmly, to direct at Risteri. "You! What have you done?!"

"It was my idea," I say, trying to head this off and hoping surely it isn't as unsalvageable as she makes it sound. "Obviously it hasn't worked out exactly as intended, but—"

Lorwyn stomps toward Risteri. "This is just cursed typical, you *never* think things through and what they will mean for anyone else outside of your own privileged bubble," she snarls.

"Oh, this is my fault?" Risteri shoots to her feet from the stool. "At least *Miyara* is trying to control her own life, which is more than I can say for *some* people—"

"ENOUGH."

I hardly know I'm the one who shouted until they both turn utterly shocked faces toward me. I take a breath, but although my voice quiets to almost a whisper it's like the words won't stop.

"I have lived as a pawn in bitter old struggles that had nothing to do with me my entire life, and I refuse to be put in that situation again." I breathe again, trying to access the calming spirit of air, but it's beyond me. I shake my head, and this time I point—to the door. *My* door. "If you cannot keep me out of your business, you will both leave. Now."

They both stare at me for a long moment, glance at each other, then guiltily away again.

I wait, unmoving, not *allowing* myself to budge a jot.

They are *not* my responsibility to manage.

Maybe this is why Saiyana was so disgusted when I chose our father as a dedication guide.

But maybe, if I'd refused to allow myself to be a victim of their political tug-of-war, I could have actually helped us all instead of settling for a useless, empty gesture.

We stand there for perhaps an entire minute before Risteri passes Lorwyn a pastry. Lorwyn takes it gingerly and then, as if steeling herself for her sleekbeetle and Nakrabi pepper tea, takes a bite, glaring at me while she chews.

As if it's my fault she's now being forced to deal with Risteri.

"Can you fix it?" Risteri asks her.

Or as if she can't bring herself to believe what horror we've wrought upon my hair.

"Yes," Lorwyn finally says. "But it would take me hours, and we don't have them. The tea master has already arrived, and the tea assessment is today. I came to let you know."

Today. I close my eyes, run my hand through my hair, and wince.

So, it was a mistake after all. I suppose I should have known taking steps to control my life could not possibly be so easy.

No tea master will ever consider me a serious aspirant in my current state. There is not a single chance in the world. I am done on this course barely after I've begun.

And so there will go my job, and thus my house, and I am back to where I started two days ago, but worse off for having squandered the goodwill of those who earnestly tried to help me.

"I'm sorry, Lorwyn," I say, bowing as low as I can, knowing it's inadequate.

"Oh, shut up," she says. "Just don't put me in this position again. What color were you trying for, anyway?"

I stand up, frowning in confusion for so long that it's Risteri who answers her. "Emerald green."

Lorwyn snorts. "Should have guessed. Well, at least after considering fabric with you for hours yesterday I can say with confidence I know exactly which shade. Turn around and hold still."

"Why?"

"I'm going to have to experiment with witchcraft on your hair after all," Lorwyn informs me with her shark-sweet smile.

My heart thumps—with fear, and with hope.

I turn around, close my eyes, and focus every iota of my being on holding completely, absolutely, still.

My gut roils in response to her magic. My scalp burns, and it occurs to me suddenly that although my hair does not feel in the same way that my skin does, I can sense it now. The sensations are not, precisely, pleasant, and I try not to think about what Lorwyn is actually doing.

"There," she finally says, wearily but conclusively, when a lifetime has passed. "Go look in the bathroom mirror."

I whirl to face her, not bothering to keep the naked hope out of my expression. Lorwyn nods gravely; Risteri's hands are clasped tightly over her mouth, but her eyes are bright with excitement.

I dash to the bathroom, and my eyes promptly fill with tears.

My hair is now a lustrous shade of emerald, cascading in waves a bit past my shoulders. It looks better than I could have imagined, and I love it instantly and without reservation.

I dry my eyes before marching back out of the bathroom, knowing it would only make Lorwyn uncomfortable, but still I bow to her again. "Thank you," I say fervently. "I'm so sorry I put you in this position, but I can't regret the result even a bit."

"You say that now," she says, and I ignore her attempt to diminish my gratitude and turn to Risteri.

"And thank you," I say, bowing, "for helping me find the courage to do this at all."

"Anytime," she says, and hugs me impulsively.

"Though perhaps we should consider research next time," I add, and she laughs.

"And now," I announce as I grab a pastry, "I think I should visit the local shrine. Could one of you show me the way?"

And this question somehow renders them both speechless in confusion.

"What in the world for?" Risteri wonders aloud.

I frown. "Because there's no shrine in this home?"

"Why should there be?" Lorwyn asks, equally confused.

Because I've run the gamut of emotions in a very condensed time frame, have no time to process them, and need to restore my sense of inner calm before what will be an extremely difficult and stressful examination that relies on that serenity.

But this is not the answer to the question they're really asking, and that they're asking it at all baffles me so much I give what I consider the self-evident response. "So I have a place to offer reflection to the spirits before this examination so much depends on?"

Lorwyn blinks. "You do that? Really?" The latter question is actually addressed to Risteri.

"*I* certainly don't," Risteri says. "I mean, some nobles do I guess, but they're usually, you know—"

She looks uncomfortable, and with a sinking feeling I think I know how to finish her phrase. "Sanctimonious," I say, "only praying for the appearance and cachet associated with spiritual piety." Risteri nods, and I turn to Lorwyn. "And to you prayer is—a luxury, I suppose, and a frivolous one at that?"

"Pretty much, yes," Lorwyn says bluntly.

"I see," I say. "Nevertheless, whatever you may think, even a brief time spent contemplating in the shrine will do me a world of good."

"Okay, I admit that I absolutely don't understand that," Lorwyn says, "but it actually doesn't matter. I mean, one of us can show you where it is later for future reference if you really want, but not right now. We should have left already as it is."

My eyes widen, and I try to quell the sudden panic. Surely it should not feel equal to the subliminal panic I lived with for ages before my dedication ceremony, and yet— "No. You can't be serious."

"The tea assessment is now," Lorwyn says, confirming my fear.

CHAPTER 8

THERE'S A CROWD WAITING outside the tea shop when we arrive. Before I've decided whether to be concerned, Risteri has authoritatively convinced them to disperse enough to form a path for us to get through. "You'll do great," she whispers in my ear, and then it's only Lorwyn and I entering the shop.

Which is also, it turns out, full of people. All of them clearly wealthy, all of them chatting with the air of people about to witness a good show.

"Oh good, Talmeri is showing the tea master off to her friends," Lorwyn mutters. "I bet that puts him in a fine mood."

While this will not be the first time I've dealt with an unhappy person in a position of authority over me, my stomach has still knotted uncomfortably.

I can't dwell on how badly this can go wrong, I can't stop moving forward, or I will be carried away by others' plans and desires the way I always have.

So I bow, without even seeing the tea master to whom I offer respect. But all Talmeri's friends are carefully angled in or against that direction.

"Miyara!" Talmeri bustles over to greet me. "I was wondering when you'd get here. What kept you?"

She stops dead at the sight of my hair, and I watch her expression move rapidly through shock, then anger, and then, taking in the effect with my formal wear, consideration.

I don't give her time to decide. "My apologies," I say, bowing again and not specifying. "I came as soon as I could. May I offer my respects to the tea master?"

Talmeri hesitates for just an instant, still eyeing my hair, but the room is too quiet; she's invited to many eyes to this show to stop it here. "Yes, yes, of course." She pulls me by the elbow with slightly too much force, but I flow into it, dropping into another bow as she leads me to where a man is dressed in a simple but traditional costume from Taresan, the nation just north of Istalam.

"You may rise," he says in a smooth, even voice from which I can detect not even a shred of what he thinks of me. But he is, naturally, impeccably polite.

When I stand up straight again, he has risen, too. He is as tall as all Taresal people are, and I have to look up at him. His skin tone is lighter than a typical Istal's—still brown, but with more yellow in it—but his hair is oddly similar to mine, thick and wavy. Though his is much shorter—but then, now so is mine.

"Master Karekin, this is Miyara," Talmeri introduces me. "Perhaps—"

"I'd like to get started," he cuts her off.

Talmeri is momentarily surprised speechless. That was downright impolite, and I get the feeling he has been offended by the spectacle she's made of his presence.

This is the man who can, solely on his own judgment, block me from even taking the final examination for tea mastery.

And he is already upset before I've begun.

"Of course," Talmeri recovers. "I can have the tea room prepared right away."

I turn a quick bow to her, remembering Lorwyn's comment that Talmeri has never cleaned a day in her life and probably has no idea what it needs. "There's no need for that, grace. I'm happy to attend to that function."

"Indeed," Master Karekin says, "and so you will. Grace Talmeri, this assessment will take some time and requires utmost focus and silence. Now that we're set to begin, I'll need everyone to clear this space."

"Leave? Oh, but I thought—"

"Yes, I gather there has been a degree of misunderstanding," he says. No smile, no note of dry humor in his voice, and *I* gather he is, in fact, furious, though Talmeri has not realized. "This sudden assessment is irregular as it is, however, and I am here on very short notice. Will you permit me this courtesy?"

It is neatly, if bluntly, done—but then, handling Talmeri requires a degree of bluntness. Nevertheless, she cannot refuse.

But it is a bit surreal to watch all those people, clearly so used to having their way, obey the tea master's edict with grumbles but not objections. I don't think my mother the queen could manage such a feat with the nobles, but this man can.

This is the level of authority over others I'm attempting to claim. I, who barely have any idea of who I am or what I should be doing.

Don't think yourself into inaction; move forward.

"Master Karekin, by your leave, I will retrieve cleaning supplies for the tea room." I bow. At least I know some basics of how to care for a tea room, and surely Lorwyn must have something appropriate I can borrow in the back.

But he asks sharply, "Clean?"

Ah.

I bow again. "It is my understanding that the tea room has not been in regular use for some time. I'm sure Grace Talmeri made arrangements to prepare the space in advance, but as I was unaware a tea master could arrive so soon I had not thought to check into them myself. My sincerest apologies."

"You've not seen the space?"

"Master Karekin, I performed the tea ceremony for Grace Talmeri yesterday morning. At that time, I employed aloia incense to make the atmosphere bearable, but I would not call the resulting state fully satisfactory."

He winces; it is the first expression I've seen from him, and it's little more than a blink. "I see. Open the door and begin airing it out properly, then. We will start with the oral assessment."

The quiet of the shop when we sit down to begin is almost like the night Lorwyn first welcomed me inside. It is amazing, how much physical and emotional noise we all generate. I close my eyes for a moment, focusing on that tangible sensation of silence, holding my center of calm.

When I open them, we begin.

And I'm immediately left reeling. I know some, because I was raised to diplomacy, and because I know how to taste.

But I don't know how to judge the quality of tea leaves at different stages in the process: the quality of the plants, or how to roll the leaves. Aside from the core tea ceremony teas, I don't know all their nutritional properties, or the reasons for the correct brewing temperatures for every kind of tea and tisane and how different ingredients affect them. I know different materials of pots can affect the tea flavor and which is best, but not always why; I need to know the stories and the history of all tea, different techniques in brewing, in making, and the advantages for each method; I need to know, mathematically, how much tea to use in any cup, and I need to synthesize that without overwriting my instincts.

It is surreal to be on the edge of the Cataclysm answering questions about tea traditions from far-away places that, to the best of our knowledge, no longer exist. There is so much I don't know, so much I barely know enough to recognize how much knowledge I lack.

Throughout Master Karekin's rapid, close questioning, he gives no further indication of his opinion than the same impatience I noted at the outset. Still, I cannot help but feel like I'm failing more with every answer.

At last, we come to the tea ceremony. I resolve not to consider the effect of my new hair at all on my movements and affect—if the tea master has not acknowledged it, nor should I.

With the tea ceremony, even now, I'm confident in my ability. I've performed for tea masters and for royalty, and if Master Karekin decides to thwart my aspirations, I'm sure it will not be for this.

So when we are, at last, finished, and I am thoroughly exhausted in every way, his response is not what I expect.

"Well. At least you can forego the training in politics and etiquette." I frown, and he rolls his eyes. "You are clearly the same Miyara lately departed from the royal house of Istalam. Did you think I would not know?"

My heart stops.

I was so worried about the assessment itself I did not even consider this possibility, but I am not, evidently, too exhausted for panic.

"Will you send me back?" I manage to whisper past the sudden constriction in my chest.

"Don't be foolish." For the first time I can hear the annoyance—the *waspishness*—in his tone. "I owe your government no fealty, and even if I did, as a tea master, I answer to no one but the tea masters' guild. I don't care if you're a witch or the retired queen herself. You either know tea, or you do not, and any other concerns are outside my purview. I only mention it so we can be honest about the serious challenge you face in becoming a tea master, and it is not learning the etiquette."

I sit back wide-eyed, somehow more shocked than relieved. "Oh," I say numbly, reminding myself I can still breathe. "I see."

He's waiting for something else from me, and although he claims etiquette is not my greatest challenge I have no idea what it is. "Thank you," I hazard.

Master Karekin snorts and continues as if I'd said nothing. "You do have a head start on many aspirants. In some categories. But you have a lot to learn."

I swallow. The oral examination is still fresh in my mind. "Yes."

"Not that," he says.

Is the ability to read minds a skill shared by all tea masters?

"Yes, you have a lot to learn, but the hardest for you will be the ceremony. I see you are surprised by that. Understand, it is not enough to be merely good, or correct; the tea ceremony must always be perfect. It's not about exact execution, nothing so mathematical. It's about the experience of the tea ceremony. Do you see?"

He waits again, for me to understand. "Do you refer to accounting for the individual guest when creating the experience?" I ask.

"No. That is also important, but you know how to listen. You have innate talent there, and you will improve naturally with practice. No. What will be difficult for you is learning to take up space."

I walk alone through a hallway of strangers, and no one can see me.

"I'm... not sure I understand," I say, though already I begin to think I may.

Master Karekin nods, as if he truly can sense this. "I admit, it's not the set of challenges I would have expected, from a princess. But you need to learn how not to make yourself smaller and more contained. You need to not pull each movement for fear of pushing too far. You need to make a space of your own, because that is how you create a path to connect with any guest. You cannot fade away in your own ceremony. Avoiding misstep, or the chance of giving offense, rather than stepping with conviction, leaves a gap in the ceremony and the experience, and no amount of perfectly executed movements will bridge it. *You* must be the bridge between your guest and the tea. Now do you see?"

I want to laugh, or maybe scream.

It is the exact same challenge I faced in the Grand Shrine, that I could not meet.

I'm now convinced he cannot simply read the thoughts in my mind, but the tenor of my soul, because he has seen me more clearly than anyone, including myself. Perhaps it has simply taken the ancient art of the tea ceremony to reveal me, the way I should have revealed myself at the dedication ceremony.

He is right: I do not, in a spiritual sense, know how to take up space. And I don't know how to learn to.

"I don't suppose," I say, "you might have any suggestions?"

Master Karekin shakes his head, though this time it is with regret. "No. This is not something anyone can help you learn. I have seen it done, but not from such as state as you're starting from. And it can take years." He waits, expectant again, and this time I know what he means me to hear.

It *can* be done.

And perhaps, the first step to knowing the space I inhabit and filling it without apology is resolving to.

"Then I will have a full three months ahead of me," I say.

If he dares prevent me now, I will not accept it.

Master Karekin considers me. "You have considerable talent and skill. You should not rush your studies. The examination can only be taken once."

I know, and that terrifies me. I can fail completely all at once, and I will have only one chance to succeed.

But. I will have one.

"I will gladly spend the rest of my life studying the intricacies and art of tea," I say. "I have no intention of stopping on this course once I'm certified."

He snorts. "Your desire to continue learning is admirable; your desire to rush less so."

I wait a moment, and then venture, "But you're going to allow me to try."

And for the first time, he smiles.

"You are equal to aspire to tea mastery," he proclaims formally. "May the spirits guide your quest."

After Master Karekin finishes my assessment, I sneak out the back and get directions from Lorwyn. I have just enough time before the tea shop opens to pick up the study materials Master Karekin has recommended to me at the bookstore.

Although Lorwyn offers to accompany me, I want to be by myself for a bit, to let my thoughts bounce around without worrying how others will take them.

And I want to take this step by myself, to prove I can.

I will find this bookstore, I will find the correct books, I will manage the transaction of purchasing them, I will find my way back to the tea shop, and I will begin to behave as though I do not need my hand held for every step of what for most people are basic, everyday facets of living.

Despite my best intentions, I do end up asking passersby for directions to the bookstore. Twice.

Still. They do not lead me the whole way there, and I count it as a partial victory.

Outside, I smile for a moment to myself: it's the same bookstore I attempted to shelter from the rain in two nights and a lifetime ago. How different would my path be now if the man that night had let me in here, if I had never continued on to find Lorwyn and the tea shop?

Perhaps the spirits are already guiding my quest. It's a comforting thought as I take the steps.

The bookstore itself is like a maze, and one I would gladly be lost in. Here I don't ask for assistance, content to wander, marveling at all the knowledge I didn't know existed, the stories I've never been permitted to read.

My time, unfortunately, is not endless. I do find a map of Sayorsen with notable destinations clearly marked, though, and I decide I'd better acquire it, no matter what Lorwyn thinks. And although she scoffed at the notion of learning to cook, I find a recipe book with plenty of drawings, too.

But I don't find the correct tea books, so I am again in a state of only partial success. Still, I steel myself, and venture to the front counter.

We will see how I do at monetary transactions. Surely, after an afternoon working in the tea shop, I can handle the other side of the encounter.

But I'm startled instantly to see the bookseller is in fact the same man who would not let me in from the rain, who thought to bring me to the police. He looks confused for a moment, too, but I don't think it's because he remembers me. Either a woman in need of shelter makes little impression, or I appear too changed for him to recognize me as the same person.

"Just a moment, grace," the bookseller says to me, with a pointed nod to a young Gaellani man beside me. "You can wait behind Deniel in line."

I glance at this customer in surprise that quickly turns to mortification, and I bow rapidly, deeply.

How have I already made such a mistake, and such a silly one? Lines, Miyara!

But although the customer doesn't say anything—as I have not—he smiles.

It's as though I feel his genuine amusement, his desire to set me at ease, and warmth suffuses me as I shyly return his smile and retreat behind him.

Perhaps I am still mentally present in my tea assessment, focused on how an individual can create a true experience for another.

Perhaps it is merely that I have become too accustomed to shark-like smiles, or smiles that convey a fiction of politeness.

But I still feel warm.

And I resolve to give as many people as true of smiles as I can.

"On to the next one of these law tomes, are you," the bookseller is saying jovially. "I was surprised when your request came in!"

"The last couple months have been good to me," the customer—Deniel?—answers in a low, soothing voice. I open my map, trying not to eavesdrop so obviously, trying to imagine what his expression must look like. "I tried to give my mother a gift, but—"

"But of course she insisted you spend for your own pet hobby before considering her." The bookseller shakes his head. "She's too good to you."

"I can't deny that," he agrees. "So I at least owe it to her to push myself as far as I can with this."

"Even though it won't go anywhere?" the bookseller presses.

There's a wry note in Deniel's voice as he answers, "Perhaps especially then."

I wish I could see his face, then. Already it's as though the impression of his thoughtful features are fixed in my mind. I realize I'm staring at the back of his head, his disheveled, ash-blond hair and quickly focus back on my map, studying it furiously.

Only to start in surprise when I see his name marked on a destination of interest in Sayorsen.

All at once I remember the potter Lorwyn taunted the spy Thiano over, the one who makes the most gorgeous tea sets, is named Deniel.

My head snaps back up, but it is now only the bookseller in front of me, waiting expectantly.

I hear the telltale chime as the door opens, and look just in time to see Deniel's slender frame slipping away.

Was he the potter? Is Deniel a common Gaellani name?

I have no idea how to ask without inviting more questions than I'm prepared to answer, and that is a lesson a princess learns young.

"You can put those up here," the bookseller says. "Did you find everything you were looking for?"

"Not quite," I say, thinking of the easy opportunity for answers I just missed. "Tea Master Karekin said I could find a few specific books here, but—"

"Oh, you're the tea aspirant!" The bookseller's smile widens. "You should have said. Welcome! I pulled them from the shelves and set them aside as soon as I heard, just to be safe. Here."

He hefts a stack of three enormous books out from a shelf under the counter, and my eyes widen at the size of them.

Learning to do, indeed.

"These will go on Talmeri's shop account, I understand," he says, wrapping them carefully. "But it looks like you found more?"

I blush. "I did. But not for any purpose I think Grace Talmeri would be willing for the shop to pay for."

He laughs. "Unplanned purchases you can only questionably justify are a common experience in a bookstore, I assure you. Let's get a separate receipt started, then."

I carefully count out the marks from my own pouch, glad again that Lorwyn showed me how—and how to save enough with lunches that I can afford to this week. Though it's clear these will almost have to be my last unplanned purchase until next week, and I begin to see why Lorwyn was so concerned about Talmeri's tight control of my funds.

Still. I did not manage the tea books myself, but I am leaving with them, and I have successfully purchased two other items that will help me learn independence.

A partial success.

A step.

And despite my exhausting morning, I feel as though I will have no trouble carrying all this weight back to my place at the tea shop.

CHAPTER 9

THE NEWS OF MY new status as a tea aspirant has begun to spread, and I spend nearly as much time carefully answering questions about the assessment and my course going forward as I do serving tea.

After two hours of this, Meristo and I retreat to Lorwyn's lab to confer.

"My presence is making everything go slower," I say without preamble.

"The gossip will die down in the next couple days," Lorwyn says, but she doesn't sound convinced.

"Then you'd better have Talmeri get Taseino scheduled double with me until then," Meristo tells her grimly. "We'll need more hands on deck to manage this."

"What about Iskielo?" I ask.

Meristo rolls his eyes. "I shudder to think what adding Iskielo to the mix would do. In the meantime, can you stay back here?"

I purse my lips. "I'm supposed to be working."

"Oh, you will be," Lorwyn assures me. "I'll help you get more oriented here, and whenever Meristo needs something you can fetch it for him. Aaand that's the front door chiming. Meristo, you're on. Miyara, with me."

And that's how I end up spending the afternoon in Lorwyn's lab.

She gives me a tour full of wisdom like "never touch this under any circumstances" and "this is where merchandise goes to die" and ends with, "But honestly, there's so little organization back here there's really no good way to learn other than having to find things."

More magical knowledge, like the locations of the tea up-front. This should not surprise me.

"I hope you've at least labeled whatever is likely to kill me?" I ask.

"Not really." Lorwyn smiles. "How do you think I keep the boys from messing with my things?"

I huff a laugh. "Well. If there's nothing else you can teach me about where things are, could you help me study?"

She frowns, very gently replacing the tea pet from the other day on a shelf, giving it a lingering pat. "I do have things to do, you know."

"Oh, I know, and please tell me if I get in the way—"

"You're getting in the way," she says, but the laughter in her eyes tells me it's a joke and I roll my eyes in response.

"I mean, I guess, could you explain some things as you do them? There are whole chapters in one of my books on the properties of different tea leaves, and more on rolling techniques—"

Lorwyn's eyebrows rise in surprise. "Well, yeah, I guess there'd have to be. You've never rolled tea leaves?"

I shake my head.

"Huh," she says, already wandering off to one of the shelves. "Okay, I have some preserved leaves here I've been meaning to experiment with anyway. I'll walk you through the basics, and if you're at least halfway competent you can be my lab assistant today."

I smile past the obscure pressure I now feel not to disappoint her. "Such faith in my ability to learn."

Lorwyn laughs. "Don't worry, you won't like assisting me anyway."

But I do. It's soothing, and warming, set up at a station next to her, learning about the leaves and how to manipulate them, watching her incorporate them into her work. She points out when my work fails in some way, but never in a way that makes me feel like a burden. And we spend most of our time working comfortably together or laughing, together.

I wonder if this is what it's like to have a friend.

Or a sister.

Lorwyn is in the middle of a careful measurement when the back gate to the lab bangs.

"That'll be a delivery," she says without looking up. "Can you go let him in?"

I wipe my hands off on a cloth, notice they're still stained hopelessly green, shrug, and go. It takes me a moment to figure out how to make the latch work, and then the gate is sliding up out of the way to reveal a pallet full of crates.

A lean young man—Istal, I think, but oddly I can't guess his likely background more precisely than that—peeks around the back. He's wearing nondescript black, but that just makes his muscles all the more prominent. I suppose he'd have to be strong, to move pallets like this around all day. He moves with a fluid grace, and something about him puts me almost instantly at ease: perhaps it's the way he moves with such confidence in his ability, in himself, as though he always knows which way to step.

It's the kind of grace I aspire to in the tea ceremony; perhaps that affinity explains it.

"I'm with South-Central Shipping," he says. "Can I bring this in?"

Lorwyn calls, "Check his paperwork! There should be a box that indicates whether they think we're going to pay them to roll it inside."

The delivery man scowls. "You think I'm cheating you?"

"Oh, I'm sure you're the sweetest man alive," Lorwyn says absently. "But your coworkers have given South-Central a reputation around here. Miyara, check the paperwork."

I bow slightly in apology, coming around the side of the pallet where the man shoves the piece of paper at me.

"Fine, here," he announces loudly.

And then as I'm scanning the paperwork, he says in a much quieter voice, "My name is Entero, and I believe I'm an acquaintance of your grandmother's."

I freeze.

I can practically feel the blood draining out of my face, but somehow I manage quietly, "I don't know what you mean."

But I do, of course I do, and my knuckles are as white as the paper I'm clutching.

They've found me.

Oh, spirits, my family has found me already.

"Miyara?" Lorwyn arrives around the side. "Is the box checked?"

I stare blankly at the man's guarded expression. "No, it's not," I say, and my voice sounds faint.

Entero says mildly, "Maybe we should take a few minutes to catch up. I'm sure we have a lot to talk about."

"Miyara, what's this?" Lorwyn asks sharply.

He knows where I work, which means he can find me at any time.

And my presence has led led him right to Lorwyn, my first friend, an unregistered witch.

If he does work for my grandmother, then I can't let him realize. He'd have to report her, and Lorwyn's freedom and possibly life will be forfeit.

I have to get him away from her no matter what.

"He says he knows my grandmother," I say. "Would you mind if I step outside for a few minutes?"

Lorwyn frowns. "Yes. You're working. What can't he say in front of me?"

Too much. But what she might reveal to him is the real problem.

"I'll be very quick," I promise, hoping I'm not lying, and jerk myself into motion, striding out the gate with my head high as if I don't believe I'm walking into desolation.

Drat, the purposeful stride along with my tenseness probably does give that impression. Too late now.

Entero follows me, very quickly taking me by the elbow in a way I'm familiar with. "Please, this way."

His touch is too rough, though, which tells me everything I need to understand about him: he hasn't been trained on how to innocuously steer a princess.

But I'm not a princess, and I don't want to give him time to strengthen his grip.

I fling my arm away from him.

He tenses, just barely, but otherwise doesn't show his surprise. "We're still in view of the shop," he says, perfectly controlled, as if he is never anything but, as if I'm the one creating chaos with my presence.

So, Lorwyn could have seen that. Curses. "I'm walking with you. But don't try to touch me."

He nods, and we walk, my thoughts spinning rapidly.

I've been worrying about being dependent, but not what my very presence means. Stupid, stupid Miyara! I'll have to divert Entero somehow, then think of a way to keep him from returning to Talmeri's. I'm not sure what my next steps are after that, but how I'll even manage that much fills me with despair.

We round a corner, then another, and soon I won't be able to find my way back.

I stop when we're in a secluded alley. "That's far enough. What do you want?"

"I told you, I know your grandmother," he said.

"Many people know my grandmother," I say. "Are you a spy of some sort? An assassin?"

"A guard."

"No, you're not." This I'm sure of.

A touch of irritation in his expression, and I'm ridiculously gratified to see a crack in his no-longer-comforting façade. "Okay, yes, usually I'm one of her spies. But I have guard training, and there's no way your bodyguards would blend in here. Are you happy? Can we go now?"

I can't say I'm shocked to hear him confirm my grandmother, the former queen, has spies. I suppose it would be unlikely for a force like her to ever truly retire. But that one of her people has found me faster than anyone else indicates an unmatched level of competence on that front, and that leaves me with more questions—about how my grandmother occupies her days, why she sent him, how he found me.

None of which are relevant right this instant. "Go where?"

Entero frowns. "Back to the capital, of course."

I expected that answer, but my stomach still drops. Suddenly chilled, I wrap my arms around myself. "No," I whisper.

"You must realize even if you're technically no longer titled, you need to be protected," he tells me. "You may not care about your own life, but you could be taken hostage and used against your sisters. Or your mother."

This, unexpectedly, makes me laugh. "How foolish. As if any of them would give in to a demand for my sake."

"That may be, but it doesn't mean people won't try to kidnap you or worse regardless," Entero says. "And it doesn't mean your family wouldn't be bothered if you were hurt."

"And so my grandmother, out of great concern for my safety, has sent you to find me and bring me back."

"Yes."

Maybe if my grandmother had been concerned about more than my physical wellbeing and how it could be deployed against the House she should have given me more specific advice at my dedication ceremony.

"Then I'm sorry to disappoint you," I say. "But I will not go back. Not with you, and not for any reason."

He sighs. "You're being unreasonable, and you know it. You followed a man you've never met before, who you think has the ability to kill people professionally, alone, down a maze, and you think you can keep yourself safe?"

I cringe. "I think my safety is my own affair now."

"And that's where you're wrong. Your grandmother has made it mine."

That's all the warning I have before he lunges forward, seizing my wrists before I've managed to dance back more than a step.

I tug him forward, hoping to off-balance him in a move my own bodyguards taught me. But he's prepared for this, using my own momentum to back me against a wall while I struggle—

And then I see a bright light in my peripheral vision. He notices it, too, his eyes widening an instant before he throws himself backward to avoid it.

The ball of light flashes in front of me, right where he had been standing. Lacking an Entero to hit, it crashes into a trash bin behind us, and the bin melts.

Just—disintegrates, as if it had never been.

I've never seen power like that.

But Entero released me rather than drag me with him. Keeping myself to the opposite wall as far away from him as I can be, I scramble further back down the alley.

Where Lorwyn is waiting, menacingly tossing another ball of witchlight in one hand.

Oh, spirits.

Entero's expression rapidly shifts from shocked alertness to something darker as he puts it together in an instant. "Witch," he growls.

And he moves.

He launches forward with stunning speed, drawing knives from somewhere on his person as he runs.

Lorwyn hurls the witchlight ball at him, but he's faster. The ground sizzles behind him as she hurls ball after ball, and he's going to gut her right in front of me—

I throw myself in front of Lorwyn just before Entero gets close enough.

Everyone freezes.

Finally, Entero demands, "What do you think you're doing?"

"My question exactly," Lorwyn snaps. "What were you thinking, following a dangerous stranger down an alley alone?"

Entero snorts in dark amusement. It's almost exactly what he accused me of.

"I was attempting to keep him from finding out you're a witch," I say with exasperation.

They're both surprised silent for a moment.

Lorwyn reacts first. "Well, try to appear less terrified next time so I don't have to follow you! And anyway, I can take care of myself."

"Can you?" Entero asks mildly.

I feel heat against my back, see him tensing again, and stomp. "Stop it, right now!"

"I will if he will," Lorwyn says pleasantly.

"I won't lose to anyone, even a witch," Entero says.

"Entero, enough," I say, and I almost don't recognize the implacable tone in my voice. "If you make any attempt to attack her again, or any attempt to report her for witchcraft, I will personally hold you still while she does whatever she must to ensure your silence. Do I make myself clear?"

"Are you mad?" he yells. "Witches are dangerous—"

"Says the assassin with all the knives who tried to kidnap a woman," Lorwyn retorts. "Who here was attacking Miyara again?"

"I said enough. Entero, you will swear an oath on the water in your body, right this instant, or so help me this day will be your last."

He stares at me, utterly shocked. Even Lorwyn is quiet.

In truth, I'm shocked at myself, too. I've never done anything like this, and perhaps later I'll have the space to wonder if he's right, and I'm mad.

But even if this is a different kind of mistake, I don't waver. He doesn't get to kill Lorwyn because I'm foolish and untried.

"You can't be serious," Entero says.

"Miyara..." Lorwyn says quietly, uncertainly behind me.

I reach behind me and tap the wrist of her throwing arm. She tenses; she's taken my warning to be ready.

"I have never been more serious in my life," I say. "You will not do anything to cause Lorwyn to come to harm. The oath or your life, now."

Entero's expression sets as he considers his options. "And what if she hurts me? I'm not just going to swear any oath you demand any time you demand it," he says.

The fact that I'm asking him to swear one is outrageous enough. Such a demand is outside the scope of bodyguard contracts for good reason: given substantial power discrepancies, guards must be protected from the dangerous whims of those they serve.

We don't have a contract, though. Even so, I still shouldn't demand such a concession of him. But I don't know him, I don't have any proof beyond his word that my grandmother sent him or that he truly is here to look out for me, and I have no other way to protect Lorwyn.

She may be untouched now, but I didn't miss the fact that not one of her balls of witchlight actually hit him.

"But you'll swear this one," I tell him. "And in return I swear not to demand an oath from you again."

"Miyara, don't do that!" Lorwyn hisses.

But it's too late: Entero stands slowly, deliberately, and nicks a finger with one of his knives. "With this drop I swear to the spirit of water I will neither physically harm one Lorwyn nor inform on her witchcraft. Happy?"

He sounds utterly disgusted.

No, I'm not happy. But I am surprised, and unutterably relieved, he swore the oath, and I make mine in turn without hesitation.

This proves that he was, in fact, sent by my grandmother and tasked to see to my safety. Otherwise he would have either left, or killed us both. I forced the issue, but it was well within his ability to take a different path; he chose to accept this limitation.

I hope our ideas of "safety" are enough in line that I won't regret removing my own ability to limit him further. But at least this way he'll never face conflict over what to do about Lorwyn; any fallout will land squarely on me.

"You realize," Entero says, "this means if she attacks you and I have to defend you, my life and spirit are forfeit."

Yes. If the oath were any less serious, I wouldn't trust him to abide by it. I glance back at Lorwyn, whose face is unreadable. "I'd appreciate it if you could make an effort to not put him in a position where he feels compelled to sacrifice his life on my behalf."

"No promises," she says, eyes narrowing. "You want to tell me what this is all about?"

Carefully, I step out of the way, keeping an eye on both of them to make sure they don't go for each other's throats the instant I'm not standing between them.

So far so good.

And now we can all look each other in the eye and speak civilly as if we have not all forced terrible decisions on each other in the last few minutes.

"Apparently my grandmother has more varied resources at her disposal than I realized, and she's concerned for my safety," I say.

Lorwyn looks at me incredulously. "Your grandmother is in a position to hire an assassin to kidnap you?"

I exchange a look with Entero. I hadn't told him to swear to keep my secret, but I don't think I need to. By his own reasoning, the more people who know I'm a princess, the more danger I'm in.

He scowls but doesn't say anything.

In fact, the scowl is so at odds with his utter ease when we first met back at the shop that I begin to wonder if it's an act. For Lorwyn's benefit, or mine?

"So it would seem," I say.

"Then you have family with enough money and resources to provide for you," Lorwyn says slowly.

Oh. "No. I mean, yes, I have family with resources, but they can't provide for me. Not officially. It's... a legal thing, basically. My family can't give me any direct support. If that became public, they would be in serious trouble, and they won't risk that for my sake. Thus, I assume, the choice to go with an assassin."

"Can he get you money? That's not direct."

"No," Entero says. "That's not how it works. No official resources can be directed to her. She's cut off."

"But her grandmother sent you."

There, that's what I've been missing.

"How exactly did she phrase your assignment?" I ask Entero.

He crosses his arms. "I won't answer that."

But he's frowning, which makes me think he's just realized the same thing I have and isn't happy.

My grandmother sent someone unofficially—and someone who can blend in. Someone with guard training. Someone who can keep me safe.

"You're supposed to guard me, aren't you?"

He pounces on that, apparently intent on salvaging something from this disaster. "And you think I can do that here?"

Lorwyn mutters to me, "Should have made him swear not to kidnap you, you dunderhead."

Entero ignores this. "My job is to guard you, and you think you'll just be able to—what, live a normal life with a bodyguard?"

I cross my arms. "If my grandmother truly chose you, then yes, I do. Will you need to stay with me?"

"What?" Lorwyn cries. "Miyara, don't you dare."

I blink at her. "Don't what?"

"You're not bothered by sharing your personal chambers with a man you don't even know?" she demands. "What kind of upbringing did you have?"

One that included bodyguards, which Lorwyn must have realized, though I don't know how much of our conversation she heard. But I've also realized, with her witchcraft display earlier, more about just how powerful she is, so perhaps she'll let that pass to avoid prying questions.

I glance between her and Entero, uncertain how to proceed. "Do people not typically share chambers?" I ask.

Lorwyn throws up her hands, but Entero answers me succinctly. "They do, but it typically implies a close relationship. Lovers, family." He shoots a pointed look at Lorwyn. "Or bodyguards."

"No one is going to assume you're a bodyguard and you know it," she says.

Entero shrugs.

"Miyara, even if you're okay with that, two things you need to consider," Lorwyn says. "First, I'm not vouching for him to Risteri. He's outside our bargain. Second, he clearly doesn't want to stay in

Sayorsen with you. How do we know he won't try to run off with you when I'm not there to watch?"

"As if you're the greatest deterrent," Entero sneers.

It's a valid point, but I admit I'm more interested in the one she didn't specify: the one where it would be decided for me how people perceive me.

"Okay," I say slowly, "so Entero doesn't stay with me."

"And how am I supposed to keep you safe if I can't even stay in the same place as you, exactly?"

Lorwyn snaps, "That's your problem, not hers."

It's both, really. By consenting to be guarded, I need to make allowances to make guarding possible. But it is his job to figure out the particulars, and I notice that, unlike moments earlier, his muscles are very relaxed right now. Which tells me he's not actually worried about it; he's pushing to see where my boundaries are.

As if I know.

But I am consenting to be guarded. That Entero swore the oath I demanded from him proves he takes his commission seriously, and I don't think he would leave if I asked. Ultimately, he works for my grandmother, and he doesn't strike me as someone who could be easily swayed from a course he's committed to.

So I will not go out of my way to make his life any more difficult than it already has to be. This situation has been forced on both of us, and until I'm ready to outright oppose my grandmother's wishes and expect to triumph, we'll have to make the best of it gracefully.

And before he tried to kidnap me for my own good, I felt instantly comfortable in his presence. My initial impressions are rarely wrong, even if I don't understand them.

"I don't think there's a good way to guard me during my time at the shop, either, unless you're inside," I say. "And people will ask questions if you simply loiter around the shop."

"Oh, that's easily solved," Lorwyn says. "He'll just have to work there. That way I can keep an eye on him, too."

I glance at her in surprise. "You think Talmeri would hire him? He's not one of her wealthy connections."

"I can get any credentials you need by tomorrow," Entero says.

"You'll need forged social references, I think, rather than credentials," I say.

He shrugs, unconcerned. "I'll handle it. Working at the same day job as you is the most logical solution."

"Be still my beating heart," Lorwyn drawls, "we can agree on something after all."

"Don't get used to it."

I ask her, "Will it really be that easy to get Talmeri to hire him?"

She snorts. "Of course it will. Free labor that comes with apparently respectable references? And, well, look at him." She gestures vaguely in Entero's direction—at the figure he cuts with all his well-honed, deadly muscles.

"I see what you mean," I murmur, and Entero rolls his eyes.

"So," he says, "what else do I need to know?"

Lorwyn cackles, and finally everyone seems to have calmed down.

Then she crows, "Oh, are you ever going to regret this, tea boy," and I pinch the bridge of my nose, resigned to an afternoon of endless sniping.

CHAPTER 10

THE SHOP CLOSES AT LAST, Meristo heads out, and after a shockingly long time spent bickering with Lorwyn, Entero finally does, too, to do whatever he needs to arrange the form his assignment has now taken.

"Don't do anything stupid until I get back," he growls at me.

I'm reasonably sure I've managed the last few days without any assassins, but he's had a long day. I say only, "I'll do my best."

Lorwyn snorts in disgust, Entero casts her one last dirty glare, and then Lorwyn and I are alone in the back again.

"Well," she finally says, stalking over to her lab. "That could have gone worse, probably, though I can't think how."

I drop onto a box nearby. "Oh, surely your imagination is better than that. I can think of dozens of ways that end with one or all of us dead."

"Thanks for reminding me," Lorwyn says. "Why are you still here? I have work to do."

"You always say that, but you somehow manage."

I meant that to be funny, so I'm taken aback by how her face tightens. Apparently I've missed the mark, and I'm not sure how.

"I thought we should talk about what happened today, now that we're alone," I say.

Lorwyn stalks around her lab. "What's to talk about?"

I frown. "A blood oath? An assassin? Fighting with witchcraft?"

"What's to talk about?" she repeats. "Everything is terrible, we're stuck with it, that's just how it goes. Are you going to help, or are you going to leave?"

"Are you mad at me?" I ask. "I thought you were scowling for Entero's benefit."

"I always scowl, because I'm always unhappy," she says. And I'm used enough to hearing sarcasm from her that I'm especially troubled to realize I'm not hearing it now.

"Then maybe *you* should leave," I say quietly.

She sets down the tea pet abruptly. "Excuse you?"

"If your situation is so unbearable—"

"You sound like Risteri," she snarls.

That's enough to tell me she won't be receptive to anything I have to say. But she sounded so serious that I can't help pushing.

She tried to save my life today.

"Either you're being dramatic, or everything in your life is terrible. In which case why *don't* you do something else? *Anything* else?"

"Oh?" Lorwyn asks, voice dripping sweet malice. "Any ideas, my homeless, jobless, totally dependent friend?"

I grit my teeth. She has a point there. "Obviously I don't have all the answers. But I'm better off now than I was."

"You were lucky," she snaps.

"Yes, and you could be too. And even if you're not—" I break off before asking what she can lose, because I do know one thing: her life. "You could enroll in mage school. You can clearly keep all your power in check."

Lorwyn laughs, and it's the most desolate sound I've ever heard.

Then she begins to glow.

And then it's as if she combusts into witchlight.

Lorwyn is definitely not an ordinary witch.

"How about this?" she asks, stalking toward me, waving her hands. "Is this a good enough reason for why?"

As her hands move, the air around her bends, like she's passed them through water. But the hair on my arms stands on end, crackling with energy.

"I can sense your power," I say in some surprise. It's emanating off her like heat.

"Yes, I'm sure you can," Lorwyn says bitterly. "Even without a display like this, though, a witch always knows another witch."

"But if you were mage-trained, you wouldn't have to hide."

"You're so naïve. Of course I would, because as soon as they knew what I was capable of, they'd kill me for sure. Even if I could somehow hide long enough, it wouldn't matter. You think I can get *in* to mage school? How, Miyara?"

"What are you talking about? Anyone can go to mage school."

"No, anyone rich can go to mage school!" She's shouting. "Anyone with the right credentials, which of course Gaellani can't get. Anyone with connections to the right people, anyone with money—and believe me, if any Gaellani somehow managed to raise the money, there's always some other fee, some other hoop too impossible to jump through. There's no way I could *ever* go to mage school even if I wanted to, which I *don't*!"

Is it really that bad? Is she just being negative, or am I really as foolish as she thinks?

Probably, I decide, both.

"I thought you liked working on your magic," I say. "I thought that was one of the reasons you worked here, so you had a place where it's safe to experiment. Why wouldn't you want to go mage school?"

"Besides that I don't want to ruin my life with impossible dreams?"

"Better an impossible dream than none at all," I say quietly.

Her face twists. "Of course you would say that. You, who apparently grew up with all the privilege in the world and threw it away and aren't facing any consequences for it. You have a place of your own, which I've never had. Almost no Gaellani is able to, here. You have the admiration of half the city for aspiring to tea mastery in three cursed months, and believe me if I tried to aspire to *anything*, not only would no one sponsor me, they'd laugh at me in the street. Who are you to judge me?"

I swallow. "Someone who thinks you deserve to be happy."

The air seems to crackle. "People like me don't have the luxury of pursuing happiness, Miyara."

"Happiness isn't a luxury that only some people deserve to be able to attain—"

"Oh, come off it! When have you wondered how you would feed your sisters? When have you wondered when you would be thrown out on the street? When have you wondered when your neighbors would come to execute you for how you were born? When have you had to worry that if you make one wrong move—"

She snaps. The witchlight around her flares, and I take a step back away from the force of it.

Conviction shines in her eyes, and she opens her mouth for what I'm sure will be a scathing pronouncement when the air around us seems to shimmer, and she falters.

There's a *pop*, like a bubble has burst, and dozens of items nearest to her on the lab snap.

The tea pet breaks into pieces.

Lorwyn closes her eyes; clenches her fist. "When have you ever had to worry if you make one wrong move, your power will destroy what you care about the most."

My stomach is in knots.

I did this. I made this happen.

I fear I may have just destroyed what I cared about most, too: her happiness. Our friendship.

"The tea pet?" I ask.

Lorwyn glances down at it, jaw clenched. "A family heirloom," she says in a neutral voice. "It's always been fragile, but they trusted it to me as a show of faith that I would always be in control, despite my power." She scoops up the pieces of the tea pet, drops them into a trash bin. "Well. Here we are."

"Is it—can it be fixed? I—"

"A break like this? No. No, it can't. It's done."

She looks done, and broken, and—small, deflated, like the spark of her spirit snuffed out. "Lorwyn, I'm so sorry."

"You know what? I don't even care." Lorwyn stares at the remains of the tea pet for a long moment, then looks at the mess around her, and her expression twists in disgust and self-loathing.

And then she looks at me, shakes her head, and leaves without another word as I stare after her, frozen.

My words started this, and forced it. So much for knowing how to listen.

It seems like my words should be able to fix it, too, but I don't know the words for that. Only that everything I've said in the last few minutes was exactly wrong.

I go to the bin and dig out every piece of the tea pet I can find, absently wiping the hot tears off my cheeks when my vision blurs.

She's right. I don't know anything.

And now I've broken everything. Her faith in herself, our friendship.

How can I fix this? Can it be fixed?

My hands tremble, and I clench them, shoving the pieces closer together so I don't drop them.

Seeing them bunched together, I have a desperate thought. Maybe I can fix the tea pet. I could get glue—

No, I can already imagine how that will go. A horribly twisted version of the once delicately crafted piece will only represent a thoughtless perversion of what once was. I don't have the skill, and I know next-to-nothing about pottery—

But there is that potter. Deniel.

Surely if anyone can fix this, it must be him. Right?

Oh, not our friendship. But maybe Lorwyn's faith in herself could in some small measure be restored with the tea pet. Maybe she could believe that it's not worth abandoning hope.

The location of Deniel's shop is on my map.

This is probably madness, but it's all I've got. I can't just sit here with the shards of her broken faith in herself, when I'm responsible for breaking it, when she's helped me through these days of finding my own faith in myself. I can't.

I find a tea tin of innocuous ingredients I recognize—I wouldn't be surprised if some of Talmeri's choice ingredients could burn through ceramic—and carefully pour the remains of the tea pet into it. I gather my things, squint at the map, and charge off into the twilight.

I thought I might be so upset I'd have trouble finding my way, but the reverse is true: I am unerringly focused. I make not a single wrong turn, single-mindedly devoted to one task: finding the potter's shop.

As an added benefit, that means I don't have to worry about what in the world I will say when I appear on his doorstep.

Despite that, I almost think I'm in the wrong place when the building resembles a cottage. Not like Risteri's grandmother's, exactly; it's in a busier area, for one thing, and shoved right up against others just like it. I can't put my finger on what the difference is—

But it doesn't matter. I'm dithering.

Wringing my hands, I approach the door, where a small sign reads only, "Deniel's." So I'm in the right place.

What are the right words to fix this?

Here I am, showing up late in the evening after all the surrounding businesses are closed, crying, begging for help, and why should he give it to me? Why should he even open the door for the madwoman on his doorstep, and if he does why not close it in her face? In fact he's probably not here at all. I could just go, and think about how to approach this rationally, and come back tomorrow.

I squeeze my eyes against the renewed spurt of tears.

Enough.

Enough, Miyara.

I knock.

And wait.

My knuckles ache from the force of my squeezing my nails into my palms, the tension of holding it in.

Deep breaths.

Swallow.

How long has it been since I knocked? Do I knock again? Has it only been seconds?

I hear shuffling inside and freeze, one fist half-raised to knock again, my eyes wide and body tense as if to bolt, which is ludicrous since getting someone's attention was the whole point.

The door opens, and there he is. The light from inside shines behind him, making stark every disheveled hair on the same man I saw at the bookstore.

Who looks totally startled to see me on his doorstep, which is utterly reasonable, but I still feel like *I* am even more startled to see him, which isn't.

"Can I help you?" Deniel finally manages to ask.

I open my mouth to speak and it's like my throat closes up on the words. I shake my head sharply, feeling tears fly off my cheeks, and in frustration, or perhaps desperation, I manage to force my trembling hands to open the tea tin.

"It—it was a tea pet," I manage to choke out. "A baby dragon."

"I see," he says. His voice sounds grave, as though it is not utterly mad to be crying about a piece of pottery on a stranger's doorstep at night, but I can't bring myself to look at his face. "I recognize the design. It was important to you?"

I have never had trouble controlling my emotions. Perhaps the space to feel them freely has shattered that forever, but whatever it is, I have to choke back a sob as more tears squeeze out of my eyes and I shake my head.

"Not me. My—my friend. My first." And then the words are spilling out with my tears. "I didn't know it was important, but I *should* have, and I—it's my fault it's broken, and now she is, and I can't *fix* it."

Deniel doesn't say anything. Maybe he's wondering how to calm the madwoman down, or let me down gently, or just waiting for me to run out of words.

Finally, I make myself look at him and ask what I should have led with. "Can it be fixed?"

He's watching me intently. "I can't make it what it once was," Deniel says. Before my stomach has finished bottoming out he's added, "I may be able to do something else. But the price is not what you may think."

My chest squeezes. Oh, spirits. "I don't have money. At least, not what this is worth. But. Please. *Please*, if there's anything—"

"There's no monetary price that would be adequate. That's not the cost."

I blink, trying to understand through the jumble of my thoughts.

When he can see he has my full attention, Deniel says, "There is something I can do. But the process is sacred, and I won't involve money in it."

I nod, not trusting myself to speak, not sure where he's going with this.

"The price," he says, "is your greatest secret. No more, and no less. Is re-making this worth enough to you that you will trust that to a total stranger?"

I stare.

It's not so much that I'm shocked as that I'm utterly floored.

It ought to feel surreal that I am crying on a potter's doorstep to save me, and he'll do so for a secret. And I suppose it does, but not as much it should.

"Please think carefully," Deniel cautions. "This is not something I ask lightly, and I would not expect you to give it."

Perhaps another person wouldn't understand the implications of divulging their greatest secret, might consider giving a less serious one even during a sacred ritual, or wouldn't consider the question of that secret thoroughly.

I am not that person.

"I understand," I whisper. "You may have it."

He studies my expression for a long moment and, at last, nods, stepping back and opening the door. "Then come in."

I follow him, no longer sure what's happening, as we pass through a room full of displays that even at a passing glance I can tell hold some of the most beautiful ceramic pieces I've ever laid eyes on.

But we leave that room, and the one behind it is very different.

Deniel gently claps on the lights and leads me to a chair, which I drop into gingerly. "I apologize for the mess. My workshop doubles as my living area. Please, make yourself comfortable. This will take some time." He kneels before me. "May I?" He gestures at the tin.

I try to hand it to him carefully, but my hands are still shaking. His are steady, though, and I swallow past the lump of relief and fear.

"My secret—" I begin, but he shakes his head.

"Not now. Take your time to think while I work. Can I get you anything?"

I open my mouth to ask about tea, but then I think of Lorwyn, and the tea pet, and I'm leaking again, covering my face in my hands.

"That's okay," Deniel says quietly. "Take your time."

This is ridiculous. I cannot keep bursting into tears because of a piece of clay.

Although evidence suggests, to the contrary, that in fact I can.

By the time I've recovered enough to look up again, Deniel is no longer in front of me, though I can hear his quiet movements from the other side of the room.

The room is large, but not spacious, as, like the ground floor of Risteri's grandmother's cottage, it appears to serve multiple functions.

Most of the space is Deniel's workshop, full of tables, equipment, pieces in various stages of development—not as many as I'd expect, so either he doesn't produce much at once or there must be more elsewhere—though he himself hunches in a corner. There's a kitchen, too, with extra ovens, along with a small table and two wooden chairs; and then there's the smallest section where I am, with a small couch, the unevenly stuffed chair I'm sitting in, clearly well-loved, and an overstuffed bookcase, much of which is devoted to books of law.

And there, in the corner, a simple pedestal atop which sits an altar to the spirits. Free of dust, the candle lit.

Deniel's life is in this room, and he has walked me into it without a thought. I want to unravel what that means, what all these pieces together mean, but that's not what I'm here for.

What is my greatest secret?

Is it really as grave and earth-shattering as Deniel is treating it?

Spirits, Entero would say so. In fact he'd probably have much to say about following a man, alone, without asking any questions—for the second time in a single day, no less—in fact asking that stranger to name any price.

It's all well and good to understand that I'm a good judge of character, but all things considered I'm not sure I should trust myself to judge *anyone*, especially now of all times.

Leaving that aside, there is still a risk in sharing secrets. Not that Entero knows what my secrets are, but he's a guard—I'm sure he'd assume divulging any is likely to make me less safe.

And that's the crux. It's not the secret itself as much as the act of divulging it. Of being willing and able to open myself that much. Of being honest enough with myself to know what it is I fear so much not a single other soul knows, and trusting that to another I *don't* know.

If it were for my own sake, I couldn't do it. Clearly, or at some time in the last twentyish years of my life I would have.

But for Lorwyn's, to fix this—

Well. No. The tea pet is, however symbolic in my mind, still a piece of clay. But symbols have only as much weight as we imbue them with, and maybe this is what it takes for me begin to own the space I inhabit, to be aware enough that I don't accidentally cause so much harm flailing to find myself.

A long time passes before Deniel is kneeling before me again.

"It's time," he says. "Are you ready?"

The first meaningless thing he's said to me. My readiness has no bearing on this.

I take a breath for the words I have managed to avoid speaking all my life, even at my dedication, and meet his gaze head-on.

"My name is Miyara, and I was the fourth princess of Istalam."

His eyes widen.

"That's not the secret," I say fiercely. "Well. It's *a* secret, but it's not the one that matters. It has *never* mattered, not really."

What is it about my inability to stop words once they've started? When did this happen?

"It's my duty to serve people. I *want* to, more than anything, and always have. But despite everything, I have absolutely no idea how. I am—I *was* a princess, and the only thing in this world and in my life that matters is the one thing I don't know what to do about."

And that's it. That's my greatest secret, the thing I've never been able to admit to anyone.

It sounds so silly out loud.

But if Deniel thinks it is, he doesn't say so. Spirits, he may not even believe me. But he nods gravely, stands, and says with the weight of ritual, "I will keep your secret in my heart."

He extends a hand to me, palm raised. It's trembling, ever-so-slightly.

But when I put my hand in his and he helps me stand, we're both balanced with each other if unsteady, and his hand is warm around mine.

Deniel brings me over to his work table, and I stop abruptly when I see the tea pet.

"What is this?" I breathe.

Because it's not just reassembled. The cracks are filled with shimmering silver. The history of the break is still there, but it's not just re-made; it's made anew into something beautiful.

But I know what this is; similar artifacts were gifted centuries ago to an Istal queen, from a nation that, as far as I know, did not survive the Cataclysm. I had no idea this tradition had.

"Just because something is broken or appears to have no function doesn't mean it has no value," Deniel says. Then he runs a hand through his hair as though embarrassed. "Though I have to admit it won't actually work as a tea pet anymore. I'm sorry, I should have warned you about that at the start."

I can't believe he thinks I'd care about that, but as I glance up to say something to that effect the words freeze on my lips.

Deniel's eyes are bloodshot, and a quick glance toward the window reveals total darkness has descended. I've been here for hours—and he had probably worked a full day before I showed up and must be exhausted.

"This is too much," I say. "The balance is not even. All you've done, what this is worth—"

"Is beside the point," he says firmly. "This is the tradition as I learned it. It's not about balance; it's about a gift."

My eyes search his. I can't imagine what the cost of the metals alone must be, especially for a Gaellani craftsman. Not to mention his time and effort, and he can't make a habit of doing this often or openly. "Why would you go to all this trouble?" I ask.

Deniel smiles wearily, a hint of mischief in his eyes through it all that tugs at me. "I'm not telling."

I laugh outright, then, and then stop abruptly, startled by the sound after everything this night. He reaches around me and carefully wraps the tea pet in a cloth and inserts the package into the tea tin.

I blush, mortified as he places it back in my hands. I can't believe I brought him a tea tin to hold something so precious.

I gaze up at him. "Thank you," I say, with as much sincerity as I can put into the words, and they are still totally inadequate.

"The honor is all mine," he says, the corners of his eyes still crinkled from that slight smile—or perhaps from the effort of keeping them open this late.

My words were inadequate, I don't know what gesture can bridge the gap, and now that I've consciously thought about weariness I'm surprised I can speak coherently at all. It will have to wait.

I duck my head, and he steps back, and somehow we maneuver ourselves back through his shop. He opens the door to a pair of golden green eyes glaring cautiously out of the darkness.

"Oh, hello Talsion," Deniel says.

The darkness resolves into a sleek gray cat that scampers inside.

"You have a cat?" I ask inanely.

Deniel glances back with a wry look on his face. "It might be more accurate to say Talsu has adopted me," he says.

A teeny mew echoes.

"I should go," we both say at the same time and exchange smiles.

The door closes, leaving me oddly bereft and certain: like I've found myself, my home, for the first time, and know how to find it again.

I'm too weary to tease that out, and my emotions have been such a jumble all night it's probably nonsense anyway.

But I'm hopeful not for what tomorrow will bring, but to meet tomorrow as myself, in a way I can't quite explain.

The moon is shining vividly against the velvet night sky when I arrive home. I clap on the lights and as I turn to shut my door I glimpse, just for a moment, Risteri, as a gust of wind blows back the hood of her cloak.

I blink, and then she's gone.

Sneaking out when the household is most likely to believe she's sleeping? If she makes a habit of it, I know how she manages to leave food for me so early in the morning, though the why is another matter.

For another time. Sleep beckons, and I shut the door on that mystery until tomorrow.

CHAPTER 11

I THOUGHT I COULD sleep forever, but I wake before dawn. As thoughts clatter through my mind, I decide I'm too restless for sleep to find me again anytime soon and get up.

When I wash my hair, I'm startled not just by the length—I wonder how long it will take my muscles to remember how short my hair now is—but by how easily I can run my fingers through it. I go to attempt combing and find that, although wet, the waves of my hair are already neatly arranged.

Lorwyn's doing, clearly. She changed more than the surface color and length of my hair, helping me far more than I deserved.

The thought of Lorwyn propels me onward, and once I reach the kitchen I remember that nearly all the food in the cooler requires cooking. I have the recipe book, but not the patience. I'm not sure what to do with myself, but I need to move.

I pull out a container of pickled vegetables from the cooler and open a package of rice crackers, which appear to be the only food that does not involve some kind of preparation, eat enough to get going, retrieve my map and the tea tin containing the remade tea pet, and head out.

For a few minutes I take in the city in the pre-dawn light as I wander. It's beautiful to me, even the parts that are worn down or poorly designed. I wonder if I'd have felt this way about wherever I landed after leaving the palace, or if the compassion I've felt from people here has colored my view. Perhaps Sayorsen is simply where I belong, but that answer seems too convenient. It may be where I need to be now; in any event, it's where I am, and the little I know of it I already love.

That reminds me that I still haven't visited Sayorsen's shrine, which should be its heart. I search for it on the map, wondering if I'll be allowed in at this time, when I suddenly remember the state I left the tea shop in last night. Namely, I'm not sure I locked the door when I fled, and Lorwyn had already gone. That must be my first stop, then.

I walk with more urgency now, hoping I do not arrive to find the shop ransacked. If anything could damage my friendship with Lorwyn worse, it would be having allowed the one space she considers safe to explore her witchcraft in to be desolated. I wish I'd thought of that last night. Perhaps I did lock the door and have simply forgotten, and I'm worrying for nothing—

The back door's knob turns easily under my hand. I swallow and carefully open it.

And let out a breath. Everything appears to be in place.

Including the undisturbed mess on the floor of the warehouse.

After a quick look for any tentacles in my path, I go in search of cleaning supplies. Lorwyn should not have to deal with the mess I left in my wake.

That taken care of, I contemplate righting the objects on her desk and decide against it. She'd take that as encroaching, not helping.

But I do set the tea pet back in the place on the shelf where I saw it previously. Let her make of it what she will without any overt presentation or my reaction to account for.

She won't want me in her space when she arrives for the day, so I lock the door on my way out. Now, *finally*, I will find the shrine.

Except that it's not on my map.

I study it carefully, squinting in the dawn light, but if it's marked there I can't find it.

At least Lorwyn confirmed there *is* one. I'll have to ask her—

Or perhaps Risteri. Another time.

What to do now, then? I'm still thrumming with restless energy. I consider returning to the Gaellani courtyard, but that, too, seems like an invasion of Lorwyn's space. Not that it's marked on my map, either.

The night market will have dissolved until tonight, but dawn is probably a good time to gawk at the wares in the Central Market without being in the way. This *is* marked prominently, so armed with my map, I set out again.

The path is empty and quiet. I take my time studying the magecraft jewelry behind the glass window of one shop when someone inside suddenly appears making shooing motions and mouthing "we're closed."

I scurry along, rubbing my wrists where the bracelets aren't.

And then I come to Thiano's. I might have expected him to fully embody his elitist persona, staying abed late even when his colleagues are beginning work, or perhaps recovering from a night of covert meetings. But instead he leans back against the open door to his shop, expression sardonic as he waits for me to reach him.

I'm too impatient, too lacking in clarity to deal with someone of Thiano's subtlety right now. Before I can gracefully back away, he asks, "What brings you here so early, Tea Aspirant?"

"Couldn't sleep," I admit after a moment. What other answer is there?

"Is there no tea for that? For shame."

"There is. Perhaps Talmeri will gift me with some at the shop."

Thiano snorts. "Your thieving plans are safe with me, for the great esteem I hold our budding friendship in."

"I'll be sure to stay out of the way of the local police, then," I quip, but my thoughts have, finally, snagged on something particular. Perhaps too revealing a question to ask of a foreign spy, but— "Thiano, what makes a good gift?"

"What an inane question to interrupt my morning with," he notes. "Even you have given gifts before."

True. I chase the thought down. "Not when the gift I should give must make up for so much."

"Ah," Thiano says. "The weight of obligation that knows no bounds."

I shake my head. "There is no amount of labor or money that would approximate what he did for me."

I wonder if Thiano will ask who I mean, or if he already knows—or will pretend to. This is not a subject I would have expected to speak with him about.

"You might be surprised by what a sufficiently large sum of money can do," Thiano says.

"Probably," I agree. "Still. A mere 'thank you' is inadequate."

"Some debts can never be paid in full, or even in part."

His tone is too carefully even. "That's true," I say. "But is it not worthwhile to try anyway? Is it better to let the past be the past and move forward?"

Thiano snorts. "You don't have enough life experience to know."

"You'll note that I asked *you*."

His breath catches.

And then he laughs, long and hard. "Oh, child. I'm the last person outside the Cataclysm you should ever ask that. But, neatly done. Come inside."

He kicks a box out of the way, and the door nearly shuts before I scramble up the steps after him.

The shop, like the man, is a maze. "What kind of gift are you looking for?" Thiano asks.

"If I knew that—"

"Do better."

I pause. "A gift that demonstrates I value his efforts on my behalf."

"So, something nice. You want him to think kindly of you?"

I start to answer yes; stop. "I don't want to give a gift so nice he'd feel obligated in turn, if that's what you mean."

He stops ahead of me, turning to cast me a look with a smirk. "It wasn't," he says. "But duly noted."

I blush, not totally sure why. Thiano's smirk widens and he begins stalking forward again.

"Have you considered baking?" he asks.

It's my turn to stop. "No. That is, I can boil water, but—I wanted something nice."

Thiano snorts. "Cooking is work—any handicrafts are, but people value what we make with our own hands. I'm going to guess there's not much you know how to make with your hands."

"There's tea ceremony," I say doubtfully.

"And tea, as you know, is an excellent gift, but it's too inside your wheelhouse; it'll seem too easy, like you didn't care to stretch yourself. Food takes care. It's something we need, but also something we enjoy."

"Baked goods are a gift because they're a luxury," I muse.

"And the thing about nonessential food is that if people don't like it, they can get rid of it without feeling bad. You come to visit a week later, the food would have gone bad anyway, so you can each maintain the fiction it was eaten and savored."

"I still have to be able to make it well, though." This is the oddest conversation to be having with a spy. Part of me is tracking the undercurrents to analyze later, but I still feel as though he is, in truth, trying to help me. I'm just not sure how, exactly, or why.

"Yes, well, try. Do work. Or is that too much for you?"

I smile. "I suppose we'll have to see. I take it you've been leading me toward something relevant?"

Thiano shifts sideways. He's led me toward more jars and bottles of spices than I could have imagined seeing in one place.

But they're ingredients I'm at least passingly familiar with tasting—in tea, particularly, but learning to taste for tea has also taught me to isolate flavors in general fairly well. I can recall desserts I've eaten and make reasonable guesses for some of the ingredients in them.

I scan the shelves, trying to think what feels right for Deniel—and what there is likely to be a recipe for in the one book I have on the subject.

"Have you ever baked?" I ask Thiano.

He snorts. "Not on your life. Wouldn't do me or anyone else a lick of good. Will he know it's your first attempt at baking?"

"He could probably guess that," I say. "Without sampling, I mean."

"Then it's likely he'll appreciate the effort regardless of the result," Thiano says. "Unless he's not worth the effort in the first place."

"He is," I say. But I wonder if what Deniel will take from my effort is that I'm still flailing: that I know so little of what I have to offer that I will try anything.

But I *will* try. I am trying, and that matters. I hope.

"You won't be able to count on that, of course, in the future," Thiano says, and I'm not sure if he's referring to the fact that it'll no longer be my first attempt at baking or that the recipient will be worth the effort.

"I'll have to develop the skills to actually help people in anticipation of that eventuality."

He's watching me intently. "You won't be able to help everyone."

"Probably not," I agree. "But I think I'm going to try anyway."

I pull a small vial of almond extract off the wall. Whatever Thiano charges, I've read enough trade reports to know it's expensive. But I'm also sure it's responsible for the rich flavor of what I want to make: something comforting but full of flavor, and, if I'm recalling the reports correctly, a highly sought-after festival food. So it will be special, but still evoke warm feelings. If I can do it right.

Thiano waggles his eyebrows and grins at me in an awful caricature of Lorwyn's shark-smile as he quotes me the price.

It's more expensive than I can easily afford, but if I can manage to cook meals with the ingredients Risteri picked out for me I should still have enough left over for a few additional baking ingredients. I think. Or else I'll have to wait until next week.

The decision grounds me: I have something concrete to do for one of the people who's helped me. Now I will go home and see how I can manage to make it possible, and in whatever time remains I will study the art of tea so as not to squander the chance Lorwyn made for me when she couldn't make one for herself.

I brace myself outside the back door of Lorwyn's lab and knock.

The door flies open instants later, but it's not Lorwyn.

It's Entero, and he looks furious. "Where have you been?" he demands.

I blink. "Was I supposed to be somewhere in particular?"

"You were supposed to be taking care to be safe." His eyes narrow. "You didn't, did you?"

In the time since I last saw him, I've angered a witch to the point where she lost control, charged out alone into the night and then followed a man I'd never met before into his home to divulge my secrets, wandered around the streets of a city I barely know, entered an open shop that could have been full of thieves, and met with a foreign spy.

Hmm.

"I think it's fair to say I failed at that rather more spectacularly than I could have anticipated," I say. "But I seem to have made it here safely enough." As his visage darkens, I add, "Could you ask Lorwyn if I can come in please?"

Somehow his scowl deepens. "Why wouldn't you be able to?"

"Tea boy, stop blocking the door and let her in," Lorwyn hollers.

Entero lingers, just long enough to make it clear how little he thinks of Lorwyn giving him orders, then steps back with one last dark glare, gesturing me in with mock-gallantry.

Lorwyn is facing away from me at her desk. "How did you get Deniel to fix the tea pet?" she asks without turning around.

Is his handiwork so distinctive, or is he the only person who knows the technique to restore pottery in this way? I want to ask, but this isn't the time.

"I have no idea," I say.

"Oh, come on. He hasn't restored pottery like that for anyone in years, and people beg him about every week. You must have done something."

I spread my hands. "I honestly can't imagine what, unless he has a soft spot for women who appear deranged. I asked him why afterwards, and he wouldn't tell me."

Lorwyn snorts. "Of course not. That's just typical."

She says nothing more, dropping the subject. But she still hasn't turned around.

"He did mention it wouldn't work as a tea pet anymore," I say. "I'm sorry."

She shrugs like this is nothing.

I know better.

"Lorwyn—"

"Spirits, do we really have to do this?" Lorwyn whirls, planting her hands on her hips. "I shouldn't have snapped at you. Okay?"

"No. With respect, I disagree," I say. Her sharp eyebrows shoot up. "I was sanctimonious, and that would be obnoxious enough if I understood your circumstances, let alone what I was even suggesting, which I obviously don't. Snapping is the least I deserved, but I should never have put you in that position. You deserve better, certainly from me. I'm sorry, and I promise I will do better." I swallow. "Okay?"

So much packed into that last word. Is this apology sufficient? Is my promise worth anything?

Can we still be friends?

Lorwyn looks totally flummoxed, but only for a moment before her expression settles into more comfortably sardonic lines.

"I'll forgive you if you can get the scowling tea boy here to crack a smile so he doesn't terrify the customers," she says.

Relief crashes through me so fast I worry my knees will buckle. But that, along with my gratitude, would make her even more uncomfortable.

I manage, "I'm not sure how many miracles I'm good for."

She huffs a laugh, and I do have to squeeze my eyes shut for a moment.

Maybe I haven't ruined everything after all. Maybe we can still be friends.

"Does that mean," Entero says with a dangerous edge in his voice, "someone is now ready to tell me who this Deniel is, and what you were doing with him?"

"Deniel is a potter," I say.

"Deniel is the best potter," Lorwyn corrects, and I nod in accord.

Entero crosses his arms. "And?"

"And I watched him do pottery," I say.

Lorwyn snorts unhelpfully.

Entero glares at me, and I return his gaze impassively.

It was sacred, and private, and as it all worked out I decide my guard doesn't need to know any specifics.

"I take it," I interject before his glower manifests as a literal cloak around him, "Talmeri agreed to hire you?"

"She did indeed," Lorwyn says. "We're officially stuck with him. Now before Iskielo gets here for his shift and I have *two* demons rampaging through my lab—because what we needed today was the two boys with the *least* training, I could strangle Talmeri—would you take him up front and make him set a cursed tea service correctly?"

"Of course," I say. "After you, Entero."

He stalks off ahead of me. Before I follow him through the door to the shop, Lorwyn calls tentatively, "Miyara?"

I turn back. "Yes?"

"Never talk to me about mage school ever again," she says. "Okay?"

So much I would like to ask, but this is what she needs from me. "Done," I say. She nods, a jerk of a motion, and turns back to her lab, and I go to train Entero.

The shop has been open for several hours, and I'm distracted attempting to explain to Entero the reasons behind the steeping time for a particular tisane as the bell rings and another customer enters. So I don't look up until Iskielo mutters beside me, "Well, I guess I'll go find the oldest, cheapest tea we can find. Assuming she can even pay. Maybe I should just ask her to leave."

My head snaps around, and I see the subtle commotion. An old woman has hobbled in, her clothes in tatters and a huge sack attached to her back that I imagine contains all her worldly possessions. A hush has fallen over the front as the customers nearest edge away from her.

Iskielo starts to slink away, and I grab his arm.

"What?" he asks. "I said I would—"

He breaks off at whatever he sees in my expression.

"You will stay *right here*," I tell him. "You will watch, and listen, and you will not say a. Single. Other. Word."

Iskielo's young face is a mask of confusion and fear, not sure what he's messed up so badly or how, and I am *furious.* I sweep away without another word, and when I reach the old woman, I bow low.

"Welcome to Talmeri's Teas and Tisanes," I say. "Please, let me show you to a seat. Is there anything I can help you find today?"

"Oh, don't mind me, dear," she croaks, though she does follow me, and after a couple of steps accepts the arm I've held out. "I just wanted to take a moment to savor the atmosphere, if it's not too much trouble. Been a long time since I smelled a good cup of tea."

I help her set the bag down gently on the floor, startled at how heavy it is. "I think we can do somewhat better than that."

She squints at me, like she's not sure what I'm angling for from her.

I bow again. "It would be a great favor to me if you would consent to sample a particular tea of ours. Please."

The corners of her eyes crinkle. "If you say so."

I return to the tea kiosk and pull down one of the rarest, most expensive teas Talmeri carries. I haven't sampled it here, but I know what it is.

So does Iskielo. His eyes are wide as he watches me, but when he opens his mouth to say something Entero's hand shoots out and covers his mouth before any sound escapes. I incline my head to Entero in acknowledgment, he nods back, and the silence in the shop is complete while I brew the tea.

When it's ready, I take a breath, and I glide over to her table with all the tea ceremony grace I can muster.

I don't perform a full tea ceremony. But I can do an abbreviated version, more flexible than the specific historical forms, and one that doesn't require privacy. With one more bow, this is what I offer her.

I want to say with a tea ceremony that she is welcome and valuable, that here is a place where she can be warm, that will offer her tea.

This, whether she meant to or not, is what Lorwyn offered me when I arrived bedraggled on her doorstep with not a mark to my name.

The old woman sips the tea at last and says, "You do me too much honor."

"Grace, I fear I do not do you enough. Is the tea to your taste?"

She smiles as she sets the cup down with a small clatter; there's a slight tremor in her hands, more pronounced the longer she holds such a delicate cup, which I should have seen. Curses. "It's the best thing I've tasted in ages."

"Then please, take your time. I need to see to our other customers, but I'll be back to check on you shortly." I bow once more and take my leave.

I check on two other tables, where the customers won't meet my gaze without false smiles. At first I think they're embarrassed by my actions, but by the second table I decide it's their own that has caused them chagrin.

The third table I visit is different. There are four women seated there, at least two of whom I recognize from the crowd at my tea assessment, which means they're wealthy friends of Talmeri's. As I ask after their tea, one of them says to me, "I can't believe you're letting that... person stay here. This is not what I expect from this establishment."

My expectations and hers are clearly out of alignment. In this, however, I'm determined that mine will take precedence.

I will make my space what it should be.

I clear the unnecessary dishes from the table with care and answer in the same way. "Talmeri's is a place for all to feel welcome," I say, "no matter their means or circumstances."

"Well, *I* don't feel welcome with her here," she says.

"I'm saddened to hear that," I say evenly. "Is there anything else I can get you today?"

"Some compensation, yes," she says. "You gave her free tea. Why should I not have some?"

Perhaps this is shortsighted. Perhaps I have the luxury of confidence that I can be utterly clear on how this will play out. Perhaps I will regret this mightily in moments or days.

I find I don't care.

"I'm sorry," I say. "I'm afraid I cannot oblige you."

"What?" The woman's arm sweeps out dramatically. "So you value a person like *that* above me? I am a longtime, *paying* customer, and *she* gets special treatment?"

"I believe everyone deserves a good cup of tea," I say. "Which you have had."

"Well, I'm not paying for it."

I incline my head and say evenly, "Then we will not serve you again."

It takes a moment for her to process what I've said, decide I mean it, and for shock to set in.

"How dare you! Do you know who I am? When I tell my friends—"

"Yes, I know who you are." This is a lie. "And you are, of course, welcome to tell your friends whatever you like about our service. But I do wonder what your friends will think of someone who will not buy her own tea yet begrudges it to another."

She gasps in outrage, but her companions do, in fact, look embarrassed. Perhaps more by the scene she has created than the rationale for her behavior, but nevertheless, it arrests her for an instant. That is enough for me to bow and take my leave.

Iskielo's face is white, which I take to mean this wealthy woman I've dearly offended is well-known in some way. Entero's expression is utterly blank, and Lorwyn at some point emerged from her lab and is lingering by the door to the lab, watching this play out. "Talmeri won't like this," she murmurs as I pass her, depositing the dishes in the to-wash bin.

"Then Talmeri should have been more specific before she left me in charge," I reply, continuing on toward the old woman's table, where she's finished her tea.

"I didn't mean to start trouble," the old woman says.

"Nor did you," I say. "The fault is mine, for failing to create an atmosphere in which you feel welcome. My sincerest apologies, and I hope you will forgive me."

She regards me levelly for a moment and then says, "Will you pull over this bag for me?"

"Of course."

She opens the end of it so wide she's able to stick her whole head inside as she rummages around.

When she emerges, she carefully unwraps a bundle of worn gray cloth. As its covering falls away, she reveals a teapot, and I gasp.

This is not just any teapot. It's a teapot that is utterly stunning. I can't imagine how human hands could shape such a thing. This teapot is shining and vibrant, its curves twisting to form the shape of a dragon with ornate precious metal detailing.

This is the sort of pot gifted to an empress, a magic-worker's craft lovingly honed after decades, a priceless treasure that should be the subject of volumes of poetry, that none of us have any business even seeing. It's impossible for me to do justice to it with words that cannot approximate the sensation of feeling as though I am witnessing something shaped by the spirits themselves.

It shakes slightly as the old woman proffers it to me. "For you," she says.

I gape.

Then I shake my head rapidly. "Oh, no. Absolutely not. I couldn't possibly. The tea was a gift—"

"So is this," she says, "with one condition."

I blink, nonplussed.

"My hands," she says, "are not steady enough anymore to handle this teapot carefully. But this is not a teapot that deserves to languish hidden and unused. So you may use it at your discretion, as long as whenever I stop by, you will always make me tea with it. Deal?"

Still kneeling before her, I bow low, my head hitting the floor. "Grace, it would be my honor."

I take the pot from her gently, and she sighs, slumping back as though exhausted—but satisfied.

"Entero, Iskielo, come here," I say. Iskielo can't control his awe, and even Entero looks grudgingly impressed. "Never touch this teapot. This woman is always to be treated to the very best service we have to offer at no charge, and if I am not at the shop when she arrives you will send a messenger for me. Do you have any questions?"

Iskielo shakes his head rapidly, practically tripping over himself to bow. Entero manages to inject his motion with utmost respect, and I remember he knows my grandmother.

And has offered the same bow to this old, ragged woman bearing secret treasure.

When the boys have retreated, I whisper to her, "I would take it as a kindness if you would never let them know you're not secretly royalty, or a spirit made manifest."

"Oh, I think I can manage that." Her eyes twinkle. "Besides, how do you know I'm not?"

CHAPTER 12

WHEN IT'S FINALLY TIME to leave the tea shop for the day, I say to Entero, "Walk with me."

He raises his eyebrows but doesn't protest. He would have shadowed me anyway, of course, but we haven't had a chance to speak alone since he first tried to steal me away. I don't know what I want to say to him, but it seems odd to know nothing about the man who has dedicated himself to my life.

Despite walking next to me and the opportunity to interrogate me on details about what really happened with Deniel—or Lorwyn, or the mysterious old woman—Entero remains quiet and watchful. It's like there are two sides of him: this, and the belligerent, prickly side that emerges every time Lorwyn enters the room. I can't decide which is truer.

For the rest of the day at the shop, the customers could talk of nothing but the priceless teapot, passing the tale of its appearance around. Iskielo ecstatically spoke of it to whoever wanted to hear him—for once, everyone—but Entero, like me, kept his thoughts to himself.

Perhaps it's his training as an assassin. But I think, like me, he might understand what we were a part of was nothing short of magical.

At the night market, I dig out a folded list from a tiny hidden pocket in my sleeve. "Have you scouted the night market before?" I ask.

"Of course."

"Do you think you could help me find flour?"

He pauses. "Is this why you wanted me to walk with you?"

"No. I'm happy to wander around and find things on my own."

Entero studies me for a moment in the darkness, expression flickering in the inconstant light from the night market's lanterns, before saying, "This way."

With Entero beside me, no one gives me any trouble. His scowl and readiness to lead me off to other stalls is also shockingly useful for getting lower prices.

"You have no idea how bargaining works," he mutters after having negotiated on my behalf for a jar of marmalade.

"I have no idea what anything costs," I counter. "And however little money I make, my situation is still, in some ways, more secure than theirs."

"They expect you to bargain," he says.

"Even so."

"No, I mean, it looks suspicious if you don't," he explains. "They're asking you for unreasonable prices, and your willingness to accept them stands out."

Oh. "I may need you to shop with me until I learn, then," I admit, rubbing my wrists absently. "I didn't realize that was the reason for their reactions."

"It's not, entirely." Before I can ask him to elaborate, he asks, "What do you need all this for, anyway?"

I hesitate, wondering if he'll laugh at me. "I'm going to try baking."

Entero cocks his head to one side. "Baking what?"

"Almond apricot bars. The festival kind?"

I'm not sure why I'm nervous about what he'll think of this, but he doesn't offer any judgment. "I'm not sure you'll be able to get the almond extract for that here," he says instead.

"Oh, I got that this morning," I say. "I think I have everything I need now."

His head twitches, like he's scented danger. "Got it where?"

I suppose if he knows the night market, he knows this too. "Thiano. The old merchant from the Isle of Nakrab."

Entero sighs. "What did I say yesterday about trying not to get in trouble?" he wonders aloud, as if to the spirits.

"The less you know about what I managed to get into after you left the more easily you'll sleep," I say. "I promise I'm not habitually so reckless."

"I don't believe you," he says seriously, and it occurs to me that after the last few days, I don't truly have any reasonable basis to argue with him. "Miyara, you need to be careful with Thiano."

"He's incredibly shrewd," I agree.

"He's cunning and completely impossible to pin down," Entero says. "Also, he's a spy."

"I did work that out," I say, "but thank you for the warning."

He studies me. "You think you can handle him. Miyara—"

"I don't think anything of the sort. I think there's more to him than you realize."

"I think there's plenty to him," Entero says.

I smile. "I know. That's not what I mean."

I remember Thiano's anguish at being asked about obligation. I know that he must have a reason for helping me, but I'm not confident it's anything as simple as Entero would like it to be.

"I'll do my best to be careful," I say, hefting my bag of baking supplies.

"Please do not let me know what your worst at being careful is," Entero says. "I may be your guard, but there's only one of me, and I'm only human."

There's enough of a grumble in his voice that I realize he's made an effort at teasing me, and I laugh. "Let's go."

With the aid of the recipe book the following morning, I manage to chop and stir fry vegetables, though I'm not convinced this is an unmitigated success. The seeds from the pepper scattered all over the kitchen, and every time I think I've found them all I step on another. The hot oil spitting at me makes me jump every time, and it's only through grim determination that I don't run away from the pan. Or rather, that I march myself back to the kitchen. The recipe book gives no indications whether this means I'm doing something wrong or that I'm simply not tough enough for everyday living.

I manage to under-cook a pot of rice, then over-cook another, before I discover the cottage has a device specifically for this sole purpose. Lorwyn probably considers this one of those unnecessary pieces of kitchen equipment, but I'm unreasonably pleased with myself for finally managing to produce a correctly cooked bowl of rice.

I've managed to feed myself, and the results were not terrible. But they were hard-earned, and I go into baking with some trepidation.

The recipe that seemed simple does not now fill me with confidence. It's all "finely slice nuts," "stir crust until mixture resembles coarse crumbs," "bake until golden brown," "add milk until glaze is at desired consistency." As if I have any idea how finely nuts should be sliced, what texture constitutes coarse when applied to crumbs, what shade of brown indicates under-baked or burnt, or what consistency of glaze I do in fact desire. I agonize and doubtfully make my best guesses.

I'm utterly shocked that my attempt appears to turn out well—better, in fact, than I had hoped, let alone expected.

They're not the painting-perfect festival bars carefully curated for banquets at the palace. The texture is less even, and there's more variation between the bars. But they smell as though they'll taste good, and I try to believe what Thiano said, that my effort will matter more than their perfection.

I'm proud of myself, which seems a little ridiculous. And I'm nervous, which is possibly more ridiculous but seems less so.

I've finished cleaning the disaster I unleashed upon the kitchen and have flopped down in a chair, exhausted, when Entero arrives to escort me to the tea shop for work.

Talmeri is at the shop when I arrive, and I know instantly by her overly sweet smile that she is Not Pleased.

"Entero, there are some things I need to work out with Grace Talmeri," I say. "Could you start setting up out here please?"

He shoots me a look, and I merely raise my eyebrows in return.

Of course I'm not supposed to try to escape my guard, but really, while Talmeri could cost me my job, she's not likely to try to stab me. I suppose she might ask me to sample poisoned tea, but only if she could convince Lorwyn to brew it for her.

Talmeri scrutinizes the figure Entero cuts dressed to serve customers and nods in approval, a speculative gleam coming into her eye.

Entero turns to do as asked without another word, and I allow Talmeri to bustle me into her office.

"What did you think you were doing?" she asks, not bothering to tell me what she's talking about.

Fortunately, it's not hard to guess. "A customer who refuses to pay is not one we need," I say evenly.

"And yet, you didn't ask the woman who brought the teapot to pay," she says.

"I gave her a gift. I think it's best the shop appear to be in a secure enough position to bestow gifts, even if it isn't."

"That's an interesting point," Talmeri says. "Perhaps those gifts should be given to *loyal paying customers* who spread word of our service to *other*, loyal. Paying. Customers."

"And," I say as though she hadn't spoken, "the woman who brought in a priceless teapot, word of which has also clearly spread, didn't expect our service to be free. I offered it. She didn't demand it. There is a difference, grace."

Talmeri's eyes narrow. "Miyara, you offended one of the wealthiest patrons I can bring to this shop. She was prepared to let it go this time, but I admit I'm disappointed in you. I thought you understood business better than this."

I furrow my brow in feigned concern. "I think there's been some confusion. My understanding is that you brought me on to bring a tea master's skill and reputation to Talmeri's?"

"You've barely begun to aspire to tea mastery," she snaps.

"If that's as far along as you think I am, you must realize your plan to save this shop is doomed," I point out, and her expression tightens. "Grace Talmeri, I did pass the tea master's assessment without any preparation, and with your patronage, I will become a tea master in truth. But grace, you must see that part of establishing the reputation you need from a tea master is establishing expectations about what kind of shop this is."

"It's the kind of shop that serves its guests! People don't come here to be treated as inferior, but to be treated as though they're special. *That* is how you ensure they come back."

"And yet you did everything Tea Master Karekin asked of you and thought no less of his service," I say. "He ordered all your wealthy guests out of your shop, and they went, and then *they came back*. If the patronage of customers like the one I offended yesterday were enough to save the shop, you wouldn't have taken a risk on me. But you did, because Talmeri's has to change. This was *your* idea."

"This is not the kind of change or risk I meant," she bites out.

"Isn't it?" I smile in a way that invites her to share the joke. "Talmeri's gains a reputation as a place that can afford to lose wealthy customers who behave badly, which means customers who behave *well* and don't wish to tolerate such nonsense will be encouraged to come here. So you grow a base of customers happy to be here, and new customers will see how they behave and comport themselves accordingly. You want people to pay not just for the tea, but for the experience. That's why you have the tea boys, and that's why you now have me."

"You're talking about a strategy that bears fruit over a long period of time, when time is exactly what we don't have," Talmeri says seriously. "We can't afford to lose any customers now. Even demanding ones."

"I think we have to, or they will choke your business to death." I rub my wrists. I've learned enough from helping Saiyana sort out business matters that affect the crown to feel confident in this as a strategy, but my ability to execute it is somewhat more in question. Theory is not the same as having a personal stake, but. "There are always more businesses they can choke. If reputation is what it takes to save your business, then this is the kind of threat we must become impervious to."

"That's easy for you, who does not see our weekly reports, to say," Talmeri tells me. "There's only so much risk the business can afford to take on at once. Sponsoring you publicly is a big one. Disrespecting our customers is too much."

"I promise I don't intend to make a habit of offending them," I say. "If it helps, you can always blame my inexperience, so that I bear the consequence for that decision, rather than the shop."

She shakes her head. "No. That only separates your reputation from the shop's, which then defeats the purpose of having you here entirely."

True. If we couldn't present a unified front, we'd damage Talmeri's reputation more than we could help it. In that, she's right that my actions have put us in an uncomfortable position, but I can't promise never to repeat them.

"Do you have time to stay and watch how things go in the shop for a while today?" I ask. "It occurs to me you've been so busy this week you haven't seen me in the tea room, and perhaps this could be an opportunity for me to learn some of the important parts of management you have much more experience with."

"And demonstrate that we work together but that I am still training you," Talmeri says, sharp as ever. "Yes, that shouldn't wait any longer."

"It may actually be the perfect time to demonstrate we won't lose customers over this, because word has already spread about the teapot."

"That is luck, Miyara, not good business practice," Talmeri says.

"I know, but it's worth taking advantage of, isn't it? Have you seen the teapot yet?"

"I have," she admits. I assume she means it's the first thing she looked for when she arrived.

But my diversion works, and she allows me to draw her away and into conversation about how running the tea shop is going. I fall into a role I know how to play too well, fading into the background, deferring to her and working around her to demonstrate I respect her authority, since I haven't agreed to change my behavior.

But I admit I'm surprised, given that I've worked here only a few days and don't consider myself adept at running the shop yet, by the aspects that seem obvious to me that Talmeri ignores.

She's marvelous at handling customers, and given how little time she seems to spend in the shop I'm impressed by how thoroughly she knows every ingredient, its history and flavor profile and cost. Talmeri knows her business. But she's very focused on the moment: she doesn't make time for washing dishes or restocking tea, and scolds the tea boys every time those tasks have not magically been taken care of in their absence while she's directed them in interacting with customers. I'm reminded again that while she has a keen business sense, prioritizing long-term strategy is not her strength.

Unfortunately, that means it will have to be mine, and I don't have time to become an expert in that on top of gaining tea mastery. For now, I focus on redirecting the tea boys to other tasks when possible without making Talmeri feel as though I'm undercutting her authority.

"Grace Talmeri!" A short, well-groomed man with a sparkling smile and a sharp glint in his eye strides in, cutting a direct path to Talmeri.

I'm instantly on alert. It's possible this is one of Talmeri's wealthy friends, but I grew up in the heart of politics.

His smile I recognize as a snake's, and the glint in his eye is malice.

I glance at Talmeri in time to see her muscles relax—which means they had tensed—as she assumes a forced smile. "Maveno, what a surprise to see you again so soon," she says.

"A pleasant one, I should hope!" He flashes a smile that says he knows it is anything but.

I don't know what this is about, but our customers clearly do; the one closest to this man has frozen stiff, and Maveno's smile spreads as he notices.

"Now, I don't want to inconvenience your customers with our talk of business," Maveno says, presumably to Talmeri, but all the while gazing at the rigid form next to him. "Shall we chat in your office perhaps, away from prying eyes?"

I may not have any idea who this man is or what he intends, but in that moment I understand that I can't let him get Talmeri alone.

I take one step, and suddenly Entero is there, grabbing my arm. I glare at him.

"You can tell he's dangerous. Think before you act, Miyara, because if he attempts to hurt you, I will hurt him definitively," Entero hisses at me. "Don't put yourself in an unsafe situation that will compel me to do that."

How did I live my entire life with bodyguards?

I didn't, is the answer. I didn't live my life. I'm not sure I even lived someone else's life. I moved through days doing nothing that mattered, and I won't go back to it.

"It will not be safe for me if you blow my cover," I whisper.

"If I blow your cover, I won't have to keep guarding you here," he points out.

I don't have time for this. I yank out of his grip, and he lets me go—I don't have any illusions about that.

But I do go.

"Welcome to Talmeri's Teas and Tisanes," I say brightly as I cross the room.

Maveno turns to regard me with languid curiosity. I imagine it's the look of a predator, when the prey doesn't realize who it's facing.

The look itself tells me a lot.

It tells me, for instance, that he's very confident no one here can stop him.

That he is confident doing things someone ought to stop.

And that he's so sure of his confidence he can be manipulated with it.

If I can manage it just right.

"Well, well," he says with that too-slick smile. "Who's this, Talmeri?"

"Miyara, could you watch the front for a few minutes please?" Talmeri asks.

Trying to get me out of Maveno's path, after all our talk of acting in accord. As if I needed further confirmation he's planned something unfortunate.

"Miyara, is it," he says appraisingly.

I bow. "At your service, grace. I'm here to assist Grace Talmeri with running the shop. Is there a business matter I can help you with?"

"It's so nice to see young people these days express an interest in business, in *responsibility*, don't you think, Talmeri?" Maveno asks, smiling at me. "They should know what their commitments are, and they should know there are consequences for failing to meet them."

"I don't know what you mean," Talmeri says. "Forgive me, I must be misunderstanding. It sounds as though I'm being accused of skirting payments, when you know perfectly well I have always paid what I owe in full. Talmeri's is a business of good standing."

"So it is, so it is! The last thing I want to do is suggest otherwise, Talmeri. You know that. It's just that there have been questions lately. You know the kind. I'm just here to sort it all out. Shall we?"

Talmeri swallows.

"Oh," I interject with wide eyes. "I'm sorry, I don't think I understand. What sorts of questions? Could you explain them to me please?"

Talmeri very nearly snarls, "Miyara—"

"Of course, of course! For the education of the young." Maveno winks. "You know, of course, that Lord Kustio of House Taresim generously leases the land on which this business sits, and in fact the building itself, for Grace Talmeri's use. And in exchange for allowing her to run such a thriving business here—"

"She rents the space from him," I interrupt innocently. "Yes, I understand how that works. I meant, what questions are there about payments? That definitely sounds like the sort of thing we ought to get straightened out right away."

"You delightful child," Maveno says. "You're quite right. Lord Kustio is generous and doesn't charge more than a grace can pay. In return, he expects them to be honest about what they can, in fact, pay." He looks at Talmeri. "There are questions about whether you've been honest about your resources, Talmeri. A priceless treasure of a teapot. New tea boys. Sponsoring a tea aspirant. A tea master in your own shop! There are questions about whether you're taking advantage of Lord Kustio's generosity, and we can't have that."

Talmeri's is struggling, and this man is reveling in it—is making it as hard as he can, trying to get every mark he can from her.

And he must be responsible for doing it to other businesses, too, because everyone but me knew what he was here for as soon as he walked in.

Talmeri is rigid. "I have been honest with you, Maveno. I have always—"

"Oh dear," I say, "what a distressing misunderstanding. I'm so glad I caught you and have a chance to clear this up, since it's entirely my fault. How wonderful that you had a chance to come by today."

I cast a glance at Talmeri. She frowns, then nods almost imperceptibly. She'll let me take the lead and do this after all, then: separate the negative reputation from the shop and take it on myself. Not a fair exchange, perhaps, but it will still create its own set of problems for her.

Maveno looks back at me, and for the first time he doesn't look wholly amused. "Oh?"

"You understand risk, grace? I mean in the sense of investments."

"I have some understanding of risk," he says, smiling again.

"I'm not only here to assist with the regular running of the shop, as Talmeri could handle that perfectly well on her own," I say. "My presence, and my tea aspiration, are part of a plan to revolutionize Talmeri's in a way that I think Lord Kustio will find most satisfactory. But as with any change, it requires substantial up-front investments and a reallocation of resources. We're confident that those investments will be exceeded, of course, or the risk would be foolish—"

"Lord Kustio prefers to lease to safe businesses, able to reliably meet their commitments," Maveno says. "If you mean to tell me you now *lack* resources, then—"

"And that's why Talmeri's has made sure its commitments are met first, before embarking on such a venture," I interrupt him in turn, and Maveno's smile has grown fixed. "If Lord Kustio believes when the time comes to renew the lease that Talmeri's cannot meet the terms of its lease agreement—well, that is why agreements have termination clauses, is it not? But I'm confident you, and Lord Kustio, will find otherwise and will be happy with the results. We'd never have entered into this arrangement otherwise."

"And yet," he says, "questions persist."

"Questions always do." I spread my hands. "Is it not the nature of the world? But anyone who wishes to claim we have acted in bad faith may take it up with the law."

His amusement is back with the glint of malice. "And who do you think would hold such claimants accountable?"

This Lord Kustio must sit on the local council, or have blackmailed those that do. Curse everything.

"The clerks who will be tasked with the mountains of paperwork, presumably," I say lightly. "Happily, it will never have to come to that, will it? Because Lord Kustio should know we understand our commitments, and as long as he is satisfied, I'm sure the questions will fade with time. Don't you?"

"We'll see," Maveno says, with a mocking little bow. "Lord Kustio will, of course, be very interested in the fruits of your investment, Talmeri. I would make sure you're ready to answer those questions. And what an absolute delight to meet your newest employee."

"I'm pleased I could help today," I say.

"Miyara, is it? I look forward to meeting you again," Maveno says.

For the first time in the last few minutes, Entero twitches.

"I'm so glad to hear it," I say. "Can I offer you some tea before you go?"

Please go, before my bodyguard kills you.

"Oh, I have other business to be about today," he says. "But I'm sure I'll be seeing you again soon."

And then he's gone, and the whole shop exhales.

Talmeri immediately pulls me into her office and grabs me by the shoulders. "Miyara, do you realize what you've done?" she hisses at me. "Now they're going to want proof of astronomical profits in three months—"

"You needed those anyway."

"Not that high!" she cries. "I needed a boost to meet the *expected* terms, and now he'll raise them!"

"Did you have enough to bribe him today, and tomorrow, and whenever else he shows up at the shop?" I ask.

She slumps. "I could have bought us one more day. I suppose either way, in three months we'd still be doomed."

My heart twists. Her expectations and terms may be strict, but she's granted me a lot of trust, too. More than I deserve.

"The shop will change, Talmeri," I say.

She looks me in the eye. "Can it change enough? In only three months?"

I don't know. I would like to reassure her, but all the knowledge of politics and economics and history I can draw on and transfer to this situation tells me it probably can't.

Which of course she knows.

But she's still trying.

She's letting *me* try.

So I don't lie to her, and she goes to put the customers back at ease and leaves off scolding me, because what's the point? We both understand what I just promised, what I can't guarantee we can deliver.

But I feel the urgency now in a way I didn't before.

Not just to save the shop—to overcome this bully, the fear he struck in the hearts of our customers with a smile. Maveno, employed by Lord Kustio—

—of House Taresim.

I stride quickly to the back and Lorwyn's grim countenance. "You heard?"

"Enough," she says.

"Lord Kustio of Taresim," I say. "How's he related to Risteri?"

Lorwyn glances at me. "Her father. He's the head of the House. Why do you ask?"

Of course. Of course it's that tangled. I remember Risteri sneaking away before dawn and have to ask. "Do you think Risteri is a part of this? This... extortion? Driving people out of their businesses?"

Lorwyn snorts. "Try out of their *homes.* Talmeri has it easy. Lord Kustio has been buying up every Gaellani district he can, charging them so badly they're forced to leave. They move in other places if they can, but he's driving the Gaellani out of Sayorsen, Miyara."

Sayorsen had one of the highest refugee populations anywhere. "To where?"

"Exactly."

Oh, spirits.

"Talmeri's mistake," she continues, "was thinking she could serve everyone and her friends would protect her."

"And when she realized she was wrong?" I ask softly.

Lorwyn glances up, then looks away again, as if embarrassed. "Nothing. She didn't change her mind. It might have helped her, but she didn't." She shrugs. "Not sure if it's because she knows she'd lose me, and then she'd be ruined anyway. She is pretty mercenary."

But not as hard as Lorwyn. I don't think that was the reason, but even so, a piece of the sudden knot in my chest eases.

But it is now an enormous knot, and I have to ask. "What does Kustio have against the Gaellani?"

Lorwyn's expression twists. "Witches, Miyara. He thinks because we survived, we're responsible for the uncontrolled witches that caused the Cataclysm. That's always the justification for anti-Gaellani bigotry."

I feel like a fool, but Lorwyn isn't done.

"So no, of course Risteri isn't a part of this," she says.

It floors me again, how two people who seem to hate each other so much can still share so much trust.

"But I also wouldn't be surprised if Risteri doesn't even know it's happening," Lorwyn adds. "She's always had her gaze so fixed on the clouds she can't see what's right in front of her. I'm amazed she's survived trips to the Cataclysm this long."

And there's the flip side.

I sigh. "Entero has already realized I'm living on the property of the richest racist in the city, I suppose."

"The most powerful one, at any rate," Lorwyn agrees. "Taresim really isn't that wealthy, compared to other Houses. Or so Risteri used to claim."

"Then something changed," I say. "Even wealthy nobles can't just go around buying up cities."

"Well, I don't know what it is," she says. "You can wonder about it later. Right now you should wonder about whether Talmeri has driven Entero to murder without you there to intervene."

"Spirits," I mutter as Lorwyn laughs behind me.

But I do wonder. And I wonder what I can do to find an answer to that question.

Later.

Today, I have plans.

CHAPTER 13

THIS TIME WHEN I knock on Deniel's door, there's still some sun in the sky. Probably any passersby can see how nervous I am, but so far I'm holding my composure substantially better.

Entero will certainly be able to tell from wherever he's watching, I have no doubt, but he's doing me the courtesy of remaining out of sight.

When Deniel opens the door, his surprise is plain. "What are you doing here?"

Oh, spirits. Maybe he never wanted to see me again, and I'm making a nuisance of myself.

It's too late to hide the box in my hands, though, so I swallow and blurt, "I made almond apricot bars."

As explanations go, it leaves a great deal of explanation to be desired. I feel my face heating.

"Oh," Deniel says, sounding totally flummoxed, and I think I might die of embarrassment on the spot.

Why is this so hard after I felt so at ease confessing my deepest secret to him?

"I'm sorry," I start to say.

At the same moment Deniel says, "Do you want to come inside?"

We both stare at each other.

"Only if it's not too much trouble," I say.

He steps back out of the doorway, running a hand through his ever-disheveled hair. "Not at all. Please."

Hesitantly, concerned I've accidentally obligated him into welcoming me into his home a second time, I duck through the doorway.

This time, there's enough light coming through the windows that I can see more of the pottery he has on display. My jaw drops in amazement. His work truly is exquisite.

Lorwyn was right. I can't imagine being able to afford such beautiful craftsmanship in my current circumstances, but I can't help gazing at the gorgeous tea sets.

My hands clench on the box of almond apricot bars, trying to forget the ungraceful baked goods I've brought him. Oh, how did I ever think these would be an adequate gift, when he shapes pieces like this?

"You came here alone?" Deniel asks suddenly.

I turn back to him, brow furrowed. "I came alone before, too. Should I not have?"

"No, that is—" Deniel lets out a breath and doesn't meet my gaze. "I heard you were escorted through the night market."

I'm not sure how to respond, and continue staring at him in confusion until Deniel looks up and clarifies, "With a man."

Oh.

This was what people in the market had been whispering about, wasn't it? No wonder Entero hadn't explained.

"His name's Entero," I say. "I wouldn't return to the capital, so apparently I have an unofficial bodyguard now, courtesy of my grandmother. He's somewhere nearby watching for trouble, but he agreed not to shadow me too closely unless he thinks I'm in imminent danger. So, yes, I'm alone. Not with a man."

I just had to go and add that last part, didn't I?

"Ah," Deniel says, and he sounds nearly as flustered as I feel. "So. You—wanted to see me?"

Time to try this again. I take a breath. "Yes," I say. "I wanted to thank you—"

"You already have."

"—and I know I don't have anything to offer you—"

Deniel frowns. Spirits, what did I say wrong?

I finish, "But I wanted another chance to say how much I appreciate what you did for me."

Deniel is quiet for a long moment, studying me. "You already thanked me, and I already said I didn't expect repayment."

"I know." My fingers twitch reflexively to rub my wrists, except I'm carrying a box and can't.

"Are you here because I'm the only one who knows you were a princess?" he asks.

"What? No, of course not." It's refreshing not to have to lie about it, but that's not what made me want to see him. If that were all—I wince. "In fact, I seem to be doing a rather terrible job of keeping that fact hidden. At least three other people in Sayorsen have recognized me on sight."

"Who?" he asks.

"Entero, whom I'd never met back in the capital," I say. "Also the tea master who assessed me, as well as a Nakrabi merchant."

Deniel nods slowly. "So, why then?"

Finally I apprehend what he's asking. I'm a former princess, and many nobles would see him as just a Gaellani, or just an artisan. I'm not those nobles, which he must know—but as far as he's concerned, since I owe him nothing, unless I want something from him there's no reason for me to be here.

So why indeed? Why didn't I just send my inadequate box of baked goods with a note via messenger, and why did I accept his invitation to come inside?

"I just—" I feel heat creeping up my face again. "I want to get to know you better. If you want."

Spirit of earth, if you would graciously swallow me whole this instant, I swear—

"I would," Deniel says quietly.

I force myself to look up and meet his gaze. His face is pink, too.

"Oh," I say, equally quietly, then abruptly can't take this anymore and hold the box of almond apricot bars in front of my face to hide. "I'm sorry. I have no idea what to say now."

I hear the steps as he crosses to me. Gently, Deniel lowers the box from in front of my face, and my face cannot possibly be more enflamed.

His eyes are crinkled with amusement. "Do you want to study with me?" he asks. Then he cringes. "I'm sorry, that must sound boring. I just thought, you have the tea mastery exam, and—"

"Oh, that's a great idea," I say. "Yes, let's study."

Surely that will keep me from continuing to make a fool of myself with conversation. Conversation may have been the point of coming in person, but evidently I'm in no position to manage it.

Deniel steps back, runs a hand through his tousled hair, and gestures for me to follow him into the back.

"Here, let me take this," Deniel says, gesturing at the poor abused box of baked goods.

I hand it to him. "I suppose I can hide behind one of your enormous books if necessary."

He flashes a grin, and my face heats again. I was definitely wrong about my improved composure.

"I'm sorry, I don't have much seating, but please sit wherever looks comfortable," Deniel says as he sets the box down in the center of his small table.

I look at the small sofa, and one golden eye squints up at me. "Oh! Is that Talsion? I almost didn't see him there."

"Ah, yes, he's been helping," Deniel says. "He likes that blanket because he blends in. You can sit next to him if you'd like. He won't bite or anything—he'll probably just pointedly ignore you, to be honest."

"Spirits forefend," I say. "I'm not sure I could cope. But I should think your chair and I are old friends by now."

I open my bag, withdrawing the one tea instruction book I have on me, and peer over at the small table in front of the sofa. Deniel has a sheaf of paper full of notes spread out next to a fat tome—the one I saw him buy at the bookstore, if I'm not mistaken.

He sits on the couch, absently petting the cat, who burrows deeper into the blanket. I'm almost overcome by how adorable they are—but also by the sudden yearning to be so casually comfortable curled up on the couch with them.

I rub my bare wrists and ask, "You study law?"

"Not formally," Deniel says, running a hand through his hair again. "I mean. I'd like to, but..."

Like Lorwyn. "Too much systemic bias against Gaellani," I murmur.

He glances up at me in surprise. "Yes. I couldn't leave my job now, regardless. But I think it would be good for the Gaellani to have someone on our side who understands the laws that work against us. And even if I can't ever become a lawyer in truth, I find it all fascinating."

He pauses. "Well. Not all of it. But I spend a lot of time studying all the same." He looks away again. "That must sound silly."

"Not even a little," I say quietly. I'm retroactively angry at the bookseller who denigrated Deniel's study as a frivolous waste of time. Even at the time I thought Deniel had handled the interaction gracefully, but now I realize it must not be the first time someone has tried to make him feel it's silly in truth.

Deniel stands abruptly. "Would you like some tea?"

"Oh!" I scramble after him, setting my book aside. "I can make tea for us both, if you'd like."

"I don't have anything fancy," he cautions as I follow him to the kitchen.

"As long as you haven't combined sleekbeetle scales with Nakrabi death peppers, I promise to consider myself fortunate."

Deniel chokes. "You have that at the tea shop?"

"Not anymore. Drinking it was part of my interview."

"I admit that would have defeated me," he says, pulling a tin of tea out of one cupboard and a kettle from another. "If you want to make tea, why don't I make dinner?"

"You can do that?" As soon as the question is out of my mouth I cover my face with my hands. "Of course you can do that. I'm sorry."

Deniel laughs. "Would you like me to show you how?"

I remove my hands from my face and, hesitantly nod. "If you really wouldn't mind."

"Not at all," he says, though his smile fades. "But you sound uncomfortable?"

I wave my hand vaguely. "It's just... out of balance. You've already done so much for me, with the tea pet, and now—"

"I should thank you for bringing it to my doorstep," he says. "I can rarely justify the ritual. But regardless, that's not how it works. Do you expect me to do things for you?"

"Of course not! But... I would like to be able to do things for you, too."

Deniel smiles. "That's why it's fine. Here, start the kettle. What do you like to eat?"

I blink as I fill the kettle with water. What do I like to eat? I've always chosen dishes with care to avoid offending dignitaries.

I stare at my bare wrists and finally say, "Not Nakrabi death peppers."

"So, sleekbeetle scales are fine?"

"We've now worked them into a lovely green tea with aloia nectar and marigold," I inform him.

Deniel laughs, peering into his cooler. "Noted. What do you think of mixed rice bowls?"

"I have no idea what they are, and I'd love to try them."

"Are you sure? I don't want to make something you don't like."

"I don't think I'm very picky," I say.

"Miyara, you're a professional taster."

I shiver slightly. Has he ever said my name before? I breathe in the scent of Deniel's tea and adjust the heating of the kettle slightly.

"Yes, but..." How to explain? "My preferences were never allowed to count, at the palace. I'm not sure I know what they are anymore." That probably won't reassure him about his choice. Hmm. "I had a noodle dish at a Gaellani market a few days ago that was delicious, but everything else smelled delicious too. I like trying new things."

There, that's true.

"Have you had a chicken and egg bowl?" Deniel asks.

"I don't think so."

"Let's try that, then. It's pretty easy to make. I'll save dazzling you with my cooking skills for another time."

"At this time any cooking skills will dazzle me," I say.

He grins. "All the more reason to wait until you can appreciate them. The tea cups are in that cupboard on your left."

I gasp when I see them. "Deniel, these are beautiful. You made these?"

He glances at me sidelong. "I mean. I am a potter. It seems silly not to make my own. I decided I liked these too much to sell."

"I can see why," I breathe, touching them with not a little wonder. "Spirits, if you can dazzle me further I'll never be able to form coherent sentences around you."

Deniel chokes. "They're not that nice."

Modesty, or does he truly not know? Just in case it's the latter, I say, "Deniel, I'm a tea aspirant, and I grew up in the royal palace. I promise you that they are." Before he can react, I ask, "Are these two cups the only ones you've kept?"

"I don't have many visitors," he says, pulling ingredients out of the cooler as I scoop tea into the pot. "I can't really justify keeping more on hand than I need when I can sell them instead."

I cock my head to one side, watching him as I wait for the water to heat. "Your friends don't come here?"

"I'm not close to many people," Deniel admits, setting another pot of water to boil and measuring out rice. I'm interested to see how he does this correctly since I couldn't, but not as interested as I am in what he just said. He seems like the easiest person in the world to be close to.

"Why not?" I ask, only belatedly realizing that's probably rude.

But Deniel doesn't seem to mind. "I was always quiet, and I got sucked into pottery young. I never spent much time with people my own age, and then I was successful enough that I could afford to move out of the Gaellani quarter. I didn't appreciate at the time how much it would help my business, but my parents did. Since I've been here, I'm even more removed from the community, not because I don't see them, but because I have the option to be removed if I want to be, if that makes sense."

"The model refugee story," I murmur.

"That," he agrees. "It's not that I don't have friends, and the people I knew still seem happy to see me when I visit. But they don't drop by unannounced."

"Success and power, even in limited amounts, are isolating," I say. "I wonder if that's truer when the perceived power is greater than the reality, or the reverse."

He meets my gaze directly, unguardedly, for a long moment, and it's like my world narrows, like I could anchor myself to his gaze and stare into his eyes forever.

Then the kettle whistles, and I tear away, busying myself with pouring water into the teapot.

"I have everything ready," Deniel says. "Do you want to watch how I slice the chicken?"

"Yes, the tea just needs a couple minutes to steep." I look over at everything he's gathered. "What are all the sauces?"

"Let's start there."

He runs through the ingredients, and when he's done I pour our tea and hand him a cup.

Deniel takes a sip and looks at me curiously. "Why does this taste better than usual?" he asks. "I didn't notice you doing anything special."

"I was careful with the water temperature and steeping time," I say. "I'm going to pay attention when you get the rice out of the pot, too."

"That does take a few bad pots to learn how to judge," he says.

"Then I'm well on my way. Except the place I'm staying has a rice cooker, so perhaps I'll never learn after all."

He smiles. "Actually, wait over there while I chop the onion. This batch is particularly potent. You live alone?"

"Yes, I happened to meet someone who was owed a favor by someone with an empty cottage. Why don't your parents live with you?"

"Parents and little sister," Deniel says. "They didn't want their presence to hold me back, if that makes sense. For their struggles to keep me from reaching greater success."

Regrettably. Istal families don't typically live together, outside aristocratic mansions, and especially not combined with their place of business. Having his family here would have affected how people perceived him, which would in turn affect his business.

He starts tearing up, and as I widen my eyes in alarm so then do I. Spirits, I had no idea onions could do this.

"Is your family doing well?" I ask.

"As well as can be expected," he says. "I help them as much as I can."

"But your mother wants you to prioritize yourself," I say softly.

Deniel glances at me sharply. "I didn't realize you were listening at the bookstore."

"I always listen. My apprehension just varies greatly." I hesitate and then add, "And I think you did realize."

His eyes crinkle. "Okay. Maybe. I didn't think you'd remember that. I think it's safe to come over here now."

So I do, and he talks me through everything he's doing. I'm overly conscious of his warmth behind me as he shows me how to slice the chicken or crack an egg.

We talk about his family. His shy sister, so many years younger than him, who came as a surprise to his parents after they'd had so much trouble conceiving him. His father, who trained as a bridge engineer before the Cataclysm and now works as a manual laborer, because no one hires refugees for respectable engineering work. His mother, who has a steady job assisting at a bakery, carrying heavy loads and working long hours.

"If you want, I'm sure she'd help you learn how to bake," he says. "It's not something I've done much."

"You haven't even tried my first attempt yet," I say with a laugh.

"I'll be honored to," he says seriously.

Part of the reason I baked in the first place was hoping he'd feel that way, but the words make me awkward again. "I'd like to learn more about baking, but I don't think I'd feel comfortable asking your mother," I say.

Deniel returns his attention to the stove. "She'd enjoy it, honestly. The bakery is steady work, but she doesn't have any creative input. I think she'd love to have a shop of her own, if she could get a loan."

"If she's that good, I definitely don't want to embarrass myself with her."

He smiles. "Not a bakery. She makes sculptures out of candy. She never finished training, so she experiments whenever she lets me give her enough extra to spend on materials, after whatever food and clothing and whatnot the family really needs."

Deniel carefully arranges the dish we've made in bowls, and I carry them to the table while he fetches sticks to eat with.

"How do you cope?" I ask him as we sit. "How do you keep from feeling guilty for all they've done, and all they still do to support you, when you can never do enough to help them?"

"I'll answer that, but try a bite first," he says.

I pause. With Lorwyn I pretended, but with Deniel— "Is there a correct way?"

"Not as far as I know. Ah, here. Watch?"

He doesn't mix it, but takes a bite that includes some egg, onion, and rice. I do the same, and my eyes widen.

"It's delicious!" I exclaim.

"You don't have to sound so surprised," Deniel says, clearly amused.

"But it didn't seem that hard!"

"Good." He smiles. "So you like it?"

"Definitely."

"Even better. So now you know one thing you like."

It's my turn to smile. "Yes, I do. Thank you."

"So, your question. You hit on part of my answer already, which is acknowledging that there's no possible way to help enough to restore any semblance of balance. My parents have supported me out of love, and although they'll accept help from me, they get annoyed when they think I'm helping them too much. Because they didn't help me in order to get help."

"But you're still ready to help them whenever you can."

"Yes, but over the years I've learned some attempts to help are intrusive. If I help more than they want, am I really helping them, or just myself?"

"So what do you do?"

Deniel sighs. "Here is where I feel compelled to point out that my solution is not necessarily the healthiest. I can't tell you what the right answer is, only what mine is."

But I realize I already know. "They supported you so you could have your own life, not so you could serve theirs. So you do everything you can not to squander the opportunity."

"Yes. They want me to be happy, and I am. But I am happiest when my work can help them, too. So I work. And it's work I enjoy, but... I do work a great deal more than they think I should have to."

I remember what Saiyana said during my dedication ceremony. That there was a lot of work, and I could do so much good if I would just put my mind to it.

How much good can I accomplish as a tea master? I owe it to a lot of people to find out.

"What are you thinking about?" Deniel asks me quietly.

I swallow, shocked by how much of the bowl I've managed to eat so quickly. I wasn't exaggerating about liking it.

"My sister Saiyana," I say. "She told me something very similar, though she meant me to take it in a very different way."

"How so?"

I sigh. "Saiyana was closer to me than anyone, but she has never really understood me. Or perhaps she understood I could never be happy with the opportunities afforded our positions. She's happy ordering other people's affairs for them, confident that she's improving them for everyone, and thinks I could do it too if I wanted. But I don't."

"You want to help people help themselves," Deniel says.

That. "But I don't really even know how to help my own self," I say, setting my sticks aside and rubbing my wrists. "I hope pursuing tea mastery will help, but I don't know."

"No one ever really knows," Deniel says. "That's the great secret. If your sister pretends otherwise, she's lying to either you or herself." Then his eyes widen. "Spirits. I probably shouldn't speak of princesses like that, let alone to you. I'm sorry."

I laugh. "Gossip is rampant at the palace. I assure you I have heard worse than you are ever likely to think, and I would far rather hear your honest opinion."

"Is that normal, for a person in the royal palace? To want honesty?"

"To want it?" Hmm. "I'm not sure. But it's certainly naïve to expect to receive it, or to offer it without an ulterior motive." Deniel has finished his bowl, too, and I decide it's now or never. "Would you like to try one of the bars?"

He smiles. "Yes, please."

I pass him a bar and watch him chew with some trepidation, but his expression turns to surprised delight. "Have you tried this?" he asks.

I shake my head. "I feared I'd talk myself out of giving them to you entirely."

"You should have one," he says, "otherwise I'm going to eat them all before you have a chance."

"That is their intended purpose," I say, daring to hope. "So they're not terrible?"

"Just try one." I shake my head again, and he rolls his eyes. "All right, I suppose I'll just bring the rest to my mother and see what the professional baker thinks—"

"You're a terrible person," I say, snatching one from the box and stuffing a bite in my mouth while he laughs.

And then I blink, staring at him with my mouth full.

"See? They're great, Miyara. Have a little more faith in yourself."

His gaze is warm, and I'm somehow blushing yet again.

I manage to swallow and say, "The texture is off, and the flavor is a touch too sweet."

"And they're still great," he repeats, "even if someday you'll improve them. Thank you for making them for me."

"You're welcome," I say, looking away. My heart is beating faster than it has any right to be.

"You're so worried," Deniel says abruptly, "about not being able to take care of yourself, because it makes you feel like you're only taking from other people instead of giving, which is what you want. So what do you need in order to feel like you're not relying on other people?"

That's a good question, but I fear the list of answers is unreasonably long. "I need to know how to feed myself, for one."

"Demonstrably fixable," Deniel says dryly. "That's not what I mean."

"I know," I say, though sometimes the sheer quantity of everyday things I'm unfamiliar with feels overwhelming. I rub my bare wrists, thinking, while Deniel watches. "I need to feel like I'm making a difference. Where I fit."

He nods slowly. "That's harder. I don't think you can know where you fit without knowing the shape of the space around you."

It always comes back to the space I inhabit, doesn't it?

"In Sayorsen, there are two things you have to understand," Deniel continues.

"The Cataclysm." It's in the background of everything here, but although I've served tea made with ingredients from the Cataclysm, its physical proximity doesn't truly seem real to me.

He nods. "If you decide to learn more, make sure you're careful about who you choose as a guide. There are a lot of questionable people who'll try to take advantage—"

"I know a guide I can trust."

A smile ghosts across his face. "Then you're better off than most."

Too true. "What's the second thing I need to understand? The refugee community in Sayorsen?"

"No," Deniel says. "You don't need to be part of that community, and in fact will never fit there."

That stings, which is ridiculous, because of course it's true, too. But I realize what he's getting at, and say quietly, "It's that I need to understand the ways people in Sayorsen are systemically oppressed, isn't it."

Deniel looks up sharply. "I was going to say it's the way our social structure works, but, yes. It's that exactly."

"And how do I educate myself about that?"

"You already are. You're listening." He pauses. "But if you want, it might help to go to a city council meeting."

I blink. It never would have occurred to me to get anywhere near the local governance, and I'm not sure how to navigate that—especially since there's a chance city leaders might recognize me. "Do you go?" I ask. "Can I go with you?"

Deniel opens his mouth and closes it again, looking uncomfortable. My chest tightens.

"Would you rather people not see us together?" I ask softly. "Because I don't know what I want or where I fit yet?"

"No, it's not that," he says. "I don't want you to feel constrained by what I can reach."

Like his parents separated themselves from him.

That's not what I need from him.

"I won't," I say.

"You don't know that."

I nod. "I will learn for certain. But I think you're wrong."

Deniel smiles, and my chest eases. "Fair enough."

Suddenly the cat rubs against my leg and then waits, expectantly. I look at Deniel hesitantly, and he nods in encouragement. I reach down and pet Talsion gently on the head, and he bumps up into my palm.

"You can give him a piece of chicken," Deniel says, tone full of resigned amusement. "Then maybe we should clean up and actually study?"

"I suppose we'd better," I say, feeding the cat with some bemusement. "Washing dishes, at least, is now firmly within my skillset."

Deniel laughs again, my toes curl in pleasure at the sound of it, and I realize I've never felt happier than I do when he smiles at me. Which is absolutely ludicrous, but nevertheless true.

I will wonder about my sanity at another time. Tonight, I am here, and so is he, and our work awaits us.

CHAPTER 14

A KNOCK SOUNDS AT my door, and I throw it open without any preamble. "Come right—"

Risteri takes one step toward me, and then a shadow flashes behind her.

She shoves the bundle in her arms at me, whirling and throwing a punch—

That misses, because it's Entero who's dropped from my roof right behind her.

But at her attack, he responds in kind.

I've barely managed to catch the sack Risteri cast my way and they're battling on my doorstep.

"Stop!" I cry as they land together on the ground, locked in a grapple.

"Miyara, get inside!" they both yell back at me.

That's enough for them to pause and stare at each other.

I run over and put a hand on each of their shoulders. "Entero, this is my friend Risteri. She's the one who arranged for me to be able to stay here."

"Where did he come from?" Risteri demands, shoving away from him back to her feet.

"He's guarding me," I say as she stares at me incredulously.

"Which means," he growls at me, "no one goes into your house before my say-so."

Ah. As a princess I had a team of guards—no one could have gotten close enough to my chambers to knock without their approval, and guards inside would have opened the door to greet them. Entero can't do the work of so many without my help.

"I'm sorry," I say. "Risteri and Lorwyn are always welcome here."

And Deniel. But surely he won't want to come to my house.

"You know Lorwyn?" Risteri asks him.

Entero scowls. "To my displeasure."

Her eyes narrow. "I don't like your tone."

"Are you going to tell me you're friends with her?"

Risteri's expression shutters, and she doesn't answer, turning her back on him. "I got your message," she says to me. "Are you sure about this?"

"Yes," I say. "Sayorsen is my home now, and this is part of it. I want to see."

"What's this?" Entero asks.

"Then let me help you get changed," Risteri says, gesturing at the bag. "I brought some of my spares, since all your clothing is so delicate."

Entero crosses his arms and waits.

"Risteri is a Cataclysm tour guide," I explain.

He shakes his head immediately. "No. Are you mad? Absolutely not."

"How refreshing," Risteri says. "A guard who says what he actually thinks of his charge. You must be new at this."

Entero flushes but stands his ground. "You're not going into the Cataclysm. It's not even a little safe."

"Well, it's a *little* safe," Risteri says. "At least the parts I'd consider taking the uninitiated to, and I've been at this a while. But you're right, that safety isn't certain. That's why I asked if she was sure."

"If I were entirely safe anywhere, I wouldn't need a guard," I say. "I trust Risteri."

"*I* don't," Entero says.

"Any reason in particular?" Risteri asks. "Just out of curiosity."

"You're carrying witchcraft."

Entero and I both watch Risteri freeze.

"Everyone inside," I say, heading for my door. When they've followed, both resolutely not looking at each other I ask, "Is it Lorwyn's?"

Risteri jerks, glancing at Entero, who is in turn staring at me.

"Yes, everyone here knows Lorwyn is a witch and will keep her secret," I say impatiently. "Well?"

"I'm not answering that," Risteri says. "He does not sound like he has Lorwyn's best interests at heart."

Entero tenses. "I won't raise a hand to her."

"Is that so?"

I sigh. "Fine, you two just keep scowling at each other, then. I'll go get dressed."

"Miyara—" Entero starts.

"I am going," I tell him. "If you have particular concerns, perhaps Risteri would be gracious enough to address them for you. But once I'm changed, I'm going."

I'm dressed in green leggings and a short gray tunic with boots big enough I've had to stuff a pair of socks into them to keep my feet from sloshing too much. Entero walks beside me in his customary black, having elected to ensure my safety personally.

We're clumped in the middle of a small tour group, where the anticipation is palpable. Almost everyone is Istal, though a couple of watchful Velasari stand toward the back, eyes gleaming.

I catch Entero's eye, and he casually edges between me and their line of sight.

Probably they're just tourists, and probably they wouldn't recognize me like this, in common clothing and with shorter, green hair. But it's Entero's job to mitigate potential threats, and he leads us away from them.

"Welcome!" Risteri calls. "My name's Risteri, and I'll be your Cataclysm guide today. Now that you've all been through the safety briefing, you're ready to go! Remember, you're going to experience a lot of strange things, but do your best not to make sudden movements or noises. If you wander away from the group, expect to be eaten before anyone can find you. So let's get to it!"

I whisper to Entero, "Do you think she realizes how much creepier that sounds in such a cheerful tone?"

"Yes," he says. "Hush."

The edge of the Cataclysm is almost invisible. I can stare off into the distance and see forests and mountains—but then it ripples, shimmering like a bubble, reflecting Sayorsen back at me.

And my own image. I stare at myself, gawky in Risteri's unfamiliar clothing.

But in my eyes, I see determination.

I poke the bubble, watching it ripple like a liquid mirror, warping the images behind, through.

I take a breath and walk into the barrier.

Risteri is calling for the group to follow her, and I stumble, trying to catch my bearings.

Of course, there are none.

We're walking through a forested path, which Risteri calls one of the few stable paths, as long as you don't wander from it. But the deeper you go, the less reliable it will be.

On one side, I see forest, but though I can't explain it, it feels not just different, but *wrong*.

Then a face forms in the bark of the tree, smiling a kindly, wise smile.

"The elder tree," Risteri explains, "lures prey in with the promise of great wisdom. The bark exudes a chemical that makes people feel special or chosen just to look at it. But that smile opens and swallows you whole. Fortunately, the chemical effect is pretty light, so as long as you're aware it's happening you're not in any danger."

The elder tree's smile widens, exposing sharp fangs and gaping void behind them.

Moving along, Risteri twists a few vines together which then emit a high screech as she holds them there for us to pass before the vines can, apparently, wrap us up and squeeze us to death.

There's the brilliant blue flower that blinds any that come too close, the stones that skip themselves over a pond, the tiny bird that projects the image of being a bird of prey to intimidate predators. The path we walk on spirals in the air, and our heads turn toward the ground, which is now the sky, and the path becomes desert.

Risteri steers us clear of a small sentient squall passing through and deftly navigates us through a maze answering the frog lord's riddle. For our amusement she makes a show of nearly sitting on a boulder that then stands up in the shape of a bear and stalks a few steps away in a huff before curling into a boulder again. When a cosmic haze descends, she rubs some liquid from a stopper on a dagger and plunges it upwards until the haze explodes into rainbow wisps.

And so we go through, one impossibility after another.

But it's clear what she meant about reality destabilizing the further we go. Some of the tourists are nauseated from all the twisting orientations, others holding hands in terror because they can't tell what's real anymore.

That bearing I lost before this excursion.

"That's as far as we go on today's tour!" Risteri declares. "Let's head back. Don't worry, the trip takes less time that direction, except when the moon outside is full."

I wonder how many moons the Cataclysm has at any given time, and as I look up my mouth falls open.

There are glowing eyes, and shimmering scales, and oh, there is a *dragon* in the sky. Or perhaps the dragon *is* the sky.

"Risteri," Entero says quietly.

"I see her," Risteri says. "Everyone, stay—"

Someone screams, and the eyes flicker out of the sky, replaced by clouds, as if they never were.

But the scream calls other things.

Thorns grow out of the ground at our feet, shooting up to waist-height as a swarm of grotesque butterflies dripping acid descends, and Risteri has her hands-full hustling the group to less actively hostile ground while a tangible wind delightedly winds itself around her.

Once there, I ask her, "What was that?"

"Nothing I've seen before, and nothing that should have been that close to the trail," she says quietly before swearing. "You! Where's your friend?"

It's one of the Velasari, and he spreads his hands in a show of distress. "Why, she was just here—oh, you don't think—?"

Entero says quietly, "She's definitely not here."

"Spirits." Risteri scans the area and waves Entero over. "Let me show you the things most likely to start up."

"You're leaving us?" one of the tourists gasps.

Risteri says, "The woman who wandered off is probably dead by now. But I'll go look for her in case she needs help, the same as I would for any of you."

"She knew the rules," another mutters nervously.

Risteri's expression is sheer disdain. "I hope you can be sure you'll never err or be in need of assistance, if all your friends think like you. Wait here, or take your life in your hands. It's your choice."

After a minute, Risteri and Entero exchange professional nods, and then she disappears.

Entero relaxes almost immediately, and I suddenly realize I've read him wrong in the past: the utter relaxation isn't comfort; it's readiness for extreme danger. It's making his muscles liquid, so that when he has to act, he moves instantly.

But he's still close to my side, despite various tourists' protests. When they crowd him, he swipes with a knife to clear space.

Because he'll protect them only because whatever comes for them will also come for me.

But I can tell that makes him angry. He'll do his duty as my guard, but not happily, and I like him better for that.

We wait, and wait, and wait.

And finally, Risteri returns and practically tosses the Velsari at her friend.

The Velsari woman is white, clothes shredded and babbling through tears as her friend goes through the motions of soothing her while watching Risteri.

Who says, "Don't let me see you in the Cataclysm again."

The Velsari nods, hauling the woman with him as Risteri leads the distraught group back to the relative safety of Sayorsen.

When the rest of the group is gone, Risteri says to Entero, "Thank you. You shouldn't have had to take that on."

Entero shrugs. "You're the one who knows how to navigate the Cataclysm. You had a far better chance of finding the dragon."

Risteri scowls. "Yeah. Not that it mattered."

"That's what you wanted to be doing? Investigating?" I ask Entero, who shrugs and looks away.

"I could kill those Velsari," Risteri mutters, kicking a pebble at her feet.

"What were they doing?"

"Scouting," she says, shaking her head in disgust. "Magical experimentation on the Cataclysm is seriously regulated, since no one really understands it or wants to take the chance of making it worse. So periodically you get people trying to go around the law, because they're so special they clearly know better than anyone else when they're so inexperienced they can't even make it through the outer rim unscathed. A lot of Velasari think they're holier because Velasar is the furthest country on the continent, so it was physically untouched by the Cataclysm."

"And because they burn witches and are proud of it," I say.

"Yeah," Risteri says. "Makes their scouts easier to spot than the Istals and Taresals, anyway, since Velasari who visit the Cataclysm rarely have anything good in mind."

"Why let them go on the tours at all, then?" Entero asks.

"Because that kind of discrimination is illegal," Risteri says. "And there's no proof. The organizers just always try to assign them to my tour group, since foreigners will hesitate to start a feud with an Istal noble house."

"But you still went to save her."

"I know how many horrible ways there are to die in the Cataclysm," Risteri says. "Stupidity and sanctimony aren't good enough reasons to abandon someone to that."

"Nakrabi never try to scout?" I ask.

"Not in my experience. Too superior to be curious about our continental problems, I suppose."

Maybe. But Thiano was still in Sayorsen, rather than another city with greater trade access.

"Risteri, do you have any plans for the afternoon?" I ask. "It's my day off, and I wanted to try learning how to cook."

Risteri hesitates. "My cooking skills are pretty slim and mostly involve campfires."

"I can boil water and reheat food on a stove, so I'm sure you're already ahead of me."

"I suppose that's true," she says. "Why me, though? Lorwyn could show you, I'm sure."

"I don't want to be shown. I want to play, and I thought you might enjoy an activity involving fire."

Entero sighs as Risteri laughs and says, "I'm in."

Much later, as Risteri and I sit full, exhausted, and surrounded by a greater mess than I could have imagined, she asks me, "So who is that guy anyway?"

It takes me a moment. "You mean Entero?"

"Yeah. What's his deal?"

I consider. "He's the bane of Lorwyn's existence."

"How do you mean?"

"Like the closer they are to each other, the chances of spontaneous combustion increase a hundredfold."

Risteri's eyebrows rise. "Oh ho, so it's like *that*, is it. That explains some things."

I frown at her. "Like what?" Risteri waggles her eyebrows at me, and it still takes me another moment. "*Oh*. You think so?"

She nods, sipping her tea confidently. "Yep. That's how Lorwyn is when she likes someone."

"Murderous?" I ask incredulously.

Risteri laughs. "Yeah. I think being attracted makes her uncomfortable, so she goes on the attack hard."

I'm still having trouble wrapping my mind around the idea that Lorwyn could like—or at least be attracted to—Entero. "How do you know?"

"I paid close attention, because I used to have the biggest crush on her."

I set my tea cup down carefully. "Ah. And she..."

"Didn't like me. Not like that."

"Does Lorwyn only like men, then?" I ask.

"No, she likes men and women. Just not me," Risteri says matter-of-factly.

Oh dear. "Is that part of the reason you two...?"

"Oh, no. Our issues are separate."

Because that couldn't have complicated matters enough. But apparently that, at least, is resolved between them, so I say, "I wonder if Entero likes her too."

"I don't have a solid read on him yet, but maybe," Risteri says. "He was awfully sensitive to her witchcraft."

I shake my head. "I can't imagine expressing fondness for someone by attacking them the way those two go at it," I marvel. "How could that ever work?"

Risteri looks at me oddly. "Okay, I'm going to bring over a stack of romance novels for you to read. Your education on what matters is clearly lacking."

I hesitate for a moment and then ask, "Will you bring them on your way out before the house wakes up?"

She looks at me too blankly. "I don't know what you mean."

"I saw you a couple days ago, and then you vanished," I say. "I assume this is whatever you bargained with Lorwyn for years ago, to hide a person in the shadow of your family home. What I can't figure out is why you need to."

Risteri stares at me.

Then she sighs, removing a metal cuff bracelet and showing me the frayed string bracelet she hides underneath it, made of faded colorful threads braided together, tied to other, newer threads.

"This used to be a friendship bracelet," Risteri says. "By the time I demanded she help me, we weren't really friends anymore, so the fact that she spelled this is... very Lorwyn. I re-tie it as I grow or it comes apart. The shape doesn't matter, apparently, just that it uses the same threads."

"And you can hide it under other bracelets," I say. My cuffs had never come off, before my dedication ceremony. It never would've occurred to me to search there.

"The spell hides me from my father or anyone that belongs to him," she says. "So I still have to sneak out, because it won't hide me from anyone else. Like you."

My eyes widen. A spell with parameters that broad should have been a huge magical working, and Lorwyn apparently performed it before she was even in adolescence, with no training. Spirits, but she was powerful.

"I know," Risteri says, interpreting the look on my face correctly. "I knew I was asking her for something serious, but I didn't really understand how serious until later."

"Would you have asked, if you had?"

She looks away. "Not the same way. I didn't mean for it to go like it did." Then she meets my eyes and says, "But I'd still have asked."

Knowing how painful their relationship has become, I have to ask. "What is so important you can't risk your father knowing about?"

Risteri squares her shoulders. "I don't just give tours in the Cataclysm."

"I assumed you must spend more time there, and deeper inside, to be able to lead groups safely through," I say.

"I try to recover treasures people have lost, when I can," she says. "I find Gaellani and Istal artifacts, mostly. I want to help ground people in what our lives are now and connect them to their roots, to be part of bringing people together and healing those old wounds. We've all lost a lot, but we're here now and all part of Istalam."

I can imagine Lorwyn gagging at this sentimentality, and I can't help but say, "It's hard to heal wounds when Istal institutions systematically foster divisions."

Risteri lets out a breath. "You sound like Lorwyn. I know that's not how oppression works."

I don't believe her. I believe she cares, I believe she wants to help, and I believe she's not afraid to work. I don't believe she understands systemic oppression, but I'm hardly an expert to tutor her in it.

So I say, "I'm sure that must appall your family, but it doesn't seem like the sort of thing you couldn't work around them without magic if you really had to."

Risteri regards me steadily. "Do you promise not to laugh?"

What? "Yes."

"Lorwyn and I used to explore the Cataclysm together, when we were children. Yes, I know it was reckless, but the thing is, one time we found people."

I can't have heard that right. "*What*?"

Risteri nods. "I know. And yes, I'm sure. The eyes we saw in the sky today? I've seen eyes like that, but not for fifteen years."

Oh, spirits. "You think there are people lost in the Cataclysm?"

"Until today, I thought they must have died. Lorwyn's thought that for years. She couldn't believe I wanted to keep wasting my time and hers searching, but how could I not? How could I know there might be people trapped in the Cataclysm and not try to help?"

I can imagine too clearly. Risteri, with stars in her eyes and righteousness in her heart and all the privilege of nobility. Lorwyn, who had to work to feed her sisters, who couldn't afford to keep being dragged away on what was probably a fool's errand and maybe one day not come back, who was already in so much danger outside the Cataclysm, who had so few resources but so many responsibilities and couldn't subsist on hope alone.

This is what started the rift between them. And once it started, it grew and grew.

"Where does your father come into this?" I ask.

Risteri looks away. "In my defense, I was a child, but it was still stupid. I told my father about the people thinking he would help me rescue them."

"And?"

"And I heard him send some of his people out into the Cataclysm, though he claims he never found them. He says it must have been a childish fantasy."

"You don't believe him."

Risteri looks me in the eye. "No, I don't believe him. I don't know what he's hiding. I don't know what happened that day. But I will never give up on finding out."

Even once Lorwyn did, once she had to, because it's the right thing to do. And Risteri can afford to lose everything, but she can't live with herself if she fails.

"I believe you," I tell her. "I'm neither a witch nor a warrior, but if I can help, I hope you'll come to me."

Risteri lets out a shaky breath, wilting. "I haven't dared talk about this in years. That you believe me is enough."

CHAPTER 15

ENTERO AND I ARRIVE at the shop early for the start of my second week of work, with plenty of time for Talmeri and me to review my work and negotiate my compensation.

But Talmeri isn't there.

I'm a little surprised, and annoyed both that I'm surprised at all and that she would forget our appointment. If she's not here by the time Meristo arrives for work I'll send him to the messenger's guild to make sure nothing actually concerning has happened.

I'm explaining how green and white teas differ to Entero when Talmeri finally bustles in without even a word about her tardiness. When we've moved into her office, she says, "How has he worked here for several days and not learned something so basic? I'm not sure he's going to work out."

"He's working for free," I remind her, actually surprised she's protesting that good fortune. "And once word gets out there's a man working here who looks like that, you know he's going to bring in a lot more customers than the boys and their service ever could."

Talmeri smiles faintly. "He is something to look at, isn't he? I suppose you're right. In that case, I assume you think he's got enough of a handle on things that you can set up tea ceremony service this week?"

I let my face go politely blank. I've spent the last week struggling to feel like I have even a marginal handle on running the shop; Entero is definitely not trained, let alone Iskielo; and I have barely begun my own training in tea mastery.

"I think this week is too soon," I say. "I'd like to have more time to study first."

Talmeri's tone is viciously pleasant as she asks, "If you're not going to perform tea ceremony for our customers, what am I paying you for, exactly?"

"To make considered decisions, and to create a thoughtful experience for your guests," I say. "Before I can do that, I need to practice the tea ceremony more. So on top of my living expenses, this week I'd like to buy a tea set."

That gives her pause as she studies me like she's looking for the catch, unable to believe that's all I'm asking for. "We have plenty of tea sets at the shop."

"A portable tea set," I clarify.

"Why portable?"

"Because I don't want to take advantage of business hours to do my studying here, and I can't invite people to my current place of residence. This way, no matter where I find myself, I can study."

There are other things I want, but I know better than to ask Talmeri for more so early in our arrangement, when she's still insecure. This has the advantage of being something that will benefit her directly, and I'm pleased with myself for coming up with a way to ask for more without feeling guilty.

Talmeri drums her fingers on her desk. "A portable tea set. That kind of craftsmanship isn't cheap. If you want me to front that cost, and you're not going to start performing tea ceremony, I think you should start working on some tasks beyond what the tea boys do."

I've been managing the shop and the tea boys, too, but I can't use that argument in my favor since Talmeri never has—she won't consider that a worthwhile skill. "What do you have in mind?"

"If you're going to manage the front, you need to understand the business side of the shop," Talmeri says, leaning back in her chair. "Obviously I wouldn't expect you to take over everything at once, but I think getting you working on inventory is a good place to start."

That makes more sense than I was expecting, and I feel a little bad about that. Understanding how inventory works will teach me a lot about the shop, too, giving me a better handle on all the tea we deal in. And since I'm getting what I want, I have no right to protest anyway. I want her to feel like she's getting a good deal, like I'm worth the investment.

So I agree, and Talmeri suggests a stipend for the week that looks reasonable and I accept that too. She gives me a basic rundown of the tasks associated with inventory—keeping track of what and how much arrives at the back and what we sell, how to cross-check that everything arrives at the correct quantity, quality, and price and what to do when it's wrong. It's a lot of new tasks at once, but manageable, and she doesn't try to overload me. I'm grateful, though I'm not sure it's out of appreciation for how much I can take on or an unwillingness to cede that much control.

We part on good terms, and I'm pleased with how I handled the situation right up until I tell Lorwyn.

"She did mention our inventory is a mess?" Lorwyn asks incredulously.

I frown. "What do you mean? I was just looking at the inventory records."

"I'm not saying the system doesn't work, but she hasn't kept it updated," Lorwyn says. "I mean don't get me wrong, I think it's a good idea for you to take this over since it's one of the many tasks she's let slip—"

I flip to the most recent entry in the inventory tracking book and show Lorwyn. "This date is from a shipment that arrived two weeks ago. It can't be that out of date."

Lorwyn peers at it. "Yeah, those numbers are made up."

"*What*?"

"Talmeri sometimes puts placeholder entries in when she doesn't have time to track properly, but she never goes back and fixes them. It's usually based on what she can remember, and I mean, if nothing else she has a great memory. But if she's not here when the shipments actually arrive and they're different from what she ordered, and she never looks at the paperwork—" Lorwyn nods toward a tall stack of paper in the corner of Talmeri's office. It's next to the bin where Talmeri told me new orders to track would come in.

I close my eyes. "What is that stack?"

"That's all the papers she hasn't literally dealt with but has entered something approximate into the records so it's no longer top priority."

I'm having trouble wrapping my mind around this. "It can't be legal to handle record keeping like this."

Lorwyn shrugs. "Outside my job description. So I take it she did not, in fact, mention any of this before you agreed."

"It can't be that bad," I try. "How could she know what to order if she doesn't know what the store has?"

"Makes it up," Lorwyn answers. "That's how we end up with things like sleekbeetle scales."

I deflate into the office chair. "It's really that bad."

"Yep."

I look around me in despair. This won't help me understand the store better, because all the records are wrong—Talmeri has no idea what's in the warehouse.

And she's just made that my problem, as though I don't already have enough to do.

"You have a few hours before the shop opens to get started," Lorwyn says sympathetically, and that does it.

"I'm going for a walk."

I'd seen several shops carrying portable tea sets at the Central Market, but what I had not paid enough attention to was the price.

Entero trails as my silent shadow as I lead us from shop to shop, my expression growing darker with each new piece of evidence until Thiano hails me.

"Day that bad already, huh," he says knowingly from the display in front of his shop. "Looking for anything in particular?"

"A full portable tea set that I can afford," I say. "I assume your prices won't be any lower than your neighbors'."

Thiano snorts. "For a full set? Definitely higher. I saw you going into the shop across the way—even that was outside your budget?"

I nod miserably. I'd hoped I could get a beautiful tea set, and as we began to see the prices I decided I could at least get a usable tea set. But even that, with the cost of the case, was outside the number of marks Talmeri had given me. I can't buy a full portable tea set at all, let alone still be able to eat afterwards.

Thiano laughs when I explain what happened that morning. "Oh, she got you good."

"I knew she wanted me off-balance so she'd get a better deal," I say. "Coming in late and then getting me to justify why she should pay me at all, defending Entero's work to lay the groundwork for me taking on more. I thought I'd managed to redirect her."

"You did," Thiano says. "But you thought too well of her. Talmeri's hung on this long because she's mercenary. Even if she wants to help you she'll take every advantage she can get. And you missed one: you assumed when she acknowledged the cost of good craftsmanship that she'd quote you a reasonable price, too."

I let out a curse that amuses Thiano further. It *is* my fault for not researching prices before going into that negotiation. But even more, I should have understood by now not to trust Talmeri's good intentions unquestioningly and taken her growing unease into account.

I'd won our exchange about the handling of the wealthy customer I offended too decisively. I should have known she'd try to find a way to regain the upper hand in our relationship, that she wouldn't consider me a partner in our endeavor to treat with respect.

"So what will you do now?" Thiano asks with a gleam in his eye that tells me he thinks I'm quietly plotting how to get even.

Is that what I want? I'm angry, but that feels like the wrong with response.

I shake my head. "I made the mistake of approaching her without sufficient forethought and preparation once already."

"Research, then?"

"Too late for that now," I grumble, and he snickers at me. "And anyway, it's not as if I can expect to know everything in advance, is there? There's too much, and I have other priorities." I sigh. "It's my wits that are the problem."

Thiano's expression shifts from amused to speculative as he cocks his head to one side. "And what will you do about *that*?"

"For a start?" I ask grimly. "Pray."

Sayorsen Shrine is dedicated to water. Someday I'll learn its history, but it seems appropriate that the shrine in a place that has experienced so much change values the adaptability of water.

It's not as empty as I feared from Lorwyn and Risteri's reactions. But it is quiet, and I settle my feet in the pool of water in the center along with other visitors while Entero hangs back.

Of course Entero knew where to find the local shrine. I should have thought to ask him days ago, and that only brings home that I'm not in control. That I'm being pushed from priority to decision, which means I'm letting others choose my course for me.

That has to stop. It won't just stop now that I'm out of the palace. *I* have to stop it. I have to make that choice, every time. Maybe someday it will become easier, habitual, but only if I practice.

Here in the water, I can admit that my fundamental difficulty in learning how to take up space is that I'm not sure I want to.

I don't want to impose myself on others, or on the world. It's why I rejected the mage training Saiyana took so naturally to. I want to be welcomed—and to believe that I deserve to be.

But who is there to do the welcoming, if I am not making my own choices?

I close my eyes, focusing on the feel of the water swirling around my legs. No matter the space, water always makes itself fit.

But it does more than that: over time, it carves out huge swaths of land. It can overcome fire. And it never stops inexorably flowing.

Unless, diminished, spread too thin, it vanishes.

Like my spirit, if I allow it.

This morning, I knew Talmeri wasn't being straight with me. I convinced myself to allow it rather than confront it, not to make trouble when I was getting what I wanted. Not to push when I already feel as though I should be grateful.

And she cornered me.

No: I *let* her corner me.

I'm surprised I'm angry with Talmeri. Perhaps that's a good sign, that I believe I deserve to be. But even more, I'm angry with myself. I'm less sure that bodes well, because it means I expect better than perhaps I'm capable of.

But Talmeri is getting a good deal already. An excellent deal, and I negotiated it myself. I don't need to break myself accommodating her, to lose myself for the sake of someone else.

At least in a negotiation like that, I'm confident I can only be cornered if I allow it. And if I allow it again, now, I'll end up no better off than when I was trapped in the palace, all my choices made for me, little by little draining my spirit away until it evaporates.

That isn't why I chose to go alone.

I want to be the undefeatable water, the water that will bend around others but still be one cohesive pool that someone can point to and say, *that* is Miyara.

Flexible, but discrete.

Someone, not anyone.

So I do have to reject this definition of reality Talmeri would impose on me, and I have to do it in such a way that I take control of myself, of my course, back.

On the way out of the shrine, Entero says, "You should eat something before heading back to the shop."

I'll need my strength. Little does he know. "Yes. But first, we need to go to the messengers' guild."

"Dinner's ready," Deniel says.

The sound startles me awake. At the jerk of my hand, Talsu opens one eye to glare at me, and I resume petting him absently.

"How long have I been asleep?" I ask, rubbing my eyes with my other hand.

"About an hour. Sorry, I know you wanted to help with dinner, but I didn't want to disturb you two." He smiles crookedly down at me and Talsu, who wedged himself into the chair with me and whom I am now curled around. If we look anywhere near as cute as Deniel does when sitting with the cat, I doubt I would have disturbed him either. I don't want to get up; I want him to join me, to wrap around me and sit here comfortable and warm. And close.

I shake my head. The book I was studying is now sitting out of reach on the small table, which means Deniel must have taken it out of my hands at some point. I didn't notice, nor did I hear him in the kitchen.

"I must have needed that nap more than I realized," I say. "Thank you."

He smiles, and somehow even that makes me blush. "My pleasure. But you should probably come to the table and eat before it gets cold. I'd bring it to you here, but then you'll have to fight Talsion for your dinner."

"Will I betray his tiny trust if I move?" I ask as Talsu curls into a tighter ball. "What if he never sits next to me like this again?"

"He's a cat, so I can't make any promises," Deniel says with amusement, "but I think the chances are good that now that Talsu understands how accommodating you are there'll be no keeping him away."

I sigh and extract myself with one last wistful pet. Deniel offers me a hand, and I take it, allowing him to help pull me up towards him.

And then we *are* close. My face is inches from his, and I'm staring wide-eyed, I can feel my pulse suddenly racing and I haven't let go of his hand—

I swallow and step back, and so does he, and somehow we manage to separate and pretend that did not just happen. I try to focus on stretching the kinks in my back as we move to the table.

To my relief, Deniel hasn't spent undue effort on my behalf. I'm too sleepy—well, not anymore!—to appreciate great culinary feats, but the food is warm and filling. We have things to do tonight, and I remind myself I shouldn't eat so much I'll fall right back asleep again.

"Why so tired today?" Deniel asks, watching me closely. "I don't think you slept the whole night I worked on the tea pet, and you were emotionally exhausted then."

"I may have taken on too many tasks, and they're beginning to wear on me," I admit. "But today it's physical exhaustion more than anything."

I summarize what happened with my negotiation with Talmeri that morning. "I'd hoped to start saving a bit to work on a personal project, but I'm already behind."

"What project?" he asks. "If you don't mind telling me."

"Just a small shrine," I explain. "The place I'm staying doesn't already have one, and I will be more balanced once I've invited the spirits into my home."

He nods like this is perfectly reasonable, and I'm relieved his reaction isn't like Lorwyn and Risteri's. "But you still can't get the portable tea set. Talmeri wouldn't let you borrow pottery from the shop?"

I sigh. "I thought of that. I've learned a lot about her reporting processes today, and I'm not convinced it would be legal, given how she's set up different business expense categories. If we were audited, which I think is likely to happen when her lease runs out, it could get us into trouble."

Deniel considers. "Possible. I'd have to see the records to confirm that, but you definitely can't show me without her permission. But in that case, I can at least help you with the pottery."

I'm so busy marveling at how confident he can sound about his grasp of the law without going to school or practicing professionally that it takes a moment for that to penetrate.

"Oh, I definitely can't afford anything as nice as what you make, and don't you dare offer to just give them to me."

He cocks his head to one side. "What about pieces I can't sell?"

I frown. "What do you mean?"

"Not every piece comes out right," he explains. "Now that I've built a reputation, I can't really sell inferior pieces without hurting that reputation overall. And I can't give them all away without hurting other businesses, so a lot of them just end up as trash, which I always feel a bit bad about."

"So I'd be doing you a favor," I deadpan.

Deniel laughs. "I promise not to foist my best pieces on you and pretend they're destined for the garbage otherwise."

I don't want to take advantage of his kindness, for him to go to any trouble on my account, and I want to value his work properly—but I can't deny this would help. "I would still need a matched set of cups," I hedge. "For balance in the ceremony."

Deniel leans back in his chair, gazing at the ceiling as if it has the answers. "I think I have a pair," he says. "Though they don't have a matching teapot."

"That would still be a great help," I say.

"Stop by once you have a portable case then," he says. "But that doesn't explain why you're so tired."

"Oh, that's because I'm getting even."

Deniel pauses. "Come again?"

"With Talmeri," I clarify.

"No, I got that part," he says. "Isn't that dangerous?"

"Not as dangerous as doing nothing," I say seriously, bracing myself for him to tell me I'm being ridiculous.

But he nods slowly. "Still tricky, though. What did you decide on?"

As we clear the table, I explain, "She made inventory my problem, so I'm taking it over."

Deniel smiles, a small, expectant and amused smile, and that alone makes me feel ready to take on anything. "Well, this I have to hear."

"I messaged all the tea boys," I explain. "They're scheduled in triple shifts for the next week to inventory everything we have in the shop."

His eyebrows lift. "How'd you get them to agree to that?"

"I promised to give them, or someone of their choice, a complementary tea ceremony once I'm certified. I may have mentioned it might be a good midwinter gift for their parents, who are the ones who insist on them working at the shop in the first place." I pause, then admit, "I'm a little worried I may have promised something I can't deliver, and that they all seem to think my becoming a tea master in three months is an inevitable outcome."

Deniel reaches over the counter as if for my hand, but I'm holding a plate and so his hand lands on my upturned, bare wrist.

I go utterly still.

"They know you're going to do everything you can, and they believe you can," Deniel says. "Let us have faith in you, even when it's hard to have it for yourself."

Then he takes the dish out of my hands and continues washing as if nothing momentous just occurred. And maybe for him it wasn't, but I continue to stare at him and his casual confidence in silence until he prompts, "You don't think Talmeri will object?"

"No," I say, pulling myself back into the conversation with an effort of will. "It doubles as marketing, for one, but it's also solely dependent on me—my expertise and labor. So I'm not taking away shop resources."

I outline the rest of the plan for him: we'll dispose of all the expired product, sell the soon-to-be bad tea at massive discounts, reorganize the back, and create a new inventory system standardized so it will be easy to see when it's wrong—which means Talmeri won't be able to enter whatever she wants and mess up the inventory without my knowledge.

"So I will be doing exactly what she asked of me, and going above and beyond, so she'll have no basis to reproach me," I tell Deniel.

"And in so doing you'll take some of her power away," he says. "If it doesn't backfire, she'll think twice about trying to sneak responsibilities on you again."

"But it might backfire. In either case, it still means that I'm going to spend the next week doing a lot of heavy lifting, not to mention figuring out how to implement a new inventory system when I've never seen a functioning one before."

"Well," Deniel says, "the good news is if you don't get it right the first time, since it's now your responsibility you'll have the opportunity to fix it in the future. That's also the bad news."

I laugh, a little hysterically. "Thank you for not telling me I'm batty."

"There are people who will take every advantage from you they think they can get," he says. "Talmeri, I think, is one of them."

I glance away. "I may not be so different from that."

"Then nor am I. Do you think I'm innocent after shamelessly introducing you to Talsion and then making you dinner?"

"That's not the same."

"No, it isn't," he says pointedly.

I laugh. "Spirits, you are a lawyer."

He smiles shyly at that and shrugs. "You have the ability to set boundaries for what you will tolerate, and you should. That's not something to be ashamed of. But don't fool yourself into thinking it isn't also a kind of work."

I wince. "So I am learning."

"Are you sure you're up for this tonight? There will be other opportunities."

"I'm sure," I say. "I'm not going to let dealing with Talmeri keep me from working on what matters to me."

Where do I fit? How can I serve?

"Then let's head to the council meeting," Deniel says.

CHAPTER 16

"ARE WE EARLY?" I ask Deniel as we enter the audience section and its rows of chairs in the large room where the city council meeting will take place.

Entero told me he'd keep watch from the upper level and promptly vanished. I don't see an upper level, so I assume this is another place he has mysteriously managed to scout in his nonexistent free time and located a secret hideout. He is more comfortable in the shadows.

There's a stage at the front with a curved table for the council members, so they'll all be able to see each other as they discuss issues. According to Deniel they rarely decide anything at these meetings—the public meeting is a holdover from an earlier era, now a token demonstration that the leaders of Sayorsen attend to people's concerns so they won't rise up in rebellion. Real decisions are negotiated in between meetings and announced to the public.

"A little," Deniel says. "The audience doesn't always fill up, but we don't want to take the chance of being turned away at the door if more ethnic Istals want to come in."

Without looking where he's going he leads me to a group of Gaellani around the middle, and as he introduces me around the few present I realize they must always sit here.

Not so close to the front that they'll be seen as impertinent, not so far back that they can be easily ignored, and close enough to the exit that they can escape if things go badly wrong. I'm sad that such consideration is necessary but also intrigued by what other tactics they employ.

The group doesn't pay me any particular attention, returning to their discussions about the issues on the meeting's agenda, which is a relief.

I'm more comfortable in the shadows, too.

A sudden thought strikes me as we sit, and I whisper to Deniel, "Will I meet your parents tonight?"

He blinks, then a small smile crosses his face. "As if you're the one who should worry about meeting the other's family."

"I disowned myself, so my family isn't likely to be an issue." I hope. If I can hide well enough.

Deniel shakes his head. "You're safe. They'll both still be working at this hour."

Most people who work long hours won't be able to attend, or they'll be too tired to; have other tasks that must be taken care of in the limited time allotted. "So the people most affected by council decisions often won't have the opportunity to speak in their own interest." I frown toward the front where council members are beginning to arrive.

Deniel hesitates and then adds, "I'm not sure my parents would come anyway."

That surprises me, when they've always been so supportive of Deniel, his work and his dreams. "Why not?"

"Because I think they may have given up. Not on change, necessarily, but—on this. But some other time, I'd—" He breaks off, shaking his head.

"What?"

"Never mind," he says. "I'll ask you later. The meeting will be starting soon."

It doesn't, but I listen quietly as Deniel consults with the other Gaellani about what subjects are likely to come up and what they should be prepared for. While some non-Gaellani stop by to greet us, no one joins the group who isn't Gaellani besides me. It can only be by design, but I'm not sure why.

The councilors have all filed in, with the exception of the seat left empty for Lord Kustio in the center. I can't decide if I'm more relieved or disappointed by his absence.

"He doesn't usually come," Deniel explains. "Which is for the best. His presence never means anything good."

But when the councilors actually start arguing about issues, I'm surprised not by their disagreement or the degree of their self-interest, but by how utterly inept several are at considering the ramifications.

Petitions made to the royal family are carefully prepared, so I've been spared many obviously flawed arguments. I know this. But as a princess, I was expected to learn the background and processes for many fields so I'd be able to adapt and judge on any issue. It's evident the councilors do not take their charge to serve Sayorsen so seriously.

It's also evident how support and precedent for some of the most trying issues we face develop.

The councilors indulge the most nebulous and bigoted of complaints with exhaustive discussion and promises to take the issue seriously while disregarding other concrete issues entirely. When they finally call on a Gaellani, who asks about antiquated fire regulations, they dismiss the subject at once and move on to another question.

This is the service Sayorsen's citizens live with every day, and I can't imagine it is so different elsewhere. I clench my hands, white-knuckled, until Deniel places one hand over mine.

"That went well," he says quietly. "We had our say."

He's *pleased* with this? "And for what?" I whisper furiously.

His grip tightens, and I look at him—and am surprised by how fierce his expression is.

Is he angry with *me*?

"Now," Deniel says, "other people have heard our piece, and they'll look into it or ask us questions. In a few weeks, when the councilors can pretend they don't remember Gaellani brought it up in the first place, someone else will raise the issue again. And we'll do that, work with people again and again, for as long as we need to. That's how this works."

Or fails to. Now I see how his parents could have decided not to support Deniel in this, how they could believe anything he put his energy into was a waste of time. I'm horrified by the disgrace of this council, but what's the alternative? My family could replace the councilors, but if the people those councilors need to deal with don't respect their appointment, still nothing gets done. If Sayorseni citizens overthrew the council, the army could be called in to quell a revolt. And with such a high Gaellani population here, I do not like to think who might bear the brunt of that.

"You bear this because you have to," I finally say. "I understand that, but allow me to hate it."

Deniel is quiet a moment.

And then he says, "No."

I glance up, startled.

"Change is slow, Miyara. It takes work. It takes time. But I don't just sit here because someone has to. I sit here because I want to be part of the change. Because we *do* create change. Slowly, yes, and it's frustrating a lot of the time. But we're inexorable. We're not leaving. Don't diminish that."

Inexorable, like the spirit of water. I search his gaze, not sure what I'm looking for. "It's so little, for so much work and time put in, against needs that are so great. Why is this worthwhile? What don't I understand?"

"That many people still don't consider Gaellani people," Deniel says bluntly. "Not really. They say or think they do, but they'll seize on any difference, any excuse to justify different treatment of us. We come to every council meeting, and we force them to see us. To gradually make them understand we're people just like them and we're not going anywhere. It takes time to change people's minds on that scale, Miyara."

"And space," I whisper, closing my eyes.

They're here, taking up space, refusing to be driven out. And here I sit quietly in the shadows of their effort—I, who, as Lorwyn pointed out, have never had to worry about my rights, *I* sit here questioning the merit of their efforts.

"That too," Deniel says. "As much as we can we pick subjects to bring up that people outside the Gaellani community are likely to have experienced issues with, to create common ground. That strategy has its own issues, and it's one we debate a lot. It's always a balance, because our power alone is limited, since the councilors are predisposed to dismiss our concerns."

Because if they can make conditions impossible enough, the Gaellani will have to leave. But even if they wished to, they have nowhere to go.

Do the councilors all really believe that's right? The Sayorseni don't seem to. But even wealthy Istals like Talmeri are being pressed by Lord Kustio's policies; they might exert enough pressure to outweigh the councilors' better judgment.

Which means there needs to be stronger counter-pressure, and the Gaellani's position is too precarious to afford to supply it.

"But I don't have that limitation," I say slowly.

Deniel frowns at me. "I thought you were worried one of the councilors might recognize you."

"I am." At the very least, to be on this council means they're wealthy or well-connected, which means there's a more than slight chance one of them will know enough to recognize me. And if they start making inquiries, and my family hears of it, they will drag me back, no matter what I want.

But if I won't risk standing up for what matters to me, then I might as well still be trapped in the palace.

So I squeeze Deniel's hand once, and let it go.

And I stand.

And I stand, and I stand, thinking all the while how I can make my statement so memorable it won't simply be disregarded, and whether that is a mistake—for my security, too, and I'm surprised Entero hasn't swooped down to make me sit again, but mainly for Sayorsen's.

If I can even manage it.

Finally, Deniel says, "If you change seats, they'll acknowledge you."

I look at him, then around us, and at the audience at large. "That's why no non-Gaellani sit with you, even those who are friendly to you. They only call on the Gaellani once."

He nods. "At most. Also if non-Gaellani sit here, the councilors only call on them. So—"

"So I will always wait for you to make your points first before standing, but I won't move and give them an excuse not to see you," I say, turning resolutely back to the front.

I understand better now why Deniel feared I would find myself too limited, being with him. Perhaps I still don't understand fully, but he's wrong.

Being with him makes me strong.

I wait, and wait, and when the tenth question is entertained past when I should have been acknowledged, I finish waiting.

I have waited for too much of my life.

Before the next audience member is chosen, I call, "With respect, I would address the council."

The audience murmurs as the council fixes its attention on me.

A councilor says, "The young grace with the... fascinating hair choices may wait her turn like everyone else. Such a bald need to be noticed will not further your goals in this chamber."

"I appreciate your concern regarding how my style choices affect how others perceive me," I reply coolly. "Happily, in my assessment Tea Master Karekin did not judge my hair color in opposition to my ability to serve. Councilor."

There is a rustle of sound as the news passes around the room that I'm the tea aspirant. Even without mastery, that matters, and tonight I will leverage it.

It is petty, but I'm pleased that the councilor who addressed me now bears a pinched expression.

"Please pardon my interruption," I say, bowing. "As I've been standing for some time, I thought for sure the council must not be able to see this section well. Shall I wait another turn?"

"That won't be necessary, Aspirant," another councilor says. "Our apologies for failing to address you more promptly. How may the council serve you today?"

My fingers tingle with nerves. I have the attention I wanted; now we'll see if I can handle what it means.

"My question is one of a unique and baffling policy I've discovered since my arrival in Sayorsen," I say. "It seems it is common to refuse to employ or serve Gaellani workers and patrons. As this practice is clearly illegal, my question is what the council is doing to curtail it?"

The room is silent.

Speaking of the practice out loud is taboo, I understand belatedly, as dozens of gazes turn on me in disbelief, and I fight the urge to apologize, to bow and shrink back into the shadows.

I stand, and I school my expression into one of calm. *That*, at least, is familiar.

The councilor who mocked me before speaks first. "While the council of course respects the position of the tea aspirant, this allegation lacks legal basis. Individuals can make choices based on who they think will best understand their business and will work hard—"

"One of my colleagues now is Gaellani, and I assure you if hard work were a racial trait you'd be silly to hire anyone *but* Gaellani," I interrupt. "And I have certainly known Istals who put in less effort."

"As you say, individuals vary greatly, and it's up to each private citizen to make their own decisions, however much you might personally disagree with them. It is not the council's place to tell people how to run their businesses."

Oh no, this is your *failure, and I will not let you eschew your responsibility.*

"With respect to the councilor, while that is generally true, it is not universally true. People are not, for instance, permitted to run businesses that fail to pay taxes to Istalam. That is law. And in this case, there is likewise an exception. I refer you to Queen Esmeri's official decree welcoming all refugees of the Cataclysm, including Sayorsen's ethnically Gaellani residents, as equal citizens of Istalam."

"A speech is not law," the councilor argues.

"The speech has been cited as the precedent for several subsequent laws," I respond without pause. "In particular, I'm sure you will remember the case that formalized Istal policy to the effect that the nation of Velasar and its people are not to be treated as holier than Istals or anyone else because it was untouched by the Cataclysm's effects. The key wording from Queen Esmeri's decree is that disaster strikes equals unequally, and that our responsibility as human citizens of this world is to reject that inequality wherever it is found, because it is humans that create it, not nature or magic. And to that end, all survivors of the Cataclysm are to be treated as equals of those—including Istals—who were lost. Allowing discrimination against Gaellani to continue when it has been found is, in fact, illegal."

Some of the councilors appear speechless. I see panic on one face and weariness on more; those will be councilors who know this is wrong but not how to fix it.

But the one who called out my hair says, "How is it that an aspirant pursuing tea studies is so knowledgeable about the law?"

I've made an enemy tonight, and he will try to find out who I am.

"Tea masters are called upon to negotiate treaties, grace," I say. "Such preparation is part of my studies. If the council wishes to verify my interpretation of the law, may I recommend *Judiciary Advances for the Modern Era* by the current court's counsel and *The Dowager Queen's Legacy* by Irota Sanevar?"

"Your recommendations will be duly recorded," another councilor says. "We appreciate your service."

It's a dismissal.

And for once in my life, it's a dismissal I blatantly ignore.

"I would also like to say, as I'm new to Sayorsen, thank you for accommodating my questions as I make my home in this fine city." *I will call your bigotry for what it is, I refuse to accept it as normal, and I'm not going anywhere.* "The policy is harmful to Gaellani specifically, but I'm employed at an Istal-owned business, and this affects our sales, too."

It bothers me to appeal to classism in this way, but while my tea aspirancy is enough to get me listened to, it won't be enough on its own to make change. For that I need allies, so at the last minute I adopt Deniel's tactic. Let them remember this, rather than my unexpected historical knowledge.

"I hear you don't need sales as badly as that," a councilor points out.

And my refusal of the rich woman continues to haunt me. First Talmeri's vengeance this morning, and now this.

"You're correct, I believe accommodating bigotry is bad for business," I say. "We are all equal before the spirits, and we are all Istalam. If I don't look out for the welfare of all the people I serve, can I be said in truth to be serving their interests? If we don't care about the wellbeing of a group of our own citizens, how can we in truth represent Istals?"

"You raise interesting questions, and the council is not prepared to issue a statement on them at this time," a councilor says.

"I thank the council for its consideration," I say, and sit down at last.

Oh, spirits, what have I done?

"That was terrifying," Deniel whispers. "Are you okay?"

Barely moving my lips I reply, "Everyone will be watching me, so I will be perfectly serene."

Deniel turns away from me, and I resist the urge to clench my jaw, my hands, *anything* as hard as I can at his withdrawal.

Then he leans back in his chair, his shoulder brushing mine, and says lowly, "I'm here. It's almost over."

I take a deep breath. He did understand what it cost me, to fall back on the behavior most intrinsic to life as a princess.

Pretending nothing matters.

Later, as I walk back with Deniel to collect my books, I ask, "Did I make things harder for you?"

He frowns down at his feet. "Honestly, it's hard to say," he finally says. "I'm sorry I can't be more reassuring. But probably nothing will come of this."

Except that councilor will have it in for me. But if that's the worst consequence, I can surely cope. If Entero forgives me for making myself a target.

"I know," I say. "But I can make their failure to serve harder to ignore."

And I can make my *self* harder to ignore.

I can make myself take up space, even, especially when it goes against my instincts, because my instincts on this are defined by a life of surviving in the palace. A life of knowing I had to hide my true self, because there was no place for it there.

Now I'll learn to make a place for it here, or I'll have none anywhere.

Deniel sighs. "Even if it does make things harder for us in the short term, thank you for that. It's not safe for Gaellani to bring that issue up. If we appear self-serving, we undo the careful work we've done before. But it makes it hard to advocate for ourselves. We have non-Gaellani friends, of course, but everyone has been afraid to approach this head-on because the fallout gets ugly."

"Whereas I can get away with it, because I'm Istal and don't have vulnerable connections here." Risteri's own father sat on the council, Talmeri moved in high social circles, and she'd never make it without Lorwyn. "And I have a bodyguard," I add.

Deniel doesn't laugh. "I hope it won't come to that."

That sobers me. "Do you have any suggestions for next time?"

"I don't think you need any help from me to handle the council whatsoever," Deniel says with the ghost of a smile, but there's a touch of sadness in it.

"I meant how not to make things worse for you," I say. "I assume drawing attention to the Gaellani isn't ideal. I tried to mitigate it at the end with an appeal to the respectability argument, gross as I find it, though that might have undercut my own point—"

"The 'it affects good old-fashioned Istal businesses too' bit, and the question of which groups exactly the council serves." Deniel nods. "Yes, you may want to appeal more broadly like that to develop credibility of the kind people will listen to."

I'm not sure that's the kind of credibility I want. But it is a kind of privilege, that I can afford to choose purity over practicality in this, and I wonder if that means I shouldn't use it—or if I should.

"I didn't realize," Deniel says into the silence, "how much policy you know."

I frown at him in the darkness. "What did you think princesses do before our dedications?"

"I'm sorry, I didn't mean I thought you were frivolous. I knew you must have studied history, but you quoted specific *phrases*, and you remember which books analyzed them without any preparation—"

Oh. "Princesses are expected to be conversant with many subjects, so we can't be blindsided by negotiating tactics," I explain. "We train our memory to remember details like that. It's one of the few parts of my training I took to naturally." Probably one of the reasons Saiyana thought I'd be an asset in her line of work, now that I think about it.

And now I can be an asset to *Deniel.*

I almost gasp, then immediately realize I shouldn't betray my excitement. I don't want him to ask for my help because he knows how much I want to help; I want him to ask only if I can *actually* be of help.

"If you ever want references to back up the points the Gaellani plan to raise in the council meeting, please let me know," I say casually.

"That's a good idea," Deniel says. "It'll help us develop our case when other people come looking for more information, too. We do refer them to books when we can find them, of course, but you can probably identify good sources a lot faster." He hesitates and then blurts, "Do you know one on the history of trade law?"

I blink. "Yes, *Traders and Traitors.* It's a collection of articles from university professors and government officials in Miteran. What do you need—oh, it's for your own studies!" I smile widely. "I'm so glad my training will come in useful for something after all."

He shakes his head in amusement, like he can't believe I doubted it. I'm more cheerful than I've been all night as I regale him with my favorite smuggling anecdote from the book, and he tells me about one of his favorite lawsuits from my mother's reign against a shrewd Velasari businessman. We both wear silly grins by the time we part ways at his house, and Entero appears at my side for the walk home.

Entero gives me a long-suffering look but doesn't say any more about my choices tonight, at least not now. Perhaps he sees my smile and thinks I'm in no mood to take such chastisement to heart.

I can do something for Deniel. Perhaps that isn't tonight's greatest victory and shouldn't be the thing about tonight that makes me happiest. I would be happier if it weren't a skill so specific to being a princess—but no, that's part of me too, will always be my past, even if it's not all of me now.

But the me of before wouldn't have been able to help Deniel.

CHAPTER 17

I RETURN TO THE Central Market with a mission. After all my pacing the day before, it doesn't take long to locate a basic, portable, slatted wooden tea tray, lightweight and with compartments to hold tea tools once I've acquired them. When I have everything but the tea, cups, and pot, for as cheap as I can find, I march over to Thiano's stall.

"How much is that bowl?" I point at a metallic bowl shaped like a leaf, threaded with veins of bright blue.

"More than you can afford," Thiano drawls.

"The blue is an indication of magical error in its creation, which anyone who could afford your prices would know. And the aesthetic of its asymmetrical curves, while elegant, are not in fashion outside of Gaellani craftsmanship, and they can't afford your prices. Are you sure you won't sell it to me?"

Thiano sizes me up and names a price. Next to me, Entero nods shallowly. So, not as low as it could be, but not as exorbitant as Thiano's typical prices. I start counting out marks before he can change his mind.

"Well look who's feeling confident again today," Thiano says, eyebrows raised. "You've sorted out your monetary difficulty, then?"

I smile faintly. "Not exactly. This may backfire spectacularly. But it's a movement forward instead of back, so I can live with it."

Thiano twitches, the barest movement in his fingertips, and he's back under control as soon as I've noticed. But something about that sentiment resonated with him.

"You don't think Deniel would make you a bowl?" he asks slyly, trying to distract me. Not so recovered after all then, or why let me know he's aware of my relationship with Deniel?

"Perhaps I shall ask, and then I will fill this one with flowers," I say. "Do you have any recommendations for where I can find a pedestal?"

He leans back. "I might be able to find something for you."

"And I'm sure I couldn't afford your prices if you did," I say dryly.

"Then why should I help you?"

"Because I'm buying a bowl."

"A bowl at a discount," he says.

"A bowl you couldn't have sold otherwise at all, so a discounted price still gains you more than zero," I say.

"And why do you think that means I'll help a competitor?"

"Because you know that I'll buy more bowls from you in the future, when I can," I say, meeting his gaze.

Thiano studies me for a long moment.

Then abruptly says, "Tell me what you need."

Too fast; I've missed something. "The pedestal, and the bowl, are for an altar in my home," I begin.

He nods. "Say no more. I will take care of it, and you will promise to pay me whatever it is I say."

I narrow my eyes, this time trying to discern *his* motives. "I think I would be a fool to trust you."

Thiano grins, slowly, and it does not reach his eyes. Entero tenses beside me. "Is that a no, then?"

Whatever relationship we are playing at, I have no doubt it will be over if I refuse this. By any standard of logic, it's a bad idea.

But I'm smiling anyway.

"I cherish the freedom I have to make such foolish judgments," I tell him with a bow.

His smile this time is genuine, if small, and something in his eyes tells me it pains him, too. Perhaps someday I'll know why.

Lorwyn opens one of the tea compartments at the shop's brewing station. "This is the best approximation of a ceremonial green tea we have that isn't exorbitantly expensive. Talmeri won't have a fit if you write this off."

"Is there more in the back?" I ask.

"In theory. We may never be able to reach it again, of course."

The back is a disaster of boxes and debris, and every time I step back there it looks worse. I'd have been upset by the chaos in a place I considered my home, but Lorwyn is oddly cheerful about it.

The bell tinkles, and Taseino greets whoever has come in while Lorwyn's eyes narrow. "That's not the kind of person I expect to see around here."

I turn casually to see what she means. The customer's long, straight hair is pulled back in a simple clip, and he's tall and lean, the robes of his mage's office draping around him. The state robes aren't fancy, but that's not what arrests me: it's that they're lined with white, a right only the most advanced practitioners ever earn.

I know who this has to be before he turns. Our gazes lock, and I freeze, only my eyes widening.

Across the room, Ostario freezes, too.

"Miyara?" Lorwyn asks quietly.

"Go to the back, right now," I say.

"I'm not leaving when you look like—"

I whirl so Ostario won't see my lips move as I mouth, "He's a witch."

Lorwyn blinks, uncomprehending for a moment, and then she blanches, the blood draining out of her face.

A witch always knows another witch, she'd said.

And this one is a mage, too, one that works for Istalam.

Lorwyn slips away behind me, Ostario watching but not saying anything. Spirits, I hope I got her out in time.

"Something I should know about?" he asks me in his rich baritone.

"Yes," I say.

He waits.

We stare at each other across the expanse of the shop.

"But?" he prompts.

"But not that you need to."

Ostario's lips quirk, and he crosses over to me.

That's *good*, that means he's not planning on announcing to the few people in the front who I am and that we know each other.

But I still clench my fists, my world narrowed on this man closing in who can ruin everything for me with a word.

I fight the urge to flee. It wouldn't help.

When he's close, he says quietly, "Saiyana must find you infuriating."

I swallow. "Are you going to tell her I'm here?"

He pinches the bridge of his nose. "Why don't we go somewhere to talk?"

I shake my head. "It will be noted if I'm seen to be on casual terms with a mage of your stature." I motion for him to follow me, leading him to the tea ceremony room. "But I can serve you tea."

Ostario stops. "Oh, no. I couldn't possibly allow you to serve—"

"You should *expect* me to serve you," I cut him off. "That's what we're for."

Ostario studies me. When I step back and pointedly make space for him to enter the tea ceremony room before me, he goes without another objection.

I turn to Taseino, whose eyes are wide. He must know what the white lining means, how rare it is for a mage to be of that caliber. "He said he wanted to talk to Talmeri," Taseino whispers.

"I'll take care of it." I hope I'm not lying. "Please see to the front until we're done. Pull the other boys from inventory if you need to. Oh, and please let Entero know that I'll be serving Mage Ostario tea, so I'll be with him soon."

Then I enter the room myself, closing the door behind me, to face Ostario.

Who's watching me carefully, like he's not sure which direction I might attack from.

That won't do. He's my guest, now.

I take a breath and begin preparing the tea. "I'm not Saiyana."

Ostario snorts. "With that kind of insight into what I'm thinking about, you might as well be."

Saiyana never knows for sure with him, and it drives her to distraction. I don't think I should tell him that, though.

"So what brings you to Talmeri's today?" I ask. "Since I gather you weren't expecting to find me."

"It wouldn't have occurred to me to look for you here," he says. "I don't know where I would have looked, to be honest, and as often as we've talked I feel like I should apologize for not knowing you better."

"There's no need." I cast him a rueful smile. "How could you know what I never let anyone, even myself, see? Even genius mages like yourself aren't omniscient."

Ostario sighs theatrically. "My air of mystery and arcane wisdom bears further cultivation, I see."

I smile a little wider. "No, it doesn't. And you haven't answered my question."

"I was told Talmeri is the sort of person who hears everything and that she's impressed by displays of power," he says.

"Ah." I nod, arranging the tea tray. "That's why you're wearing your official robes for once."

"I often wear them on assignment," Ostario says. "It's an efficient way to cut through nonsense."

I kneel in front of him and begin the motions of the ceremony.

"Your High—Miyara, you really don't need to do this."

I meet his eyes, not pausing. "I know. I want to. It's my pleasure to serve you."

That startles him, and in his silence I flow into the tea ceremony.

I wonder if he's more startled that I want to serve him, or that I have expressed a want of anything. He was years ahead of me in mage training, and we do not know each other well, except through Saiyana. But he could not have become so accomplished as a mage without being discerning.

Like Saiyana, who I also managed to fool my whole life.

Or perhaps I didn't, and that's why he knows enough to be patient now.

It's a struggle to clear my mind, and the ceremony does not flow as naturally as usual. There is certainly more of myself in it, I suppose, but not, I think, in a useful way.

But when I look at Ostario as he sips his tea, his face is blank, like he's fighting a strong emotion. I can't decide if that's good or bad—for either of us.

"Can you tell me what you were going to ask Talmeri about?" I ask, settling across from him.

He takes another bracing sip. "Unregulated magical items."

Whatever I was expecting, it wasn't that. "Come again?"

Ostario nods. "Normally it's hard to smuggle magical items, but these aren't registering as magical even though they are. So we have dangerous magical items the crown can't track, and you can see the concerning implications of that, I'm sure. So since this is an unprecedented magical occurrence..."

"They suspect something to do with the Cataclysm, which means an investigator must be sent to Sayorsen, even with nothing more concrete to go on and the likelihood there's nothing to be found here."

Ostario raises his teacup as if to mock-clink glasses. "I assume this is the first you've heard of it, then?"

"Yes," I say. "Ostario, why are you being sent out on such a flimsy excuse for an assignment?"

"It's a serious problem."

"And I'm not unhappy someone competent is on the case, but you're the most promising mage talent of our generation. An assignment like this seems—"

"Beneath me?" Ostario suggests, amused. "Setting me up for failure? You don't need to worry about me, Miyara. This is hardly the worst my mage superiors have thrown at me, and I promise I can handle my career."

"I know," I say, "but I will worry regardless. It is my nature."

Ostario laughs. "You *are* different than Saiyana."

"Not as different in this regard as you'd think," I say. "I don't think she'd be quite as intent on controlling so much if she didn't care deeply."

"A royal family that actually cares," Ostario muses. "That may be the best kept state secret of all."

"I wonder if we haven't done people a disservice with that secrecy. Of course I see how it could be used against us to take political advantage, but... I wonder if isn't important for people to know that there is someone who cares, in a position to do something about it."

Ostario leans back on his hands, staring at the ceiling above us pensively. "I'm not privy to a lot of court gossip," he finally says, "but I *do* hear about what the mage corp is up to. Saiyana has refused to speak about you at all."

My chest tightens. I should have expected that. I knew she'd be upset. Still. "I see."

"There were a few mages who spoke against you, though, and what you did, which I'm sure won't surprise you," Ostario continues. "But

I thought you might like to know that Saiyana also challenged each of them to mage duels and wiped the floor with every one."

My eyes sting with sudden tears. "I wish I hadn't made this so hard for her," I whisper.

"Don't be like that now," Ostario says gently. "You're more yourself today than I've ever seen you. I imagine everyone who knows about your choice wonders at it, but now that I've seen you here, I don't."

Now I *am* crying. I bow my head.

He's the first to have known me before and seen me after. That the change in me should appear so obvious to him is a reassurance about the rightness of my choice I hadn't known I craved.

Ostario continues, "Saiyana will continue to best everyone who opposes her, because that's what she does. But that's not you."

No. *No*, it isn't, and I am beyond words that someone has finally acknowledged and had the nerve to say that to my face.

"Saiyana hasn't bested everyone," I manage past the tightness of my throat. "She didn't convince me to follow in her footsteps, and I know it's always bothered her that she's never definitively bested you in magework."

Ostario's eyes twinkle. "How tragic for her. We shall both have to see that continues."

I laugh, perhaps harder than is truly merited. Especially since there is one substantial issue still between us.

I meet his eyes and ask again, but calmly this time, "Will you tell Saiyana?"

Ostario smiles. "Unofficially, I'm supposed to report your whereabouts, because you're part of the royal family," he says. "But you see, there's a logical flaw with this charge, because if you're part of the royal family..."

"Please do not tell Saiyana or any of the royal family I'm here," I request quickly.

He flashes me a grin.

"But that is very shoddy logic," I add.

Ostario shrugs. "The order isn't official, which gives me some leeway. My dedication as a mage entitles me to act in the country's best interests as I perceive it, as well. I'll manage."

"Thank you," I say. "Truly."

"My pleasure," he says. "Now, I regret to bring this up, as you were finally relaxed there for a moment, but I thought you should know that your hair color has been changed permanently."

I still. "Oh?"

"As it's not a spell that will fade with time," Ostario says, looking directly at me, "if you wish to have it changed back, or changed in any other way, you'll need to speak to a witch."

Oh, spirits, he realized after all.

...but he isn't saying so directly.

"Thank you," I say, standing. "I had wondered if that was the case. But since you mention spells, I wonder if I could prevail upon you for a preservation spell—"

"Certainly," he says smoothly, rising to join me. "A favor for a favor."

Uh oh. "I'll let you know if I hear anything about the smuggled magical items."

"I appreciate that, but—hypothetically speaking, you understand—if you happened to know an unregistered witch, I would like for you to keep her out of my path."

I have no idea how to respond to that and just stare.

Ostario sighs. "I'm going to be investigating in Sayorsen until this situation is resolved, which means for the foreseeable future. As long as your hypothetical friend isn't involved, make sure she's not in a position where I am forced to notice her. If that's what you think is best. Though you might wish to mention that I'm qualified to give mage lessons. If she were interested."

I'm still gaping and make myself close my mouth. "Hypothetically," I say, "I doubt such a person could pay you."

"That's often the case," Ostario says. "I'm confident we could work something out. Would you like to show me where you need the preservation spell?"

In something of a daze, I start toward the door to show him my portable tea tray—but before I open it I turn abruptly and hug him, hard.

"Thank you," I whisper.

Gently, he returns my embrace. "It is my pleasure to serve you," he says.

Once Ostario has taken his leave, Entero appears at my side like a shadow.

"I didn't need protection," I say without preamble. "The worst thing he could have done would have been what you want anyway."

"I know," Entero says, surprising me. "Ostario isn't a threat to you. I was going to say, please go tell Lorwyn he's not a threat to her, either, because she's scared all the boys away and I can't tell if my presence is making her more nervous or less."

I blink. "I wish I'd known you were so confident about those things before I talked to him."

"Then you should actually talk to me about your security sometime, instead of assuming you have to fight me about it," Entero says pointedly, and I wince. "But later."

"Later," I agree, and go to see Lorwyn.

I pause just inside the lab. Lorwyn is sitting still, facing away. So still and stiff she could be a statue.

"I wasn't sure you'd still be here," I say quietly, crossing over to her slowly. "He's gone from the shop, and he won't come back unless I invite him."

"That's why you're always so careful to point out witches aren't always women," Lorwyn says, still not moving.

I would like to think I would be so careful even if I hadn't known Ostario for years, but all I say is, "Yes."

"You were right," she whispers. "I even felt his witchcraft when he walked in, and until you told me I *still* didn't understand. All the witches I've ever known are women."

Ostario doesn't speak much about his past; his air of mystery may be constructed, but it's effective. But I know he entered mage school in part because he didn't think he'd be able to hide his witchcraft. I remember watching from the audience at Ostario's mage trials when he'd been asked about being a witch sympathizer.

"Not only can I pass unscathed, I can now pass judgment," he'd explained to the mages, and I remember thinking he'd seemed sad. "No witch will ever trust me now."

And it hadn't escaped me, then, that the mages judging him that day might not ever trust him, either. Because he'd been born a witch, and because he'd chosen to leave them.

"Maybe now," I say to Lorwyn, "you'll know others, if they feel safe coming to you."

"Witches never feel safe," Lorwyn snaps. "You were right, okay? You were right, and it shouldn't have taken a witch who has power over my life for me to admit it. I hope you're happy."

"No," I say quietly. "I'm not. But you can trust him not to turn you in as long as he can pretend not to notice you."

Lorwyn buries her head in her hands. "How do you know? How do you know him, anyway?"

I ponder possible answers to that. "He was in my older sister's mage class," I finally say.

"And you know all your sister's friends well enough to vouch for their trustworthiness, I assume? Ha!"

"I'm not sure they would consider each other friends," I say, wedging myself into Lorwyn's work area casually, so she can't keep not looking at me. "More like rivals."

"How encouraging."

I sigh. "Truthfully, I'm reasonably sure my sister's in love with him."

At that, Lorwyn finally looks up at me, startled.

And then thoughtful, like that makes sense to her.

Oh, Risteri's right after all about Lorwyn liking Entero, isn't she?

"So," I say, "what are we going to do? He's powerful enough that if he meets you again, he won't be able to pretend he can't tell you're a witch, and he'll have to bring you in. And he'll be able to."

"I'm powerful too," Lorwyn says grimly.

I shake my head. "Your determination might lend you extra strength, but Ostario has had years to practice openly. I'm reliably informed by someone dead set on beating him that he's the most talented mage alive. Someday soon he'll probably be the best. That's *without* witchcraft." I pause, trying to think how to bring this around.

Lorwyn slumps. "Whatever you're not saying, just get it out already."

Fine. "I have reason to believe he'd be willing to give you lessons as a mage—"

"Absolutely not." Her voice was firm. "Then I would *have* to register. I don't care if you like him and he likes you, I don't trust anyone who's sold out. It's historically turned out badly for witches, so don't try to tell me I'm prejudiced about nothing."

I purse my lips. She's wrong about Ostario, but she's not wrong about history. Since I'm confident he won't turn *me* in, though, it's also not my life on the line here. "I won't. But Ostario knows you exist, and he's not turning you in."

"Yet," Lorwyn says darkly. "He knows where to find me, so he can always blackmail me later."

So, no mage lessons. I cross my arms, thinking. "Can you make something for yourself that'll work on him like Risteri's bracelet works on her father? That will hide you, but just from him?"

Her head snaps around to stare at me. "*What?*"

Oh. "Risteri didn't volunteer the information, if that's what you're worried about. I figured it out."

"Your ability to find out absolutely everything does not make me feel any better," she snaps, but I can see that it does: she's already leaning back in her chair, frowning as she considers the problem.

Leaving me a moment to blink at that summation. Do I have such a talent for ferreting out information?

I startle at a sudden thought. My grandmother who I now know has a secret employ of spies had told me, "There will always be work for those who know how to listen."

Is *that* what she'd meant?

"Tricky, since he's a witch and a mage," Lorwyn mutters, reaching up to where the tea pet sits and pulling a small shard down. She shrugs at me. "You missed a piece, but that's fine. No one will ask why I'm wearing a piece of my family's heirloom." She shoves around her desk until she finds a box full of string, and she says, "Let me work on this alone for a while. I'll let you know when it's safe to send the boys back."

Something in me eases. She'll be okay. We both will.

I hope it will be enough.

CHAPTER 18

I STAY LATE, WORKING on inventory until Lorwyn tells me she wants some privacy in the back and shoos me and Entero out.

"How are you feeling?" I ask Entero. He's been uncharacteristically quiet in the face of Lorwyn's temper this afternoon, and I'm not sure if it's out of consideration for her or if he's worrying over something else.

But he looks at me like the question itself is silly. "What do you have in mind?"

"I was going to go to Deniel's," I explain. "I didn't have a chance to pick up the teacups before work today. But if you're tired, I don't have to stay—"

"It's fine," he says. "Don't worry about me." He eyes the sky. "Might rain, though."

I can't tell what he's noticed; the sky is clear. "Well, if it starts raining, feel free to knock and come get me."

Entero studies me. "You don't think you'll notice the sound of the rain?"

I glance away as we walk. "When I'm alone with Deniel I have a tendency to forget my surroundings."

"Hmm." He doesn't sound as upset by that as I expected, and I risk a glance at him. "You really like him," Entero says.

Was that a question? "Yes," I say. "I really do." And then impulsively add, "What about you?"

"You mean, what do I think of Deniel?" he clarifies.

I *am* interested in that, but I say, "No."

"Ah." Entero looks up at the sky for a moment. "You're my charge, Miyara, and I'm your *only* guard, which means you always come first. Even if I had the time, I don't think I'd ever feel comfortable being with someone who I couldn't make my priority. Who would always know that she could never be first in my mind. I'd want her to know I'd always be there for her and for to never have reason to doubt that. But I can't offer that. So you don't have to worry about me getting distracted."

I close my eyes. "I'm sorry, Entero."

"I signed up for this," he reminds me. "It's not as if my position would be better as a spy. I don't think I'd feel comfortable being with someone I always had to lie to, either. And I wouldn't want someone who'd be okay with the lies."

"What if you could do something else?" I ask. "Have you ever wanted to?"

Entero rolls his eyes. "People don't tend to end up in my line of work when they have lots of options, Miyara."

"That's not what I asked."

"Fine." He looks at me directly. "No, I haven't ever wanted to do something different. This life has always suited me, and I'm not ashamed of my choices."

"And if that changes?" I ask him quietly. "If you decide you do want something different, what then?"

Entero shrugs. "Probably nothing. We can't all just quit one life and start over fresh. And, as I said, I'm not sorry about who I am."

"Even if it means being alone."

"Wouldn't want to be with someone who couldn't handle all of me anyway," he says. "Are you satisfied?"

"Never." I smile. "But I'm glad you're at peace with yourself. You *have* been doing a lot of thinking today."

He snorts. "You can't leave anything alone, can you?"

"I will if you ask," I say honestly.

"But you'll worry about it anyway," Entero says, resigned.

"Yes," I admit.

He's quiet for a minute, and I think we're going to leave it at that, when he abruptly says, "Don't tell her."

"I would not," I say seriously. If he's not willing or able to fight for this, I will not push.

And who am I to judge the lines he has drawn for himself, the choices he's made? Lorwyn made that clear to me; maybe to him, too.

"Thank you," he says.

"I'm not sure this deserves thanks."

"Given how hard it seems to be for you to keep your fingers out of anything, I will take it," he drawls.

That startles me into a laugh. What Miyara have I become, that my own guard should expect me to push so? "If there's ever anything besides silence I can give you that would help you find happiness, I hope you will let me know," I say.

"I'll keep that in mind," he says, "but don't wait for it."

All through this conversation, he has been confident, assured. He knows who he is, and has for some time. I won't wait for him to change.

But if he decides to, I hope I'm there to witness it.

Deniel is breathless as he opens the door. "Sorry," he says.

I blink. "For what?"

"Oh." He runs a hand through his hair. I now know it is not *always* disheveled, but it has returned to its natural state tonight. "Nothing. I was distracted, so it took me a bit to come to the door. Please, come in."

I hadn't noticed it was that much longer than usual, but now I'm curious. "Distracted by what?"

"Oh, just work," Deniel says.

This late? "Something special?"

"Just busy," he says.

It takes me a moment to realize he's being evasive, which is so unlike him I'm not sure what to make of it.

"I'm sorry, it sounds like you've had a long day." I fiddle with my wrists. "Should I come back another time?"

Deniel stops and turns around abruptly. He reaches over and takes my hands in his, gazing at me intently. "I'm sorry," he says again. "I'd like you to stay. If you want to."

Suddenly shy, all I do is nod. Deniel's thumb brushes over my bare wrist, a flutter of a touch, as he releases my hands, and I'm frozen like a statue, not even daring to breathe, not sure why.

Deniel holds out an upturned palm. Everything suddenly feels so surreal, so important and fraught, but like I'm stepping into a whole new world, I place my palm in his, and our hands close around each other.

I'm blushing, but I make myself meet his eyes.

I'm not sure what the look in his eyes is. It's intent, but warm, and somehow fragile. I squeeze his hand, and he smiles.

"Let me show you what I found," he says, and leads me forward.

Two teacups sit on his dining table. They're clearly a pair, though not identical: the shapes are slightly warped in different ways, and the deep green paint at the top drips down the sides in unique patterns.

I love them immediately.

"I didn't realize how I'd messed them up before I fired them," Deniel confesses, running his free hand through his hair. "So then I thought I'd try a different way of glazing to mitigate the effect, and it exacerbated it instead."

"Are you sure you can't sell these?" I breathe. "They're incredible."

His smile is rueful. "Maybe someday I'll be able to afford to let people know I have a fondness for strange experiments, but not yet."

I glance up at him. "How much more successful could you possibly need to be?"

"It's not about success, or even skill, as much as it's about establishment," Deniel explains. "My shop has a good reputation, but it's not at the point where that's just... accepted as a matter of course, I suppose. Without that security, there's nothing to keep me from being well-known one day and out of work the next."

That must be especially true for him, being Gaellani in a city whose leaders were allowing the Gaellani to be forced out. He couldn't afford to take those kinds of risks in his position.

"Well," I say, "when you get to that point, remember to describe those pieces as 'eccentric' rather than strange. People are very comfortable paying for eccentricity from artists."

"That's true," Deniel acknowledges with a wry smile. "But they really are strange, and I'd like to be able to call them that openly. Someday."

His voice ends on a wistful note, and I squeeze his hand. "Someday."

He glances down at our hands, then back up at me uncertainly. "Do you want to try them out?"

Could he be worried I don't like them in truth? "Very much so," I say fervently. "I just. Ah. Do not especially wish to hurry to release your hand."

Deniel bursts into laughter. Then he lifts our joined hands and bows over them.

His eyes flick up to mine, a question in them, though I don't know what it is.

Gently, he kisses the back of my hand.

My eyes widen, and I am amazed I don't combust on the spot.

Perhaps I'm wrong—I certainly *feel* as though I'm entirely aflame.

But Deniel is blushing, too, as he unlocks our hands with a smile. "I'm not going anywhere," he says, and it feels like a promise.

Oh, certainly, I will definitely be able to focus now.

I carefully pick one cup up, turning it around and getting a feel for the weight of it in my hand, then the other, studying its grooves from all sides and trying to think how I can present each best during the ceremony.

I set them down with an absent bow and pull out my new portable tea kit. Opening the compartment, I'm relieved to find that the cups will both fit inside easily, and I barely have to adjust the interior padding at all to keep them from bouncing around.

Deniel has been watching me silently, and I'm not sure how long it's been because I really do lose track of my surroundings with him. He doesn't seem to be waiting for anything from me in particular, just... watching, and I find myself blurting, "May I perform the tea ceremony for you?"

He blinks, startled. "Are you sure you don't mind?"

"Not at all," I say. "It would be my pleasure to serve you."

He nods, shyly. "Then I'd like that."

All at once I'm filled with a combination of excitement and nervousness—the combination of feelings is no longer strange to me around Deniel, but it is definitely acute.

"Let me try with my tea set, if you don't mind," I babble, and when I notice my hand is shaking slightly from the jolt of nervous energy I turn my back on him briefly to take a breath.

I've never served him tea before. Not really; not like this.

I've been studying, but he's gone to so much trouble for me, and—what if I'm not any better?

It's not that I mind serving Deniel. It's that I want too badly for it to go well.

I want to impress him. And that will interfere with shaping an experience that's about him, not me.

Earlier, when I served Ostario, I could feel a change in the ceremony, like I was finally part of it. But not as a bridge; something was off, there.

Here, I don't know how I can keep myself out of the ceremony, because it's Deniel, and I can't stop focusing on him, and so many of my thoughts about him are bound up, selfishly, with myself, and my own desires.

Why do I want to impress him? Aside from the obvious?

I want him to think I'm wonderful, even if I don't believe it—no, I want to *be* wonderful, for him. I want him to think I'm worthwhile, that I'm not wasting my time, or his. Because *he's* wonderful, and I want him to know that, to know that I know it.

There.

I relocate to the floor opposite the small sofa table. The tea ceremony can only properly be performed on the ground. Deniel settles gingerly across from me, and then his jaw drops when I withdraw the dragon teapot from the tea set.

"Is that—?" he whispers, eyes going wide and words breaking off like he's strangled.

Already I've managed to eclipse myself, but at his failure to form words I can't help but smile.

"The old woman did say it was a gift to me." I shrug. "If Talmeri wants me to continue displaying it at the shop, she can give me enough marks to purchase its equal."

"No such thing," Deniel breathes, reaching out and then aborting the gesture.

"No, there isn't," I agree, watching him. "You can touch it. I'll let you know when I'm ready."

Deniel can still barely bring himself to touch the pot, and when he does, his touch is reverent. Like he can't quite believe this magic is within his reach.

Finally, I withdraw it from his grasp, smiling at how totally awed he looks at me. "I'm not going anywhere," I echo him. "But for now, let me serve you."

I begin, flowing into the ritual movements of the ceremony.

The ceremony is different from the start. I can feel it, though I can't pinpoint exactly how. I try to focus on each movement, perfecting it, though I falter more than once. It's not the unfamiliar tools; it's my own nervousness, the pressure of my own desire to make Deniel's experience as wonderful as he deserves at odds with my conviction whether I *can* make him feel that much for himself.

As I bring the ceremony to a close, I find I'm no less a mix of excitement and nervousness than I was when I started.

Deniel sips his tea, not looking at me. I sit still, not sure what to do or say now.

And Master Karekin thought I didn't need any help with the etiquette portion of tea mastery. Ha!

When I'm about ready to erupt from my skin, Deniel finally looks at me.

There's a part of his expression that's like the warmth in his eyes earlier, and the awe from seeing the dragon pot, and a strange hint of—sadness? Like when he couldn't believe that magic was before him.

"Miyara," Deniel says. "I... honestly don't know what to say. That was amazing."

Wonder. That's what his expression is.

"I didn't understand the tea ceremony could be like that," he says. "I knew you had to be good, obviously, but Miyara, that—"

"It wasn't that good." My performance doesn't merit that degree of praise, and it makes me uncomfortable to accept it from him. "I slipped several moves, and the flow broke—"

"No, don't you dare," Deniel interrupts me so sternly I do break off in surprise. "You were the one who told me these teacups I gave you were incredible even though they're not perfect, weren't you?"

"It's not about that," I say, rubbing my wrists absently. "It's the *experience* that has to be perfect."

"And it *was,*" Deniel says, gaze holding mine fiercely. "It was perfect in part *because* of those flaws. Listen to me. I don't know as much as you about tea ceremony, but I know art, Miyara. If you let yourself focus too hard on just the craft, the art suffers."

"But the craft is what I can control."

His expression turns wry. "Yes. And the craft matters. But a technically perfect piece of art—or a performance—won't be as meaningful as a heartfelt one. The craft is the skeleton that carries your art, but without spirit it's empty. People can always tell."

As soon as he says it, I know it's truth.

Minute mistakes in craft—well, I should endeavor not to make them, but they aren't, ultimately, what breaks the ceremony. Which also means executing them perfectly won't *make* the ceremony, either.

"I'm not sure if that's reassuring or terrifying," I say.

Deniel smiles slightly. "Then we may make a professional artist of you yet."

I let out a breath that's half laughter, taking a bracing sip of my own tea. Lorwyn was right: this is very close to the traditional blue dragon's blend.

We sit there quietly, drinking tea, watching each other, *being*, as the rain starts to fall.

And then, all at once, to pour.

I hear a thump from the roof, and Deniel winces. "Excuse me. I should go make sure the bowl upstairs is in the right place." He looks embarrassed. "The roof leaks when the rain comes down hard."

"I don't think that's what that sound was." Now I'm embarrassed. "As much as I've been enjoying the way our evening has been going, would you mind terribly if I invited my guard inside?"

Deniel blinks. "He was on the roof?"

"Likely. He's overly fond of dropping down from high places."

He peers at me. "You're not joking, are you? Yes, of course. No one should be exposed in weather like this."

He's right, which is why I asked, but my silly dreams of curling up with Deniel are still dashed. I open the front door, stepping out of the way as Talsu darts inside as a blur of gray, and call over the shockingly loud rain, "Entero, come inside!"

He drops down in front of me instantly, and I back up to let him inside quickly. The wind whistles, and as I struggle to shove the door closed against the wind hands appear on both sides of me to help.

A pair of hands on each side, in fact.

Deniel and Entero eye each other warily.

"Deniel, this is Entero, my guard. Entero, this is Deniel, my—" I break off, not sure how to finish the sentence. We are friends, I suppose, but I don't want to term us *just* friends.

Entero comes to the rescue. "If you ever do anything to hurt her, I will make sure there are too many pieces of you to ever be put back together."

Or not. I whirl to face him, blocking his view of Deniel, my eyes narrowed. "Deniel, if Entero gives you so much as a paper cut, I will find a witch to cast something that will cause him no end of trouble."

Entero's eyes narrow at me in return. "You wouldn't."

"Make myself invisible and watch you fret yourself silly trying to locate me?" I ask evenly. "No, I probably wouldn't."

His eyes widen, and he scowls, realizing even if I won't abuse the bargain I made with him before how very hard I can still make his life if provoked. "I didn't think you were the type to play that game."

"I'm not," I say. "I'm the type that won't stand for unwarranted disrespect."

Entero leans sideways to see Deniel. "Do you feel better knowing where we stand now?" he asks, then smiles at me, the wickedest smile I've ever seen.

My jaw drops, and I know I'm blushing furiously again.

Behind me, Deniel says dryly, "I did wonder what your relationship was like. I see you get along well."

"Is it too late to send him back out into the rain to drown?" I ask.

"Much," Entero says easily, dodging out of the way before I've even thought of lifting a hand to mock-swipe at him. "Deniel, could I use your washroom for a few minutes please? I don't want to soak your house."

"Of course," Deniel says. "I can bring you a change of clothes while they dry."

Entero nods his thanks easily, like it is totally expected to give clothing to strangers in need.

Perhaps it is. The priestess at my dedication didn't hesitate to give me her own slippers. But I'm still surprised to see Entero taking easily to any part of "normal" life.

"When the rain stops," Entero says, "I can fix your roof for you, if you want."

Is *that* a normal offer, too? But no, Deniel seems taken aback as well.

Entero catches my incredulous eye and shrugs. "You learn a lot of strange skills in my line of work."

"If it wouldn't be too much trouble, I'd be glad of the help," Deniel says simply.

Now they're both getting along, and I feel somehow more at sea than I did when Entero threatened him. When did I go mad?

"I'm going to make another pot of tea," I say.

The rain lasts long enough for the three of us to have time to make dinner and eat together, with Talsu tucked in a corner of the couch watching us suspiciously as though we're to blame for the rain. Entero knows his way around a kitchen, too, though he looks slightly abashed when Deniel and I stare at the speed at which he chops vegetables. I knew he was good with knives, but I have a new level of appreciation for that level of precision with *all* knifework.

After dinner, even though Entero appears to nap on the floor, I can't shake the feeling that we have a chaperone. Which perhaps is just as well: I don't know where things were going with Deniel tonight, and I want to take care with him.

So Deniel and I study until Entero abruptly sits up and says, "The rain has stopped."

"We should go then, before it starts up again," I say regretfully, closing my book.

"You can keep my clothes for now, since yours won't be dry yet," Deniel offers to Entero. Then glances at me with a smile. "I imagine you may have an occasion to bring them back."

I smile back. "I certainly hope so."

"So, tomorrow then," Entero says dryly and bows. "Thanks."

Deniel bows in return. We catch each other's eye, and there's a spark there, and an understanding, but I don't know what to do with it.

I follow Entero to the door, and then on an impulse I whirl and wrap my arms around Deniel.

He staggers back a step in surprise, but before I can be mortified for longer than a moment he quickly hugs me in return.

I have never felt so warm, not even falling asleep in Risteri's grandmother's bed my first night here. And I have never been so aware of the pace of my heartbeat.

Finally, reluctantly, I let go. "Goodnight," I whisper.

His smile is crooked and perfect. "Goodnight, Miyara."

"Well?" I ask Entero as we leave.

"Now you're asking what I think of him?"

"I'm going to strangle you," I agree.

Entero snorts. "I like him. He's not intimidated by you, and only a little by me."

"He isn't stupid."

"I know. That wasn't a criticism." Entero thinks for a moment, then shrugs, abandoning the effort to locate the correct words to describe his thoughts. "You two move well together."

Or perhaps he found them after all.

"Thank you," I say simply. And then, "Does this mean now you'll actually knock on the door when you start falling off the roof?"

Entero glances at me sidelong. "Depends. Am I going to be... interrupting?"

I blush, looking away. "No." I take a deep breath. "I'll let you know if that becomes a concern."

I might die of embarrassment having that conversation, but not as hard as if he appeared while Deniel and I were—

"I'd appreciate it," Entero says. "Some things I'd strongly prefer not to walk in on, even in the name of duty."

I sigh. "You are never, ever going to stop teasing me, are you."

"I had no idea how easily the unflappable Miyara would fluster every time I as much as mention him," Entero says cheerfully. "It's possible the novelty might wear off with time."

Would the idea of Deniel and I together ever not make me feel like this? I… am not sure I'd want that.

Which Entero, smirking at me, must realize.

"That's it, we're going to the Night Market," I announce, and Entero sighs dramatically.

And I realize that if we had the introductions to do over again, while I'm still not sure how I would name Deniel, Entero I would want to introduce as my friend.

At the Night Market, Entero helps me bargain for a nice, simple candle that I can use for my altar.

And I pick out the fluffiest, warmest pair of socks I can find, and add them to my portable tea kit. A silly place for them, but I intend to carry it with me everywhere, and I never want to be without such a luxury again.

I'll never forget what I promised myself my first night in Sayorsen, and it's time I start making good on it.

With Ostario's preservation spell active, I pick up two rice dumplings, too, and add them to the kit. I'll never be without food, either, to have myself or to offer to someone else who's hungry.

The portable tea kit is full now, and heavy, the weight of it uncomfortable.

I'll learn.

After Entero escorts me to my door, I pause, weighing how tired I am. Then I take a moment to scoop up a handful of small rocks from outside, stones just like the ones Lorwyn had thrown at Risteri's window that first night.

I rinse them in the kitchen, then layer them in the bowl I purchased from Thiano and fill it partially with water. Last the candle, wedged carefully up by the stones, and though my eyelids are heavy I dig around in the kitchen until I find a lighting tool, because this matters and I will see it done.

There.

In the quiet of darkness, I bow, feeling, at last, like I've come home. "Spirits of earth, water, and air, be welcome in my home."

CHAPTER 19

FOR THE REST OF the week, I drive myself to exhaustion reorganizing the inventory system at the shop and studying for tea mastery in all the hours I can snag before and after. More than once Deniel wakes me for dinner, but tonight it's my turn to wake him for another council meeting.

I pause frowning by the couch where he's fallen asleep next to Talsion. I haven't studied many people as they sleep, but I'm surprised he doesn't look peaceful. Even asleep, Deniel looks tired and tense, his face pale and drawn.

I reach down and pet Talsu first so as not to startle the cat. He opens one eye to consider me, then tucks even more tightly where he lies on Deniel's stomach.

I kneel down next to Deniel and gently prod his shoulder. "Deniel, it's nearly time—"

Deniel's eyes flutter open, and he blinks at me.

And smiles.

"Hi," he says quietly.

"Hi," I answer slightly breathlessly, realizing how close our faces are. I take a breath and sit back on my heels.

"Is everything okay?" Deniel asks, forehead creasing in concern.

"Are you sure you should come to the meeting tonight?" I ask. "I think you might be sick."

He frowns. "No, I don't think so."

"Then you're working too hard, and maybe you should rest," I say seriously. "You've been so tired every day this week."

"So have you," Deniel points out, reaching down to pet Talsu, who inexplicably scrambles away. "And you still plan to go."

"We both know why I'm tired, and my inventory project is at an end," I say. "Is this really just ordinary work busyness for you?"

"Miyara, I'm fine," Deniel says. "You don't need to worry about me."

"You do not look fine," I say. "And I *am* worried."

He sits up, regarding me seriously, earnestly, the Deniel I've come to know.

"I'm fine," he says. "I promise."

And he lies.

I nod and stand, going to bring him a cup of tea.

Whatever is going on, he doesn't trust me with it, and I don't know why. I thought he would know he can come to me if he's in trouble. Perhaps he doesn't think I can help.

Perhaps he's right.

It's so small, in the scheme of things. But I feel betrayed. Not because I think whatever trouble he's in has anything to do with me—I *do* trust him, even if the reverse isn't true.

And that's it: I have never once lied to him, and I did not think he would ever lie to me. I feel more at sea in whatever is going on between us now than I did when it was moving so fast, because perhaps I should not burden him with all my thoughts, if that's not the sort of relationship he wants.

Even if I do. Even if I never want to hesitate with him.

He's not required to want or need me, or my help, or the same things I do. I won't force myself where I'm not wanted. That's not what I left the palace for.

"Miyara?" Deniel comes up behind me. "I'm sorry, I'm not trying to worry you. But hosting another council meeting so soon after the last one isn't normal, and I think it's important to be there. Even if I'm tired."

I can pretend to believe him, if that's what he needs. For him, whom I never want to pretend with, I will pretend.

"Have some tea before we go," I say. "It will help you wake up."

We're early, but already there's a crowd gathering outside the meeting space. Entero appears beside me and Deniel.

"I'll join you in the audience tonight," he says.

Deniel looks at him in concern. "You think something will happen that you'll need to be close to Miyara for?"

"Something feels different tonight, and I don't trust it," Entero replies, glancing at me.

Deniel is too tired to notice it's not an answer to the question he asked, but I'm not. Entero's anticipating trouble for the Gaellani, and he's putting his body in a place where he can be a deterrent, where he'll be forced to defend them because of my proximity.

"Thank you," I say.

Entero shoots me a quelling look. "Just doing my job."

I smile and let that pass.

We join the Gaellani group in the same place as last time, though it's grown. I'd have expected fewer to make it in, given how packed the room is, but they must be as worried as Deniel about what this sudden meeting means. Glynis, displaying her messenger patch, narrows her eyes at me as I pass where she's lurking on the side, ready to dart out with a message.

We take our seats just in time for the reason for the sudden meeting to emerge, as a nobleman escorts Ostario to a seat at the council table.

I lean closer to Deniel. "Is that—"

"Lord Kustio of House Taresim," he confirms grimly. "He technically presides over Sayorsen's city council, but he almost never bothers to come to meetings. For him to show now, so soon after the last meeting he missed, does not fill me with optimism. But I don't know who—"

"That's Ostario, the mage I told you about," I say.

Deniel frowns at the stage for a moment and then passes that onto the group.

I study Lord Kustio as he makes a show of welcoming the impassive Ostario to Sayorsen. Like Risteri, Kustio is built athletically. His sleek dark hair hangs loose against the sharp panes of his face, and his robes are so finely made it's impossible to mistake his wealth. I narrow my eyes at them: they are, in fact, far less understated than I'd expect of someone in his position, which tells me he is either newly flush with money or else trying to make a statement to people he thinks might miss it otherwise.

"I called this meeting," Kustio is saying in a tone so casual it menaces, "to introduce Mage Ostario officially to our people. We will all cooperate with any legal requests."

My eyebrows shoot up, and my gaze flicks to see how Ostario has taken that implication.

But he only inclines his head to Kustio and says, "I appreciate the support, and I'm glad to be made known to Sayorsen. I will endeavor to interfere with everyone's day-to-day lives as little as possible."

Next to me, Entero whispers, "Kustio doesn't know what he's investigating, and he's upset Ostario has the gall not to tell him."

I nod. That's my read, too.

"There is some other business that I wish to discuss with my people this evening," Kustio says to Ostario. "I trust a mage such as yourself has more important concerns to occupy his time."

Ostario pauses. "On the contrary, I think perhaps I should know more about Sayorsen and its citizens' concerns."

"Then I would be honored for such an illustrious mage to join us here, unless you think this will interfere with your affairs?"

Ostario regards him. "I'm not here to pry into any business outside the scope of my investigation."

I clench my fists and let out a hiss of frustration.

"What happened?" Deniel asks.

"Kustio set that up neatly," I whisper. "If Ostario had refused to stay, he'd look aloof, which would make people less likely to help his investigation. If he refused to keep sitting there, he'd make enemies of the council, but now that he's agreed it positions things to look like a powerful mage with the capital's authority supports whatever Kustio is about to do." I shake my head. "Ostario must have seen it coming, but he walked into it anyway."

"Quiet," Entero hisses. "Here it comes."

"One of my fellow councilors," Lord Kustio begins gravely, "has informed me of some concerns raised at the last meeting I was sadly unable to attend."

The councilor whom I'd made an enemy of is looking right at me.

"I expected he'd come for *me*," I say quietly to Entero.

"He did make some inquiries," Entero murmurs. "They did not bear fruit."

I cast him a look. "Are you certain that's part of your job description?"

"I could be persuaded to accept a bonus," Entero says. "But only after we see what it means that he thought it was worth bringing Kustio in when he couldn't make trouble for you himself."

"I had planned," Lord Kustio says, "to renovate Sayorsen at a slower pace. You've all had a chance by now to experience a taste of the positive changes to come. I had wanted to give people time to adjust, but I don't think it's good for any of us to give resentment time to simmer. I think, perhaps, it may be time to speed up the process. Don't you think that would be easier on everyone?"

The room erupts with sound as Kustio looks down on the audience, his threat unmistakable.

Deniel has gone quiet, though, glaring at the front as he thinks. "He can't increase the timeline on that scale," Deniel says. "Too many people have held out against his plan."

Kustio beckons, and a nondescript aide emerges into the light and, bowing, begins passing out some pages to all the members of the council.

Another councilor is apparently thinking along the same lines as she cuts in carefully, "Lord Kustio, even if that would be easier, it will take a great deal of time and effort to arrange the necessary permits—"

She breaks off as she sees what's on the page in front of her, mouth snapping closed.

"I am happy to pay to expedite the process, if that is what it takes to improve Sayorsen," Kustio says. "But as you can see, I don't think that will be necessary."

"I... apologize, Lord Kustio." She swallows. "I was not aware you had acquired the necessary rights to such a percentage of the city already. Have these forms gone through the standard regulations?"

"Never fear, councilor, your office is not at fault for oversight," Kustio purrs. "They'll be on your desk soon enough."

Someone from the audience calls, "What percentage?"

The councilor scans the document. "Judging by these numbers, my guess would be approximately seventy percent. Does that sound right to you, Lord Kustio?"

"Seventy?" Deniel whispers faintly. "Oh, spirits, no."

"How can he afford that?" I ask incredulously.

Deniel closes his eyes. "I thought there was enough resistance to keep him from moving so fast, but it must not have been sufficient. Rich people can get away with a lot, Miyara. They always have some illicit form of income that will never be scrutinized the way it would if I tried to spend such money."

I shake my head, speaking when he starts to explain further. "No, I don't disagree, Deniel, but the amount of money we're talking about here is simply far beyond what that explanation can compass. Entero, do you know—"

"I checked, but no," he admits. "Kustio definitely has some kind of operation running, but he's been careful."

His lack of knowledge startles me; so quickly I've come to expect him to be aware of every undercurrent. It's unreasonable—I'd never have expected another guard to know so much—but Entero, and his skills, are different. "You don't know where it starts? How it works?"

"He's careful," Entero repeats. "I'd need more time to get close, and you're my priority."

There's a note of frustration in his voice, and I look away. More and more I'm certain that, at least where Entero is concerned, I'm a liability. Guarding me is in the way not just of his happiness, but also of utilizing his remarkable skills.

Another councilor's voice is raised. "It's only natural for people to have concerns about what changes on this scale will mean for them, and we should make sure we take the time to address their questions."

Stalling. Oh, spirits forgive me, I'm grateful to this council's long practice at refusing to make decisions at these meetings after all.

"Councilor, I am spending my own money to improve conditions in Sayorsen for everyone," Kustio says. "Is it right that I should be lambasted for my generosity? Is that fair?"

A citizen toward the front totters to his feet, and the room goes silent.

After a pregnant pause, Kustio deigns to acknowledge him. "Does the citizen have something to add?"

"Yes, grace, I do," the old man says. "Lots of folks are happy with the way their lives work now, and your plan is going to force them into changes they don't want or need. You have to understand—"

"Just because people think subpar conditions are acceptable does not mean we should allow people to live in such a lowly way," Kustio cuts him off.

"And what, grace, of those who can't afford to live in accordance with the standard you'd impose on them?"

Kustio lifts his brows. "If people aren't willing to contribute to the common decency for everyone, they can go elsewhere. Sayorsen is committed to lifting all of its citizens up. Anyone who doesn't wish to be part of that is no true Sayorseni."

And in case there could be any mistaking his meaning, Kustio lets his gaze rest on the Gaellani section of the audience.

"Do you have any further questions, citizen?" Kustio asks.

"No, grace," the old man says. "I understand you quite clearly."

"He's extorting the entire city," I breathe, and ask Entero, "Can you report this?"

His expression is dark. "Yes, but it won't help in time, since my presence here isn't official. There aren't any open cases against Kustio or Taresim—I told you, I checked. Without cause, the crown can't just show up to investigate."

I close my eyes. "And since he's a noble, we could count on Istalam's court going up in flames the moment the crown moved unilaterally without that cause. Spirits."

"What would you have done... before?" Entero asks. "Could you have fixed this?"

As a princess.

I stare down toward my clenched hands.

It's the first time I've doubted my path.

I don't know.

I don't know what I could, or would, have done.

In a way, that's its own kind of answer.

Deniel, I realize, is watching me closely, though for what I don't know.

"It's too late for that," I finally say. "I made my choice. I'll have to find a way forward as I am now." I look at Deniel. "What will happen now?"

He shakes his head slowly. "I don't know. What he's doing isn't clearly illegal, as far as I understand. A few of the councilors have been slowing him with paperwork, but they can't get enough public support to make such a risky lawsuit worthwhile. On the surface, Kustio's gentrification plan does seem to improve things for the people who are already comfortable. There's not enough outrage, not among the people who Istal systems are designed to serve."

"Or else there's too much fear," Entero adds quietly.

"Aside from the Gaellani, he targets people and businesses individually," I muse, scanning the room. "It makes it harder for them to rally together."

"People aren't blind to what he's doing," Deniel says. "But as long as they think it doesn't affect them personally, they don't care."

How can we change that, fast enough to matter? It's like the problem at Talmeri's multiplied: she doesn't need just any tea server, she needs to change the game to counter the scope of what Kustio is doing.

According to Deniel, communities within Sayorsen have been working on building community empathy for ages, but whatever progress they've made isn't enough to stand up to Kustio's plan. The Sayorseni may be a distinct community, but they don't feel responsible for the dreams and disasters of their neighbors.

I watch the councilors and audience members argue with each other, and Deniel's right: many are in favor of what Kustio is doing.

But Entero's right, too. People are afraid, and rightfully so. If they stand up, Kustio will target them, and no one who can will stand with them. Not unless they all stand together.

Can I bring them together?

As soon as I think it, I know the answer is no.

I'm not part of Sayorsen's community yet, not really, and an outsider can't hope to bring them together. If someone could, I imagine Kustio has rendered them impotent by now.

So what can *I* do?

"Entero," I say.

"I already don't like the sound of this," he says. "What are you doing?"

Not what I want to do, what *am* I doing.

"How would you feel about my making myself a target," I say.

"What?" Deniel turns to me sharply.

I smile at him. "I wanted to come to these meetings to see where I fit and how I could serve, remember?"

"Miyara, can I get some more specifics please?" Entero asks patiently. "What kind of target?"

"The inconvenient kind," I say. "The kind he can't dismiss easily."

"A diversionary tactic, then," he muses. "Drawing fire."

"And attention," I say.

"Yeah, my professional opinion is this is an extremely bad idea." The frustration in his voice is plain. "Kustio has the resources to hurt you, and he has the resources to figure out who you are."

Deniel starts to say something to me, but the Gaellani on the other side of him grips his arm painfully, and we look to the front.

"I understand some questions were raised at the last meeting," Lord Kustio asks, eyes boring into the Gaellani section, into *Deniel.* "Would anyone like to discuss them now?"

What is my freedom for, if not to serve however I can?

I stand.

"Lord Kustio, I believe you may be referencing the matters I am responsible for bringing up, and since you have offered so graciously I would, in fact, like to raise some particular questions in your hearing. Could you explain the metrics by which you determine how rents are raised?"

On stage, Ostario's eyes widen.

"Ah, you're dissatisfied with the terms of your rental agreement, is that it?" Kustio asks. "And you think it's appropriate to make your personal grievance the responsibility of the public?"

"On the contrary, my rental terms are quite favorable," I say. "My landlord, by all accounts, is very generous."

Entero doesn't even twitch.

"Is that so?" Kustio asks. "Will your rates go up soon, then, I wonder?"

Sloppy. "That seems unlikely, my lord. We have not been introduced, but I am a tea aspirant. As I'm sure a nobleman such as yourself is aware, that makes my situation unique."

"I'd forgotten about that," Deniel whispers to Entero. "Kustio could face steep sanctions if he were found to have interfered directly with the development of a tea aspirant or the affairs of a tea master." He pauses. "But it also means no tea master will step in, now that an aspirant has."

If they need a tea master, then I will do my best to give them one.

"I deeply regret," Lord Kustio says, "we have not had the opportunity to be introduced before now, Aspirant. Sayorsen is, naturally, honored to host you during your studies. Do tell me, from your... outside perspective, do you believe you can know Sayorsen's needs better than those residents who've lived here for years?"

That question's barbs are more careful; it is common to question tea masters on what they observe from the outside. Until now I don't think I fully appreciated this aspect of tea masters' service. I knew tea masters tended to travel, but their ability to be invited inside yet remain apart is unique.

"As a new resident, I have many questions," I say. "Do you believe, Lord Kustio, that one person, however knowledgeable or well-intentioned, should have the right to decide the course of a whole city?"

"As our queen decides the course of our nation?" Kustio returns. "This has long been our tradition, in the service of the spirits."

"Queen Ilmari leads with the support of a council, as do you," I say. "I am dismayed your council seems to have been unaware of the extent of your plan. For such all-encompassing change, do you not think your fellow councilors might render useful insight in that capacity? Like the nobility, the councils are part of Istalam's tradition of service to the spirits, too."

"Would you have me withhold help when people are in need?" Kustio asks.

"I'd love to see your study of which people, precisely, these changes will help, and how," I say earnestly. "Has the requisite impact study previously been made available for discussion at these meetings?"

"The impact study will be filed in due course," Kustio says.

"Legal," Deniel murmurs next to me. "There's a grace period."

And by then the results will be skewed, because all the Gaellani will have been driven out.

I stand there among them, allowing time for that thought to filter through the room. I am silent, but still I stand here, taking up space, and that, I think, more than anything I've said, draws people's discomfort.

Kustio appears to sense a shift in the room as he says, "But perhaps you're right. I do wish everyone to understand how these changes will help us all. I hope we can work together on that course moving forward, and we should consider how best to make that happen. Perhaps you, as a new resident, might consider as well."

"It is my honor to serve," I say, bowing, and only then do I sit.

Deniel grips my hand tightly, and I close my eyes, taking deep breaths.

Entero says, "You made him back off tonight, but I don't think you won that encounter, Miyara."

He's right. Kustio remained too collected, which means he has cards I don't know about. I made myself an inconvenience, an obstacle, but not an obstruction. "What do you think he's going to try?"

Deniel says, "Lord Kustio has bought up so much of the city he can effectively do whatever he wants. I really don't know what more he can do than he's done."

"What he can do," Entero says, "is consolidate his support or eliminate his enemies. Or both."

"Do you think he sees me as the latter?" I ask.

Entero shakes his head. "I think he's too arrogant to. Yet. But don't let that change, Miyara. There's only one of me."

Deniel's hand tightens on mine. "A tea master should not need a bodyguard in order to speak truth," he hisses.

I cover our hands with my free one. "*No one* should need such force, no citizen of Istalam or anywhere else," I say. "But there's no one to hold him to account."

I narrow my eyes, toward the front where the council is bringing the meeting to a close.

Unless.

I edge out of my seat and catch Glynis before anyone else has a chance to.

"I'm not going to lead his people to where you're staying, if that's what you're worried about," Glynis tells me.

"I know," I say. "I need you to take a message to the mage. Tell him it's from me—we met at Talmeri's."

She fights to keep her expression impassive, but I can tell by the glint in her eye I have her undivided attention. "What's the message?"

"Tell him I thought it might be of interest to him to know that no one seems to be aware of how Lord Kustio's aggressive takeover is being financed."

Glynis' eyebrows shoot up. "It may take me a little while to get to him when he can hear that privately. You waiting on a response to that?"

"That's fine." I smile. "If the mage wishes to respond, you know where to find me."

She considers me anew. "You have guts. I'll give you that."

As she zooms off, I reflect that may be my favorite thing anyone has ever said to me.

Late that night, Glynis pounds on my door.

"Here you go, for all the good it'll do you," she says, thrusting a sealed scroll at me with a scowl.

"What's wrong?" I ask.

She glares at me. "Giving me a magically sealed message? As if any messenger can't be trusted to be discreet? What do you think is wrong?"

"Oh," I say. "It's not a matter of personal or professional distrust. That's the official procedure all mages on active assignment are expected to follow, for all their communications."

Glynis takes that in. "It's weird that you know that, when you didn't know how the messengers' guild works."

Spirits, she had noticed. "With wits like that you'd make a fine mage yourself."

"Ha," Glynis says. "Don't want to."

The speed with which she spouts off that answer reminds me of Lorwyn, and I say, "Be that as it may, I hope if you did want to, you would."

I study her a moment.

"What?" she demands.

"Do you want to watch me open it?" I ask.

Suspiciously, Glynis asks, "I thought you just said it was some secret mage thing?"

"Well, *I'm* not a professional mage," I say.

In truth I'm not much of a mage at all, but that answer satisfies her.

I scoop up a handful of pebbles and motion Glynis to follow me inside. I arrange them in a careful structure first, setting the scroll inside, and once everything is set I un-work the seal.

The seal cracks open, and I pick up the scroll.

"That's it?" Glynis asks.

I'm not sure if she's surprised or disappointed. "A lot of mage work is pretty easy," I say. "I meant you'd be good at the harder stuff I'm not."

"Hmph. Well, what's it say?"

That Ostario needs evidence before he can violate Kustio's privacy or use magic against a citizen not directly challenging the crown or attacking civilians. Any use of magic in the pursuit of his investigation has to be justifiable to a court. Magecraft is tightly regulated, and especially as a witch, Ostario can't afford to use it whenever he'd like.

All facts I knew, but not what I wanted from him. Whatever Ostario thinks to do, he won't help with this.

"He promises he'll find the truth, but he has to follow policy," I say, dropping the message into my fire and watching it burn.

Glynis sighs. "I was hoping for something more exciting than that."

"Me too," I admit, gathering the pebbles from the floor.

"Well?" she asks. "Anything else?"

"No," I say. "I have my answer."

I chose to make my way alone, and I will do so.

CHAPTER 20

"I GOT YOUR MESSAGE to pick up cleaning supplies on my way in," I tell Lorwyn when Entero and I arrive in the back. "I put the cost on Talmeri's tab." I heave them down on the floor, taking deep breaths.

"Why isn't Grace 'My Muscles are Chiseled from Stone' Entero carrying any of this?" Lorwyn demands.

I can't tell if Entero is amused or irritated as he replies, "I'm a guard, not a cargo animal."

I put in, "After last night, Entero thinks it's best to keep his hands as free as possible."

Lorwyn frowns. "How do you already know what happened last night?"

I pause. "I'm talking about the council meeting last night, where I may have made an enemy of Lord Kustio. What are you talking about?"

"You did *what*?"

I glance at Entero, second-guessing my assumptions and assessment. "I admit I thought that might have been noteworthy enough to have spread."

"It has," he says. "It's not you who's the odd one here."

Lorwyn says, "You'll have to forgive me if I take some extra pains to distance myself from people when there's a real possibility a mage may shortly come for me and then my family."

"He won't," Entero and I both say in tandem.

Lorwyn rolls her eyes. "I expect that kind of naiveté from Miyara, but you, Entero? Come on."

"That should tell you something," Entero says.

"Yes, that you've taken leave of your senses, too!"

I interrupt, "Lorwyn, what did you think I knew?"

She gestures around the lab. "Look around."

The shelves are messier than I thought they'd been when I left last night, but they've certainly been in worse states.

Entero, however, swears, and Lorwyn nods in grim satisfaction.

"Yeah," she says. "Someone broke in. So far it doesn't look like anything was taken, and it's not like we have many extremely valuable things here anyway. But they also didn't go to any trouble to make sure we didn't know they'd been here." To Entero she adds, "Don't worry, I made sure the place was clear before you got here."

Entero snaps, "Why don't you have protections on the shop to keep this from happening in the first place?"

"Oh, should I just post an iridescent sign advertising a witch works here, then?"

"What about the tea pet?" he asks intently.

She blinks. "Well I can put protections on *some* things."

Entero relaxes a fraction. "Just not on the whole shop. That would be too obvious."

Lorwyn narrows her eyes, not sure what to make of this. "Yes."

"So does someone want us to know they can break in?" I ask. "Or did they just not find what they were looking for?"

"Not sure," she says. "We don't have much that's valuable here. Basically, at least right this second everything seems fine."

"It's not," Entero says.

"I realize," Lorwyn snaps. "But what I'm getting at is, since you're about to go negotiate with Talmeri for this week's salary, you should know that she's in a *mood*. So, you know. Spirits guide you and all that."

"My uncle is so excited to have a tea ceremony from a real live tea master," Iskielo is crowing to Talmeri when I enter the front.

Talmeri looks venomous.

I cross quickly over to them while Entero checks to make sure there's nothing amiss Lorwyn wouldn't have noticed.

"Lorwyn just told me what happened," I say. "Iskielo, have you had a chance to check whether anything is missing, or have you been cleaning the whole time?"

"Both," he announces. "The inventory is so easy to check now! I'm almost as fast as Taseino, and Meristo told me that would take *months*."

"And was anything missing?"

"No, nothing."

"Except," Talmeri says, "the dragon teapot, which Lorwyn tells me you took with you."

"Ah," I say. "Yes, I'm so glad I took it with me. Perhaps that's what they were looking for."

"Miyara," Talmeri says with a small, tight smile, "I do hope you're not serious. I'm sure you know that you can't simply take things from the shop."

"Oh, but look, she brought it back," Iskielo says quickly as I extract it from my case and put it back on the shelf. "That's just borrowing, right? I accidentally brought a towel home once."

"I appreciate your support, Iskielo," I manage to say without a hint of dryness in my tone. He must be utterly hopeless at keeping out of trouble. "But Talmeri would be correct that this is inappropriate."

"Would?" Talmeri echoes, dangerously pleasant.

"This teapot was a gift to me, not the shop," I remind her. "I'm sorry, I didn't realize my taking it would come as a surprise to you, given the compensation we worked out last week and that you understood what I was working toward."

Her smile vanishes. "Is that what this is about? You're unhappy with the terms of our negotiation? That is why we established that every week—"

"We will renegotiate, yes," I say. "But I think perhaps we should adjourn to your office? Iskielo—"

"Keep doing what I had you working on," Talmeri cuts me off.

"Yeah, sure." Iskielo bobs his head, apparently untroubled to find his managers arguing in front of him.

I follow Talmeri into her office, and she slams the door behind us.

"Let us keep one fact very clear," she says. "You are not in charge here."

"I'm aware of that," I say. I knew she would take my overhaul of inventory as a challenge to her authority.

I counted on it.

"Do you? Because that means you don't decide," she continues, "who works here when. You don't use *my business* to promise favors."

"I didn't promise any favors from you, since those are not mine to give," I say. "I promised them something I *am* solely responsible for. You made me responsible for inventory, grace, and I have taken that responsibility seriously. I'm sorry we seem to have had a misunderstanding about how this was supposed to work. Perhaps, in the future, if you don't want me to be so responsible for a task, could you give me more specifics when you task me with it? Maybe that will help alleviate potential future confusion."

I hold her gaze steadily, not bothering to mask my expression or tone.

Talmeri narrows her eyes. "Perhaps before we go any further we should take some time to discuss the scope of your position."

"I agree," I say. "Fortunately, the new inventory system is helping the boys serve customers more efficiently, so I think it's time for to open the tea ceremony room."

Talmeri frowns. "Already?"

"No time to waste," I say, not giving her time to regroup. "I got the portable set to practice, and so I have been. I have some thoughts for aesthetic changes to make to the room that I'd like your feedback on before we discuss the advance, but more to the point you're much more familiar with both running this business as well as the shop's clientele. I thought perhaps we could discuss the best way for the shop to present this new avenue and work that out together."

Talmeri studies me, clearly suspicious, probably thinking I hold a grudge after last week and want to steal her ideas.

But not, ultimately, so suspicious to outweigh how much she wants this for her shop right away.

"Let's discuss, then," she says.

In the end, we decide I'll start offering two ceremonies in each shift to begin with, at a discounted rate since I'll still be practicing—and that will also serve as part of her marketing scheme to help entice people who will then spread the word, the prospect of enacting which has brought out her shark smile.

And in the end, I don't have to exchange any further words with her on the subject of my compensation and how she deals with me. The substantially heavier weight of the bag of marks speaks for itself.

Talmeri sticks around for a while after our meeting to work on her plans, though she bustles out of her office regularly to help customers.

So she's on hand when Iskielo starts to greet a new customer and freezes.

Maveno saunters in.

"Maveno," Talmeri greets him with an admirable approximation of warmth. "What a surprise to see you again so soon. How can we be of service to you?"

"Oh," he says smirking, "not to me."

He holds the door open with a flourish.

I understand an instant before Lord Kustio himself enters the tea shop.

All our customers are on their feet at once, bowing. Kustio savors their deference for too long a moment before dismissively waving it away.

I step away from the tea kiosk toward Kustio—but not all the way. And bow, only slightly more deeply than one grace would to another.

"Lord Kustio, what an honor to meet you in person, so soon after our introduction last night," I say. "Iskielo, will you fetch Entero from the back, please?"

"No need to trouble yourself to bring backup on our account," Maveno says.

I bow again. "I will endeavor not to disappoint such faith in my abilities, but I'm sure the lord's business will command much of my attention. I would hate for our other customers to go unattended while I'm occupied. Iskielo, please."

Iskielo flees. He'll blurt out who's here the second he's in the lab, and Entero will make sure he doesn't follow him back to the front.

"Lord Kustio," Talmeri says, crossing the room to bow herself. "I'm humbled to have you grace our establishment. To what do we owe the gift of your presence?"

"Nothing to fret over, Talmeri, I assure you," Kustio says kindly, turning his gaze to me. "I was interested in meeting the tea aspirant in more... private circumstances, and when I heard about the unique piece that's recently come into your possession I decided to make the long trip downtown."

As if it's such an arduous journey from his estate, when I walk it every day.

"You must mean the dragon teapot," Talmeri says, not quite masking her relief at a request she can meet, as Entero enters the room.

The movement attracts Maveno's attention, and he studies Entero. Except for a perfunctory bow, my guard appears to ignore him.

"Entero, please keep an eye on the front while we assist Lord Kustio and Maveno," I say.

"Of course." The customers won't protest when he does the bare minimum.

I cross the room to where Talmeri is regaling Kustio with a much-edited tale of the teapot's arrival, where Kustio's whole expression has sharpened on the image of the teapot itself.

I arrive just in time for him to ask to have it, her to hold it out for him unthinkingly, and me to pluck it gently from her hands.

"I'm afraid this teapot is not available," I say with a bow. "My sincerest apologies."

Talmeri tenses. "I'm sure Lord Kustio meant to ask to hold it for a moment, nothing more, Miyara."

"On the contrary," Kustio says, focusing on me, and I grip the teapot a little more tightly. "Grace Miyara has the right of it. Can you not make a gift of this teapot? To me?"

Talmeri hesitates. "This... is highly irregular, my Lord."

Behind us, Maveno says, mildly, "And?"

He says nothing else, and neither does Kustio, waiting expectantly, but nor do they need to. The threat is clear.

Talmeri clenches her jaw and won't meet my eyes. "I suppose—"

"I truly regret that it's not possible," I say. "As Grace Talmeri described, this teapot was given to me, not the shop, and it came with a condition I will be unable to meet if I pass it on to you."

Kustio watches me, almost amused. "I would very much like this teapot," he drawls. "I'm confident you can work something out to meet any other... conditions."

"I am pleased by your confidence." I bow. "Nevertheless."

Maveno prompts behind me, "Nevertheless?"

Talmeri jumps. I don't take my eyes off Kustio.

"The teapot is mine, and I cannot be persuaded to part with it," I say.

"Do you think," Kustio says, "you are being entirely reasonable?"

As if he is behaving reasonably.

Then again, his guard is entirely in favor of his intimidating behavior, while my guard is glaring daggers. But he has not employed any actual daggers, nor tried to intervene, so it's possible the daggers he glares are as much for Kustio as for me.

Entero's instincts, truly, are not those of a bodyguard.

"I admit," I say, "I am quite curious about your sudden attachment to this object you've evidently never encountered before. Does it hold some special significance for you, my Lord?" Beyond being a means through which to publicly demonstrate he can bend me to his will.

"I believe an object of such value should be treated with the utmost care," he says. "I have the resources to provide for such, when even a respectable shop like Grace Talmeri's might encounter... difficulties."

Does he mean the break-in, or is he threatening to raise her rent again? "There are many kinds of care," I say. "Monetary support is one, of course, but so is time, attention, and experience. And I suspect I am not so greatly burdened with treasures to care for as a person of your stature."

"Is that so," Kustio muses. He runs his hand along a shelf like it belongs to him. "Perhaps when you have so few things, they become more precious to you. Harder to share. I suppose it's true of people as well, isn't it?"

"I don't own any people, my Lord," I say. "Nor do you."

Talmeri sucks in a breath, and Maveno chuckles quietly behind us.

The tea room, I suddenly realize, is too quiet.

I glance toward Entero, and he promptly drops a tray carrying a full tea set. All the customers turn toward him, begin offering to help clean up.

Spirits bless him, he was already prepared for the moment I wouldn't want them to hear whatever Kustio was about to say to me.

"Don't we? Are there not people you would claim as yours? Our family," he says, idly toying with another pot that sits on the shelf.

I scarcely dare to breathe, waiting for him to reveal that he knows, of course he knows, how many other people in Sayorsen know I was—

"Our friends," Kustio continues, and glances back at me, "and theirs. The owner of that exquisite tea pet, for instance. I do wonder what Mage Ostario would make of it."

I was so prepared for a different axe to fall it takes me a moment to recognize what he actually knows, to process that the reality is even worse than what he could have known.

Beside me, Talmeri's eyes widen, and I watch her whiten as she realizes what he must mean.

I risk a glance, in time to see Entero deftly cutting Maveno off from entering the back door.

Maveno smiles.

As evenly as I can, I say, "I don't believe Mage Ostario has time to appreciate lost pottery restoration arts."

"I think in this case," Lord Kustio says, "he could be persuaded to make the time. I think he would be very interested to see an object so... magical. One way or another. Don't you?"

Until that point, I was, if on edge, still calm. And I am, still, somehow. In a way.

But I am also incandescent with rage. He thinks to trade Lorwyn's safety for a *teapot*?

No.

No.

May the spirits guide me, but I will not continue on as I have.

"Are you so concerned with winning the investigator's favor, then?" I asked. "How curious. Perhaps you should consider your family. I'm sure your daughter would be happy to help anyone she considers hers."

"Ah, my daughter." Lord Kustio shakes his head gently. "My daughter thinks she can come and go as she pleases, but she was not so careful as a child, you know. She did not have so many friends it took significant resources to work out how she was managing it. I have, I assure you, deeply considered my daughter in this matter."

That bodes poorly, but I'm not sure he realizes what she's really doing in the Cataclysm. I'm certainly not about to draw his attention there. "I had wondered why," I say, "with her considerable skills, Risteri chooses to return people's stolen objects. I begin to apprehend what she is attempting to compensate for."

Talmeri's voice emerges strangled. "Miyara!"

"Now, now, grace, I think we are finally beginning to understand each other," Kustio says, looking down his nose at me with a smug smile.

"We do indeed." I've learned what I can; it's time to end this. "And I regret to inform you that teapot is the only one I own, and I have been using it to practice for my tea mastery. I require continual access to it, so any attempt to part me from it would interfere with my training."

"Are you quite certain it's so crucial?" His eyes glitter. "I would hate for a contested claim among the tea masters' guild to cost your prospects. You have such... promise."

"I'm afraid within the guild, the word of a tea aspirant can only be gainsaid by that of a tea master," I say.

And the prospect of that censure is enough to give even this awful man pause.

But not to back off; just to try another mode of attack.

He bows, mocking, and steps in closer to me. "You are new in town," he murmurs in my ear, "so I will warn you this once. I always get what I want, in the end."

"I will take that under advisement," I say. "Good day, Lord Kustio."

The entire tea room barely dares to breathe as Lord Kustio, haughty and undaunted as ever, and Maveno, smirking, take their leave.

Talmeri spares a smile and a few words of social easing nonsense for our customers before dragging me into her office.

"Miyara, I know you don't like him," she begins fervently.

"An extreme understatement," I say.

"But that doesn't change the fact that you just made a very bad mistake making an enemy of him. And you're clever enough to understand how bad."

"Yes," I agree.

"But it's not too late to fix this," she says. "We'll let some time pass—not too long, mind you, we don't want to give him time to set anything else in motion—but we can set up a meeting, later, and you can apologize—"

"No."

"—and *hand over the spirits-cursed teapot—*"

"I won't let him bully me," I say. "Never again."

"Oh, well, there's a fine principle," Talmeri snaps, "but a teapot is not worth Lorwyn's life!"

She does understand. I'm relieved to know that she wants to do what's right, that she knows what that is. But even Talmeri cannot afford the risk she senses, and her apprehension of what's at stake is not misguided.

I cover her hands with mine. "The tea pet can be hidden," I say steadily. "If Kustio had any other hard evidence against Lorwyn, he'd have used it to threaten his daughter with years ago."

She tears her hands away. "Don't you understand? He'll just make something up!"

"Exactly," I say. "Which means that whether I give him the teapot doesn't matter. And so I won't give him anything."

Talmeri shakes her head. "Mark my words, Miyara, making trouble for a man like Kustio can only backfire."

"Don't worry. You can always fire me, which will please him, and I know you can spin that in a way that will keep any fallout from blowing back on the shop."

"This isn't about the shop!" she cries. "It's not safe, Miyara, for *you.* You don't understand what he can do to you."

"I do," I say quietly. "But I'm not here to have a safe life. I'm here to have a meaningful one. He is not the first person to pressure me into being someone I do not want."

"Oh, is that so? Was that before or after you showed up here with nothing to your name?"

Talmeri meant that to sting; it doesn't. "Before, of course." I smile. "And I won what mattered."

"Then I'd hate to see what losing looks like," she snaps.

"And you won't."

Disgusted, she storms out of the office.

I take a breath, pull my portable case from where I'd set it earlier, and carefully set the dragon teapot back inside.

"I hope," Entero says, closing the door behind him, "you don't think you're going to keep carrying on your person the thing he actively wants to steal."

It had to have been Kustio's people who'd broken in, if they knew about the tea pet hidden in the back under magical protections.

"You missed the other piece," I say. "He suggested the tea pet as an alternative magical item."

Entero's eyes narrow. "He came here looking for the teapot and found the tea pet."

"He came here looking for magic," I say, "and he found it."

"You think this is one of the pieces of contraband Ostario's tracking the source of?"

"I'll tell Ostario just in case, but if it were, I don't know why Kustio would be trying so hard to get it," I say. "It seems like that would just implicate him in the smuggling operation, doesn't it?"

"Which means," Entero says, "Kustio knows something about this teapot neither Lorwyn, a shockingly powerful witch, nor Ostario, both a witch and a shockingly accomplished mage, do."

"Or suspects," I agree. "And if the teapot is something he wants, it's something I'm going to go to great pains to keep."

Entero watched until I'd finished sealing the tea case. "What are you planning?"

I close my eyes. "It's not enough," I whisper. "It's not enough to stall Kustio. It's not enough to resist him."

"He threatened Lorwyn," Entero says darkly. And then after a moment he adds, "And you. But I don't think you care about that."

"He threatened Lorwyn," I agree. "And he did so at least in part to punish Risteri. But if he ruins Risteri's or my prospects here, we will be able to recover. Lorwyn doesn't have that luxury."

"She doesn't belong to you, no matter what Kustio says," Entero tells me. "And she will hate you if she finds out you put yourself in danger to protect her."

"Oh, I don't intend to hide it from her. It's time to find out where Kustio's money is coming from." I meet Entero's now gleaming eyes. "It's time to take him down for good."

CHAPTER 21

"WOW," RISTERI BREATHES ONCE I've finished performing the tea ceremony for her in the cottage. "You really are good at this."

"Not good enough, yet," I say. The deprecation is out before I can stop it, so I wince and add, "But thank you."

Risteri nods. "Yeah, a tea master performed the ceremony for me once," she says. "You're not quite there, but I can definitely tell you're good enough to be there soon."

I let out a breath. It's an odd kind of relief to hear her echo aloud what I know rather than heaping false praise. This I can accept more easily, and perhaps that is its own kind of failure.

The cottage door bangs open. "You called?" Lorwyn demands, then freezes when she sees Risteri.

She turns on her heel to walk right back out, but Entero blocks the exit.

"Move," Lorwyn says.

"I have faith that you can manage to contain your natural urge to lash out for a few minutes," Entero says.

"And why do you think that?"

"Because I'm still here," he says, closing the door behind them both.

Lorwyn crosses her arms and glares at me. "Talk fast."

"Yes," Risteri says, setting her cup down and turning from watching Lorwyn with Entero to watching me with narrowed eyes. "I also didn't know this was a setup."

Lorwyn scoffs, and Risteri rolls her eyes.

"She did not," I confirm, for whatever chance there is of Lorwyn believing me. "I apologize for inviting you both here under false pretenses, but this pertains to you both."

I take a sip of tea, centering myself, or perhaps bracing myself for what I'm about to start.

"Risteri," I say, "are you aware that your father has bought up nearly seventy percent of the city to force gentrification to drive the Gaellani out of Sayorsen?"

"What?" Risteri echoes.

But so does Lorwyn. "Seventy?" she demands. "Since when?"

"The city council was surprised too," I say.

Risteri is shaking her head. "No. He can't possibly have."

Lorwyn shoots her a look. "You've met your father."

Risteri glares back. "I'm also a scion of House Taresim. I know what assets he has access to through the House, and there is no way he could afford something that."

"But," Lorwyn says, "you're not surprised that he would."

Risteri looks away. "Not as surprised as I'd like to be. I have, as you pointed out, met my father."

"But of course you didn't know."

"I believe you," I tell Risteri.

"Oh, I believe her too," Lorwyn says. "That's the problem."

"The point," I say with a quelling glance at Lorwyn, "is that no one seems to know where Kustio's funds are coming from. Not the city council, not a member of his own House, and not... Entero."

Lorwyn and Risteri both regard Entero, Lorwyn frowning, Risteri speculative. Neither seems surprised that this is the sort of thing he would know about.

"Kustio has an underground operation of some kind, but I haven't penetrated it yet," Entero says, leaning back against the door casually.

"And coincidentally," I say, "Mage Ostario is here to investigate a smuggling operation of untraceable magical objects."

"Which may actually be a coincidence," Entero says, "since it's likely Ostario was sent here for unrelated political reasons."

"But Kustio did show up at Talmeri's yesterday to demand a very special teapot from me," I say. "Which I'm sure is at least in part because he knew it was mine. But it might also be because he knows something else about it."

"Wait, stop right there," Risteri says. "Why is my father interested in you at all?"

Ah. "Because I had the gall to publicly suggest he shouldn't be allowed to discriminate against Gaellani."

Lorwyn throws up her hands in disgust. "I should have known."

Risteri has gone rigid. "Miyara, no," she says. "I mean, obviously I support that worldview, but you have no idea what he can do to you."

"He can't," I say.

"You don't understand."

"I'm a tea aspirant," I say. "I leveraged that to pit myself against him, which affords me a certain amount of protection. What he can do to me isn't the problem. The problem is that I hadn't realized he knows about Lorwyn. If he can't get at me directly, he's going to go for her."

The blood drains from Risteri's face.

"Breathe," Entero says quietly, and I glance at Lorwyn in time to watch her expression move from shock, to fear, to anger.

"That is the fourth time my witchcraft has been discovered since you came to town," she snarls.

"No, it isn't," I say calmly, though with Lorwyn I fear she may take that worse. "Kustio's daughter started vanishing from underneath his nose, and she was previously known to have a public association with exactly one person. He's known for years, and he's been keeping quiet, waiting to blackmail Risteri with it for years. Which makes me ask, why issue the threat now?"

"Spirits take you, I DO NOT CARE," Lorwyn spits. "And if you expect me to be grateful that you've deigned to tell me my life and that of my family is in danger—"

Definitely worse. "I don't—"

"Save it," she snaps. "I'm getting out while I can." She whirls on Entero and says dangerously, "Move."

He does not.

Instead my guard looks her in the eye and tells her, "If I thought you were in imminent danger from Kustio, he'd already be dead."

That arrests Lorwyn, long enough for Risteri and me to exchange alarmed looks at all the implications there.

Long enough for Entero to continue, "You should know I don't share Miyara's worldview or her privilege, and I don't expect you to. If you want to run, I won't stop you."

Lorwyn starts, "How very generous—"

"But if you stay, we can fight him. And we can win."

Lorwyn stares at him for a long moment.

Then she turns to me and says flatly, "Get to the point. Fast."

She's still here, and listening. I bow quickly and, keeping my face impassive, say, "Kustio has wanted Risteri to stop acting out for years now."

Risteri nods in confirmation. "So if he hasn't threatened me with exposing her before, he must have been saving it for something."

"And if he's willing to reveal it now, it means something has changed," I say. "Since the city can't stop him from taking over, it must be Ostario's presence. He'll sacrifice this play he's been holding onto for years to keep Ostario from finding him out."

"Great, fabulous, my witchcraft is his favorite huge secret and he's up to no good," Lorwyn says. "The point, Miyara."

"The point is that no reason has been enough for him to come forward with that before now, because he needs to keep knowledge of what he's up to from getting out. And since the only person before now who would care if he went public with your witchcraft is his daughter, he's been holding onto that expecting that one day she would find out what he's been hiding and it would matter to her."

"The people in the Cataclysm," Risteri breathes. "He does know where they are."

"Oh, come on," Lorwyn says.

"Risteri," I say, "has spent years looking for them in the Cataclysm and hasn't been able to find them."

"Because they're not there."

"That may be, but something is, or someone," I say. "Weeks ago we saw the same eyes Risteri remembers in the Cataclysm. And if Kustio, with all his resources, used magic to block whatever he has going on there, of course Risteri can't find it alone, no matter how well she can navigate the Cataclysm. But you, a witch, might be able to."

"Oh, so this is somehow my fault again?"

"Obviously it's Kustio's fault," I snap. "But Ostario is here because there are magical objects that can't be traced, which means they're unknown magic, which suggests they could have come from the Cataclysm. Kustio is worried what Ostario will find, and he's been waiting to blackmail the two of you specifically for years. Are there other potentially world-altering secrets you both stumbled on as children?"

They exchange a long look.

"So we find whatever he's hiding," I say. "And we end him with it." My heart is beating rapidly, but my voice is calm. "We end the grip he has over the Gaellani, and the city, and both of you." I meet Risteri's wide eyes with my own. "If you think you can do it. It's no small thing, to betray your family."

Here is the next obstacle. It's a risk, making clear to her that my plan involves her deliberately opposing her family. But she deserves to know before she chooses.

And Lorwyn isn't wrong: she should have known before.

Risteri shakes her head. "He betrayed me, and if you're right, it's worse than I ever knew." She closes her eyes. "Or worse than I was willing to believe. But I don't claim anyone as family who would do what he has. I won't." She takes a breath, squares her shoulders. "I'm in. Lorwyn?"

Before I've had time to take a relieved breath, Lorwyn says, "No."

"Lor—"

"What's your plan, cut off his money and then turn him over to the police?" she asks me. "So then he gets arrested, blames everything on the witch, and he goes free while I get executed. Do you think I was born yesterday?"

We're all silent.

I'm not sure anyone in this room can protect her from that. I'm neither a princess nor a tea master, and my word vouching for her won't make a difference. Risteri's might, if she gains favor by turning her father in, but she could just as easily lose favor for betraying her family, or for being tarred with the same brush as House Taresim. And if Entero tries to go public, given his real line of work and the secrets he could expose, I wonder, uneasily, if he'd even be allowed the chance to.

Lorwyn snorts. "Yeah. That's what I thought."

Entero says, "I can forge a trail that indicates you registered years ago."

Oh, sweet spirits, I'm ridiculous. Here I've been dwelling on death and honor and justice. I restrain the urge to smack myself in the face, instead praying a brief thank you to the spirits for Entero. At least someone here is practical.

"Oh, and I'm supposed to trust you?" Lorwyn asks.

He shrugs. "You can't change what Kustio knows, Lorwyn. You're going to have to deal with it somehow."

"Wait," Risteri says. "*Can* you just change what he knows?"

I blink, arrested by all the implications of that question.

"No," Lorwyn says shortly.

"But what if—"

"I'm sure."

Risteri pauses. "Did you try on me?"

"Of course not," Lorwyn snaps. "I'd have melted your brain. I'm sure it's possible for some witch, but my witchcraft works best on physical things. So I could melt your father's brain, but that's not likely to convince anyone there shouldn't be a witch hunt." She closes her eyes. "And if Kustio figured out our connection that easily, it's too much to hope for no one else could."

"Oh," Risteri says. She purses her lips, and then asks Entero, "Could you just kill him? That seems like it would solve our problems."

Perhaps I should be dismayed that everyone around me is quite so practical.

Perhaps I should be dismayed the notion doesn't offend me more. Perhaps I am less concerned with justice than vengeance, after all, and perhaps it's past time I visit the shrine again to evaluate what I am in truth coming to stand for.

Entero doesn't look at Lorwyn when he answers. "Even outside of House Taresim, your father's security is tight, and a lot of it's magic-based. I'm confident I could kill him, but I'm less confident I would survive the attempt."

Lorwyn stares at him, no doubt realizing what he's just admitted in light of his earlier promise.

"It would not be my first choice of plan," Entero says, "but it makes for a solid backup."

Lorwyn erupts. "Don't be stupid!"

"I'm not," Entero says, still not looking at her. "I'm making a rational assessment of the risks involved."

"You—"

"In any case," I interrupt, sensing that argument rapidly morphing into one I should not be overhearing, "if we can't find what Kustio's hidden in the Cataclysm on our own, we might need him alive."

And then I frown in concern at Risteri, who, of all possible reactions, is laughing.

"I knew it," Risteri manages to say, looking at Lorwyn in some combination of fondness and sadness. "I knew someday something would matter to you besides your own skin. Even if it wasn't me."

Lorwyn snarls, "And I knew someday you and your obliviousness would be the death of me, and here we are."

"So are we agreed?" I ask. "You'll help find whatever Kustio has hidden in the Cataclysm?"

Lorwyn and Risteri exchange a long, weighted look.

A knock sounds at the door, and we all jump.

All, that is, except Entero, who says, "It's Glynis."

"How can you possibly know that?" Risteri asks.

"Recognize the footsteps," Entero says.

"See how infuriating he is?" Lorwyn mutters.

"Does anyone have an objection to letting her in?" I ask.

"She's already interrupted our portentous moment," Risteri says. "Might as well."

Lorwyn nods, and Entero opens the door.

Glynis darts inside, and as the door shuts behind her she looks the group of us, one at a time.

And sighs. "Well. I guess it was inevitable, then."

"What are you on about?" Lorwyn asks.

"I have a message from Talmeri," she says grimly to me. "It's for Miyara, but I think you all need to hear it."

My heart jumps into my throat. Whatever it is, it can't be good.

Probably it's something else, but part of me can't help worry he's found out about me and this is how Risteri and Lorwyn will learn of it. Then how will they trust me? And why should I deserve it?

"Let's hear it," I manage.

Glynis takes a breath. "Kustio has filed a motion with the city council to move up the lease termination date on Talmeri's shop," she says.

"What?" I gasp. "How? Can that work?"

"I don't know, you'd have to ask Deniel, but Talmeri thinks so," Glynis says. "At least for the legal explanation. As far as interfering with your tea mastery training, apparently this also checks out, so there's no out there. And Talmeri also told me to tell you nothing she said could change his mind."

"What does that mean?" Risteri asks.

"That she volunteered to fire me," I say, thinking fast. "Possibly also that she volunteered to steal the teapot from me for him."

"What? Wait, you didn't give him the teapot?"

"Of course not."

Lorwyn cuts in, "Why did she try to fire you, for him?"

"It was my idea," I explain. "As a backup. Apparently not a sufficient one." Spirits, I'd underestimated him. This wasn't good. "Glynis, how long does Talmeri's have before—"

"A week."

We all freeze.

"A week?" I echo faintly.

"One week. And then time's up."

One week.

One week, and then Talmeri's will be gone.

And so will my job—I'll be back to having no money, and no chance of getting another job in Sayorsen, not if Kustio has anything to say about it. And he will.

But what matters more is that I'll lose the support Talmeri has given me to become a tea master. I won't just fail her and the shop; I'll fail Sayorsen, leaving the people here neither a tea aspirant or tea master to stand up for them.

One week, and Lorwyn will lose her haven.

One week, and Kustio will win.

It seems like such a silly thing to dwell on, but my chest constricts with the knowledge that in one week, I'll have failed myself. I finally decided to do something, finally decided I wanted it, and tried—and in just one week, I will have failed. Just like that.

"So," Glynis says, "I guess I see the answer on your face, but the last part of the message is Talmeri asking if you can be ready to take the tea ceremony exam next week."

My heart thumps.

Risteri says incredulously, "She wants Miyara to what?"

"Well, Talmeri's officially lost it," Lorwyn mutters. "This whole situation must have driven her fully mad."

One week. One week to master the art of tea.

"Well?" Glynis asks. "Want me to tell her no?"

"I'm thinking," I say.

Risteri and Lorwyn both pause, looking at me, then at each other. Probably thinking I've gone mad, too.

But what do I have to lose?

Entero answers before I can. "By your own logic, this means Kustio must think he has at least a week of grace to get you. So everything else he's planning will be on hold for at least that long, too."

"Do you think I can do it?" I ask him.

"What I think about it has never mattered," he says. Reminds me, perhaps.

One week, to succeed in full, or to fail, completely.

I look at Lorwyn. "I think I may need some help."

"You think?"

Mindful of Glynis' presence, Risteri says, "I have some preparations to make before we can... do what we were talking about anyway. That kind of, uh, trip, is a little different than my usual fare. But I can start working on it while you two... try."

One week, to determine whether I can, and will, be able to make my way alone.

I meet at each of my friends' gazes in turn, see the belief in them.

Not that I'll succeed.

That I won't give up.

That I can be the person that I want to be.

One week, to follow my chosen path. To serve.

One week.

"Tell Talmeri," I say to Glynis, "I'll be ready. Let's get to work."

CHAPTER 22

A FEW DAYS LATER, I knock on Deniel's door. As has been the case over the last weeks, he's slow to answer. Not just slow: there's rapid clattering in the background that makes me wonder what I've interrupted, and why he's scrambling to hide it.

When Deniel does make it to the door, he's surprised. "Miyara! I wasn't expecting you."

I raise my eyebrows. "I can tell."

He blushes and ducks his head, running a hand through his hair, and that reaction more than anything he's said makes me feel better about whatever he's caught up in. He's still being secretive, but maybe not as truly in trouble as I'd feared.

"Is this a bad time?" I ask.

"No no, it's fine," he says, stepping back. "I just didn't expect you to have time to come over this week."

I still wish he would be honest with me about whatever is going on, but I'm too tired to push. Instead, I wearily heft the sack I'm carrying. "I brought dinner."

Deniel's eyebrows shoot up as he ushers me inside. "And you have enough time to cook?"

"Oh, definitely not," I say, traipsing over to the dining table. "No time to work at the shop, even, let alone to dine out, or shop for groceries, or do my own laundry, so certainly not to learn how to cook."

"Ah," Deniel says, smiling. "The neighbors have stepped in?"

"I suppose," I say, unpacking two packed boxes full of food from the bag and following Deniel into the kitchen. "I'm not sure where all of it's coming from. A lot seems to be Gaellani food."

Deniel nods, fishing out chopsticks and the cups while I start the kettle. "It's often the people with the least who give the most," he says.

"If it makes you feel any better, they did something similar when I first set up shop here."

I pause. "That does, actually. I think they were coordinating to some extent, but it's not just the Gaellani anymore. I have more food than I know what to do with. Even Glynis is beginning to whine about how much time she's spending on deliveries to and from my place."

"Glynis isn't bundling deliveries?"

"She is, but Entero wants Lorwyn to check everything first. In case Kustio goes that far."

"I'm surprised Entero can't check for poison," Deniel notes.

"He can, but Lorwyn has worked at Talmeri's a long time, and has more experience with the ways magic from the Cataclysm can go wrong," I say. "If I'm right about Kustio having access to strange magic from the Cataclysm, nobody's more likely to catch it than her."

I'm not sure if Deniel knows Lorwyn is a witch—other Gaellani seem to, but that's not my secret to tell.

Maybe there are other reasons he's hiding whatever is going on than his personal trust.

"Anyway, it's unlikely, since I'm sure Kustio believes the barrier he's set me is so impossible to clear he doesn't need to do anything else," I say. "But there's hardly any point in having guards if they don't get to indulge their paranoia from time to time."

The water boils. Deniel opens the cupboard to pass me the cups and teapot, and blinks. I already have everything ready.

"When did you even move?" he asks.

"I have become all about efficiency in the last few days," I say, though in truth I'm slightly flustered by how comfortable I've become in his kitchen. "No wasted movements, no wasted moments."

Deniel narrows his eyes. "I see."

I sigh. "I did consider refusing the gifts, but Lorwyn and Entero both told me I was being stupid. And since they agreed on something—"

"You let it go, even though you privately disagree still." Deniel nods. "They are, of course, correct."

"Why?" I ask, frustrated with how obvious this seems to be to everyone else. "I may have singlehandedly failed everyone in this city. I pushed until Kustio threatened to do worse. I was the one—"

"Miyara, sit down," Deniel says, exasperated.

I carry the tea cups over to the table, set them down. Pause. Rotate one slightly.

"Miyara."

I sit down and try not to glare. "I don't deserve their kindness or support."

"It's not about deserving. You don't decide whether you're worthy of what person who gives a gift has to offer. They do. You know that."

"Do I? You've tried to give your parents gifts, and they've managed to not accept them because they believe they don't merit them."

"And that bothers me."

"Oh, and since finding out I was a princess, you've never tried to convince me that spending time with you isn't worth my while? That I deserve different opportunities than being with you can give me?"

Deniel pauses abruptly. "Not very hard. And that's not exactly the same."

I wait.

After a minute he sighs. "Miyara, you stood up for people in a way no one else can, or will. The consequences are falling on your head. Yes, I know they're not just for you. But let people express their appreciation for what you've tried, even if you fail. Let them do something to help, when for so long they've felt like they couldn't do anything. The gifts are for you, yes, but they're also for them: they're a way for them to say what kind of people they are. Let them be the kind of people who choose to support their neighbors in their struggles."

I look away. "It feels wrong. When I've done so little, to take so much. Especially when people have so little to give."

"Some things are worth putting in more than you can spare for," Deniel says.

"Even if I fail?" I ask, my voice quieter than I meant it to be.

"Perhaps especially then," Deniel says gently. Then: "You're worried you're going to let them all down. Don't be. Hope matters, even if it's fleeting."

I jam a bite of rolled egg into my mouth to keep the frustration from erupting. The packed boxes are full of small bites of dishes, many of which I don't recognize.

Deniel doesn't speak into the silence, instead eating from his own box, waiting for me.

"I'm doing everything I can," I say. "I wake up and study cultivation techniques with Lorwyn. I eat and drill properties of different teas. I pack my head as full of knowledge as I can, as fast as I can, focusing on all the details I don't have time to internalize, and I know it's not going to be enough."

Deniel fiddles with his chopsticks. "I wasn't going to say this before, but that sort of over-focus on efficiency and facts is probably not helping with what you need to improve on in the ceremony itself," he says. "You need more of yourself, not less."

"*I know.*" Abruptly I'm near tears and furious about it, because I don't deserve to be. I set my teacup down too fast. Take a breath. "I know. You're right. I don't have time to be here. But I've been practicing the ceremony, and the last time went so badly I wanted to smash the dragon teapot into a million pieces, and I decided I'd just make things worse if I tried any more tonight. So. Here I am. Not being economical."

"Probably wise," Deniel says after a moment. "I know time is of the essence, but breaks and processing are part of art."

"Forgive me if I'm not happy about that."

"I do, and as someone who has no choice but to wait in between steps for pottery to come out, I do hear you," Deniel says. "But I think your unhappiness is keeping you so tied into things it's even harder to get the perspective you need to do well at the ceremony."

Letting go, when I'm trying with all my might to hold on, to this.

I try to savor the fried rice ball; fail. "Do you have any suggestions?"

Deniel is quiet for a minute. "I think I do," he finally says. "But finish eating first."

I dutifully take a bit of pickled radish. "What do you have in mind?"

"I'm not telling," he says, taking my teacup and raising his eyebrows in challenge at my surprise. "I've never seen you make a pot of tea with less attention. Don't even pretend you were appreciating that cup."

I blink. I don't even remember what I brewed. So bemused I'm not even embarrassed I ask, "Was it that bad?"

"No, of course not," Deniel says. "But since I've regularly had the benefit of tea you've put care into now, the difference was notable. Keep eating."

Deniel bustles around the kitchen. From here I can't see what he's making, so I dutifully focus on eating. If I'm going to accept food from people, I at least should eat it.

An awful grinding sound starts up in the kitchen, and Deniel waves away my sudden concern, heading for the door. By the time he's back, he has a grumpy looking Talsion with him, who promptly squirms out of Deniel's arms, jumps up on the tea table, and lies down stiffly, giving Deniel his back.

I finish eating, tidy up the remains of our boxes, and head over to the couch to pet Talsu, who refuses to relax, pointing his nose in the air and looking away from me.

After a few minutes during which I fear I will explode from frustration of not doing anything useful for anyone—failing at tea ceremony, failing at putting in every moment I can, failing at taking a break—Deniel comes into the kitchen carrying two steaming mugs.

"What's this?"

"Not a tisane, exactly," he says. "But I think you'll like it."

I've reached the point where the prospect of drinking anything that *isn't* a tea or tisane sounds wonderful, and also decadent.

But I am also, still, touched to eat or drink anything that Deniel has made specifically for me and my pleasure.

Which I realize is the point.

He sets the mugs down on the tea table, where Talsu gives them an experimental sniff and then sits up on his haunches, and tugs over the blanket Talsu always sleeps on.

"Here," Deniel says. "Get comfortable on the couch and I'll cover you."

That done, he deposits Talsion on the blanket next to me. The cat paces in a circle, considering, and then ultimately curls up next to me, using my leg as a pillow.

"Well," I say. "I suppose I'm stuck here for a little while now."

"I will fetch you provisions as needed," Deniel says, handing me one of the mugs.

I blow on it gently and take a sip. It's rich and sweet; my whole body tingles with the sudden warmth, relaxing just a fraction.

But I still can't help teasing out the notes. "Cinnamon?"

"I go through the sticks slowly, so any purchase lasts me a while," Deniel assures me. "I do mostly drink water."

"And there's water in this, and sugar obviously, nuts, and..." I frown, concentrating on the base. "Not just nuts. Rice?"

Deniel smiles. "Correct as always. Thiano dropped a hint once about a beverage like this in Nakrab, I'm sure to tempt me into the cinnamon. He never gave me a recipe, though, so I experimented. What do you think?"

"I love it and wish to sip it all winter," I say, snuggling further into the couch, earning a side-eye from Talsu.

Deniel laughs and pulls a book down from his shelf—not a law book, though.

"May I sit here?" he asks, gesturing next to me on the couch, holding my gaze.

My heart thumps. "It is your couch," I say.

"That's not what I mean," he says gently. "I also have this great big chair, and I am quite fond of it."

I stare, my chest all of a sudden tight, and I nod, quickly, before the moment stretches too long, before my cheeks finish heating at the implication, at his consideration.

Deniel settles in carefully next to me, only one small cat between us. He takes a sip of his drink, sets it down, and opens the book.

"This is the story of a cat adventurer who solves mysteries, beginning with the tale of the vanishing fish snacks," he announces. "May I read it to you? Talsu has heard this one before, of course, but it's one of his favorites, so I'm sure he won't mind the repetition."

I can't stop the smile spreading across my face. It's like Deniel has poked a hole in the dark knot of frustration at my core, and as it drains away only warmth fills it. "You bought a book for Talsion?"

"It's actually the book I learned to read on," Deniel admits, showing me the well-worn spine with a rueful look. "My sister too. When Talsu first started visiting he got anxious when I was quiet for too long. I tried reading my law books aloud, but I swear he thought they were boring. So I asked if any of the kids were using this book, and, well." He shrugs. "Now we just keep it here for me and Talsu until someone asks for it."

As if the sight of the book alone is enough, Talsu has begun purring.

"Sometimes," Deniel says, "when you've been making a lot of art, it helps to take some art *in*, too. I'm not sure why. I don't think it's that we run out of art inside us, but the intake helps... center, somehow. Bring clarity. If that makes sense."

Like receiving the tea ceremony, and taking in the tea.

"It does," I say.

"And," he adds, almost apologetically, "it is Talsion's favorite. And I did just rudely drag him over for us."

"Well, if it's Talsu's favorite, I can't wait to hear it," I say, watching Deniel over the lip of my mug as I take another sip. "As a cat, his taste is, naturally, impeccable."

Deniel flashes me a grin and begins to read.

So I let myself be distracted, just for a little while, by the sound of his voice, by the warmth of his body so close to mine, by the purring cat and blanket and non-tea warm beverage he's arranged to care for me.

When I arrive back at the cottage that night, Entero stills outside. "Wait here for a moment." He darts away.

It's too dark for me to see where he's gone, but he returns a moment later, motions me to silence and to continue waiting, and opens the cottage door.

I stay there until he gestures for me to come inside, and his face is grim in the dim lighting inside. It takes me a moment to understand why, and then I see it.

There's a pedestal, sitting exactly where I wanted my altar, the bowl on top of it.

"No one is here," Entero growls, "but someone came in while we were out. That's the only change."

I take a step toward the pedestal, entranced. It's gorgeous. More gorgeous than anything I could have imagined—intricate work and smooth lines and perfect balance among all its twists.

It is also more expensive than anything I could have imagined.

And like a fool, I promised to pay Thiano whatever he asked for. Which means he wants something extraordinary, some price he knows I can't afford.

Or won't be willing to.

Depositing the pedestal in my own home, without my consent, is a message about the consequences of our bargain, too.

I close my eyes, breathe deep. "How early can we call on Thiano tomorrow?"

"Dawn."

"Dawn it is, then."

Entero studies me. "You're awfully calm."

"Tomorrow, I'll prepare to fight the world again. But tonight, I'm going to rest up for it."

Entero bows. "Then sleep well."

When we arrive at Thiano's the next morning, Thiano doesn't pretend to smile like we're friends, like I have no reason to be angry for his betrayal of my trust, privacy, security, like he hasn't just made our relationship explicitly political and fraught and dangerous. He's not cruel; he doesn't rub anything in. He just opens the door, and steps back, and without saying a word I storm inside.

When the door clangs shut behind me, I whirl, Entero a silent shadow behind me. "What do you want."

Thiano crosses his arms. "I want you to stay out of this Kustio thing."

Of all things, *that*? "A little late for that," I snap.

He continues as if I haven't interrupted. "I don't want you to just pretend you'll stay out of it and walk away, though I don't think that's who you are. You're a person who keeps your promises, in letter and spirit."

"That's why you set up the bargain that way," I say softly, furiously.

"Drop the whole thing," Thiano says. "That's the price."

I can hardly even conceive of what he's asking. Of course I can't just drop this. What does he want, for me to take Entero right this moment, vanish from town, go into hiding, and never be heard from again? Lock myself in the cottage with my altar to the spirits and refuse to come out until the week has passed, and then go wherever I choose because I obviously couldn't stay here? Let Kustio bully me, *everyone*, and abandon them? How could I possibly?

But I swore an oath.

If I break my word like this, Thiano can do whatever he wishes—seize assets, force labor—until the price we agreed upon is met. Perhaps that is what he was after all along, a foreign princess at his service, but it seems too obvious.

And while that *should* be what I'm concerned about, in truth my worry is what does it mean for me, to be a person who breaks their word? How can I serve anyone with integrity without honor? How can I believe in myself if I know that's all my word means?

But how can I go forward as myself if I meet the price he has demanded?

"I can't," I say. Entero shifts behind me. "I can't do that. Take the pedestal back."

Thiano steps forward suddenly. "That wasn't our agreement. There were no conditions of your acceptance of my choice relative to the payment you owe. You will meet my price, or you'll break your word. Your oath, before the spirits, to me."

Him, a foreign spy—an *old*, bitter one, who could only have gotten that way by seeing and knowing things I can scarcely dream of. One who has demonstrated he can access my home, who can get to me whenever he pleases.

I understand, full well, what I am doing.

"I appreciate," I say, "the work you did finding and acquiring the pedestal. It's exquisite, more perfect than I knew to dream."

"Oh, I know," Thiano says. "That's not what we're discussing."

"It is," I say. "I want you to know that I value your effort on my behalf. But while I swore my oath in good faith, I will not do as you ask."

My heart rate is climbing, but I keep my gaze cool on Thiano. I can't hear Entero moving, which means he will be ready for anything, if needed.

Thiano slides his hand along one shelf, picks up a small metallic ball, and tosses it from hand to hand, the ball making a heavy *thwap* sound each time it lands.

"I know who your friends are," Thiano says idly. *Thwap.* "I know the secrets you would protect—" *Thwap.* "—theirs and your own." *Thwap.* "I know where you sleep, and of all places in your current situation, it's on Kustio's own land." He draws up close. "You *will* do as you agreed."

I smile, and I know it is Lorwyn's shark smile.

I've learned many things in my time in Sayorsen.

"No," I say. "I will not. And if you come for my friends, I will stand between you, even if it is the last thing I do."

Thiano frowns down at me, and for a long moment, all I can feel is the pressure of my own heart, the weight of the air between us, waiting to the move that pierces it.

And then Thiano rocks back on his heels. "Good. I had to be sure," he says cryptically.

I try to take a normal breath. "Would you care to explain that?" I ask, my voice falsely pleasant.

Thiano grins at me ferally. "You don't get to be as old as I am without a few tricks up your sleeve," he says. "I happen to have learned that Kustio will be visiting his little project in the Cataclysm tonight. You'll want to round up the witch and the tracker now to make sure you can follow him. Oh, and don't get separated from your... bodyguard, yes, that's definitely what you are." He waggles his eyebrows suggestively.

Somehow, before I have managed to formulate a coherent response, he has shooed us out the door and slammed it shut behind.

I stare at it, and then at Entero.

Who sighs.

"I don't like him," Entero says grumpily, "but all my instincts are telling me that was the truth."

"That doesn't mean it's a good idea," I say. "It could be a trap."

He shrugs. "You're going to do it anyway, and I'm not going to stop you. So let's stop wasting daylight."

He's right. There's no way I'm missing this chance, and I'll have Entero, Risteri, and Lorwyn with me if anything goes wrong. A comfort and a fear.

But I think about Thiano's test, how long he's been planning it, what he really meant.

I wonder how long Thiano has been looking for an excuse to hope.

Perhaps today will mark a day of hope, and clarity, and new beginnings for us all.

CHAPTER 23

"ARE YOU SURE YOU need to come?" Risteri asks me. "Of all of us you're the only one who doesn't know how to protect herself, and we're going deep inside the Cataclysm. That there'll be something you need protection from is certain, even if it's not my father."

I glance at Entero. His face is impassive—not denying her argument is valid, but not pushing me, either.

His respect for my agency and understanding that I will sometimes put myself in harm's way on purpose have spoiled me for all other bodyguards.

"I'm sure," I say. "Thiano said I needed to go, and I don't think he would say that for no reason. Even if the reason is that Entero is the one who'll be needed, and he can't leave me alone in case..." Perhaps impolitic to suggest her father might have something untoward planned for me. "In case."

Risteri shakes her head. "It's not like the edges, Miyara. You don't understand what we're going into."

"I know," I say. "I mean, I know that I don't understand. But I am going regardless."

I nod at Entero, and he returns the gesture, gravely, stepping forward. "Miyara is my charge," he says. "I'll take responsibility for her."

"Sure, but what about yourself?" Risteri asks.

I want to ask why we can't treat this as a team endeavor, rather than every person for themselves, but I don't want to give Risteri any further concerns about my apprehension of the situation.

When Entero says, "I'll manage," she accepts his word without question.

Then we plan.

I am nearly superfluous to this plan. It's not a position I relish, but I know my strengths, and infiltration, trailing, and tracking are not among them.

Though after formulating the plan, I am keener than I'd have expected to acquire them.

Lorwyn enchants a bean sprout for each of us. (Her glare dares Entero to comment on her choice, and he does not disappoint.) Snapping a bean sprout once will cause the others to point unerringly toward its location, so we can easily reconvene and follow Kustio's party into the Cataclysm, wherever they go.

A second snap will indicate dire distress, in which case we will come running.

A more advanced communication spell is impossible for Lorwyn, at least without a great deal more preparation, and I won't try to involve Ostario again until I have evidence. So we're on our own.

With her invisibility charm, Risteri stakes out the Taresim manor. Entero needs no magic to hide at a place he's determined is a base of Kustio's illicit operations.

Lorwyn and I, meanwhile, are lurking by the city offices, and I hold her hand so as not to lose the camouflage she's cast a camouflage over us. There's no reason to think Kustio will assemble his people here, but since it's the only other place he visits regularly we watch it anyway. We are, at least, not too far from the others, so we won't have far to go to catch up.

Except Kustio strolls out, and Maveno is at his side.

Lorwyn and I exchange a look. She squeezes my hand, and I nod.

We're going to follow them.

Lorwyn knows the limits of her spell, so I follow her lead as she guides us along walls slowly.

As soon as Kustio and Maveno cross a wide street, I realize first that the trouble with camouflage is it works best against unobtrusive physical objects, and second that stealth is less Lorwyn's strength than it is mine.

But I know how to walk without making a sound.

I know how to diminish myself so that no one can see me, even when they think they're looking.

I know how to stand in the middle of a crowd and fade into the background with no witchcraft camouflage at all.

So I tug on Lorwyn's hand until she meets my eyes, mouth *follow my lead*, and weave us through the street.

When we reach the other side, Kustio and Maveno have collected a powerfully built woman in Taresim livery and continued onward.

A few blocks later, another.

Then a third.

"If this is a diversion," I whisper to Lorwyn, "it's a very convincing one."

She glares at the bean sprout in her hand, considering.

"Curse it," she mutters, and snaps it.

Kustio's head jerks, and I duck us around a stall as he whirls to look in our direction. He scans for a moment, consults some object in his palm I can't see, scans again with a frown, and then motions for his group to continue on.

"Can he detect witchcraft?" I whisper to Lorwyn.

"Not with magecraft," she answers, eyes narrowed. "And I'd know witchcraft if he had any on him."

"Another kind of magic, then," I say, easing us into the flow of the crowd. It was logical to assume Kustio had something to do with the black market magical objects of Ostario's investigation, and this banishes any doubts I had.

Soon enough, though, we leave the busy city streets. There's not only less of a crowd to hide amongst, there are fewer people to notice or comment on Kustio and his entourage, because it's only in such an abandoned part of town that they become noteworthy.

"We're nearly at the barrier," Lorwyn whispers.

I nod, distracted. Kustio's group has slowed down. My ability to stay hidden is largely dependent on what people are unwilling to see. But here there aren't people to see, or more importantly, fail to see, at all.

I stroll along as if there's nothing out of the ordinary, as if there's no reason to pay any attention to me, as if I'm just trying not to make a bother. But the fact is my presence at all is the antithesis of all those things.

Heart beating rapidly, I edge us around the corner of a building as surreptitiously as I can.

But the movement is enough. Maveno is paying attention, always watching for prey, and his head whips up.

In the same instant my stomach roils so violently I gag. But silently, recognizing the sensation as witchcraft.

Lorwyn breathes heavily. "We're invisible," she hisses. "Don't move."

Maveno's eyes search where he knows he's just seen someone, and then he smiles, a nasty smile. He says something to Kustio I can't hear, though it's not hard to guess.

Kustio glances over his shoulder, curls his lip.

And vanishes through the barrier to the Cataclysm.

I jerk, and Lorwyn's hand tightens on mine.

"Stop," she rasps. "I didn't have time to do this gracefully. If you move, they'll see us."

"But on the outer edges of the Cataclysm, they can go through the barrier and then head in any direction, and we won't know—"

"*They will see us.* They have more people and unknown magic. Trust Risteri. She'll find them."

Lorwyn scowls, as irritated by her own words as I am by being so close yet unable to follow. We watch as their whole group vanishes into the Cataclysm—all except for one.

"Can you take him?" I ask Lorwyn quietly.

"Not and hold this invisibility," she says. "And we don't know what's on the other side of that barrier."

Then there's a streak of black, and Kustio's guard falls.

"Okay," Lorwyn says grumpily. "I guess you can trust Entero too."

Entero vanishes across the barrier, reemerging moments later with another guard, tossing him in a boneless heap on top of the first.

He glances down at his hand, looks in our direction and says, "You can come out now."

With a sigh of relief, Lorwyn drops the pocket of invisibility and releases my hand, wiping hers on her pants. I do too: our nerves have made us both sweat.

Risteri comes tearing around a corner, stopping suddenly and gasping for breath when she sees us. "What happened?" she puffs.

I fill her in, and her eyes narrow. "Will you be able to track them?" I ask.

"Oh, yes," she says without hesitation. "Knowing where they entered the Cataclysm is enough for me to pick up the trail, and it won't have faded yet. Unless they have some kind of magic to confuse it." She looks expectantly at Lorwyn.

Who sighs, and offers her hand to Risteri.

"What's this?" Entero asks.

"Witch's aura," Lorwyn says.

"Which is?"

"Only of limited use, but this is one of the few occasions."

Entero crosses his arms. "I thought you were only good at witchcraft with physical manifestations. Aura doesn't sound very physical."

"It will be," she says. "It's a physical manifestation of my witchcraft, that will perform exactly one purpose."

"We used to use it to find our way through the Cataclysm," Risteri explains, "before I learned to navigate it."

"But that's not what you're using it for today," I say.

Risteri and Lorwyn exchange a look. "No," Risteri hedges.

Lorwyn lifts her chin and meets Entero's eyes. "It will nullify any magic other than my own within the sphere of my aura."

Entero's eyes widen.

No wonder she's never mentioned that ability—if mages knew it were possible to thwart their magic in such a way, their witch hunt would be a hundred times worse.

"Okay, I'm impressed," Entero says. "What's your range?"

"Not far," Lorwyn admits. "That's why I'll need to stay close to Risteri, to make sure nothing interferes with her tracking. So you watch Miyara."

"Will your aura destroy the Cataclysm, too?" I ask in concern. And not just for the trail such destruction will inevitably leave of our passing—terrifying as it can be, the idea of leaving a barren wake through the Cataclysm makes my heart hurt.

Lorwyn glares at Risteri. "You explain."

"Think of it like a pencil eraser rubbing out a drawing," Risteri says. "Lorwyn's aura will erase some lines, but the Cataclysm is always drawing new ones, always shifting shape. It'll fill in the picture behind us as we pass through almost instantly. Anything living either draws out of the way or sprouts right back up after we pass. No damage."

I take a breath. This is it, then. "We're ready?"

Nods all around.

Entero moves into position just behind my shoulder, and with Lorwyn and Risteri in the lead, we cross the barrier into the Cataclysm.

Immediately, a cloudy sphere surrounds Lorwyn and Risteri, the two of them glowing in the center like their natural coloring has been rendered iridescent in the midst of a deep, swirling charcoal canvas.

Our trip through the Cataclysm begins like my last one: occasional dangerous plants, illusions, and obstacles that Risteri navigates through absently. She's focusing on something I can't see, which doesn't surprise me.

What does surprise me, as we move into increasingly weird and surreal territory, is that after a decade apart, Risteri and Lorwyn work together wordlessly. They walk in step, moving around each other like they're executing a choreographed dance, each knowing their part and performing it around, no, *with* the other.

Entero is never far from my side, watching Risteri move and imitating her to bring us both through the Cataclysm, which gets increasingly hard to do as we go deeper in.

And deeper.

And the Cataclysm changes.

At the edges, it's almost whimsical. A dangerous edge, but stable. Predictable.

We pass farther inside, where that edge takes a turn.

Here the Cataclysm is more active, and more deadly. Magical beasts that try to vacuum our blood out of our skins from paces away, shadows that shade us until they become tangible air we can't breathe, echoes of phantom children's cries pulled from our minds to tempt us into the hungry earth.

And we pass farther inside still.

The Cataclysm's interior is not, to put it mildly, stable.

This is what Risteri wanted to protect me from: not the physical horrors, exactly, but the metaphysical ones, the ones my mind has no words for.

We walk through air and water, upside down and sideways, and sometimes we swim, or fly. The vista of the world changes with every instant, sometimes teeth, or a forest, or a vortex of luminescence.

I can't tell who is beside me; I can only trust it is Entero and not a manifestation of the Cataclysm attempting to devour me.

I can only focus on the witchcloud in front of me, where Risteri and Lorwyn continue to shine, and follow, and follow, and hope this one sense remains.

I can only let go of my ability to control anything, to do anything other than continue to move forward and trust that my feet will still be under me.

I can only hold onto myself, and move, as the world slips and morphs around me.

But the world does, finally, slowly, stabilize.

And I've seen enough to realize that's uncommon.

"You both okay?" Lorwyn asks, glancing over her shoulder, her hair damp with sweat.

"Yes," I say, looking around curiously as beside me Entero nods. He's broken a sweat, too, but his breathing is even, so I'm not worried.

It's like we've landed on an island anchored in a galaxy, a wide open plain with rocks and mountains in the distance, and wind. My legs shake slightly underneath me, like they're no longer sure how to cope with solid ground. How long were we traveling?

"Of course neither of you is even winded," Lorwyn says, rolling her eyes. "You're both unnatural."

Risteri is stomping around and glaring, so Entero asks, "Does the trail end here?"

"No," Lorwyn says. "I mean I couldn't track anything to save my life, but come over and look at this."

I let her tug me inside her witchcloud aura, and the sound of the world becomes muted. But Lorwyn points, and I see the world as composed of shimmering light, with brilliant threads of color weaving together.

Which is noteworthy, because the threads aren't weaving so consistently everywhere. In most places they're knotted, or tumbling around, and in our stable pocket here many are even, like they've been combed. But where Lorwyn points, they're binding themselves over a line.

Lorwyn releases my hand, and I stumble out.

She holds a hand out to Entero, and their gazes lock in a moment so taut I'm amazed I can still breathe air so full of the tension between them.

He takes her hand, and she pulls him in, and they stand there together, silently, hands clasped tightly.

Feeling like a voyeur, I edge over to Risteri. "The Cataclysm's magic is being harnessed somehow to hide Kustio's magical trail?" I ask her.

"Yes." She kicks a rock. "This is unbelievable. I've been in this place a hundred times over the years and this pocket has never been here. Or rather, the Cataclysm has been made to hide it from me. What a waste!"

She's been this deep into the Cataclysm, alone, in this one direction, *a hundred times*? *Spirits.*

"You're here now," I say, "and all that time means you know the Cataclysm better than anyone, well enough to bring people with you without flailing, demonstrating clearly how Entero could keep us from being killed. Are you ready to continue on?"

She sighs, glancing at Lorwyn's bubble where she and Entero are still standing holding hands, eerily still. "No point in waiting around."

I can do this much, at least, and do, interrupting Lorwyn and Entero, separating them, so Risteri doesn't have to put herself between them. They step away from each other without a single backward glance, unable or unwilling to acknowledge what it means for them.

We continue.

This is harder, in a way, trudging along barren ground in a journey that seems endless.

But finally, hidden by mounds of boulders, we hear voices. Lorwyn and Entero exchange a glance, and Lorwyn dispels her aura, washing a camouflage over us all in its place.

In the shadows of the boulders, we peek out so we can have a clear view.

And stare.

Because it's not just Kustio and his people here.

There are more, dozens at least, and they look like no people I've seen before.

Their skin is not just pale, but white as alabaster, a stark contrast to the black of their hair spiking off their heads, and many appear androgynous. And their eyes—

Risteri's breath catches.

A fierce, striking woman's eyes that I know instantly are the same as the eyes we saw in the dragon in the sky.

A community of *people*, people who are *dragons*, living, *surviving* in the Cataclysm. How is this possible? Is it because they're dragons? Or—

"We have been over this a hundred times," Kustio is saying, his tone patronizing.

"And the answer," a deep voice resounds softly in an accent I've never heard, "remains unsatisfactory, because it remains unchanged."

The man Kustio faces is taller than his brethren, shrouded in a cloak black as night, his spiky black hair streaked crimson, his eyes glowing a luminous gold.

Kustio sighs impatiently. "You know the reasons, Sa Rangim. Preparations are underway, but our resources are limited. As the speaker for Istalam, I must be able to demonstrate the Te Muraka will not burden our people."

My hackles rise. "Speaker" implies not just that he intercedes in matters concerning these people, but that he speaks on behalf of Istalam. All of which is false.

"And to do this," the man with the crimson streaks in his hair, Sa Rangim, says, "to demonstrate our lack of danger, you ask for magic that conducted in stealth. How curious, that your people should consider such items the opposite of dangerous to them. I worry, old friend, we may give the wrong impression."

Neither his tone nor his gaze matches his words, and Kustio's eyes narrow.

"I must be able to demonstrate that the Te Muraka are in full control of your baser, chaotic natures," Kustio says.

My mouth falls open in outrage—do these people know the insult he has dealt them so casually? I look at all the impassive Te Muraka faces, at how the glow of their eyes shines, in many of them, ever so slightly brighter.

Oh, they know.

"This magic is regarded as subtle, intricate, and careful," Kustio continues. "It is exactly the correct impression to give. Old friend, if I didn't know better I'd think you'd begun to doubt me. You recall that it was I who brought you magecraft to stabilize your ground and keep your people safe. Who helped hide you from the worst of the Cataclysm."

And that is another part of the how. My mind reels.

"And hid us from your people, as well," Sa Rangim agrees. "And from everything in the Cataclysm that sustains us, too. The life of this pocket is draining, Lord Kustio."

Kustio arches his brows. "You mean you have drained it. And you wonder about the concerns regarding your control. Are you telling me such small magics as I ask are now impossible for you?"

"I am telling you I require assurance not just that you will keep your promise, for I have no doubts about your integrity, but *when*."

My fists are clenched so hard my nails dig painfully into my palms. No, I don't think anyone here misunderstands the nature of Kustio's integrity.

Sa Rangim continues, "We cannot judge the magic needed to sustain us without that context."

"And I cannot give you a time—"

"Then you may find that all of the stealthy magics we have created for you over the years are, very suddenly, not so stealthy," Sa Rangim says.

Kustio steps forward. "You threaten me? I, who have spoken for you for years?"

"Have you?" Sa Rangim asks. Idly; pointedly.

Kustio's draws himself up angrily. "I have interceded on your behalf countless times. I alone tethered your oasis in this madness, tethers that, if you recall, will need to be renewed soon if they are to remain."

Sa Rangim bows. "I do recall. I recall everything, Lord Kustio. And so we keep our promises. But never think it is a lack of friendship from us that causes the magic to fail. They will last as long as the magic."

"Then you had better ensure," Kustio growls, "the magic lasts. Hadn't you?"

Lorwyn tugs my hand. I follow her further behind the boulders, where I see she's already led Entero without my noticing. Quickly, she goes back to pull Risteri back, and I feel the problem: my stomach is settled, which must mean the camouflage has faded. Lorwyn's stamina for sustained witchcraft is exhausted.

Around the corner, Lorwyn tries to tug Risteri back—but Risteri shakes her head, resisting. Lorwyn pulls harder, and Risteri yanks her arm away.

Risteri's shadow flickers in the Te Muraka's eyes.

None of them so much as turn a head, but Maveno does.

He whirls, shouts, and only then does the spell break.

We flee.

I've never run so fast in my life. We run through the plains, Kustio's guards chasing us, and after a minute Risteri grabs my hand while Lorwyn takes Entero's and yells at us to jump.

I am in the habit of following her instructions, so I don't think about why.

But once we're in the air, everything changes: it's like we'd reached the edge of the plains, a cliff, and jumped off—but at the same time it's not like that at all. It's like we jumped into the air, and the world flipped.

Just like that, we're out of the stable pocket, free-falling into the abyss.

"You got us out faster than you got us in," Entero says to Risteri as we trudge up to my cottage in the darkness.

"I knew where we were," she says wearily. "I only needed Lorwyn's witchcraft to find it, not to leave. The route we took in wasn't the fastest. I wonder if my father even knows that."

Lorwyn split off from the group as soon as we were through the barrier. With only the three of us here no one bothers to point out that speed wouldn't have been of the essence if Risteri had been willing to put Lorwyn's assessment of the situation above her own. But I'm confident that we're all thinking it.

"He does," Maveno says, and as my brain rushes to process what that means he adds, "There are quite a lot of routes you can discover, over time."

And then we're surrounded.

Or rather, I am.

Risteri lashes out and is soon grappling a guard while I stand frozen with no idea what to do, trying to recall my childhood training for such a scenario.

One of the other guards surges towards me—

And then she drops.

Not unconscious, but as if her knees buckled out from underneath her. Already she is trying to rise.

I move forward.

Hoping she isn't clever enough for a ruse, I stride up and kick her in the head with all my might.

She falls back, but she's still conscious—my foot might hurt more than her thick skull.

But then she falls sideways like something struck her, and this time she stays down.

I glance around to see Risteri has taken down a second guard, and nearly all the rest have fallen, too.

I watch the last guard double over strangely, never seeing what hit him or how.

Then out of the darkness Entero emerges.

Maveno's eyes have widened in understanding as Entero appears in front of him. "You—"

He never finishes the sentence.

"What took you so long?" Risteri gasps sarcastically.

"Harder to leave them alive than dead," Entero answers.

Risteri stares at him, taken aback.

"Kustio knows all of us were in the Cataclysm tonight, and he must know now Miyara has been staying at this cottage, which means neither of you can stay here," Entero says, spinning my shoulders around to face the other direction. "Let's go."

I follow, but I say, "I'm not going to a safe house."

Entero's hands tighten on my shoulders. "Miyara—"

I shake him off. "There's no time, Entero. If I understood even a fraction of what we saw in the Cataclysm, you must realize that. I don't have time to be spirited away. I don't have time to not be here, fighting this, fighting for *them.*"

He doesn't ask who I mean. "You'd bring this down on Deniel, then?"

My stomach flops. Because of course, where else could I go tonight that Kustio might not know to look for me?

"I think Deniel will understand," I say, even as my insides twist further.

I believe that, but I also believe I shouldn't bring him into it anyway.

But there's no *time.*

"Think he can spare another blanket?" Risteri asks, her tone light but her voice tight, and I close my eyes. I haven't dared to think what this has cost her.

She's probably known those guards all her lives. She hasn't just fought them—she's seen the betrayal they've lived with her own eyes.

Not to mention her father.

"Yes," I say. "I'm so sorry."

"Don't be," Risteri says. "I'll figure out a way to get your things from the cottage. The servants will probably take pity on me."

Deliberately misunderstanding me, but I let it pass.

I am homeless again, with nothing to my name.

Except friends beside me, and my tea kit, because I've carried it with me everywhere. I clutch it now.

"I can get a message to Glynis discreetly," Deniel says once explanations are done and we're all huddled in his living room. "I know how to trigger an emergency council meeting without Kustio's permission. A council meeting is your only chance at stopping Kustio before this goes any further. Tell everyone what he's done. They'll listen to you."

But Deniel would be on the hook, associated with me. I purse my lips, then grab him by the hand and drag him into the front pottery display room.

"I don't want you involved in this," I say baldly. "This is my problem, and you have so much to lose, and I—"

Deniel covers my mouth with his hand. "I'm already involved, and happy to be so," he says. "And this isn't just your problem. I have been studying the law and attending council meetings in Sayorsen for years, Miyara. Trust me to do my part in fighting this."

I swallow. I do trust him; *I* am where everything is most likely to go wrong.

"I do trust you," I say. "I'm trusting you with everything, and I'm going to risk everything. The way things are going, there's no way I'll be able to stay free of my past much longer." I swallow. "Will you still not tell me what's been bothering you lately?"

Deniel blinks. "No," he says, sounding surprised, like it hasn't occurred to him that whatever has been exhausting him so badly, and his refusal to disclose it, signifies in comparison. "Not yet."

"There may never be another time," I say.

"There will be," he says. "I'll have a messenger tell you the moment the meeting time is decided. I'd better get going."

He looks away, and I feel our moment slipping away, the strange conviction that our time is up.

"I'll take care of Risteri and Entero here," I say by rote, and that's another shock—an irrelevant one, but one that hits me perhaps more deeply.

I know his home so well I didn't stop to think before that statement.

Deniel smiles, and my chest tightens the same way it has since the first time I saw his crooked smile—if anything, the feeling has grown more pronounced with time. "I know you will," he says, as if it's the most obvious thing to him in the world.

I stare after him as he leaves, the world shifting beneath my feet and leaving me topsy-turvy more confoundingly than when I'd been in the Cataclysm.

I can practically feel the moment my orientation shifts, and falls into place, leaving me rocking with the sensation that I've moved through the void and finally found a stable pocket I'm not sure how to stand on yet, a pocket that may become untethered at any moment.

I'm home.

CHAPTER 24

ENTERO SHAKES ME AWAKE, and his grim countenance has me sitting bolt upright on Deniel's couch in seconds.

"What happened?" I ask. "Was Deniel not able to call the meeting?"

"He hasn't been back," Entero says. "As far as we know he hasn't encountered any unforeseen problems."

"Then what?"

"The tea master is here," he says.

My eyes widen. "*Here*?"

"Not here as in Deniel's house, here as in at Talmeri's," Entero clarifies. "To test you for mastery."

I stare, my heart thundering in my ears.

"You mean today," I say. "You mean *now*."

Entero nods, his brow creased in concern. "Are you ready?"

"No," I whisper, meeting his gaze. "No, I'm not."

If I fail before the council meeting, no one will take my word seriously. If I fail to take the test, the same, and I may never have another chance.

"So what are you going to do?" Entero asks. There's no judgment in his tone, and I can't decide if that makes everything easier or harder.

Easier, because it alleviates the feeling of external pressure, lets me step back and see that, in this moment, I have not yet failed.

Harder, because the greatest pressure has always come from within, and I know what I have to choose. Not just for Sayorsen, but for myself.

"I will try," I say. "I will do whatever I can, to the best of my ability. It will have to be enough."

And though I wonder if anything will ever be enough for me, I know how peacefully I sleep in this place surrounded with the people I have come to know, who have believed in me, and I know I will move forward, no matter what.

That is who I am, and that is what I must bring to this test.

"Then make yourself a cup of tea," Entero says. "I have breakfast nearly ready, and Risteri went to fetch Lorwyn."

I smile. He always knew what I would choose, and that is a comfort, too. A friend who sees who I am and accepts it. "What for?"

"Your clothes," Entero says. "All but what you're wearing is at the cottage, and Risteri says Kustio has it locked down. I could probably get in, but I'm not leaving your side today. Apparently we don't have time to wash your current outfit or get you a new one, so the witch will prepare you for the test."

I look down at my rumpled clothing. I wear emerald green that complements my hair, embroidered with leaves the shade of white tea and shimmering—or at least, they were—pants underneath.

I have flown through the Cataclysm in these clothes, found heightened emotions and peace and myself. I am dressed for tea.

Tea Master Karekin is already kneeling inside the tea ceremony room when I arrive at Talmeri's. "You are late," he says.

He is not simply affecting sternness with me; he is displeased.

"My apologies," I say, "but I think perhaps I am in fact early."

His glance is cutting. "Indeed."

I bow, and wait.

"I permitted you to aspire to mastery under already unusual circumstances," Karekin says. "And now, after only weeks, you seek to test. Would you make a mockery of my allowance?"

"The circumstances have become even more unusual than that," I say.

"So I hear." His tone is unimpressed.

Still bowed, I shake my head. "You cannot have heard in full, not yet."

"Do you think that matters?"

I pause. "I do believe details matter. But as to my choice to be here, now, no. I will test for mastery, at your discretion."

Karekin snorts. "Before you are ready."

"Perhaps," I say, "but it remains to be seen."

"I will warn you only once more," Karekin says. "You have promise, but you may only test for mastery once. Do not let outside forces push you into wasting your choice."

I smile, and rise. "I have chosen this for myself, Master. Come what may."

Karekin closes his eyes, takes a breath.

And gestures, imperiously, to the seat in front of him.

"More fool you," he says quietly. "Be seated. We begin."

The test for mastery mimics the form of the test for aspiration. The oral exam is as grueling as before—but I have learned, and grown. I have focused on the details, and I know them better than I realized.

But of course, the details were never my problem. They are legion, but they were never what would cost me mastery.

With sufficient study, anyone can learn to brew a perfect cup of tea, or recall all the minutiae about tea from memory. Tea mastery is more than that.

A true test of tea mastery requires performance of the ceremony.

So I'm glad the oral exam goes well, so as not to make me doubt myself further. But the tea ceremony requires different skills, and I know my focus on details may have interfered with them.

"It's time," Karekin says implacably.

I take a breath, choose the tea.

Yes. Yes, it is time.

When I carry the tea tray over and bow, I believe myself to be prepared for anything.

And then the door to the room opens, and Glynis steps in with a bow.

"How dare you," Karekin snaps. "We are not to be interrupted."

"My sincerest apologies," Glynis says, and though I keep my hands steady my stomach knots at her sincere tone. "I was previously instructed to come right away."

"Instructed by whom?" Karekin demands, because no order should countermand a tea master's.

"The aspirant," Glynis says, and looks at me. "Miyara, the emergency council meeting is happening. It's happening immediately. If you leave right away, you might make it in time, but it has to be now."

My hands do tremble then.

"Miyara, what is this?" Karekin asks, voice low.

I close my eyes. Deniel's knowledge is secondhand. Lorwyn cannot speak without endangering herself. Risteri's complaint will be disregarded. Entero cannot go on record.

Without my presence, Kustio will win.

I will be thwarted not by villainy, or even my own personal failings, but timing.

"Miyara," Karekin growls.

On one hand, the tea mastery, the purpose and power to serve I've yearned for my whole life, nearly within my grasp despite the impossible odds.

On the other, people. My people.

"Miyara," Glynis says urgently.

"I know," I whisper. "I know."

I set down the tea tray, and bow.

"My sincerest apologies, Master Karekin," I say. "I must go."

His expression is a storm. "If you leave now, you will fail. You can never retake this test. Would you throw this chance away so lightly?"

"Not lightly," I say. "Never that. I wished for this with all my spirit, and I will continue to practice tea and serve for all my days." My eyes mist, and I choke the word, "Somehow."

And unable to face this a moment longer, I flee.

I slam open the doors to the council meeting, Entero and Glynis in step behind me.

I have failed to become a tea master. I cannot fail in this.

At least I have one grace: no one besides me and Glynis knows yet that I have failed in tea mastery. As far as the Sayorseni are concerned, I am still an aspirant.

I will use whatever power I can grasp.

"How nice," Kustio says from the dais, "for you to join us. I understand we have you to thank for being here?"

"No," I say. "We have you, Lord Kustio. And your treacherous conduct."

The audience rustles. It is fuller than I expected.

"Bold words," my enemy among the council members says. "I do hope you can back them up, or you will find yourself in deep trouble, Aspirant Miyara."

Already, the words that gave me such fierce pride have become a weapon.

Leaning forward, Kustio says, "Just so."

The council needs an excuse to go against Kustio, but give him a moment and he will remind them what they have to fear from him. I cut to the chase.

"Lord Kustio has been smuggling objects from the Cataclysm," I say.

The council member who has been trying to stall Kustio sighs. "Aspirant, I would be shocked if those words did not apply to every Sayorseni in this room. *Children* bring objects out of the Cataclysm."

"They do not bring magical objects intended to be disguised from crown regulations," I say. "My apologies to Mage Ostario, if he is in attendance, for betraying the object of his inquisition."

After a moment where the council waits for Ostario to show himself—he does not—the council member once again regards me.

"Do you have proof?" she asks.

"I am a witness," I say. "As a tea aspirant, my statement is sufficient to require an inquiry. Specifically, an inquiry into the source of Lord Kustio's finances, as he has been using illegal magic to finance his plans for Sayorsen. His monetary promises are in bad faith, and so is his business."

The crowd erupts.

And then, through the din:

"Is that all?"

Kustio has risen.

"It is enough," I say firmly, though my heart rate accelerates. I've missed something. "And what an official inquiry will find will be even more."

"You cannot prove I possess illegal objects, or that if I do they have come into my hands knowingly," Kustio says.

"It will be easy enough to prove how you came by them, when the people you've trapped in the Cataclysm testify," I snarl.

Gasps all around.

The councilors call for order, but in the wake of my claim it takes minutes for the crowd to settle enough for anyone to be heard.

"There are no people in the Cataclysm," Kustio says. "That is due to its nature, and, as the aspirant must be aware, among the reasons refugees were accepted into Istalam. Because it is not possible to live in the Cataclysm. Spending too much time there warps people beyond recognition and destroys whatever it is that makes them human."

When I open my mouth to dispute that understanding is obviously incomplete, Kustio holds up a hand, eyes glittering. "Are there *beings* in the Cataclysm? Of that there can be no doubt. But people? People who can testify in an Istal court? No, Miyara," he purrs. "No such people exist."

Realization slams into me. I search, find Deniel in the crowd, but he won't meet my eyes, already looks devastated and broken.

There is a reason making Gaellani citizens of Istalam was such a momentous ruling for my grandmother, even if those citizens are treated unequally under the law. *They are treated.*

Kustio's framing of the Te Muraka as beasts is not just looking down on them, not just accidental bigotry. It is calculated to keep them as less than people, with none of the rights.

Istalam must welcome people into its borders, but not so any magic from the Cataclysm.

Without proof of illegal behavior, the inquiry I would start will end in Kustio's acquittal. Not least because as soon as they learn I'm no longer an aspirant, I'll have no grounds to bring it.

I will fail doubly, exponentially, in one fell swoop.

Because the people who helped me get here will not be spared.

And the people in the Cataclysm will still be trapped. Maybe not forever, but how long do they have?

The council member who hates me asks, "Aspirant Miyara, do you dispute Kustio's claims?"

Yes. But how?

The answer is obvious—terrifying.

Moving forward as myself, and all that means.

"Lord Kustio is partially correct," I say. "I regret that in my haste to expose him, I did not arrive today with the proof the council must have to render justice."

"Then why have you wasted our time with baseless accusations?"

"They are not baseless, and time was of the essence," I say. "You must take Kustio into custody immediately before he can interfere more than he already has with the course of justice."

"We *must* do nothing of the kind—"

"If I am proved right, to do otherwise will see you charged with negligence."

"If you could be proved right, we would not be having this discussion."

I take a breath, and steel myself. "Graces of the council, I humbly ask for one day. See the lord of Taresim confined, as comfortably as you may, for one day, and if I cannot produce proof in that time, I will submit to your judgment."

It will mean my imprisonment. It will mean the loss of my freedom, forever.

I lift my chin.

The council members exchange looks. I ignore Kustio's haughty one.

"I am innocent according to the law," Kustio croons. "You will not prove otherwise. Why waste this time? Miyara should submit to judgment now."

The councilor who has done the most to block Kustio stands. "In the face of such serious accusations, the council grants you one day to gather evidence to back up your charge. Return at this time tomorrow, or you will be judged in contempt." She turns. "Lord Kustio, if you would please follow me."

My enemy among the councilors studies me closely. Will his hatred of me and sycophancy win over self-preservation? If he still believes

Kustio's side is the winning one... I can't count on this temporary arrest to prevent Kustio from moving to thwart me.

"This is preposterous," Kustio says, but like he's mildly annoyed, not like he's worried.

I glance once more toward Deniel, but he won't look at me.

He's already given up. Our time has passed.

I turn on my heel and tell Glynis, "Find Risteri and Lorwyn, and tell them to meet me where we came out yesterday."

"What in the name of all the spirits happened," Lorwyn snarls when she arrives.

Risteri has been stiff and silent, unwilling to hear the answer, unwilling to even look at me except with anxious glances cast sidelong.

Entero is watching me closely, like he's unsure exactly how mad I've gone.

The answer is extremely.

"I had to leave in the middle of the mastery exam, which means I failed," I say, and Risteri sucks in a breath.

"What else?" Lorwyn snaps.

"Kustio has not technically broken any laws," I say.

"Are you kidding me? He—"

"I know what he's done," I say. "He's certainly broken the spirit, but not the letter, and the letter is what counts in court."

"Oh, you've had some long regretful conversations with darling Deniel I see," Lorwyn says.

"I didn't—"

"Isn't it too bad that there's nothing to be done, the spirits-cursed law just won't allow—"

"Lorwyn, stop it."

"I trusted you!" she shouts. "You said you could take care of this, and now it's all for nothing? Worse than that, it'll cost everything? I don't—"

"Oh *will* you shut up," I snap.

"Excuse you?"

Of course everyone has given up on me, and why shouldn't they? I've failed, repeatedly, emphatically.

"There *is* something to be done," I say, "and I am going to do it. But I need your help."

"Oh, this should be good," Lorwyn scoffs.

"Will you just listen?" Risteri asks. "Maybe it's not as dire as you think, and if someone can solve this—"

A laugh cracks out of Lorwyn like a whip. "This from you? You, who has never listened in all your life?"

"I don't—"

"You knew who your father was, and what have you done? Gone traipsing after treasures as if that means anything?"

"I just wanted to do something to help," Risteri says quietly. "What else was I supposed to do?"

"*Listen*!" Lorwyn shouts.

I step between them. "Enough."

"Oh, I'm just getting started," Lorwyn says.

"Too bad, because I wasn't finished," I say amicably, bluntly, and *that* finally gets Lorwyn's attention.

She steps back.

I look Risteri in the eye. "You knew what your father was, and you didn't know what he was doing. You didn't look, because you didn't want to know."

"I couldn't have done anything!" Risteri cries. "I barely have any freedom as it is—"

"And the people in the Cataclysm have none," I say. "You could have organized an inquiry from the nobility. You could have accumulated evidence. You could have stood in his way. To make yourself feel better you believed it couldn't possibly be so bad, and now we'll never know what you could have accomplished, because you never tried."

Risteri steps back.

"And you," I say, turning to Lorwyn, my voice calm and deadly soft. "You just keep giving up."

After a moment, she says, "How dare you."

"How dare *you*," I say.

"You think I wanted to abandon people?"

"No matter what you wanted, I think you *did* abandon them, but no, what I really think is that you abandoned yourself," I say. "I think you let other people convince you that you were a victim until you made yourself into one. How accommodating of you. How nice it must be, to know you've isolated yourself from anyone and anything that could hurt you, sheltered yourself from daring to live, until you lost yourself. What comfort, what joy, what a life you have made by rejecting the possibility of any other."

"You have no idea—"

"Do you think I don't?" I ask softly. I look at her, look at Risteri. "Do you think I don't understand the decisions you've both made, too well? I know, because I've made them, and I am *done.* I am done talking you both into daring to help instead of blaming each other forever. I am done giving up. I am done not facing my problems. If I only have one last day of freedom, I will spend it chasing what matters, and if you have a problem with that then you can both go home and hide and pretend forever. I'm done."

The wind gusts past, loud in our silence.

I am out of time to be gentle; the stakes are too high, and they're now.

I turn and walk toward the Cataclysm, and pray the spirits will guide me.

And then a sigh.

"Spirits, you are a tea master, no matter what happened with the exam," Risteri mutters. "Reading spirits and eviscerating people with them."

"You're worse than the Nakrabi ghost pepper tisane, and I should have let you freeze," Lorwyn adds.

"Nothing is worse than that tisane," I say, my voice tight. Barely daring to hope.

"Entero is," Lorwyn says lightly, and then pauses. "Speaking of, why don't we get a diatribe about his many flaws? That only seems fair."

Entero rolls his eyes. "Because I'm her bodyguard, so my help is taken as given, obviously, and yours isn't."

I turn back to them. "Because Entero knows who he is, and what it means," I say softly. Sadly.

His whole body tenses, like he's scented the danger at last. "Why am I going to hate your plan?" Then he pauses, swallows; realizes what he will hate more than anything else I could ask of him. "No."

"I'm sorry," I say.

"After all that, you had better come out and tell us what the plan is," Lorwyn growls. "I assume you need Risteri and me to take you back to the people we found yesterday."

"The core of Kustio's defense is a legal fiction that the people we saw in the Cataclysm are not, in fact, people," I say. "We're going to destroy that notion."

"How?" Risteri asks.

"I'm going to negotiate a treaty with the Te Muraka."

Everyone is silent for a beat.

Then Lorwyn erupts, "That's it? *That's* your grand plan?"

And Risteri says, "Miyara, I know you were training to be a tea master, but I don't care how much diplomatic training you have, no one will ever accept—"

"I'm the fourth daughter of Queen Ilmari of Istalam, and they will." I swallow. "My grandmother is still influential in politics, and she knows not just how I have been trained, but that I understand how to listen. She will trust my work."

A different shocked silence. This time I watch their faces, trying to conceal my anxiety, wondering if they'll hate me now.

"I don't suppose," Risteri says, "anyone thought to bring liquor?"

"I cannot believe you," Lorwyn says. "All this time, and you're a spirits-cursed *princess*?"

"No, I disowned myself," I say. "The day we met. But I was."

"I'm going to *blast* you," Lorwyn says.

I wince. "I can't say I don't deserve it, but could it wait until tomorrow?"

"I'll consider it," Lorwyn says dangerously.

"I really have been ignoring what's right in front of me, if I didn't see this coming," Risteri says.

"Spirits, of course you're a princess." Lorwyn rolls her eyes. "What else could you possibly be?"

"A tea master," I say without thinking, then close my eyes. "Not anymore, I suppose."

Someday I'll have to deal with what that means, decide who I can be if not that.

But first I need to make sure there is a someday.

"Why didn't you just say you were a princess?" Risteri asks. "This all could have gone a lot faster—"

"Because it shouldn't have mattered," I say. "The fact that I was a princess should not define how you treat me. It doesn't make me different in the way—"

"It certainly makes you different in the way that you think you can negotiate a treaty with dragon people you've never met before and that the crown will stand by it," Lorwyn says dryly and glances at Entero. "And I assume you came to bring her back to her family, and that's why Miyara told me she needed to hide from authorities and the nobility, so her family wouldn't know where she is?"

"Wow," Risteri says. "You have done a spectacularly bad job of that."

I sigh. "Extremely bad, yes. And this will be the final blow. The treaty will lead them straight to me, and I won't have the power to resist them. So this is the last thing I'm doing with my freedom."

Maybe my utter inability to hide who I am is a sign from the spirits. I'm not a princess anymore, but that will always be part of me. I can't hide from my past, and I won't hide from myself any longer.

"So," Risteri says awkwardly. "Are we going, then?"

I look at Entero.

"Don't ask this," he says.

"You arranged to have physical references transferred from the palace to Sayorsen in less than a day, which means you'll be able to covertly get the physical copy of the treaty there before tomorrow," I say. "I'm counting on you."

"The palace?" Risteri asks.

"He works for my grandmother," I explain.

"The dowager queen Esmeri," Lorwyn says faintly. "Right. She employs assassins. This is normal."

"You're a witch," I remind her.

"Oh, shut up."

Entero's jaw works. "To make the arrangements, I won't be able to come with you."

I look at my Risteri and Lorwyn. "Can you get me through the depths of the Cataclysm in one piece?"

They exchange a glance. Something passes between them that leaves their eyes glistening, but they turn back to me and nod.

"We'll meet here when it's done," I tell Entero.

"Don't die without me," he says, but to Lorwyn, and she frowns after him as he vanishes before our eyes.

"I hate when he does that," Lorwyn mutters.

I swallow and turn away.

Facing the Cataclysm, I hold out my hands, and Lorwyn and Risteri each take them. "Let's go bring them home."

CHAPTER 25

THE WORLD LOOKS DIFFERENT inside Lorwyn's magic.

I can see all the same things as my friends, but I still can't understand how we progress. I don't know what track it is that Risteri is following, I don't know what Lorwyn does to counteract magical interference—only that she does something, as my stomach is a riot of sensing witchcraft—and I don't know how they both apprehend the manifestations of the Cataclysm in our path and circumvent them.

I watch them move, circling around me in a dance, never letting go of my hands.

And I don't let go of theirs.

I match their rhythm, and I move forward, drawing us all inexorably through the shining abyss.

Finally we arrive, just as before, Risteri and Lorwyn shaking from the exertion of protecting someone who cannot protect herself so deep in the Cataclysm.

I'm safe with my friends, even without Entero to guard me. Which is good, considering what's to come.

Then darkness passes over us, a cloud blocking the light.

I hear the snap of enormous wings and look up to see their shadow dissipating in the air.

A woman drops in front of us, slamming into the ground hard enough to leave a small crater. Dust billows into our faces.

When I can stop using my arms to block the dust from my eyes, I see it's the same woman we noticed before.

The one whose eyes we saw in the shape of a dragon weeks ago.

She is staring, intently, at Risteri.

"You returned," she says in a throaty voice.

Risteri swallows. "I was always returning," she rasps out.

"Why?" the woman asks, and tilts her head, studying Lorwyn's aura. "What is this?"

"Lorwyn, let it go," I say.

"Do you really think that's a good idea?" Lorwyn asks, eyes narrowed on the woman whose attention has turned to us.

But Lorwyn is willing to follow my lead, and Risteri waits for my decision, too.

This is my task, now, and they're trusting me not to get them killed.

I nod, and before my eyes have finished adjusting I know the moment Lorwyn drops it because I feel heat emanating off the woman before us like she's a fire.

I gather myself and bow. "It is an honor to meet you. I am Miyara of Istalam, and I would speak with your leader."

Her eyes narrow. "I am Sa Nikuran, and I say again. Why?"

"I would hear from Sa Rangim how I may serve you," I say.

She blinks.

And then says, "Follow me."

We do. I try to exchange glances with my companions, but Lorwyn is studying Risteri, whose gaze is fixed firmly on Sa Nikuran. It's not hard to see why: against the bland landscape, Sa Nikuran is like the slash of an ink stroke, perfectly executed, her features sharp but her movements smooth.

We reach a set of boulders like a gate, and another Te Muraka steps out. They exchange words with Sa Nikuran and vanish.

She leads us through the boulders to an arched tunnel of rock, which we pass through to a wide circle enclosed by stones.

Sized, perhaps, for a dragon.

"Wait now," Sa Nikuran says.

"For what?" Risteri blurts.

Sa Nikuran cuts a glance at her. "Te Murak."

It is soon clear what she means, as Te Muraka file through the archway and take up positions behind stones, and I count as best I can. They number in the dozens.

But not the hundreds.

Then the sky darkens, and I look up to see it is filled with dragons, soaring in.

They circle high above us, and some descend to land behind their brethren outside the circle, each alighting a boom that shakes the very ground.

"Miyara, I hope you know what you're doing," Lorwyn whispers in my ear.

"Indeed," Sa Nikuran says, stepping in front of us.

Her form blurs, and she launches into the air.

And right above us, she transforms into a crimson dragon.

The first pump of her wings sends such a torrent of air down that we're flattened on the ground.

I already understood that these people are dragons, or I thought I did. But now not only is the evidence incontrovertible, I begin to feel, in my bones, what that means.

By the time I'm able to take to my feet again, Sa Nikuran is directly above the circle. Her head draws back, and she exhales a jet of flame.

Frozen, I can only watch in awe as the flame hits the rocks that surround us, starting from the arched gate. Sa Nikuran turns, meticulously breathing her precise flame around the circle, leaving us sealed in radiant obsidian.

And with that display of the degree and discipline of Te Muraka power, only then does Sa Rangim enter.

He is as imposing as I remember. But although I feel his heat, it is more muted than Sa Nikuran's—not a slap, but a controlled burn.

And, I understand, more dangerous for it.

"I am Sa Rangim, of Te Murak," he says, inclining a bow toward me.

At the perfectly correct angle for a ruler greeting a foreign dignitary. I bow in return, two shades deeper, covering my surprise. Given their acceptance of Kustio's arguments, I'd thought them largely ignorant of Istalam, but that is apparently not a complete picture.

"I am Miyara of Istalam," I reply. "My companions, Lorwyn and Risteri. Thank you for your grace in meeting us."

"Your companions," he rumbles, "do not merit your place name?"

"They merit whatever names they choose for themselves," I say. "Names are more than places; they are families and homes."

"An evasion."

"A courtesy," I say, "to them."

Sa Rangim waits expectantly.

Lorwyn says, "Lorwyn, Witch of the Gaellani."

"I see," he says, and turns to Risteri.

After a moment, she says, "Risteri of Sayorsen."

"You hesitated," he notes. "Do you not customarily introduce yourself thus?"

Risteri looks at me in query, and I nod. "No. Until recently I introduced myself as Risteri of Taresim."

The name registers. "You are with Lord Kustio, then?"

"No. But he is my birth father."

"You renounce him, then."

"Emphatically. But the city of Sayorsen is my home."

Sa Rangim circles all of us, studying. I'm close enough to see the tiny hairs on the back of Lorwyn's neck standing on end, be it because of magic or her natural sense of danger.

But although I have deduced Sa Rangim is not to be trifled with, my hackles are not raised. Which is curious and not, clearly, reciprocal.

How can I make him see we are not like Kustio? Because that is where we must begin, if we are to move forward.

"And you, the witch, the Gaellani," Sa Rangim says. "You do not claim Istalam either."

Lorwyn scowls, and I silently urge her not to slam Istalam in front of all the Te Muraka. "Istalam's welcome of witches and Gaellani has varied," she bites out.

I dare to breathe. A far more diplomatic response than I would have expected—or than Istalam may deserve.

But then Sa Rangim's attention is back on me. "But you claim Istalam," he says.

"I do," I say. "I am a daughter of the queen, and serving the people of Istalam is my purpose."

There is a rustle at that, and only then do I realize not just how eerily silent the Te Muraka have been, but now that even from a distance they can hear us.

"You keep saying you are here to serve," Sa Rangim says. "How do you propose to do so?"

Tomorrow, I don't know.

Today, I do.

I set my tea case on the ground and bow over it. "Sa Rangim, if I may, before we continue meeting each other, I would be honored to serve you tea."

He cocks his head, considering me. "The tea ceremony," he says. "I witnessed one, long ago. You are an adept at its practice?"

"I am."

The ease of the certainty in my words startles me a little, but at the same time I feel as though a lock has clicked into place inside me.

I will never claim the title of tea master, now. But I am adept, certification or no.

"Very well," he says. "How do we begin?"

I bow. "Could I prevail upon you for water?"

"We will provide water," he agrees, and instants later a Te Muraka appears at his side with a glass pitcher. "Will this be sufficient?"

"More than," I say, and turn to Lorwyn. "Will you heat it for me, please?"

"How will she heat it?" Sa Rangim interrupts.

"With your permission, with witchcraft."

His eyes narrow. "We can create fire for you."

"I do not need fire," I explain. "The pieces I have on hand will not tolerate an open flame. I need the water heated to a specific temperature to correctly brew these particular leaves."

The blue dragon's blend. Perhaps it is best not to name aloud, now. Lorwyn can see what it is clearly enough.

She puts in, "It will barely take any magic. I doubt you will notice the difference."

"I will," Sa Rangim says, "but you may proceed."

"Then please, be seated," I say, and glance over my shoulder. "Both of you too, please." The Te Muraka can lurk if they wish, but it will not create a good experience for the guest if all of us are looming.

I carefully set out the tea set, shuffling the sweet buns and socks inside so as not to interfere with my impression, and reflect on what I am about to do. This is no private ceremony, and the guest has little idea of what to expect. This is no tea room, and I can't control any of the atmospheric variables.

I can control myself.

But I won't.

This is the tea ceremony in its barest form. There is no bridge but what I make, what I bring, so I must bring all of myself.

And I am not afraid.

I am a surging wave.

Sa Rangim takes in the image of the teapot, and me behind it, watching me through a heavy-lidded gaze.

Spirits guide me.

"Ready, Miyara," Lorwyn says quietly.

I bow, holding the tray steady.

And begin.

And from the beginning, I know this is right.

I've listened, and listened well, and I know what of me my guest needs to see in return. He needs to see service, and welcome, and commitment, and fight.

I know who I am today, and I am all of those things.

I perform the tea ceremony, and I feel as though every nerve is alive and dancing within me, conducting the flow of the magic of the ceremony through me, and my guest, into the dragon teapot and its witched water.

And when I pour the tea, a cluster of steam rises into the air.

I offer a cup to Sa Rangim, and only then do I see that the steam has stopped rising.

I blink, almost dropping the teapot.

The steam has clustered in the shape of a miniature dragon.

And as I watch, the lines of the dragon fill in, turning blue.

A baby dragon, floating before me in the air.

It turns golden eyes on me, then shivers.

Flaps its wings ineffectually.

And falls.

Without thinking, I drop the teapot, reaching out to catch the baby dragon.

The crash never comes, because the instant I moved, so did Sa Rangim, reaching underneath to catch the priceless teapot in a move as fast as Entero.

The baby dragon nuzzles my hand, and I gape, feeling its soft, smooth, warm scales in my hands and not understanding.

"Is this your magic?" I whisper.

"No," Sa Rangim says, his eyes now glowing. "It is yours, and all of ours."

The dragon shivers, then huffs out a breath through its nose made of smoke, flickers of fire in it.

"If they can breathe out fire, how can they possibly be cold?" I wonder.

"Perhaps it is cold outside the steaming warmth of your teapot," Sa Rangim suggests.

It probably speaks poorly of how well I am coping with the suddenness of this strange magic that such an explanation sounds completely logical to me.

The baby dragon crosses its hands and feet, trying to warm them themself, and I sit back abruptly. Setting the dragon in my lap, I dig into my tea kit and produce the socks.

Fortunately, they are loose for a human, so I'm able to gently slip the baby dragon's clawed hands into one sock and its toes into the other. It chirps at me, curling in my lap contentedly. Another source of warmth.

I look up at Sa Rangim. "I have some questions."

His eyes are still glowing—warmly. "You do not know what your teapot is, I take it."

My eyebrows lift. "Evidently not."

"It is made with arcane magic," Sa Rangim says. "I am not an arcanist, to shape raw magic thus, and I cannot tell you more than that. How did you come by it?"

"It was a gift," I say, staring at the shimmering teapot. "From someone of whom I perhaps should have asked more questions. But I have never produced a dragon with it before."

"I suspect you were not in the Cataclysm, before," he says. "Nor were you performing the ceremony for me. Pure acts of art, like what you just performed, have always created spirits, even if you can't see them. Tea has always been sacred among your people, has it not?"

The traditional blue dragon's blend, refined centuries ago. "Made from earth, formed in water, released into open air," I say numbly. "But that means—I made them?"

"Your familiar is female," Sa Rangim says.

I bow quickly. "My apologies, she is acting like a certain male cat of my acquaintance and I did not wish to presume. How can you tell?"

"It is a sense, with some beings," he says. "That is one of the changes we experienced."

"The changes?" I ask.

"Are you well?" Sa Rangim returns. "You appear to be shaking."

"I magically created a baby dragon familiar," I say by way of explanation. "Perhaps tea will help."

I bow, and we each reach for our cups.

After a bracing sip, Sa Rangim says, "Once upon a time, the magic of the Te Muraka was channeled through our ability to forge connections with spirits. When the shockwave that created the Cataclysm came, those who could reach out to the spirits did so intuitively, and we survived. The rest of our people did not." He gestures around the circle. "We are the Te Muraka who remain."

My eyes fill with tears. So many, in a sense. But also so, so few.

"Our connection to the spirits kept us alive, allowed us to survive as stable beings in the Cataclysm, but it also changed us," Sa Rangim says. "We had to take in magic, to become part magic, to keep from being warped. This is how we differ from your mages and witches, as I understand."

"They channel magic, through structures for mages but directly for witches," I say. "A mage's skill comes through training their mind, but a witch's ability is innate."

"But they do not possess magic; they draw it to them. It is their capacity that is determined by ability. I have seen mages work, and now I have seen a witch. They are not comprised of magic. They do not need to eat magic to sustain them. Like spirits, we do."

"That's why this place has grown barren," I say. "You've eaten all the magic."

"We've rationed the magic," Sa Rangim corrects me. "And the magic that sustains food in the Cataclysm. But we do not have the ability to stabilize forms in structure. We must accept Kustio's hollow promises that he will ready your world for us, because without his mages we will not last."

"But you've been preparing," I say. "You speak Istal fluently. You know our etiquette customs."

"I have bargained for books from Kustio when other favors were not forthcoming," Sa Rangim says. "We will be as ready as we can."

"Why wait at all?" I ask. "Why not cross the barrier into Istalam now?"

"To be killed? To be persecuted by those who are too weak to survive us, or too close-minded to allow us the chance to live?" His hands encompass the circle around us. "This is all of us, daughter-of-the-queen Miyara. This is all we have. We have learned to drink magic out of the air, to control the fires that burn inside us, but how will we change outside the Cataclysm? Who will grant us the space to grow?"

Trying to protect his own people, but also ours. At all costs.

That, ultimately, is all I needed to know about him.

"But you must rejoin human society," I say quietly. "Because there are too few of you here."

Sa Rangim nods. "If we stay, we will die. Individually, and as a people. I believe we are still human in the ways that matter. But I do not know for certain, nor what it will mean."

I sigh. "Well. That explains clearly why, aside from his financial motives, Kustio never intended to welcome you into Istalam."

Sa Rangim's eyes narrow. "By which you mean?" he says in a low, angry voice.

"Kustio is using the money he has made from the objects you've given him to attempt to exile the Gaellani, whom he hates for being different."

"And for witches," Lorwyn murmurs behind me. "Never forget that."

"He would never welcome more difference into a sphere he thinks he can control," I say. "In his own words, he does not consider you people."

Sa Rangim's eyes flash with fire.

I hold up a hand.

"Kustio does not speak for Istalam, only for himself," I say. "I do speak for Istalam, and I do, obviously, understand you are people. Which I have already told an Istal council."

"What are you saying?" Sa Rangim asks.

"I, Miyara of Istalam, wish to welcome the Te Muraka to Istalam and offer you refuge, now and in the future," I say. "To be full citizens of Istalam. To provide you that space. And I wish to do so today, because we are not as delicate as Kustio has led us to believe, nor are you so dangerous."

"You don't know that," Sa Rangim says.

"I know everything I need to," I say, stroking the calm baby dragon in my lap. "I promise the support of the crown, and I promise my personal support, in whatever you need for Istalam to become a home for you all."

"And in exchange?" Sa Rangim asks, voice barely audible.

"I really would like to finish this today," I say apologetically.

Sa Rangim frowns. "Why?"

"In brief? Ruining Kustio. He's conspired against you as well as the Istal people, and I wish him to face justice."

"Why," he repeats.

"So he can never hurt anyone ever again," I say. "I want him stripped of his power. And I want to use the systems he abused to do so, to demonstrate our commitment to the best parts of those systems, the parts that help and protect people, instead of the worst."

Sa Rangim sips his tea, places the cup down. Considers the people around him, my companions, the dragon in my lap.

Me.

He, too, knows all he needs to of me.

"I am amenable to your proposal," Sa Rangim says.

"I'm pleased to hear it," I say. "Shall we negotiate the details of the terms now?"

Sa Rangim's answer is lost among the thunderous cheers that erupt around us.

But he's smiling. A gentle smile, but the gleam in his eyes nonetheless reminds me of Lorwyn's shark-like expression.

"A shared bite, to celebrate," I say, withdrawing the two steamed sweet buns from my case.

The dragonet's eyes pop open, head twisting around backwards to gobble one right out of my hand.

I blink.

Sa Rangim laughs outright, and carefully splits the one remaining into two halves, holding one out for me.

"A shared bite indeed," he says, and we toast with tea.

To new beginnings, together.

CHAPTER 26

SA RANGIM ALONE JOURNEYS with us back through the Cataclysm, and his awe taking in the world when we step through the barrier is wonderful and painful to behold. We don't have much time, but I don't want to interrupt this delicate moment.

Given the task ahead I'll be glad to have his calm, assured presence at my back, but Lorwyn, always skeptical, breaks the poignant silence to ask, "Are you really not worried about risking your people's leader?"

Sa Rangim smiles at her. "If there is a risk, better it should be to me alone. If I have been so badly wrong to be now overcome, my people will deserve different leadership than I can provide."

"How did you come to lead the Te Muraka?" I ask.

His smile edges, becoming decidedly sharklike.

I fear my choice of friends has developed a troubling consistency.

"There are reasons," he says only. "Your comrade approaches."

Sure enough, seconds later Entero appears before us. His expression is wooden, completely closed off.

"What's wrong?" Lorwyn asks. "Did we do all this for nothing after all?"

Something flashes in his eyes, but he squashes it. "Then you succeeded?"

"Entero, this is Sa Rangim, leader of the Te Murak," I say. "Sa Rangim, this is—"

"Entero," my guard cuts me off. "Covert operative for the dowager queen Esmeri."

Sa Rangim's eyebrows lift, though he bows politely. "I see."

Entero holds a hand out to me.

My chest tightens. He hates it, but he's chosen.

Chosen the kingdom and its people over me, whom he swore to protect.

And chosen his oaths over his love, for whom he would have done anything to stay, though she'll never believe it.

"I have to go in person," Entero says, "to guarantee it's delivered safely, fast enough, to the correct hands, and to account for its existence."

"I understand," I say, and place the scroll of our treaty into his hand.

"I don't," Lorwyn says. "Why do you both sound like someone's dying?"

Entero shoots me a quelling look and says to her, "It won't be me who brings the validation back to Sayorsen. There will be questions in the capital, and I'll be gone for a while." His eyes are intent. "I won't be here to fulfill my promise to you."

Lorwyn's eyebrows lift. "I'll still be here," she says, "with or without your protection. If that's all, you'd better get going."

They hold each other's gaze for a long, fraught moment.

Then Entero turns away, vanishing into the darkness.

"Miyara," Lorwyn says, "what did he not want to say to me?"

I close my eyes. "That he's not sure if he'll be able to come back at all."

"Why?" she asks, too calmly, as Risteri begins to swear.

"He's failed to guard me, and he's allowed his priorities to become compromised," I say. "I gather he owes a great deal to my grandmother, and his choices are not his own. Until recently, it was a bargain he had no cause to regret, but he is still bound by it. If there is any way for him to return, I am sure he will find it."

"I'm sure," Lorwyn says, still calm.

Then she blasts a flare of witchlight.

A squad of Kustio's guards whom I hadn't seen emerge drop where they stand.

That councilor must have helped Kustio somehow after all.

"Let's move on," Lorwyn says flatly.

I wish I could reassure her that if anyone can find a covert way around bindings if needed, it will be Entero. But I can't reassure her that my grandmother will be lenient, or that he will be able to circumvent her. As this was my plan, I doubt she'll want to hear anything from me.

But if we get through today, I will do whatever I must to create a chance for their future.

The council reconvenes.

I walk through a hallway to a room full of my neighbors. People who've disagreed with my concerns; people who've brought food to sustain me. People whom I've seen daily, and heard their troubles, and served tea. People who have seen, and heard, and served, me.

And I do not walk alone.

I walk at the front of a group of friends, each as unlikely and outcast as me, each at least as formidable.

Today, I reach the end of the hall, and I know I am not alone.

We process in, and I set the pace. I need no one to guide me, and even with all the eyes on me, not only do I not falter: I surge.

Today, I know my path is true, and I have no doubts about myself.

I walk to Deniel, whose expression I cannot read but he is *looking* at me. I walk among my home, my heart.

Today, I have a baby dragon curled on my shoulder, and all eyes are on me.

Including Kustio's, who, seated in the center of the table, has moved from astonishment to fury to calculation in the space of my steps.

"How dare you bring such a creature before us," he says.

I ignore him.

"Greetings, graces of the council of Sayorsen and my neighbors," I say with a bow. "Allow me to present Sa Rangim, leader of the Te Muraka, a people whom Kustio has systematically imprisoned and extorted in the Cataclysm for a decade."

"I am honored," Sa Rangim says in clearly enunciated Istal, "to stand free before you now."

The outcry is deafening.

And we're just getting started.

"How dare you entertain her manipulative nonsense," Kustio shouts over the din, his anger palpable, and the audience quiets. "After all I've done for you, you would believe such lies? No people could survive in the Cataclysm, as all of you should know perfectly well. She seeks to defame my name with these false accusations. Just look at what she has on her shoulder—is that what you call a person?"

A reminder about what he can do to them and dehumanization in one go. He is not subtle, but he is effective.

"My apologies to the council; I had not finished my introductions," I say, stroking the baby dragon's back, who curls around my neck, lashing her tail. "My companion is not Te Muraka. This is Yorani, a spirit of tea."

The councilor whom I made my enemy sneers. "A *spirit of tea?"* he echoes mockingly. "*This* is how you hope to convince us of your sincerity?"

"Your pardon," an authoritative voice brooking no argument says from the side of the room.

It's Tea Master Karekin.

I manage not to clench my fists, though Yorani senses my tension and scrambles again to one shoulder to watch Master Karekin closely.

"Do you mean to claim," he says to me, "Yorani was birthed in the course of a tea ceremony?"

If Karekin contradicts me here, this will spiral out of control quickly. But all I say is, "That's correct."

Karekin studies the baby dragon, Sa Rangim, and me, taking us all in over a long moment.

Then he says, "How remarkable. It has been many years, but I am confident the tea guild will recognize Yorani as a spirit of tea and your familiar. Congratulations."

My eyebrows shoot up; it's all I can do not to gape at him, for I've never heard of such a thing. "Will they truly?" I ask vaguely.

Mildly, Karekin replies, "I have not yet had occasion to induct you into the tea guild."

I have so many questions, but I recognize what he is allowing me here: time.

Time before he announces I'm no longer an aspirant and will never be inducted into the guild. He has managed not to address me so far, and every moment I allow the council to be distracted is a moment where someone can call me to account.

"We are not here," my enemy-councilor spits, "to discuss myths and stories."

"Indeed," I say coolly, "we are here to discuss treachery. I have, as promised, brought proof."

"Proof?" the councilor scoffs. "The presence of a man with quaint hair styling and a unique costume is your proof?"

Karekin speaks again, striding to the council platform. "Indeed not. On behalf of the crown, I have been asked to vouch for the authenticity of the documents I now present before you." He unfurls the scroll dramatically, letting it sweep across the length of the table. "This is a copy of a treaty negotiated between Istalam and the Te Muraka, signed and sealed by her Majesty, Queen Ilmari of Istalam, welcoming these people as citizens of Istalam. I trust you will not be so unwise as to contest *her* word—or mine?"

The Sayorseni don't clamor at this; they remain hushed, the silence pregnant as everyone waits for Kustio.

"This is absurd," Kustio says. "There's no way you could have negotiated a treaty like that in one day—"

"Are you saying it must have existed before, then?" I ask. "That would be unfortunate for you, I imagine."

He glares. "This proves nothing. Even if this treaty is real, you can't prove I knew—"

"About me?" Sa Rangim interrupts. "My old *friend*, there are now any number of citizens who may testify to your behavior."

"Which is convenient," Tea Master Karekin adds, "as Lord Kustio has been summoned to appear before the crown to account for his actions."

Kustio slams his hands on the table and stands. "I do not have to listen to this ridiculous conspiracy to attack my character. You will learn—you will *all* learn—not to trifle with me, and you will regret what you have attempted today." He turns to storm away.

Bars of light appear around him, and in seconds Kustio is trapped in what looks like a birdcage made of magic.

Ostario steps out of the shadows.

"I believe our business overlaps," the mage croons. "I must insist on escorting you personally."

"You have no grounds—"

"After yesterday's events I had the grounds to investigate your operations, and despite your extensive magecraft defenses and the efforts of your goons, I did so while you were away," Ostario says. "You are, it turns out, *extremely* guilty of everything Miyara's accused you of. So I will be taking you into custody, and I strongly recommend you not resist."

Kustio turns to glare at me balefully—and his eyes fall on Lorwyn.

"This is witchcraft," he says in a low, furious voice. "Witchcraft, to ensorcell so many against me—"

"I had no need of witchcraft," I say, and because I have only an instant to distract him from revealing Lorwyn add, "I am Miyara of Istalam."

And though Kustio is not subtle, nor is he stupid. His eyes widen as he understands, immediately, finally, what I mean.

"You," he snarls, and reaches inside a pocket.

The magecraft cage bends like light, then ebbs away as if a sudden shadow cast over to dispel it.

Kustio holds a small metal object in his hand—a smuggled, undetectable, dangerous magical item from the Cataclysm—and with a shout thrusts it into the air.

And then is thrown sideways as Risteri tackles him.

They wrestle for only a moment before I hear the crack of his skull against the ground.

Risteri, after all, is a noble who's never been afraid to learn how to work with her hands.

She wrests the object from her father's hands and gets to her feet.

But it flies out of her hands, high into the air.

Risteri throws a knife at it, to no avail.

Too late, I think, as the object twists around and focuses right on me. Targeting.

I take a step to the side, and it swivels with me.

A searing beam builds, like a gathering of thousands of golden threads from the Cataclysm wreathed in flame.

I look at the people behind and around me who see it too, some mesmerized, but mostly recognizing the danger and diving for cover.

Too late, I think again, knowing there's nowhere I can dodge where people won't be behind me.

Nowhere except where I'm standing, as they've already fled.

So I plant my feet, and hold my ground.

A shaft of magical power erupts out of the object and hurtles toward me—

And hits a shield.

Luminescent and transparent, I recognize the roiling shadows within as Lorwyn's witchcraft immediately.

"I never should have let you in that night," she growls behind me. "You've brought me nothing but trouble. Hold still."

"I love you too," I say, hardly daring to breathe, let alone move. "Can you stop it?"

"Definitely not," she says. "I don't know how much power is in that thing, but it's all I can do right now to push against it."

The power, building up pressure against her shield, explodes outward. I cry out, but wordlessly, soundlessly, so shocked and devastated I don't know how to cope with the sudden knowledge that all the people I'd hoped to protect will be victims after all.

But as I turn to them, I see there is a bubble, a sphere in whirling colors absorbing the power inside, protecting everyone outside of it but me, Lorwyn, Yorani, and Sa Rangim.

And behind it, Ostario, his hands raised and a look of fierce concentration on his face.

"Show off," Lorwyn says.

"Training," I say.

"I'm still going to blast you."

But the power is still surging out of the metal object, and the surface of the bubble is beginning to warp.

"Allow me," Sa Rangim says in a low voice behind me.

I turn to look at him, see him raise a hand, a ball of sparks fritzing above it.

He shoots a bolt of lightning that passes through the shield, straight through the beam of power, and cracks into the magical object at the other end.

Which falls.

And all is silent.

"Lightning," I say quietly enough that only my companions will here, "not fire. This is a reason you're leader."

Sa Rangim smiles, just barely. "It is a reason, yes."

Shakily, Risteri picks up the magical object and carries it toward us. “Can you do something about this?” she asks. “Make sure it’s turned off?”

Sa Rangim reaches for it, but Yorani stretches her head around faster.

And chomps it. One, two, three bites, and the object is gone.

I blink. “Well.”

“I did mention spirits eat magic,” Sa Rangim says, sounding almost embarrassed.

I cast a glance around the room, at people huddled and wide-eyed, scared and confused, and I step up onto the platform.

I bow.

And I begin to speak.

I apologize for the danger of this afternoon and reassure my neighbors it has passed. I thank the council for their work on our behalf and charge them with the enormous task of unraveling Kustio’s scheme—the extortion, the evictions, all of it. More than one pales at the prospect.

I am calm, and my steadiness radiates out of me as the people of Sayorsen return to their seats, as they settle into order, as they dare to hope a bright future may be possible.

Throughout it all, I feel Tea Master Karekin in the background, watching me.

Ostario resets his structure, takes the unconscious Kustio into custody and announces, “Grace Lorwyn, my apologies about your cover, but thank you for your assistance in this matter. We’ll debrief upon my return.”

He vanishes, the stones of his structure falling aside, a showy bit of magic that it does the audience good to see: powerful magecraft, on their side, against Kustio.

Which is a mask for his real gift, the veneer of legitimacy so Lorwyn won’t be mobbed by Sayorseni who’ve connected what she must be, by acting as though she was working for him all along.

I close my eyes, silently thanking the spirits for Ostario’s foresight and dangerous generosity, and it’s in that moment Tea Master Karekin takes to the platform once more.

“There is another order of business yet unsorted,” he says.

I brace myself. I no longer need the tea mastery to save Sayorsen or Talmeri's, nor even myself, but the official proclamation closing the door I wanted—*want*—so badly to pass through will still hurt.

"I am pleased to name Miyara tea master," Karekin announces, "and on behalf of the tea guild, I bid her welcome."

My eyes snap open, and I stare at him in blatant astonishment as the whole room cheers for me.

"What?" I breathe. "But—"

"You did not complete the traditional exam, it's true," Karekin says only for my ears. "So this will have to be a provisional mastery, pending further evaluation at a later date. But as I had not yet rendered judgment, there was room to maneuver. That you created the first tea spirit in centuries tells me what I need to know about your ceremony." He smiles. "Listening to you here tells me the rest."

So stunned I can't formulate words, I bow, as low as I have ever bowed.

When I rise, Karekin is already striding away.

He says no more, but nor does he need to.

We'll see each other again, and soon.

"There is," the council member who has tried to halt Kustio says, "a further order of business, Tea Master Miyara."

My head is still spinning, and I can't guess what she means.

"As always, I am at your service," I say, and the room quiets once again to hear what she has to say.

"With Kustio's removal, and I have no doubt it will be permanent, there is an open seat on the council," she explains. "Normally, by tradition, that seat would pass to his heir—"

Risteri assures her, "Oh, I will formally renounce Taresim's claim in writing if you need. The house has absolutely violated the public trust."

"Thank you," the councilor says. "That will save me a great deal of paperwork. But the fact remains, a seat is open, and it falls to the council to choose a new member to fill it. My colleagues and I," she cuts a contemptuous look at my enemy among them, who scowls, "have reached an agreement. There is no one whose judgment is more trustworthy than yours, Tea Master Miyara."

I should have seen that coming, but of course I'd had no idea I'd be named tea master. Without that air of legitimacy, I doubt the verdict would have been quite so easy for them.

But I know how to respond, smiling and raising a hand to stop the customary applause beginning to build at that announcement.

"I am grateful for the council's regard," I say, "and since you hold my judgment in such esteem, I hope you will honor my wish that the seat be instead bestowed on another who is better suited to the role."

I look out of the crowd and locate with ease the onc face I am always drawn toward.

"Deniel," I say, "would you come to the front, please?"

The whole room, it seems, gapes at me.

Deniel schools his expression, striding toward the platform surrounded by profound silence.

The council member's expression is perplexed. "This is—irregular," she says.

"Yet necessary and right," I murmur in return.

When Deniel reaches the front, I say, "You all know Deniel, not just because of his craft, but because he has lived in Sayorsen for years and made his presence known. He has supported his community. He has attended city meetings without fail. He knows the needs of Sayorsen, and the laws and processes that govern it, better than anyone." I look frankly at the council member. "He also knows the needs of the Gaellani, and of Cataclysm refugees who make their homes here. That understanding is vital to solving the problems Sayorsen currently faces."

She purses her lips, taking my point. It's past time a Gaellani was invited to participate in politics, and with Kustio's targeting of them to un-work and the integration of the Te Muraka imminent, the council will need Deniel's help desperately.

Deniel, however, hisses at me, "What are you doing?"

"I don't know how to represent this community, and I don't know how to do the work. You do," I say. "You can help clear the way so maybe next time, the council will choose deserving people on their own, without outside intervention."

He searches my face. "Why, Miyara? Didn't you want to help people? This is how."

I shake my head. "No. Not for me." I smile, not sure why I'm tearing up. But, no. This is a divergence, and he knows it. "I know my place, Deniel. It's as the outside intervention. And for that I have to be outside the system."

That was, after all, what I chose: to make my way alone. Not as part of something.

I think I'm beginning to understand the true nature of that burden in a way I didn't when I dedicated myself. Instead of leaving loneliness behind, in a way I've committed myself to it forever.

I don't regret it.

The councilor waits until it's clear neither of us have anything more to say to each other, or perhaps tires of watching us stare into each other's eyes, and, obtaining Deniel's consent, grudgingly confirms him as the new city council member for Sayorsen.

As this momentous meeting finally draws to a close, she asks me, "So what will you do now?"

"Continue to serve," I say. "In whatever capacity I may."

"And that means?" she asks impatiently.

"Serving tea," I say with a placid bow. "And also working to integrate the Te Muraka into Sayorsen."

Her eyes narrow, and then horror dawns. "*All* of them, *here*?"

"Of course," I say serenely. "Sayorsen's proximity to the Cataclysm makes it the natural place to begin. I look forward to working with you, councilor."

She stares at me in consternation, then shakes her head with a low chuckle. "Oh, this should be good."

As I promise to visit her offices forthwith to begin making arrangements, Deniel catches my hand.

"I know you have a lot to do," he says.

"So will you," I say.

"I know," Deniel says. "I know. But—come see me? When you can?"

What more needs to be said? Or are we going to talk at last? Do I care?

I sigh.

Of course I care.

"When I can," I agree.

"I'll be waiting," he says, and my breath catches, because in his voice I hear the underlying promise of forever.

But with that I take my leave, and escort Sa Rangim of the Te Muraka and Yorani the tea spirit to Sayorsen's shrine, to introduce them to the spirits, who I hope will watch over them as they have me, and to give my thanks.

And thence to the Gaellani courtyard to introduce them to their first noodle bowls.

EPILOGUE

THE NEXT FEW DAYS pass in a whirl of activity, punctuated by a few momentous exchanges.

At first, my only priority is serving the Te Muraka. And Yorani, but she's content to turn what I'm coming to know as her unique brand of mischief on them for long stretches of time. Sa Nikuran finds her amusing, fortunately, and is happy to dragon-sit. I'm relieved there are breaks to be had from my sudden and unexpected role as dragon parent.

The day after the historic council meeting, a formal delegation arrives from the capital to help settle the Te Muraka. None of my family is among those sent, and none of them appear to realize I'm the former princess. But I know it's only a matter of time before my family comes for me.

That's a fight for the future. For now, life goes on.

When Ostario comes into Lorwyn's lab, I immediately requisition one of her burners and put a kettle on. Yorani, just as promptly, hops up to sit on top of it, basking in the warmth.

"I need to speak with Lorwyn alone, Miyara, if you don't mind stepping out," the mage says.

I rummage through Lorwyn's things until I find leaves I'm satisfied with. "When a dangerous man arrived here with the intention of doing what was best for me," I say, locating a mostly clean cup, "she wouldn't leave me alone with him either."

Lorwyn tenses a fraction, but she doesn't gainsay me.

I don't think she's spoken Entero's name aloud since he left. So far, there's been no word.

"Very well," Ostario says equably enough. "May I assume we can speak frankly, then?"

"I know she was a princess and you're a witch," Lorwyn says flatly.

"And so are you," Ostario notes. "We'll have to do something about that."

I sigh. "Ostario. Really."

"Something that is not killing you," he clarifies, rolling his eyes. "Obviously."

"Oh, obviously," Lorwyn echoes. "What's it to be then, indentured servitude? Torturous experiments?"

"Lessons," Ostario says, "in magecraft *and* in witchcraft. I felt how much power you were able to pull, and consistently, to shield against that blast. If you were trained, it wouldn't have mattered if I was at that council meeting at all."

"And in return," Lorwyn presses, "I assume I'll be at the state's beck and call."

"Oh, worse than that, you'll be at *my* beck and call," Ostario says. "You'll learn what I tell you to learn, the way I tell you to learn it, because I'm forging a trail for you to make it look like you've been registered and safe all this time. Since we both know you're emphatically not safe, and I've risked my reputation for you, teaching you is now my problem."

That is a curious way to look at it. But it's also, I think, one Lorwyn will accept more readily than any professions of altruism.

"Why are you smiling?" Lorwyn demands of me. "This is blackmail."

"He's already forging a history for you," I say. "Just accept the lessons."

"If you'll recall," Ostario says, "I did offer you a chance without blackmail attached first, but I suppose I should have known, given witches, how that would go."

"What," Lorwyn says, "because we're all rightfully suspicious? Backward? Criminal?"

"Because witches always have to do everything the hard way," he says, smiling a little sadly. "I should know."

With that, he begins making his way out.

"Why are you doing this?" Lorwyn calls after him. "Don't tell me it's just out of the goodness of your heart, or about helping witches, or even Miyara. What's in it for you?"

Ostario pauses at the door. "Maybe someday I'll tell you. You're not ready for that level of magic yet." He smiles more broadly. "Until next time, my apprentice."

He takes his leave, and Lorwyn just stands there, staring after him, like she can't make any sense of what's just happened and what it means for her. I gently push her into her chair, and she collapses into it, still staring numbly.

"Congratulations," I tell her. "You're going to be the most unwilling mage in history."

I hand her a cup of tea, and she sips automatically.

"You're a menace, and I should never have let you inside that night," she says again, and I laugh.

Risteri manages to claw herself free of dealing with the shambles Kustio has left of House Taresim's affairs and joins me as I walk, once more, to the council offices.

"You would not believe how deep it all goes," she says. "Well, no, I suppose you would. But it's going to take a lot of work to salvage the House, and it's work I have basically no experience doing. So that bodes well."

"Your grandmother will be coming to take charge, won't she?" I ask, struggling to resettle a certain baby dragon spirit differently on my shoulder. No one has yet explained to me what a familiar means for a person who doesn't perform magic, other than a great deal of adorable bother.

Risteri shudders. "Spirits, don't remind me. She's going to be furious with me."

"The actions you took against your father are ultimately what will protect your House from the worst of the fallout," I say. "Your grandmother will recognize that. It will matter."

"I know," Risteri says. "But it'll all take a while to sort out, and honestly, it'll be a while before I want to have any more to do with the House than I have to."

"I thought you had friends among the servants?"

Risteri sighs. "I'm friendly with them, but real friendship is hard when there's that much power disparity, too much potential for one side to hurt the other. Even if it's just perception. You know that."

"I do," I say softly.

"I'm making sure they're provided for, at least until everything finishes shaking out," Risteri says. "We'll see who comes out the other side unscathed and what the House finances look like then. But everyone who stays on has to *stay*, because of the investigation, and I can't deal with being trapped there. Never again."

Risteri and I have far more in common than I suspected when we first met.

"So where will you go?" I ask.

"Well," she says. Looks at me; glances away. "Since it's not like you'll be able to stay in the cottage anymore, I was wondering if you might need a roommate?"

I stare at her, arrested by the notion.

"Unless Deniel—" Risteri starts.

"I'm not moving in with Deniel," I say. "And I would *love* to be your roommate."

"Really?" she asks, voice tentative.

I take her hand. "Really," I say, and we grin at each other stupidly. "Just think how much fun we'll have with fire without supervision."

Risteri laughs. "We are going to have to work on our cooking, aren't we?"

"That is one kind of fire you'll enjoy playing with," I agree serenely.

It takes Risteri a moment to realize I'm teasing her about Sa Nikuran—I suspect I need more practice at teasing—but when she does, instead of blushing, she lets loose a full-bodied cackle, the loudest and most carefree sound I've ever heard.

When she can breathe again, Risteri says, "I'll be able to talk the tourism guild into paying me a salary for my work, but what about you? I thought Talmeri wouldn't pay you enough for rent."

"That was before," I say. "She will now. Leave it to me."

After we arrange a dragon-sitter for Yorani for the afternoon, Risteri drags Lorwyn off to help her look for apartments, leaving Talmeri alone with me.

It doesn't take long to renegotiate our terms.

I get everything I want, including a raise for Lorwyn, and in the end Talmeri is nearly as happy with the new arrangement as I am.

I have plans for this tea shop, and I have plans for my role in it.

My grandmother was right: there is work for those who know how to listen, and I finally believe I know what that work is and my place in it.

I leave, feeling bright and strong, which I'm unreasonably glad of, because I finally have time to walk a very familiar path.

As I approach Deniel's house, I pause, because Thiano is leaving it with a covered box.

"So," I say, "did it all turn out how you plotted?"

He smirks at me and shakes his head. "You give me too much credit."

"I don't think I do," I say.

Thiano laughs. "Then give me the credit of assuming I always have plots yet to satisfy, Tea Princess." He winks, and saunters past with a wave. "Until next time."

I watch him go and wonder if I'll ever know where his lingering sadness comes from, and how it drives him. But that's a mystery for the future, too.

Today, I steel myself like I have so many times before not knowing what to expect at this door, and knock.

There's no hesitation.

The door nearly flies open, and Deniel is waiting there, hopeful and breathless. "You're here," he breathes. "Please, come in."

I follow him to the back, unsettled. "How is everything going with the council?" I ask.

"Busier than I've had time to process," he says. "I'd love to tell you about it later and hear your thoughts about the council politics. If you want? But first, I have something for you."

He goes into his work area and returns with a small wrapped box.

"What's this?" I ask.

"For you," he says, which I had gathered, but I suppose it was an inane question.

I untie the ribbon, then the cloth underneath, which Deniel takes from me so I have both hands available to hold the box and lift the lid.

Inside rest two dazzlingly fine silver filigree cuff bracelets.

I stare.

"I noticed," Deniel says nervously, "when you were over here, any time you got nervous about your place, you'd start rubbing your wrists, like it bothered you that they were bare. I figured it was something from your time at the palace you couldn't take with you, but I thought maybe having new bracelets, from your new life, would help you feel more settled. Wherever you go."

The old bracelets were the cold security of reliable shackles. But this is... a familiar comfort, but with a new meaning. Every time I touch them I'll be reminded how different my life is now. My fingers tremble as I touch them.

"Miyara?" Deniel asks uncertainly.

He saw me. All along, he saw me.

"This is what you were hiding from me?" I whisper.

"Thiano procured them for me," Deniel explains. "His services... well, we bargained for me to pay him in a few special tea sets, since I've refused to sell him any before. That was what I was working on."

"Why wouldn't you *tell* me?" I cry. "I thought you were in trouble and didn't trust me!"

"Oh, Miyara, *no*," Deniel says, taking me by the shoulders. "I'm sorry. I didn't realize that was what you thought or I'd have said something. It was just that—you already felt so indebted to everyone around you, felt like you could never repay them. And after knowing what the bracelets cost, I didn't want you to feel obligated to me." His face softens. "I never want you to feel obligated to me."

Tears fall down my cheeks, and, gently, he brushes them aside.

But.

Wherever you go, he said.

"You pushed yourself to make them in a hurry," I say, "because you didn't think I'd stay."

Deniel freezes. Swallows. "Miyara, you were in hiding, but—"

"I never was very good at it," I say. "And I was never sure I would be able to stay. A reckoning is inevitable now."

"That. But also." He takes a breath. "Miyara, you never had a chance to explore. You came here on accident, not by choice. Now you're a tea master. You can go anywhere you want, and if you want to, you *should*. I want... I don't want to lose you, but I want you to always feel like anything is possible. I want you to feel free to walk your own path, even if I'd be... sad."

Now his eyes are glassy with tears. "I would be sad, too," I manage.

Then I slide the cuff bracelets onto my wrists.

I feel, uncannily, like the spirits have aligned.

"They're beautiful," I say, looking down at them.

Deniel tilts my chin up to meet his gaze again. "So are you," he says. "But if you secretly hate them, I promise I won't be offended if you toss them out the window."

"Deniel—"

"I mean it," he says. "I never want you to feel constrained or stifled with me. I want you to be happy, whatever that means."

"Even if," I say, "that means I'm going to stay by your side, no matter what you think is best for me? Even if I just bring you trouble?"

"Especially then," Deniel whispers, cupping my cheek.

And then he kisses me.

I stare, wide-eyed into his dancing eyes, for a stunned, thrilled moment.

And then I drop the box and close my eyes, leaning into Deniel as our arms wrap around each other.

After a long, wonderful moment, we separate, each breathing heavily. I know I must be flushed bright red, but I am reassured that Deniel is, too.

"I have no idea what I'm doing," I confess.

He smiles his perfect, crooked smile, running a hand through his hair.

I stop resisting the urge and let myself follow the course his hand has taken, patting the hair sticking up back into place.

Deniel's breath catches, and then our gazes catch, and we are kissing again.

This time when we separate, Deniel says, "Neither do I. But I think we can figure it out together. If you want."

"I would," I say, "very much."

And we smile, utterly ridiculous smiles at each other, and I cannot imagine being happier than I am in this moment.

Which is, naturally, when Talsion mews from our feet.

"Our chaperone," Deniel jokes, untangling himself to reach down and pet Talsu, leaving me a clear view of his altar to the spirits.

I smile, and bow, and offer a silent prayer.

For the future. Our future, together, as ourselves.

"Just wait until you both meet Yorani," I say as Deniel straightens. "She grows smarter and bolder with every day."

"I'm sure Talsu will have opinions of her," Deniel says.

"I'm sure Yorani will have opinions of you," I counter, and he laughs.

My favorite sound in the world.

"I will endeavor to measure up to her standards," Deniel says.

He reaches for my hand.

"Do you have time for a cup of tea?" he asks.

I take it, and hold on.

I am exactly where I'm supposed to be.

"Always."

THANK YOU

Thank you for reading!

I started posting Tea Princess Chronicles as a web serial in 2017, Kickstarted the whole series (and funded in an hour and a half!) to transform them into books in 2021, and now here we are. Whether you've been part of this journey for a while or are just joining in, thank you for being here.

If you enjoyed reading this book of the Tea Princess Chronicles, I hope you'll tell someone about it or leave a review!

For a FREE, newsletter-exclusive Tea Princess Chronicles short story, sign up for my newsletter at caseyblair.com! Subscribing will keep you in the loop on free fiction opportunities, sales, and new books.

Happy reading!

Casey

About the Author

Casey Blair is a bestselling author of adventurous, feel-good fantasy novels with ambitious heroines and plenty of banter, including the completed cozy fantasy series Tea Princess Chronicles , the fantasy romance novella *The Sorceress Transcendent*, and the action anime-style novella *Consider the Dust*. Her own adventures have included teaching English in rural Japan, taking a train to Tibet, rappelling down waterfalls in Costa Rica, and practicing capoeira. She now lives in the Pacific Northwest and can be found dancing spontaneously, exploring forests around the world, or trapped under a cat.

For more information visit her website caseyblair.com or follow her on Instagram @CaseyLBlair.

Also By

Tea Princess Chronicles

A Coup of Tea

Tea Set and Match

Royal Tea Service

Tales from a Magical Tea Shop: Stories of the Tea Princess Chronicles

Stand-Alone

The Sorceress Transcendent

Consider the Dust

Printed in the USA
CPSIA information can be obtained
at www.ICGtesting.com
LVHW030345140524
780146LV00007B/590